Falling for the Nanny

SUSAN MEIER

MICHELLE CELMER

BARBARA McMAHON

First Published in Great Britain 2016
By Mills & Boon, an imprint of HarperCollins*Publishers*
1 London Bridge Street, London, SE1 9GF

FALLING FOR THE NANNY © 2016 Harlequin Books S. A.

The Billionaire's Baby SOS, *The Nanny Bombshell* and *The Nanny Who Kissed Her Boss* were first published in Great Britain by Harlequin (UK) Limited.

The Billionaire's Baby SOS © 2013 Harlequin Books S. A.
The Nanny Bombshell © 2012 Michelle Celmer
The Nanny Who Kissed Her Boss © 2012 Barbara McMahon

Special thanks and acknowledgement are given to Susan Meier for her contribution to THE LARKVILLE LEGACY series.

ISBN: 978-0-263-92062-8

05-0416

Our policy is to use papers that are natural, renewable and recyclable products and made from wood grown in sustainable forests. The logging and manufacturing processes conform to the legal environmental regulations of the country of origin.

Printed and bound in Spain
by CPI, Barcelona

THE BILLIONAIRE'S BABY SOS

BY
SUSAN MEIER

Susan Meier spent most of her twenties thinking she was a job-hopper—until she began to write and realised everything that had come before was only research! One of eleven children, with twenty-four nieces and nephews and three kids of her own, Susan has had plenty of real-life experience watching romance blossom in unexpected ways. She lives in western Pennsylvania with her wonderful husband Mike, three children and two over-fed, well-cuddled cats, Sophie and Fluffy. You can visit Susan's website at: www.susanmeier.com.

CHAPTER ONE

ALL the ornate boardroom doors that Matt Patterson had faced hadn't been as intimidating as the ordinary brown door before him.

Dysart Adoption Agency.

His chest tightened. His palms began to sweat. His mouth went dry.

Still, he never shirked a responsibility. He opened the door and walked inside.

Wood-paneled walls, an empty reception desk and a soft powder scent greeted him. So did the sound of a baby's laughter. High-pitched and filled with joy, the little-girl giggles and squeals of delight rolled up the hall.

Nine chances out of ten that was his baby.

His baby.

Man, this was going to put a cramp in his love life.

And his traveling.

And his staff.

Good God! The housekeeper, Mrs. McHenry, would have a fit when she discovered they were going to have to add a nursery and a nanny to his already-busy household.

He followed the sound of the giggles to an office at the end of a short hall. Her back to him, a slim woman held a baby in the crook of her arm. Her glossy chestnut-brown hair was swept up in a neat, professional chignon and her red dress rode her curves like an Italian sports car took the turns at Le Mans.

His eyebrows rose. "Somehow I'd always pictured the women who worked at adoption agencies as gray-haired old maids in tacky white blouses."

The baby stopped laughing. The woman at the window spun around.

For the first time Matt could remember, he was speechless.

Huge round brown eyes dominated her face. High cheekbones showcased a pert and proper nose and full, lush lips.

"Can I help you?"

He walked in slowly, his interest piqued. She was exactly the kind of woman he wined and dined, seduced and then left with the gift of a diamond bracelet. But before he could open his mouth to flirt, the baby in her arms squawked. Bella. Oswald and Ginny's daughter. His, because he'd agreed to be godfather to his ex-wife's baby.

Sadness stole over him. This time last week Ginny had called to make dinner plans for when he returned to Boston. Now she and Oswald were gone. He'd never again see Ginny's pretty smile or hear Oswald's goofy laugh. He'd lost the ex-wife he loved and her new husband, who had become a good friend.

Bella screeched again. The woman looked at the baby, then gasped slightly as her gaze jerked back to him. "I'm Claire Kincaid, Bella's caseworker. Are you Matt Patterson?"

Shoving his hands into the pants pockets of his handmade suit, he ambled into the room. "Yes."

"My God. In four days, Bella's hardly responded to anybody. She doesn't even cry. She eats and sleeps and laughs when I tickle her. But you're the first person she's spoken to."

"Spoken to? Sounded like a squawk to me."

She laughed. "Squawking is how babies talk."

Her pretty brown eyes glittered with humor and his gut tightened. She was *incredibly* beautiful.

"She knows me." He paused. "A bit."

"Because you're a friend of her parents?"

He nodded and took another cautious step toward the woman and Bella. Dark-haired, blue-eyed Bella strained toward him, reaching for him to take her.

Surprised, he jerked back.

Claire Kincaid's smile faded. "She wants you."

"Yes. And I fully intend to care for her but I—" He paused, sucked in a breath. His instincts insisted he should flirt with the beautiful woman. His brain, however, reminded him this wasn't a pleasure trip and he'd better get his head in the game. Somehow or another he'd ended up with a baby and he didn't have a clue what to do with her. "I can't hold her."

"Excuse me?"

He pulled his hands from his pants pockets and raised them in a gesture of total helplessness. "I don't know how."

She took a step toward him. "It's really quite simple."

Her sweet and polite voice matched her nearly perfect face and sent tingly warmth through him. But when she stepped toward him, offering the little girl, he backed up again.

She frowned. "This child is yours."

"And I will take care of her. Next week." He shook his head. "No. That doesn't work for me, either. I have to go to Texas for some family reunion thing—"

The woman holding Bella stopped him with a wave of

her hand. "I don't care if you're the king of the world and you have to hold court. Bella is yours now." She smoothed a hand down the baby's back. "Besides, there's nothing to be afraid of. She's such a sweetie that caring for her will come naturally." She held the baby out to him, and again, Bella strained toward him.

His nervous system rattled like the old-fashioned ticker at the New York Stock Exchange. He'd known for four days that his ex-wife was dead and he was to be Bella's guardian, and he hadn't panicked. He'd handled it the same way he handled everything in his life. He took it one step at a time. But with the baby in front of him, it all suddenly became very real. For the next eighteen years, this child was *his*. He'd have to raise her. Get her through toddler years and preschool, then elementary school, middle school—*teen years*.

"I—" He wanted to take her. He really did. But this was *Ginny and Oswald's* baby. A baby who deserved to be loved and pampered. He hadn't loved or pampered anybody in—well, ever. That's why he'd lost Ginny. He wasn't the pampering, wine and roses, long walks on the beach and talks all night kind of guy. Worse, the people who might be able to help him—his staff—were all out of town.

"Really. I can't take her now. I've been in London for three weeks. When I heard about Bella, I came home early. But I'd dismissed my household staff for the six weeks I was supposed to be away. They're in places like Aruba taking a much-needed break. Even if I called them home, they wouldn't get back before Friday. And I," he said, pressing his hand against his chest, "have absolutely no idea how to care for a baby."

"You don't have nieces or nephews?"

He winced. "No, but even if I did, let's just say I'm not much of a family man."

Though Claire straightened as if she were about to rain down the fire of hell upon him, she protectively rubbed her hand along Bella's back, soothing her. "You agreed to parent a child when you have absolutely no idea of how?"

"I agreed to be a godfather. I didn't realize that also meant I'd be the baby's guardian if something happened to her parents."

"How could you not know that?"

"In some circles *godfather* is a purely honorary term."

Her pretty face softened. "Apparently, your friends took it seriously because you're named Bella's guardian in their wills."

"Yes. But they never told me that and I am just not ready for this."

"You still have to take her."

Disbelief and anger at the injustice of it all reared up in him. Ginny dead. Bella his. It didn't make any sense. Mostly because he wasn't qualified to do this—any of it. He couldn't hold her, let alone change a diaper. And he was the last person who should be assigned to love her.

Bella began to fuss and Claire Kinkaid rubbed her cheek against the baby's, comforting and quieting her.

Inspiration struck like a band of angels singing the *Hallelujah Chorus*. "You're pretty good with kids. What are you doing tonight, Miss Kincaid?"

"It's Claire." She moved her gaze away from his, straightening the collar of Bella's little pink blouse. "And I'm busy."

His eyes narrowed. Busy? She was pretty enough to have a date on a Monday night. If she'd been able to hold his gaze, he might have bought that. "So what you're really saying is that you don't want to help us?"

"We're an adoption agency, not a nanny service." She walked to her desk, pulled out some business cards. "But these are the names and addresses of some well-respected agencies. You could get a stellar nanny from any one of them."

As Claire held out the cards to Matt, Bella blinked slowly. Her long black lashes fell to her cheeks and lifted again. Tears filled her pretty blue eyes, as if she understood she was being shuffled off again.

Sympathy for her swelled in Matt's already tight chest. He had been young, maybe three, when he'd felt odd about his dad—as if he and Cedric Patterson didn't fit together—as if somewhere deep in his subconscious he had always known that he wasn't really Cedric's son. And he didn't belong in the Patterson family. Though Bella was a lot younger, he'd bet that somewhere in her subconscious all of this was being recorded. He could see in her eyes that she might not fully comprehend what was happening, but she was afraid. If nothing else, she hadn't seen her parents in almost a week. She was alone. Frightened.

And though it didn't make sense from a practical standpoint, her emotional well-being suddenly meant more to him than worry over dirty diapers.

He slid his hands into his pants pockets again. "I don't want a nanny. At least not yet. I don't want to leave her with another stranger."

And right now Claire Kincaid was the one person in the world who wasn't a stranger to her.

He caught Claire's gaze and offered the only workable solution. "I'll pay you anything you want to spend the next week with me."

Claire knew the offer was for her nanny services, but her face warmed and her stomach tightened. Matt Patterson might not know how to care for a baby, but he was one good-looking guy. Six foot one if he was an inch, he didn't tower over her, but he was tall enough that even in her heels she had to look up to him. His hair was a shiny light brown, cut short, professional, businesslike. His wicked green eyes smiled when he smiled, and grew stormy cold when he didn't get his way. But happy or stormy they always had a quality of…assessment. As if everything she said or did was of vital importance. And every time he caught her gaze, a lightning bolt of attraction shot through her.

She hadn't had a response to a man in years and her body picked *now?* And *this guy?* A man who'd left his baby with an adoption agency for four days? A man who didn't seem to want to take Bella now? Was she crazy?

"I'm sorry, Mr. Patterson, but as I said before we're an adoption agency. Not a nanny service."

He took a lazy step toward her, sending her pulse into overdrive. The way he looked, everything he did, was just so male. "You're pretty good with her, though."

She took a step back. "Yes. Well, I love children."

"You're better than just somebody who loves children." Studying her face, he frowned. "I'm guessing you got into this business because you were a nanny at some point." His frown deepened and he looked at her even more intently. "Probably when you were in school. Which wasn't too long ago."

Her heart shivered in her chest. He was so close she would only have to lift her hand to touch him, and for some strange reason she itched to raise her hand. Feel his skin. With all his attention focused on her, her body began to thrum.

Stupid hormones! Why pick now to wake up?

She swallowed and took another step back. "I put myself through my first three years at university as a nanny, Mr. Patterson. There is no deep, dark secret about my past."

He smiled. His full lips bowed upward and his green eyes lit with pleasure. "Too bad. Pretty woman like you should have a secret. It makes you mysterious and…" His smile grew. "Interesting."

Her face reddened. Tingles of attraction raced down her spine. Damn, he was gorgeous. And charming. But she knew what happened the last time she got involved with a charming man. She ended up in a bad relationship. A relationship that broke her heart and caused her to stay away from men for five long years.

She forced the business cards for nanny services into his hand. "Dysart Adoption Agency was hired by the attorney for Bella's parents to keep her until you arrived. You have arrived. Our responsibility had ended."

He squeezed his eyes shut. "Fine."

Refusing to fall victim to the helplessness she heard in his voice, she became all business. "Do you have a car seat?"

"My driver picked one up and installed it."

Still holding Bella, she bent and grabbed the diaper bag beside her desk. "Great." She handed it to him. "Those are all the things she's needed for the four days I kept her at my apartment. I imagine there are more things at her parents' house."

"Things?"

"Like a crib. High chair. Baby swing. The things she needs for daily life." Brisk and with purpose, she headed out of the office and up the hall, expecting him to follow her. "I will go with you to your car and help you strap Bella in."

When she reached the office door, he opened it for her

and followed her out, but he didn't say a word. He didn't say a word in the elevator. Standing in the box packed with people, their shoulders brushed. A current of electricity crackled through her.

As inconspicuously as possible, she peeked over at him. With his sloping cheekbones and sexy green eyes, he *was* gorgeous. But she'd met other good-looking men and never felt this. He had power, but power had never been particularly attractive to her. Yet something about him called to her and he wasn't even reacting. Though he'd flirted a bit, it was because he wanted her help. The attraction was clearly one-sided.

She sucked in a quiet breath, glad to be getting away from him. In two minutes, he'd be gone and she wouldn't have to worry she'd say or do something stupid because her hormones insisted she and Matt Patterson should… should… Well, she knew what her hormones wanted.

And that was wrong. Good grief, she'd barely dated since her big mistake her senior year at university when she'd fallen for one of her professors. They'd had a secret affair that started off wonderful and ended when he introduced her to his wife at graduation, humiliating her. Looking back, she realized she should have seen the signs that he was married. He'd pulled her away from her friends, insisted they meet at her place even though he made fun of her condo and never took her out in public. But loneliness after her dad's death had made her vulnerable, needy, and she'd missed the signs.

Which was why, for the past five years, she'd been a woman in control of her emotions. She'd never be so foolish as to fall so fast or be so smitten that she let a man walk all over her. Being overwhelmingly attracted to a guy she didn't know was so out of character it scared her.

The elevator bell dinged. They strode across the building lobby. He pushed on the revolving door, motioning Claire through, into the crisp late-September afternoon. He followed her out into the busy Boston street and paused in front of the black limo parked there. A uniformed man raced to the back door and opened it.

Claire peeked inside. A bar and a television sat across from a curving white leather seat that looked like a plush sofa. But on the sofa sat a car seat.

She quickly passed Bella to Matt Patterson—so quickly he didn't have time to protest and their fingers didn't even accidentally brush. "I'll slide inside, then you hand Bella to me. I will strap her in the car seat, and you can be on your way."

She climbed in. He passed Bella to her. She put the baby into the car seat and secured the straps. As she pulled away, she looked at the baby's pretty face. Blue eyes. Pug nose. Cupid's bow mouth.

Her heart twisted. She'd had this baby with her twenty-four hours a day for four days. Caring for her. Teasing her and playing with her to help her accept her new circumstances. Walking the floor with her as she sobbed all night because she missed her mom and dad. Bella had cried so hard the first night that Claire had cried with her. A baby couldn't understand or deal with death. All she knew was she missed her mom and desperately wanted the comfort of her arms.

Claire swallowed. This poor sweet baby would never see her mom again. Just as Claire hadn't seen her mom after she died.

She pressed her fingers to her mouth. How could she leave this sweet baby with a man who didn't know how to care for her?

She couldn't.

She scooted across the seat and out of the limo. Though

fear trembled through her, she faced Matt Patterson and held out her hand. "Do you have a business card?"

He frowned. "Yes."

"Does it have your home address?"

His eyes narrowed. "Are you planning to do some kind of surprise inspection?"

"I'm going to lock the office, then meet you at your house."

He smiled. Those beautiful green eyes of his lit with so much pleasure, a corresponding pleasure tugged at her stomach. "You're going to help me?"

God help her. "This evening, yes, to get you settled in. Then you're on your own."

CHAPTER TWO

THE rhythm of the car lulled Bella to sleep and she napped through the entire drive home. But when Jimmy, Matt's driver, stopped the limo to punch in the code to open the big black wrought-iron gate for his estate, the baby awoke. She glanced around sleepily. Her little mouth turned down. Her nose wrinkled and she let out with a yowl that went through Matt like an icy wind blows through barren trees.

Pretending not to notice, Jimmy drove up the brown brick driveway. Little Bella's wails filled the back of the limo. She didn't see that the grounds were manicured to perfection. Or that the leaves on the trees had begun to change colors and swatches of red, yellow and orange guided them along the circular driveway to the front of the stately stone mansion.

She didn't care when Matt said, "Shh. Shh. Please stop crying."

She simply continued to wail.

Jimmy appeared at the back door, opened it with a wince. "Quite a set of lungs."

"Indeed." Matt smiled ruefully. "You wouldn't know how to…" He paused, searching for a proper phrase and finally settled on, "Make her stop."

Jimmy backed off. "No, sir. Confirmed bachelor." He

tugged both ends of his bow tie jauntily. "Happily single. Not daddy material."

Remembering what Claire had asked him, he said, "No nieces or nephews?"

"Several but I don't take to them until they're old enough to go the bathroom on their own and get into the casinos in Atlantic City."

He sighed. "An excellent plan." His plan. Until circumstance changed things.

Bella's screams grew louder. He raised his voice to be heard above the sobbing. "So how do we get her into the house?"

Jimmy stepped back again. "Sorry. Not in my job description. In fact, I think I'll go make sure the limo's place in the garage is cleared."

He raced away and Matt scowled. See if the place in the garage is cleared? What a line.

He turned back to the baby. "So…what? You want food? A bottle? Some Scotch?" He knew she didn't want the third, but the terror riding his blood right now had him giddy. *He'd* like a Scotch. But he knew he wasn't getting one. Might not ever get one again until this child turned eighteen.

With Bella wailing beside him, he knew he had a choice. Sit in this limo for God knew how long until the adoption agency woman arrived. Or get Bella out of her car seat and into the house.

A cold wind blew alongside the car. The open door caught it and sent frigid air swirling into the limo. A few drops of rain pelted the limo roof, then the rain started full force.

"Crap."

He reached for the door and slammed it closed. Bella's wails echoed around him.

Jimmy suddenly appeared at the driver door. "Let's get this in the garage!"

"Good idea."

The sound of Bella screaming competed with the drumming of rain on the roof, making a horrendous racket. Matt squeezed his eyes shut, popped them open and turned to Bella. "Come on, kid. You knew me at the adoption agency office." He pointed at his chest. "I'm Mommy's friend."

Her crying only increased when they pulled into the garage. Being indoors seemed to cause the sound to ricochet off the walls and reverberate through him.

He peeked at her face. Little blue eyes watery and sad. Her nose red. Her lips trembling.

He scrubbed his hand across his mouth. He couldn't stand to see her like this. He had to do something!

Noting that Jimmy had disappeared as soon as the limo lurched to a stop, he reached for the buckles of her car seat. Once he had her out of the car seat, he'd carry her into the house and maybe the movement of walking would calm her down?

He found a clasp at her belly that, when opened, allowed him to raise two straps over her head. A buckle by her hip released the bottom strap. When he jiggled the padded half circle around her, he discovered it rose, too.

But with all of her trappings gone, Bella fell forward. He just barely caught her. And when she plopped against him, she wiped her wet face in the lapel of his silk suit.

He groaned.

She clung to him. Using his lapels like a rope ladder, she climbed up and burrowed into his neck.

His heart knotted with confusing emotions. Fear and misery wanted to dominate. He had no idea what to do with this kid. Barely any idea how to get her into the house.

But sympathy snaked through the fear. She was alone. Lost. He knew what it was like to be alone and lost. Except he could also add unwanted. The morning after their legendary fight, Cedric might have retracted his demand that Matt leave the Patterson home, but too many harsh words had been spoken. Up until then, Matt had called Cedric Dad, believed they were blood. But in that awful fight, Cedric had let loose of the big family secret.

Matt and his twin were not Cedric's children. His mother had been married before. She'd left her first husband not knowing she was pregnant, and Cedric had taken her in, raised her children as his own.

It explained why Matt had always felt a distance between himself and Cedric, always felt a nagging sense of not being wanted, not really having a place, not having a home—

He looked at Bella. Orphaned. Alone. With a guy who didn't even know how to get her to stop crying, let alone how to feed her. She could have heard the conversation he'd had with Jimmy about not wanting kids. Not being daddy material. And though he knew that on a logical level she didn't understand a word they'd said, on an emotional level, she'd recorded it all.

Did she feel unwanted?

He pressed his lips together and closed his eyes. His chest shivered with regret. Then he popped his eyes open again, caught Bella beneath the arms and lifted her so they were eye to eye.

"I am sorry for everything that has happened to you in the past few days." His eyes squeezed shut again, as his own grief over losing Ginny and Oswald swamped him.

"Very sorry. I'm going to miss your mama, too. But you're mine now. And that means something."

He wasn't sure what it meant. He *knew*—to use Jimmy's phrasing—that he wasn't daddy material. The best he could do for this kid might be to hire a great nanny or a team of nannies—or maybe find the best nanny on the planet and give her every cent of his money to raise this little girl. But whatever he decided, Matt Patterson didn't abdicate responsibility or say die without a fight.

And as soon as he figured out how to fight, he would fight.

He slid out of the limo, Bella in his arms, and headed for the door into the mansion.

With his resolve in place, he noticed Bella's crying but he reacted to it differently. Something was wrong. He had to fix it.

Unfortunately, he didn't know how. She didn't feel wet. She wasn't generating any god-awful smells. So he steered clear of the diaper area. He asked about food. Mimed feeding himself. She only cried harder. He tried dancing. A couple waltzing twirls caused her to blink in confusion and quit crying for a few seconds, but when he stopped dancing she started crying.

He danced again. Around and around and around the foyer they went. Back to the den where he deposited the diaper bag, took off his jacket and rolled up the sleeves of his white shirt—all while dancing a baby around the sofa.

They danced through the empty kitchen. Up the hall. Around the dining room table. Across the sunroom. Until he felt dizzy and his legs became rubbery.

Where the hell was the adoption agency woman... Claire? Where the hell was Claire?

As if she'd heard him, the gate buzzer sounded. He raced to the com unit and hit the button. "Claire?"

"Yes. It's me."

Her musical voice sent sensation skipping down his spine, bringing her pretty face and sensual body to mind. If she were any other person, if he'd met her any other way, he would date her—

Oh, who was he kidding? He'd sleep with her. But needing her the way he did for Bella, he couldn't even consider sleeping with her. Technically, once she began helping him with the baby, she became an employee.

A smart man didn't hurt a woman in his employ. Especially not one he so desperately needed.

Regret tumbled through him as he pressed the com button. "I'm opening the gate now."

He hit two more buttons and Bella patted his cheeks, as if trying to get his attention.

"What? You want to dance some more?"

She giggled.

What went through Matt's heart was so foreign he couldn't describe it, but it felt like tug of longing crashed into a wall of truth.

He couldn't raise a child. For Pete's sake! He was the Iceman on Wall Street. Unyielding. Intractable. The only thing he knew was severity. Hard truth. He didn't have an ounce of softness in him.

Bella patted his cheek again, squealing with delight, obviously trying to get him to dance some more.

Yearning surged through him, but before he could capture it, it hit that wall of truth again. He was hard, cold. No matter how much he wanted to be the one who showed this child she was loved, that she didn't have to be afraid, he knew he couldn't. His family had taught him that people lied. His ex-wife had shown him that even when he wanted love he didn't know how to accept it.

So how could he show this little girl she was loved?
He couldn't.

After parking in front of Matt Patterson's mansion, Claire
got out of her little red car and popped her umbrella.
Standing in the cold rain, staring at the residence, she
suddenly understood what it meant to be a billionaire. Her
entire condo building could fit into his house.

She hesitated at the sidewalk. Her heart tumbled in her
chest as the reality of what she'd just agreed to hit her.
For the first time in five years she was attracted to a man
and she'd agreed to spend the evening in his house, helping him care for his baby.

She straightened. This fear was ridiculous. She was an
adult. Back when she'd fallen for Ben she'd been a starry-
eyed ingenue. She now knew how to control herself.

Plus, this situation was totally different. Matt Patterson
wasn't a professor she looked up to. In fact, *she'd* be teaching *him*. There'd be no danger that he'd sweep her off her
feet by impressing her with his brilliance. When it came to
baby care, Matt Patterson had no brilliance. She'd be fine.

Even before she got to the wood front door with the
brass knocker, it opened. Matt stood before her, his hair
oddly disheveled, his jacket removed and shirtsleeves
rolled up to the elbows. It looked like there might be a
thin sheen of sweat on his forehead.

"Come in. Come in," Matt said, all but dumping Bella
into her arms after she closed her umbrella and angled it
by the door. "I've changed my mind about the nanny. I
think we need to get one now."

"Okay." Bella on her arm, Claire slid out of her coat
and walked into the foyer. A huge crystal chandelier dominated the space. Her heels clicked on the Italian marble
floor. The sound echoed around them.

"I have the cards you gave me in my jacket pocket in the den." He turned and headed down a hall.

Claire followed him.

"But it's all so confusing." He stopped in front of a closed door. "I've never even considered hiring a nanny before." He peeked back at her. "Do I get somebody who's old…old and cuddly…who might want to retire before Bella hits four? Or somebody who's young and sophisticated who might not love her enough. Read her stories. That kind of stuff."

"You're overthinking."

"That's because this is very important to me." He opened the door and led her into a neat-as-a-pin den that could double as an office given that there was an overstuffed sofa and chair in front of a big-screen TV, as well as a heavy oak desk and tall-backed chair on the far side of the room.

He went to the desk and plopped on the chair. But before Claire sat, she sniffed and frowned. "You haven't by any chance changed her diaper in the past hour."

"She wasn't wet."

Her nose wrinkled. "I think she is now. Where's the diaper bag?"

He pointed to the overstuffed sofa where the baby's bag leaned drunkenly against the arm, beside his jacket, which had been tossed haphazardly on the sofa back. "There."

"Okay…so…" She peeked at him. "There wouldn't happen to be a nursery in this house?"

He snorted. "Not hardly."

"Okay." She looked around again, knowing she could make do. "How about a blanket?"

He rose from his chair. "Blanket I can help you with." He frowned. "I think. I know there's a linen closet upstairs somewhere."

"You get a blanket and I'll rummage through the diaper bag for a diaper. Hopefully by the time I'm ready to change her you'll be back with a blanket."

He nodded once and left the room.

When she was sure he was gone, Claire waltzed Bella around the desk once. Rocking the floor with the baby, she'd discovered dancing was the only way to get her to stop crying, but it was also fun. Sort of their point of connection.

"So how's it going with the new daddy so far?"

She screeched and Claire laughed. "You're right. He's green. But think of him as a diamond in the rough."

She danced the baby over to the sofa and poked through the diaper bag until she found a diaper.

She tossed it to the sofa, then danced Bella around again. As the room spun by, she realized how cold and sterile it was and a worry flitted through her. How could a man who lived in such a formal house ever care for a baby? "There's not even an afghan to lay you on."

"Here we are," Matt said, walking into the room. In his hands was a thick blue blanket.

Not wanting to be caught dancing with the baby, she turned her waltz into a step that looked something like she'd been pacing and said, "Lay it on the sofa."

He did as instructed and Claire made short order of Bella's diaper. But even though Matt had meandered away from the spectacle, she caught him peering over a time or two.

A light of hope lit. He might be green and his house might be cold but he was curious. "Want to learn how to do this?"

He pulled back. "No."

"You sure? It's not difficult."

"My hour alone with her was enough to remind me that I don't have the skills to care for her."

"What are you going to do when your nanny takes a day off?"

"Get help from the maid?"

Though that made her laugh, it didn't bode well for sweet Bella. Still, that wasn't her business. The point of her being here this evening was to help him adjust to having a baby, but since he'd mentioned changing his mind about a nanny—thank God—she could also assist him with calling an agency that could provide someone temporary for the night. And Bella would be well cared for.

So she said nothing as she rooted through the few things in the diaper bag until she found a set of clean clothes. One of the four or five sets she'd been alternating with pajamas and washing over the four days she'd kept the baby.

"At some point, you're going to have to go to your ex-wife's house and get Bella some more clothes. I have several sets of pj's and outfits for daytime in the bag, but it's really only enough for two days. I've had to do laundry twice. Plus, we don't have any of her toys. Things that might make her happy." She glanced around. "You'll also need her high chair and crib and walker and swing."

"I don't even know what half those things are."

She rose from the sofa. "That's okay. That's why I'm here. To help you get set up. What do you say we call your driver and go over to Bella's mom's house and get her high chair and crib, more of her clothes and all of her toys?"

Matt stepped back as a sickening feeling gripped him. Go to Ginny's, when she wasn't there? Knowing she'd never be there again? Knowing he'd pushed her away? Reminding himself of everything he'd lost because he was cold, heartless and the one person who shouldn't be raising her precious baby?

No. Absolutely not.

"I have a better idea. Why don't we just order a new crib and high chair and whatever else she needs?"

Claire laughed. "Why buy new when she already has them?"

Only one of his eyebrows rose.

"Oh, I get it. You're one of those money-is-no-object people."

"And this is bad because…?"

"It's not bad. It's just that it might comfort her to have some of her own things around her."

"If she's been without them for four days, she's probably forgotten them." Guilt warred with pain as he turned to the desk. He knew Claire was right. Having her own things would comfort Bella. But he just couldn't face going to that house. If he had to be strong for Bella, some concession had to be made for him.

"It's been a very long day. This time yesterday, I was in London. Today I'm here…with a baby. Let me get on the phone and make a few calls and buy a high chair and a crib. Tomorrow if she still needs *her* things, I'll make a run for them."

She frowned, as if thinking, and Matt froze. He'd given his best argument. If she disagreed, if she pushed, he had no idea how he'd talk her out of going to Ginny's. Because he couldn't go. He absolutely couldn't go.

Before she could say anything, Bella grabbed Claire's pearls, wrapped them around her chubby fist and stuck her fist into her mouth.

Claire gasped. "Have you given her a bottle lately?"

"I asked, but it didn't stop her crying so I assumed she didn't want it."

She groaned. "You don't *ask*. You show her a bottle." She walked over to the diaper bag, pulled out an empty bottle and kissed Bella's shiny black hair. "Let's go get you something to eat."

Matt raced after her. "I don't have anything for her to eat."

"We're just talking milk here." She stopped, pivoted to face him. "Although we probably should feed her something before we give her a bottle."

"I told you. I don't have—"

She stopped him with a look. "Do you like oatmeal?"

He grimaced. "No."

"Any cooked cereal at all?"

"No."

She frowned and Matt's heart sank. He was going to be a terrible father.

"Pudding?"

He brightened. "Yes! I love the little pudding cups. It's a secret vice."

"A secret vice that's coming in handy." She turned to walk away, but stopped again. "Where is the kitchen?"

He led the way down two halls, and after pushing through double swinging doors, they stood in his restaurant-size stainless-steel kitchen.

"Let me guess. There's a ballroom somewhere in this house."

"Not a ballroom," he said, walking to the first refrigerator. "A party room."

But he stopped and looked around, suddenly seeing what Claire saw. The house was big and beautiful, but it was also cold and intimidating. A child could get lost in here. And feel alone. He did not want Bella to feel alone. He did not want her going through what he went through.

Still, that was the whole point of getting a nanny.

Though he might have to do more remodeling than just a nursery, the nanny would keep Bella busy, happy. As long as he didn't get overwhelmed, he would work all this out.

He pulled open the refrigerator door, reached inside and came out with two little pudding cups. "Chocolate or vanilla?"

"Vanilla for now. Then one of us is going to have to go to a grocery store for real baby food."

"Or we could call."

"Call?"

After getting a spoon from a handy drawer, he directed her to a little table at the far end of the room. "Have a seat."

She sat, settled Bella on her lap and took the pudding cup and spoon from his hands. Bella cooed and reached for it.

As Claire popped the lid, he headed for the desk in the other corner of the kitchen and sat in front of the computer. With a few strokes on the keyboard, he said, "Ah."

She dipped the spoon into Bella's pudding. "Ah?"

"I found our grocer." He made a few clicks on his cell phone and put it to his ear. "This is Matt Patterson. I need to place an order." He waited for his call to be transferred. When someone answered, he said, "This is Matt Patterson. I have a six-month-old baby at my home. I'll need some baby food." He paused, giving the clerk a chance to write down what he'd said. "And some milk." Another pause. "For delivery. Thank you." Then he hung up.

Sliding a spoon of pudding into Bella's eager mouth, Claire said, "You didn't even tell her what kind of baby food you wanted."

"She's paid to know. It's an upscale store."

Bella smacked her lips and grabbed Claire's arm as

if to direct her to give her another bite. Claire laughed. "She's really hungry."

"I see that." He ambled over to the table. "Hey, kid." He crouched so he was eye level with Bella. "You like that?"

She giggled. His first sense of relief in days flowed through him and he smiled. He might not know exactly what to do, but he did have enough money to hire people who did.

He rose. "So diaper is taken care of. Food is handled. I guess it's time we order that crib?"

Bella screeched and slapped her chubby hands against the table. Claire quickly fed her more pudding, then she looked at him. "Yes. We should at least get a crib…and a high chair—oh, and a swing. And a baby monitor for while she's napping. Once we go online and get item numbers—" She made a whirling motion with her hand. "Then you can call whoever it is you call for furniture and baby things and have them delivered."

"Sounds like a plan." A good plan. A wonderful plan. His common sense would carry him through. There was nothing to worry about.

Bella squealed happily, reinforcing his confidence, but a weird sensation tumbled through him. Sort of like he was forgetting something. But he couldn't quite put his finger on it. Still, if it was important he would remember.

He hoped.

CHAPTER THREE

AFTER only five minutes, Bella fell asleep on Claire's arm.

"I think we should go back to the den so we can lay her down while we look for the crib and high chair."

"I can do all this from my phone, if you don't mind looking at this little screen together?"

Their gazes caught. A picture popped into her brain. Them, huddled together, looking at his phone. Her heart would shiver. She'd probably get breathless. All because her hormones had a mind of their own.

"I think the computer in the den is a better idea."

Carrying Bella, she followed him through two ornate rooms, both of which could have been formal living rooms, but at this point she was beginning to see her understanding of houses and architecture was incredibly limited.

Walking to the den, she saw more crystal chandeliers, oriental rugs, hardwood floors and art—everything from paintings to sculptures, vases and blown glass—than she'd seen in her entire lifetime.

She glanced around uneasily. "How do you live in here?"

He opened the door and they walked into the overly neat den. "How do I live where?"

"In a house that's more like a showplace than a house."

"Because of rooms like this," he said, passing the sofa, leading her to the desk with the computer.

She frowned. If he considered this room to be normal, comfortable, he was in worse shape than she'd thought.

He stopped suddenly. "You wanted to lay the baby down."

She pointed at the sofa still holding the blanket from the diaper change. "We just need another blanket to cover her."

He nodded and headed off. She sat on the sofa, Bella sleeping on her lap. Her little pink blouse and baby jeans snuggly fit her healthy body. Her fine, dark hair peaked in little tufts. Her black lashes sat on her cheeks.

In her high school and early college daydreams, Claire had always seen herself as having her own baby by now. And a house. With a wonderful, loving husband who wouldn't work all the time the way her father had. Somebody who'd be home for happy suppers and cozy nights with a storybook to read to their baby.

She snorted a quiet laugh. Yet another reason *not* to be attracted to Matt Patterson. He might be more outgoing than her quiet, quiet father, but he was cut from the same cloth. Work was his sport of choice. Money was the way he kept score. That was probably why he'd so quickly changed his mind about a nanny. Ten minutes in the car with Bella and he'd probably seen how much caring for her would interfere with his life.

Not that she was complaining. As nice as it would be for him to care for Bella himself, a clueless man needed a nanny. Still, it would be wonderful if he did get into the habit of spending a little time with Bella so she wouldn't be as alone as Claire had been as a child.

She swallowed back the lump of sadness and regret that clogged her throat. How she'd longed for a little of her dad's time and attention after her mother died. The lonely days and nights she'd spent flashed to her mind. Nights when she and her businessman father "shared" dinner but didn't speak. Nights when she'd yearned to be tucked in her bed and kissed on the forehead, but never was. Pouring cold cereal for herself for breakfast. Coming home to a quiet house with a maid who didn't like children.

Empathy for Bella rumbled through her. She hoped Matt Patterson wouldn't be a cold, distant dad, but the odds were once he got a nanny he'd slip away. He'd only have contact with the baby when he absolutely needed to. Not because he was bad, but because he didn't know how to be a dad.

He walked into the room, carrying the blanket. "Here you go."

Claire laid Bella on the blanket already on the sofa. When Matt handed the second blanket to her, she opened it enough that it could easily cover the baby.

"There."

"She's okay there?"

"We'll watch her from the desk. But I think she's fine."

"Okay."

With Bella sleeping soundly on the sofa, Matt led Claire to the computer and took the seat in front of it. She stood looking at the screen over his shoulder.

But soon tiredness set in. She'd left the office at four. The drive to Matt's estate had been at least an hour. They'd probably spent another hour changing Bella, feeding her, ordering her food. This on top of a full day's work—and a night of walking the floor with a baby who missed her mom.

She eased her hip to the desk, but Matt's gaze slid over to her rounded bottom. Tingles of awareness floated through her, along with a complication. All this time she'd thought she was just attracted to him.… What if he was attracted to her, too?

He probably wasn't, but just in case, she slid off again.

It wasn't long before her legs pulled at her. She'd been in heels for over ten hours. She eyed his chair longingly, then her gaze caught the sturdy leather arm. Thickly padded and wide, it could accommodate her weight.

Plus, he'd really have to twist and turn to see her butt, her legs, any part of her, because she wouldn't be beside him. She'd be slightly behind him.

Casually, carefully, she eased herself onto the chair's arm. Her feet sighed with relief.

Then her arm brushed his soft silk shirt, she smelled the masculine scent of his shampoo and tingles of electricity shot straight to her middle.

She almost groaned.

He faced her and their gazes connected. Looking into his pretty green eyes made her breathless—but also suddenly curious. He was gorgeous, yet not taken. He had money enough to attract any woman he wanted, yet he lived alone—

Of course, his bossiness probably turned most women off.

So why wasn't it working for her?

They found the product numbers for a crib, high chair, baby monitor and swing. She eased herself from his chair and sat on the sofa, by Bella, as he made a few calls.

Bella began to cry, so she lifted her to her lap. The baby rubbed her tired eyes, clearly feeling the effects of four sleepless nights.

When Matt hung up the phone, Claire said, "So how long until we get the crib?"

"An hour at most."

That surprised her so much she smiled. He was quite the optimist. "Really?"

He rose and headed for the door. "Yes. Give me ten minutes to talk to Jimmy."

"Jimmy?"

"My driver. He'll be the one assembling everything... since I assume cribs and high chairs don't come assembled."

"Probably not."

"Then give me ten minutes to bribe him into helping me."

She laughed, but caught herself, not sure if he'd meant that as a joke. Could stiff and formal Matt Patterson know how to joke?

But Matt wasn't back in ten minutes. In fact, he didn't return to the den for over an hour. Bella had once again fallen asleep in Claire's arms, so Claire put her head back and drifted off.

When Matt popped his head into the den saying, "Delivery truck is here. Jimmy and I will handle this," she bounced up, not sure if she was more embarrassed that she'd fallen asleep or that he'd caught her.

So she didn't immediately go out to the foyer to see what was going on. Instead, she reminded herself that she was only here a few more minutes. They'd put together the crib and lay the baby down—then she'd help him with the call to the nanny service and be gone.

No reason to be embarrassed that she'd fallen asleep. No reason to be bothered about an attraction. In twenty minutes, she'd get in her car, drive off his property and never see him again.

Or Bella.

Her heart constricted at the thought, but she knew that was life. People came and went. Attachments hurt.

She hoisted herself from the sofa and headed out to the hall. When she reached the foyer, it suddenly struck her that she had no idea where he had gone. He'd said he was going with Jimmy to assemble the crib. Which probably meant he was in a bedroom. She glanced around, guessing there could be as many as fifteen bedrooms in this house.

Before she took the thought any further, Matt appeared at the top of the stairway. "Crib's assembled. But we forgot to order sheets."

"Did you notice any flat sheets in the linen closet you found?"

"Yes."

"We'll just use one of those. Tomorrow you can order crib sheets."

"Sounds like a plan."

She carried Bella up the stairs. At the top, Matt pointed down the hall. "This way."

He guided her down two corridors and stopped at a set of double doors. Rich with grain that came through the red mahogany stain, they gleamed at her. He took both knobs, opened the doors and walked inside.

Claire stood on the threshold, her mouth gaping. A huge bed sat on a pedestal in the back of the room, near a bank of windows covered in elegant drapes that looked to be silk. What seemed like half a football field of space sat between the door and the bed, and in that space were a fireplace, white shag area rugs and two club chairs in front of a big-screen TV.

But that was it. The place was so open that gleaming hardwood floors dominated the room.

"This is your nursery?"

"I don't have a nursery, remember? This is my bedroom."

"*Your* bedroom."

"She's going to cry and get up in the middle of the night, isn't she?"

"Yes. But I assumed you'd have the nanny get up with her."

"Not tonight. It feels too much like I'll be abandoning her. That's why I put her crib—" he pointed at an open door to the right "—in there."

"You put her in a closet?"

He snorted a laugh. "No. That's an empty room beside mine. I was going to put an office in there but changed my mind. So it will come in handy tonight. With the door open, she'll be close enough that I'll hear her cry and she won't feel alone."

Gratitude tugged on her heart. She didn't know why this man so easily empathized with Bella's situation, but she was glad he did. Still—

"Do you know what to do when she gets up?"

"Change her diaper and give her a bottle." He headed out of the room. A few minutes later he came back with a flat sheet and walked through the open door into the room beside his. "I watched what you did with the diaper. It didn't seem like rocket science and neither does getting her a bottle."

"I just don't see you walking the floor." She glanced around and took in all the…space. She swore she could fit her condo in the front of his bedroom. "Though there's plenty of floor to walk a baby in here." She glanced around again and finally followed him into the room where the newly assembled crib stood. "My God. Your room is huge. Like a high school gymnasium with better furniture."

"It's adequate." He arranged the sheet on the mattress in the crib.

"It's empty."

"I don't have any need for more than a bed, a few chairs and a TV."

Seeing no point to arguing his personal choices, she laid the baby in the crib. "Whatever. But you still have to consider the hours you'll be spending walking the floor when Bella cries."

"She cries a lot?"

"Nights are the hardest for her."

He combed his fingers through his hair. "I don't want anything to be hard for her. This transition has to be smooth."

"Well, we don't have to make any decisions now. Let's call the nanny service. Maybe there'll be one who won't mind sleeping in the room with the door open?"

"She's going to sleep in the room with the crib?"

"Well, you could give her a suite in another wing, but then she wouldn't hear Bella cry."

"So I have to put a bed in there for her, too?"

"Unless you want to drag one of your chairs over there and make her stay awake all night, watching Bella." She caught his gaze. "And she's probably going to ask you to close the door while she's sleeping."

"Great. That sort of defeats the purpose."

"Not really. Trust me. That close, you'll still hear Bella cry. Plus, you have to make some concession somewhere," she said, leading him out the door.

"I know, but something inside me says I can't leave Bella. I want to be with her tonight. I want her to know she hasn't been abandoned."

Claire's heart swelled again. Her worries that Matt was going to be like her dad, ignoring Bella the way her father had ignored her, lessened a bit. For all his faults, he truly wanted to care for this baby.

They walked out into the hall, but the second the door

to Matt's bedroom closed behind them, they heard a soft cry. By the time they opened the door and returned to the little room with the crib, Bella was sobbing.

As naturally as breathing, Matt reached in and pulled her up into his arms. "Ah, Bella. Don't cry."

Claire's eyebrows rose. He hadn't hesitated. He hadn't deferred to Claire. He'd automatically taken Bella into his arms.

He really wanted to care for this baby.

"You could be very good with her."

"Right," Matt said. His voice rose to be heard above the sobbing. "As you can see, my picking her up really stopped her crying."

"Not yet. But it will. Once she gets accustomed to you." She walked around Matt, noting that his hold on the baby was secure but not a death grip that would frighten Bella. Though his shirt would be permanently wrinkled where Bella leaned against him, he either didn't notice or didn't care. And the baby had her arm on Matt's shoulder, her hand stopped just at his neck. She was beginning to trust him. "You hold her easily, naturally, as if you've done this before."

"I did have her by myself for an hour."

"Hmm." She walked around them again. "You held her the whole time?"

His face reddened a bit. "Yes. Once we got out of the limo I held her."

"And walked to keep her from crying?"

He licked his lips. "Yes. We...walked."

"So maybe you *can* handle her all night on your own."

He glanced down at Bella, who still sobbed in his arms. "I'd rather the baby in my care not cry all night. If a nanny can get her to sleep, then I say we need to bring in those reinforcements."

"Okay. Let's go downstairs and make the call."

They made it as far as the stairway before sobbing Bella leaned out of Matt's arms and toward Claire. Once Claire took her, her crying turned to sniffles, then hiccups, then nothing.

Leading them down the hall to the den, Matt turned. "Amazing. That's at least the second time she's stopped crying for you."

"She's been with me for the four days it took you to return from London."

In the den, he headed for the office section in the back. Claire sat on one of the chairs in front of the desk, Bella on her lap. Bella immediately reached for her pearls.

Leaning in Claire whispered, "Stop that."

The baby giggled. Claire tickled her tummy. "If you want to play, there are more fun things to do than suck on pearls."

Bella squealed.

Claire tickled her belly again. Bella's giggles filled the room.

Matt said, "Okay, dialing now. Everybody might want to put a lid on it so Daddy can hear."

Claire's gaze snapped up. Had he just said Daddy?

"Yes, good evening. This is Matt Patterson. I got custody of a baby today and I'm going to need a nanny."

He leaned back in his chair, obviously listening to what the person at the nanny service was saying, but Claire studied him.

With his perfect hair, sexy green eyes and disarming smile, he didn't look like the kind of guy who would refer to himself as Daddy. Especially not immediately. Ultimately, he'd probably accept the title, but at this point Claire thought for sure he'd fight it.

Something was up with him. Something caused him to see this little girl's plight and respond to it.

But if he got a nanny, a strict one, someone who wouldn't let him help with Bella tonight, someone who wouldn't let him assist with feedings or bath time, he could easily slide out of Bella's life. Grow to depend on the nanny. And then he'd be like her dad. A cold, distant father.

And Bella would have a childhood like Claire's. Lonely.

"You're right."

Matt's gaze snapped to her when she spoke. He put his hand over the receiver. "What?"

"You're right. You can't let her be with the nanny tonight. You have to get up with her. She needs to see you and you need to learn how to care for her."

Matt took his hand off the receiver and answered the person on the phone. "Yes. I'd need someone temporary for a few days while I choose a permanent employee."

She stood up, reached over and pressed the button down to disconnect his call.

"Tomorrow you can get a temporary nanny. Tomorrow we can also ask them to fax some résumés of permanent candidates. Tonight, you need to continue to bond with Bella."

He leaned back in his chair, those sexy eyes holding her gaze. "That had better mean you're staying."

She nodded as the implications of that tumbled through her. "Yes. I'll stay and help."

"And sleep in the room next to my bedroom?"

She lifted her chin. "We're adults. Both of us have the best interest of Bella in mind. Besides, there's a door."

He smiled. "So, I can trust you?"

Her mouth fell open. "Of course you can trust me!"

"Just checking."

But his gaze involuntarily fell to her breasts, then her hips and down to her feet. It was the second time he'd "looked" at her. First the subtle peek at her butt when she sat on the desk. Now a full-scale examination.

She swallowed and turned away, pretending to be preoccupied with Bella to give herself a second to resurrect her common sense. So he was attracted to her? She was attracted to him and had absolutely no intention of acting on it. He was a man too much like her father for her to even consider being interested. And she was a woman who refused to settle for anything less than a loving, wonderful husband.

Neither of them had any worries.

She hoped.

CHAPTER FOUR

CLAIRE faced Matt with a crisp, professional smile. "Since I'm staying the night, I'll need to go home to get some clothes."

Memories of his hour alone with Bella caused him to freeze with fear, not just because of the noise and the feeling of impotence, but because the baby had been so upset. He couldn't stand to see her sob like that again.

He rose. "Are you taking Bella with you?"

"You'll be fine for an hour."

"I think it's too soon to risk it." He didn't want to admit that he couldn't stand to see Bella cry. His feelings ran too deep, connected with too many personal things. Things he didn't care to discuss with a stranger.

So though he didn't lie, he was happy to have the perfect excuse to make sure he wasn't alone with the baby again. "Besides, the car seat is in the limo. We'll all have to go together."

"Fine. I don't care how I get to my house. I just want a pair of jeans and a T-shirt and to get out of these shoes."

She held up her leg to display her red high heels and Matt's gut tightened. He didn't have a shoe fetish, but he did know a good set of legs when he saw them and hers were classic. She was a beautiful woman with great legs who was helping him with his baby. If the odd flutter that took over his stomach any time she was sweet with Bella ever combined with the hot need that exploded through him every time he looked at her, he'd be in big trouble.

Especially since her agreeing to stay for Bella's sake was the kindest, nicest thing he'd ever seen anybody do.

Wincing internally, he told himself not to think like that. Claire was a nice woman and he needed her. He couldn't hurt her. And that's what he did—hurt women. Ginny hadn't hated him after the way he'd destroyed their marriage because he came to the rescue of her second husband, gave him the leg up he needed to become successful. But every other woman he'd dated had. So he didn't date anymore. He had lovers. Women who knew the score.

He texted Jimmy and led Claire through the house to the garage. When he opened the door and motioned her inside, she gasped. "All these cars are yours?"

He barely glanced at the two rows of cars. Everything from a Bentley to a classic GTO. "Yes."

Jimmy suddenly appeared at their right. "And he only lets me drive the limo."

"That's because I'm perfectly capable of driving the other cars." He turned to Claire, motioning to the driver. "This is Jimmy."

"How do, ma'am."

She smiled. "I'm Claire. It's nice to meet you."

Matt said, "We're going to Claire's apartment." He faced Claire again. "Give him the address."

She rattled off the location of her apartment and they got into the limo. She secured Bella in the car seat and just as she had in her first limo ride, Bella fell asleep.

Claire shifted uncomfortably. "So…" Obviously searching for something to say, she finally settled on, "This is a beautiful car."

Matt squelched a sigh. He already liked her. He already

experienced waves of attraction just looking at her. He didn't want them…communicating.

He snorted in derision. "Most limos are beautiful."

"Okay." Clearly getting the message he'd intended to send that he didn't want to make conversation, she turned away, pretending great interest in the scene outside her window.

He looked out the opposite window.

Still, though they rode in silence, his gaze fell to her legs, which were primly crossed at the ankles. With a little flick of a few eye muscles, his gaze could travel from those ankles the whole way past her knees because her skirt had bunched a bit—

Damn it! He wasn't just imagining letting his gaze take a trip up her legs—he had taken the trip!

"She's such an angel."

He jerked his gaze up to Claire's face. She hadn't noticed him gawking at her legs because she stared lovingly at Bella. His gut twisted again. His feelings for Bella were getting tangled up in his feelings for Claire, and strange emotions and yearnings pumped through him. Like desire interwoven with…something. He'd call it contentment but what the hell did contentment have to do with having a baby? She'd been nothing but trouble….

Except now she was sleeping. Her long black lashes sat on her puffy pink cheeks and her sweet mouth curved upward, filling his heart with the warmth of satisfaction.

He cleared his throat and gruffly said, "Yes, she's an angel," just as Jimmy pulled the limo to a curb and faced them.

"You're not thinking about letting that angel sleep in her seat while you go do whatever it is you have to do here?"

Claire laughed. "Not much of a baby fan, are you?"

"No, ma'am."

But instead of getting angry with the cheeky driver, Claire laughed again. Her pretty brown eyes shone with delight. "At least you're honest."

Matt glanced from Claire to Jimmy and back to Claire again.

Were they flirting?

A surge of jealousy caught him off guard. Since when did he get jealous?

As if only now realizing the limo had stopped, Bella woke and began to cry. Annoyed with himself for being jealous, he reached for the tummy snap, the leg strap and had the round padded thing lifted before Claire could make a move to help him.

"I see you've done this before."

"No thanks to you."

She slid across the seat. "I'm helping you a heck of a lot here. A little appreciation would be nice." Outside the limo, she faced him. "Or maybe we should just go back to your house and I'll get my car so I can come home for real."

Matt's stomach plummeted to his toes. And it wasn't just because he worried about being alone with Bella. He suddenly realized if she left him now, he'd probably never see her again and his heart squeezed.

Good God! He'd known this woman a couple of hours. How could he be jealous, and, worse, afraid of not seeing her again?

He passed Bella to Claire and started across the seat. When he got out of the limo, Claire was halfway up the walk.

Holding the door, Jimmy chuckled. "Better be nice to her unless you want to hear this kid screaming all night."

As Matt entered the building, Claire patiently waited

at the old iron freight elevator of the factory converted to apartments that she called home. She almost wished the thing would have come before he reached her so she could leave him behind. But no. He ambled toward her, looking rich, sophisticated and sexy.

She nervously tried not to notice the exposed brick and pipes that provided a bit of "chic" to the supermodern condos. But every detail popped out at her like objects in a three-dimensional movie. Ben had hated this place. He'd made fun of the pipes, asking if the contractor had run out of money before he could buy materials to cover them. He'd hated the exposed bricks because they were old. He couldn't believe anybody found anything about a factory appropriate to be seen in a residence.

And supersexy, superrich, supersophisticated Matt probably would snub his nose at her condo, too.

She just hoped he had more tact than Ben and wouldn't say his thoughts out loud.

The elevator arrived, she stepped inside and so did Matt.

He didn't say a word as they rose to her floor, but her relief was short-lived when she realized he was probably angry with her for threatening to leave him. Well, she didn't care. Let him stew a bit. She wasn't about to let him talk down to her. After Ben, she'd promised herself she'd never go through that again. And that was one promise she intended to keep.

The old metal doors opened noisily. She stepped out into the hall, once more seeing the brick walls, exposed pipes and hardwood floors. Her resolve strengthened. She loved this building. Loved her home. Let him hate it if he wanted. Let him make fun of it. She didn't care. His feelings meant nothing to her.

Still quiet, Matt followed her down the hall. She held

Bella on one arm as she marched to her door, fishing her keys out of her coat pocket. Before he reached her, she had the door open and was inside.

The exposed brick walls and hardwood floors continued throughout her open-plan apartment. Her kitchen was new, dark cabinets with slim silver handles and stainless-steel appliances. The chic dining area, including a table and trim buffet, flowed into her living room space, which had red sofas facing each other and an overstuffed red print chair with matching ottoman.

"Wow."

She spun to face him. "Wow?"

"Your apartment." He glanced around. "It's so modern." He looked around some more. "I really like it."

Nerves prickled her skin. Her breath whooshed out. She hadn't wanted his opinion to matter, but it had and that bothered her. He might be a nice guy with Bella, but he was also blunt and self-important. Guessing he was only trying to make nice after being rude to her, she grudgingly said, "Thanks."

"I had a similar condo for a while." He smiled as if remembering. "Right after I got my first job. Thought I'd hit the big-time because I started off earning six figures."

She gaped at him. "How does somebody 'start off' earning six figures?"

He strolled around the room. "I went to my interview with two five-year plans. One was for the company interviewing me. The other for their competitor."

She frowned. "So?"

"So, it never hurts to understand what the other guy is probably thinking." He chuckled. "They said I showed initiative."

"It sounds like initiative but I wouldn't know. I've never

been a businessperson, never even thought about wanting to be one."

He strolled over. "You're more of the sensitive type." He took a step that brought them so close she could almost feel the heat from his body. "But we've already discussed this."

"Yes…" She hated the tremble in her voice. He was just so damned good-looking. "We have."

"But we're really not even, you know."

"Even?"

"About what we know about each other. You have a nice condo. You like working with kids. And that's all I know about you."

"I don't exactly know a lot about you."

He chuckled. "You've been through my house." He caught her gaze. "In my bedroom. You know I was divorced but my ex-wife and I stayed close enough that she gave me custody of her child. You've seen my car collection, met my driver. Know that I give my employees long vacations when I travel for business. You know more about my personal life than most women I date."

Her skin flushed. A pulse started low in her belly. So did an unwanted sense of anticipation. It meant something that he was telling her things, or letting her see things about his life through his home. And right now, they stood so close he could kiss her—or she could kiss him, if she wanted.

She swallowed. Suddenly grateful for the protection of the baby on her arm, she said, "Why do you want to know about me?"

"I think you know."

"Because I know so much about you?"

"Because there's something between us." He took another step, forcing her to shift Bella to the left or let the poor baby get squished.

"I don't like unusual things. I don't like unexpected or unpredictable things."

Her breath lodged in her throat. They absolutely could not get any closer.

"So you don't like that you feel something for me?"

"No. I do not."

"Well, thanks."

He chuckled again. "You *should* thank me. You shouldn't want me to be interested. I don't date. I have lovers. I hurt women foolish enough to feel anything for me."

She took a step back, putting plenty of space between them, believing the air had been cleared and they were moving on. "Thanks for the warning." She handed the baby to him, but stopped short of giving her over. "You know, we've been carrying Bella around all day. It might be a good idea to let her roam a bit." She stooped and put the baby on the white shag carpet between the two red sofas. "How's this, sweetie?"

Patting the thick carpet, Bella gurgled up at her.

"Are you sure she'll be okay down there?"

"I've had her on this carpet plenty of times." She rose. "But you're going to make sure she's okay while I'm gone."

"I am?"

"Yes. I'll be five minutes, tops, while I gather a few things. You just have to make sure she doesn't go too far or bump her head or anything like that."

He glanced around. "Okay." He caught her gaze again. "But we're not done talking about this attraction."

"I think we are. You've warned me off enough that I'm not even worried about it."

"Liar."

She snorted a laugh. "What? You think you're so irresistible that—"

He caught her by the waist and hauled her to him. Before she could take her next breath, his lips were on hers. Soft yet demanding, they moved over her mouth until she found herself opening her lips beneath his. He took advantage. His tongue plunged into her mouth.

Desire ripped through her as her body became boneless. Her arms snaked around his neck. He tightened his grip on her waist and the kiss went on…

And on…

Sending sensations careening through her body, making her long for more.

Until Bella screeched.

Claire bounced away like a teenager caught kissing on the front porch by her parents.

Matt sucked in a breath. "Sorry."

With arousal pulsing through her, his apology didn't make sense. She blinked at him. "Sorry?"

"The kiss wasn't supposed to go that far. It was to prove a point." He rubbed his hand across the back of his neck. "I was hoping that…" He winced. "I thought if I kissed you we'd see the attraction was ordinary, and we'd…"

His words acted like water on a campfire. "You hoped I was a really crappy kisser?"

He winced. "Something like that."

She made a sound of disgust. This guy couldn't be any more infuriating if he tried. How could she be so attracted to him? "I'm going to get my things."

She turned to walk away but he caught her arm.

"I am sorry. But everything's getting confused. I'm trying to tell you that I'm not a family man, not the settling-down kind. Being with Bella is making me look like I might be…or maybe I should be. But I'm not."

Her face grew tight with an emotion so strong yet so foreign she couldn't even describe it. She'd never had a man tell her he was attracted to her as he tried to talk himself out of it. She wasn't sure if she was humiliated or infuriated.

"I get it."

"I don't think you do. The family reunion I'm going to in Texas is a joke. My family is riddled with secrets and lies.… No, I take that back. My family was *built on* secrets and lies. I became calloused to survive and I have survived. I've thrived. You're not like the sophisticates I date. And if you get involved with me, you will end up hurt."

She straightened her shoulders. What did he think she was? A lovesick schoolgirl? Ben had cured her of that. "Got it." She turned to go, but pivoted around again. "And just for the record, you might be a great kisser, but I'd already realized you're not a great catch. You're blunt. You're rude. You're absolutely positive you're always right. Well, this is one time you aren't. I wouldn't date you on a lost bet. You're everything I avoid in a man. I learned that lesson young because my dad was exactly like you. Cool, efficient. Silent most of the time. And if that isn't enough, I had a boyfriend who used me. So don't think I'm helping you because of your supposed charm. I'm helping you for Bella's sake." She took the two steps that separated them and got in his face. "You…are…perfectly… safe…with…me."

With that she walked away and Matt scrubbed his hand across his mouth. Well, that hadn't gone well. He'd had the best of intentions when he'd warned her off. She was a nice girl and she was attracted to him. And he didn't want her to get hurt. Yet his good intention of sparing her feelings had actually ended up making her mad.

He blew his breath out on a sigh and walked over to

Bella. Stooping down so he was on her level, he leaned in and whispered, "She'd probably kill me if I told her that she was even sexier when she yelled at me."

Bella squawked. He picked her up and rose with her. "What? You don't like the adults not paying attention to you?"

She laughed and patted his face and he smiled at her. But his smile quickly faded. Claire was right. He really was getting accustomed to this kid. He hadn't thought twice about picking her up. Didn't mind holding her now.

So maybe this was going to work? Maybe he could be a good dad?

Claire came out of her bedroom carrying a small duffel bag. Matt hardly noticed it. Seeing her hair down around her shoulders, fat curls that bounced when she walked and her plain top that hugged her curves before it stopped at the waistband of her low-riding jeans caused his mouth to water. Memories of their kiss thundered through him. Had he been a bit hasty in warning her off?

No. He'd been fair. He needed help with Bella and Claire was obviously providing it. Because she cared about Bella—not him. Not even his money. Good Lord, she hadn't even hinted about compensation.

He frowned. It was the first time since he'd gotten rich that somebody had just helped him.

Grabbing a bright red leather jacket, she said, "Let's go," and headed for the door.

He scurried after her. His gaze automatically fell to her bottom showcased in low-cut jeans, and inwardly he groaned. But he hadn't made a mistake in warning her off. He needed her. Her reward for helping him would be that he wouldn't hurt her.

When they reached the limo, Jimmy jauntily opened

the door for Claire and she smiled at him, said, "Thanks," a little breathlessly, and Matt's blood pressure rose.

He handed Bella into the limo and Claire strapped her in the car seat as he settled on the seat across from her. A bit miffed that she'd sort of flirted with Jimmy again, he decided not to talk to her.

But after ten minutes of silence in the car, he realized *she* wasn't talking to *him*.

His heart squeezed. But he ran his hand down his face. This was ridiculous. They'd both outlined very good reasons why they should stay away from each other. Hadn't his heart and hormones been paying attention?

Claire tapped on the round padded thing that kept Bella securely in the car seat. "Hey, sweet girl."

The baby gurgled a laugh.

"We should have remembered to bring something for her to play with."

He grudgingly peeked over. "Like what?"

"She came with a bear and I bought her two rattles and a chew toy. They're in her diaper bag."

"We'll give them to her when we get back."

She smiled. "Okay."

He simmered. She seemed very happy. Relaxed. Almost as if their kiss hadn't happened. Or maybe she was happy that they'd cleared the air between them?

Well, fine. He was happy, too. God knew he had a million other things to think about, worry about, stress over, if he wanted to be stressed.

His already unhappy family had been increased by four half siblings. The children his real father had had with the woman he married after Matt's mother had returned to New York. And he had to meet those people in nine short days. For his sisters' sake, he'd promised to be nice.

If he wanted to obsess over anything, he should be

figuring how he intended to keep his promise to Ellie, Charlotte and Alex. Having all recently settled down—Charlotte with a baby even—they were now all about family and wanted him to be part of that, too. He shouldn't be worried that the current woman in his company was the first woman in a long time to not only reject him, but also to stand up to him.

Great. Now he was thinking about her again.

Maybe the mistake was agreeing to let her spend the night…

In the little room next to his bedroom…

This was going to be peachy.

CHAPTER FIVE

BY THE time they arrived at the mansion, it was dark. Jimmy drove the limo into the garage, and as soon as it stopped, Claire reached for the buckles and snaps to free Bella.

She carried Bella to the door as if she'd been to his house a million times, walked through and headed to the kitchen.

Matt stayed on her heels, not exactly sure what he was supposed to do. She took a bottle from the diaper bag, rinsed it, filled it with milk and walked out of the kitchen up the hall, toward the curved stairway in the foyer. "First a bath, then some milk, then it's into bed with you, Missy."

"It's only eight."

Walking up the stairs, she faced Matt. "She's a baby. Babies go to bed early."

"Did you ever stop to think that if you kept her up until ten, she'd sleep through the night?"

"You're wishful thinking."

She walked into his bedroom and stopped at the three side-by-side doors along the left wall. "Which door?"

"For?"

"The bathroom. She needs a bath, remember?"

"Middle one."

She opened the door onto his master bath, and though

she started to step in confidently, her foot faltered. "Good God."

He ambled up behind her. "What?"

He didn't think it was the Italian marble floor that stopped her. The double sinks were special, especially since there was a waterfall that ran down the brown, gray and white stone tiles behind them. But they didn't usually earn a gasp. The huge shower was cool. He loved the showerhead that felt like rain and the jets that shot water out of any side or corner of the shower he wanted, but most people didn't notice the wonders of the shower until they were in it.

So, she had to be gaping at the old-fashioned claw-foot tub.

Sitting on a one-foot marble rise with a solid-gold faucet, beneath a skylight that probably right now had a great view of the stars, the tub could be a showstopper.

"You bathe in that?"

"Well, I don't want to walk around smelling like a wildebeest."

"I guess you feel like Napoleon when you're sitting in that thing."

"Actually, I fancy myself more like Julius Caesar." Happy to finally be in control again, he said, "I light a cigar, lay my arms along the rims, put my head back and look at the stars."

She cautiously walked over to the tub. Her head craned back until she saw the skylight. "Ah."

He snuck up behind her, whispered in her ear. "Pretty nifty, isn't it?"

"This bathroom is bigger than my entire apartment."

"Want to see the rain shower?"

She faced him, swallowing. "I'd just like to see a normal tub where I could bathe a baby."

"She'd probably fit in the bowl sinks."

"In front of the waterfall?" She glanced around again. "Sheesh. Man. Do you really need all this stuff?"

"It's my reward."

"Well, you must have worked your butt off to feel you deserved all this."

"I did. And it makes me happy."

It really did. Being in this room reminded him that this was what he'd been working for his whole life. The freedom to live his life as he wanted. His mom had lied to him about Cedric being his father. He'd never felt he fit into his own family. He had even become distant from his sisters, who didn't care about real dads and pretend dads and bloodlines or lies. But he fit here. He was happy here. And some five-foot-seven slip of a woman wasn't going to make him "think" he wanted something else out of life. Especially not after only a few hours.

Besides, she was here to help him with the baby, to show him the ropes. He didn't want to waste this opportunity.

He strolled over to the first sink where she ran water while she pulled out a diaper and one-piece sleeper from the diaper bag one-handed.

"Here. Let me hold her."

Not meeting his gaze, she handed the baby to him. "Thanks." When the baby was securely on his arm, she said, "Is the linen closet around here?"

"What do you need?"

"Towels. A washcloth."

He walked over to the corner, pressed a button and the wall opened. He pulled out two fluffy white towels and a washcloth. "Here you are."

While he was gone, she'd removed a pink bottle, a

little yellow bottle and a taller white container from the diaper bag.

"What are those?"

Taking the baby from him again, she said, "Lotions and powder. Baby wash. Nothing special."

He frowned. Had that been a quaver in her voice?

"Are you okay?"

Removing Bella's one-piece outfit, she said, "I'm fine."

But not chatty. He knew he'd discouraged conversation in the limo, but she'd seemed fine, bossy even, until... He glanced around. Until they'd started talking about his tub? This bathroom?

Maybe he'd flaunted his wealth a bit too much. Or maybe his casual comments had seemed to her as if he was rubbing her nose in his success.

"Look, I'm sorry if I came across as an idiot talking about my tub. I didn't mean to upset you."

"I'm not upset."

"Your voice says you are."

She sighed and sat naked Bella in the sink she'd filled with water. "Okay. I'm not upset as much as reminded of some things I'd rather not think about."

"Ah. The bad boyfriend."

"No, the distant dad."

"Your distant dad had a big claw-foot tub?"

"Among other things." She rinsed water along Bella's tummy, and made the baby laugh. "My father was a successful businessman." She slanted him a look. "Not anywhere near your caliber, but he did okay." She shook her head. "He lived for the deal."

Yet another reminder of why he shouldn't get involved with women. He lived for the deal, too. And Claire's current sadness was the reminder of the fallout of that kind of life. "I bet that thrilled your mother."

"My mother died when I was six."

"Oh." That news shifted through him oddly. He could picture her. A little girl with big sad brown eyes and long brown ponytails, left alone by a dad who didn't know how to care for her.

His stomach knotted and he understood why she was so sympathetic to Bella. Right then and there, he strengthened his commitment to be the best father he could for his little girl, even as his chest tightened with sorrow for Claire's loss. "I'm sorry."

She poured one of the gels onto the washcloth, worked it into suds and leisurely ran the cloth over Bella's soft skin. "It's certainly not your fault."

"I was apologizing for bringing up unhappy memories."

"It's okay."

It really wasn't. Not just for Claire, but for him. He'd spent most of his adult life upset over his mother taking him away from his real father and saddling him with a stepfather who didn't want him, and then angry that his biological dad never tried to find him, to meet him—to anything.

But after hearing of Claire's losses he felt like a heel.

He pointed toward the bedroom. "I'm going to go check on the crib, make sure that sheet is okay."

She nodded. "Okay."

Inside the bedroom, out of Claire's sight, he ran his hand down his face. He got it. Lots of people had lives worse than his. But that didn't diminish the fact that he had some problems. Not only did he have to meet four half siblings, but the twin and half sisters he'd been raised with would be in Texas, too. He had to meet his new siblings and deal with the old ones, when he was turned inside out about raising a baby because he'd lost Ginny. The one person who'd always loved him. Any other ex-wife would have been happy to be rid of him, but she'd kept him as a friend, made sure he had a part in her life even after she remarried. There was no one like Ginny who'd understood the real Matt Patterson and still liked him. True, she couldn't be married to him but they had been friends. Good friends.

But now she was gone. And for the first time since he'd met Ginny, he was alone in the world.

Truly alone.

Claire lifted Bella out of the sink and rolled her in the thick fluffy white towel. She tickled her tummy and played with her a bit, but inside she was dying. The loneliness she'd felt after her mom's death rolled over her as if it were yesterday, not decades ago. And she wished… well, she wished Matt would have comforted her. After that kiss, it was clear they both were attracted. Neither one could deny it. But he couldn't find it in his heart to stay in the room and comfort her…or even really talk about her life.

Still, that was her luck with men. Her friends found good men, strong men, who knew how to love, how to comfort. She always seemed to be attracted to the self-absorbed guys.

Like Ben. He hadn't really loved her. But she'd thought he had. And she'd loved his company. She loved having somebody to spend time with, somebody to think about the future with. But when he'd introduced her to his wife at her graduation—the day she'd believed he would propose to her—her whole world had fallen apart. Instead of proposing, he'd broken up with her. And not by saying, "I'm sorry. It didn't work out." No. He introduced her to his wife. A not-so-subtle way of saying, "Now, that you're leaving the university, I have no need of you."

Discovering he was married and realizing her loneliness had driven her to a bad relationship didn't ease the pain of being alone after he was gone. Her bed wasn't just empty; her life was empty. She had a fancy condo, new car and a degree, but her life was empty.

And that was what she saw when she really looked around this house—Matt's house. Everything was perfect, beautiful, but untouched.

She rolled Bella into clean pajamas, telling herself Matt Patterson's "untouched" house wasn't any of her business. But she knew he was lonely, and his beliefs about relationships would keep him lonely. At least she was up front about her loneliness. At least she was trying to find real love in her life.…

She snorted a laugh that made Bella giggle. Trying to find love? She hadn't been attracted to a guy since Ben. Five years. And the first guy she's attracted to is cold and unfeeling.

Yeah. She was brilliant at picking partners. Brilliant at working to cure her loneliness.

Still, he'd warned her he wasn't the kind of guy who settled down or wanted relationships. She would be a good soldier and believe him.

She lifted clean and dressed Bella from the counter and nuzzled her neck. Matt Patterson might be a crappy choice for a boyfriend, but like it or not he had to be a dad. For Bella's sake, she'd do whatever she could tonight to help him learn how to love this baby.

She carried Bella out of the bathroom and walked her into the room beside Matt's bedroom to find Jimmy helping Matt put together a single bed.

"What's this?"

"Well, I certainly didn't want you sleeping on the floor."

She hadn't forgotten she was sleeping in the room next to Matt's, but watching them put together a bed made it all very real.

"I called Jimmy and we brought this bed from storage."

Jimmy inclined his head in greeting. "Brought your duffel bag up, too."

She smiled. Jimmy was a funny, nice guy who didn't put up with any crap from his boss, who seemed to have a knack for making her laugh. "Thanks."

As they put the bed together, she carried Bella to one of the club chairs in front of the TV in Matt's room and fed her a bottle.

When the bed was together, Jimmy left. Bella finished the last of her milk, her eyes drooping. Matt left the room for a minute and returned with clean linens.

Realizing they were for the bed she'd be using, Claire rose from her chair with sleeping Bella. "I'll get those."

"No. I'm fine." He dumped the sheets on the single bed. "You take care of Bella."

"She's asleep." Claire laid her in her crib, wondering how the heck this rich guy who wasn't quite sure where to find a blanket knew so much about sheets. Not only was he making her bed now, but he'd put the sheet on the mattress in Bella's crib. "And my work with her is done. So I can get those."

"How about if we both do it?"

She walked over to the bed as Matt opened the fitted sheet, billowing it across the bed so she could catch her end and hook the corners over the mattress.

When it was on, Matt did the same thing with the flat sheet.

Uncomfortable with the silence between them, Claire said, "We really are running out of clothes for Bella."

"We can buy new."

"I know but she probably has tons of her own things. Wouldn't it be nice to have some of the pretty things her mom picked out for her?"

Matt's heart somersaulted. He knew Claire's intentions were good, but every time he thought about Ginny his sadness got worse.

"Especially for that trip to Texas you're taking. She's going to be in a new environment again. It would be better for her to have some toys and her own clothes. Comfort things."

Matt sniffed. "Comfort things?" He shook his head. "I'm the one who needs the comfort things. The whole trip-to-Texas family-reunion thing is going to be hell."

"Hell?"

He stuffed a pillow in a pillowcase. "I haven't really been involved in my family for a decade and this 'reunion' is all about meeting half siblings I didn't even know I had."

"You have stepsiblings?"

"*Half* siblings. It's a long story."

She glanced at sleeping Bella. "We have time."

"My family doesn't matter. I have Bella now. She's my family. My life is busy. I have too much work to do to get involved with those people. In fact, the smart thing to do would be just not go to Texas. That way I won't have to worry about Bella adjusting to more new people. We'll stay here with her nanny, adjusting to the world she's going to stay in, not visiting a bunch of people she'll never see again."

Shocked, Claire gaped at him. "Just like that, you're giving up family?"

"My family isn't the white picket fence, nice guys who sit around a Thanksgiving table counting our blessings. We keep secrets. We hide things. I'd rather be alone than be with them."

He sucked in a breath. "Bed is made. Bella is sleeping. If there's nothing else for me to do, I'd like to go downstairs to make some west coast calls."

"Sure."

He headed for the door, but stopped. "Make yourself at home. Shower if you want. Get yourself some cocoa or a snack in the kitchen."

She nodded.

He walked out of the room, closing the door behind him.

She glanced at Bella, sleeping soundly in the crib, and lifted her duffel bag from the floor beside the bed. She rummaged around until she found pajamas and her cosmetics case and took those into the big bathroom.

After pulling out her body wash, shampoo and other shower essentials, she stripped and walked to the big shower. She smiled. Good grief. Such luxury! She'd given up being pampered almost a decade ago, but suddenly a shower with sixteen body jets seemed like a lot of fun.

But when she was in the cube, being pelleted with warm water, the echo of the spray in the shower brought her up short. When she stepped out and dried herself in the ultrasoft towel, the sound of nothing—not another person, not a car on the street, not a TV or radio or CD player…nothing—assaulted her.

This was how he lived.

This man who rejected family, who said he didn't need people, who said he loved his life, lived with servants and silence.

CHAPTER SIX

DRESSED in her pajamas and robe, Claire took Matt up on his offer and made herself a cup of cocoa in the cool, impersonal stainless-steel kitchen. Her every movement echoed around her in the quiet, underscoring the emptiness of the house.

A huge ball of empathy for Matt lodged in her tummy and the temptation was strong to go in search of him—if only to provide company. She suspected he was in the den, but with the size of his home, she also knew he could have a totally different office in another wing somewhere and her trip would be wasted.

Still, she stopped at the bottom of the stairs in the foyer. Her intimate knowledge of the pain of loneliness wouldn't allow her to let anyone else suffer. But he didn't want help and she didn't want him to think she was interested in him romantically. They might have kissed and both enjoyed it, but they'd agreed they wouldn't pursue their attraction. Plus, as he'd said, he had Bella to be his family. He didn't need anyone else. What business was it of hers to think that wasn't enough? Why should she care that he had family he didn't wish to see?

She shouldn't.

The wise course would be to simply do what she was

here to do—help him care for Bella tonight—and leave him tomorrow.

She climbed the steps, walked through his bedroom to the single bed near the crib and removed her e-reader from her duffel. Curled under the covers, she read for an hour, so engrossed in her book she didn't even feel time passing and suddenly the bedroom door opened.

Matt walked in. "Hey."

She set down her e-reader. He looked tired and sad. Longing to make him happy rose up in her. But they'd agreed not to get any further involved than they had to be for Bella.

So she said, "Did you get your calls made?"

"Yes." He rolled his shoulders as if exhausted. "Bella still sleeping?"

"Soundly." She glanced at the crib and smiled. At least something was going right. "In the four days I had her, she usually woke around ten. Since she slept past that, I think she's happy with the new crib."

He breathed a sigh of relief. "That's good."

Claire narrowed her eyes. If he'd been worried that the baby wouldn't like the new crib, why had he insisted they buy one? They could have easily gone to his ex-wife's home and retrieved Bella's old one. So why had he argued?

He motioned toward his room. "I'll just take a few minutes in the bathroom—brush my teeth and stuff—and I'll check on you guys again."

Once again telling herself that things about him and his life were none of her business, she simply said, "We're fine. You don't need to check on us."

He nodded and left the room. But in the bathroom, he leaned against the sink. He could smell her. The scent of flowers saturated the entire room. It could have been her soap or her shampoo. It didn't matter. Whatever it was, it swirled through his nostrils, tickled his senses and awoke needs he didn't want to feel for a sweet woman like Claire.

He shook his head. Could she have picked more prim and proper pajamas? Pink like cotton candy, the pants went the whole way to her ankles and the top buttoned at her throat.

He might have thought she'd dressed so primly to make a point, but something in his gut told him pajamas like those were what she regularly wore to bed. She wouldn't try to entice a man.

He frowned. She didn't have to. For some reason or another her proper clothes were sexier to him than the slinky red and black cocktail dresses worn by women with long nails and big ideas for how to pass the time until dawn.

With Claire he'd be the one doing the seducing....

Groaning, he told himself to stop thinking about her. He stripped, showered and brushed his teeth in record time. He walked to the closet at the back of the room and rummaged until he found an old pair of pajama bottoms, a gift from Charlotte, and slid into them, along with a robe.

If she wanted to be proper, he would be proper.

He strode through his bedroom, to make one more check on them, but Claire only said, "Good night," and rolled over onto her side.

Okay. Fine. She wanted to go to sleep; he would go to sleep. It was late. After eleven. He didn't have a problem with that.

Still, he tiptoed toward the crib for one final look at sleeping Bella. Her lashes rested on her plump rosy cheeks. Her lips were bowed in a smile. He wondered if she was dreaming about her parents and his heart skipped a beat. Even with all the trauma in his life, he couldn't imagine what she was going through. He prayed he would be a good dad to this poor sweet child.

Then he left the room, shrugged out of his robe and climbed into bed—his bed on a pedestal.

Unable to relax, he sighed, plumped the pillow. He'd slept in this exact bed for years, lots of years, and suddenly tonight it seemed wrong for him to be in this big bed, like some king.

He wasn't a king. He was an outcast. An outcast who'd used his wits and education to best every competitor who came his way.

He'd won.

Yet, tonight it didn't feel like he'd won. Caring for Bella made him feel ill-equipped and vulnerable. And merely considering breaking his promise to his sisters, Charlotte especially—the only person in his family he still spoke to—and not meeting the family he didn't want to meet, had also put him on edge.

Which was probably why he'd let some things slip to Claire when she'd asked about his family. He'd never wanted to talk about them before. But suddenly, with her, it was so easy to spill his guts. He blamed it on nervousness over the upcoming trip and once again considered not going. He didn't want to know these people. He was fine on his own.

But what about his promise? Was he bound by a promise he'd made to his sisters in a moment of weakness?

He flounced onto his side, annoyed with the direction of his thoughts. Especially when he began to consider all the possibilities for fights and backbiting when the Calhoun and Patterson clans got together. Technically, he was the oldest of the Calhoun children, but his "brother" Holt ran the family ranch, watched over the family holdings and "distributed" profits. With no will specifically naming Holt leader of the pack, Matt could come in and assert his rights. After all, who better to manage a family's fortune than a man who'd made one for himself?

He didn't want to think about how they probably planned to intimidate him into falling in line with Holt's wishes. He'd rather think about Claire and her pretty pink pajamas not trying to seduce him but making him crazy with wanting her.

It was no wonder he'd kissed her.

Remembering the feeling of her soft mouth against his, the mating of their tongues, the intense heat that whooshed through him, he almost groaned. But she was in a bed only a wall away and, if he groaned, she might hear him.

And she would ask what was wrong because she was considerate like that, and God only knew what he'd say this time.

He pulled the covers over his head. What the hell was wrong with him? He never wanted to talk to anybody! Why did he suddenly want to talk to her?

He was letting her get too close. That was what was wrong. She was here to help him with the baby and he was out of his element, so in his vulnerability he was making mistakes. But no more. He would learn what he needed to know as quickly as he could so this unwanted vulnerability would go!

Bella's crying woke Claire at around three. She'd slept an hour later than usual, which was good, but she hadn't slept through the night.

Realizing all this was new to Matt and that some of it had clearly overwhelmed him, she rolled out of bed and sped to the crib.

"Shh. Shh." She reached in and pulled out Bella. "I've got you! Give me two minutes to change your diaper and we'll race to the kitchen to get your bottle."

"I'll get a bottle."

Matt's voice from behind almost made Claire jump out of her skin. She whispered, "You scared me!"

Matt headed for the door. "No need to whisper. With her lungs, Bella could have the whole household up by now…if anybody was here."

She went to reply, but Matt opened the door and left before she could. No matter. She took the baby to the bathroom, found a diaper and had her changed before Matt returned with the fresh bottle of milk.

As he walked over to her, she sat on edge of her bed. But instead of handing the bottle to her, he took the baby. "We need a rocker in here."

Shocked that he'd taken Bella and had arranged her on his arm to feed her, she gaped at him. "What are you doing?"

"Feeding her."

"I can do it. You go back to bed."

"I need to learn how to do this and I am."

Respect for him rose up in her. Her father had passed everything to the various maids they'd had over the years. But Matt really wanted to care for Bella. She patted the bed beside her. "You'll get a rocker tomorrow. Until then, you can't stand to feed her." She grimaced. "Well, you could. But it takes a few minutes for her to eat, so you're better off sitting."

He grunted, brought Bella to her bed and sat on the spot Claire had patted.

Bella gulped greedily and Claire laughed. "Are we a little piggy tonight?"

Bella grinned around the bottle's nipple.

Matt slanted her a look. "Are we allowed to talk to her?"

"Sure. It's like dinner conversation. It helps you to bond." She paused, smiled at him. "Try it."

He quickly glanced away. "I don't know what to say."

"Say anything." She paused. "Why not tell her about the new family she's about to meet in Texas?"

He rose. "She's getting done really quickly. We don't have time to talk."

Disappointment skittered through her. It wasn't good for Bella to have him running hot and cold. And when it came to family he was definitely hot and cold. So she moved them off the topic of the Texas reunion and said, "You should probably burp her."

He spun to face her. "Burp her?"

His incredulous question made her laugh. "If you don't burp her the gas will wake her up."

"The first thirteen years of my life I heard nothing but don't burp...now you want me to get her to burp."

"Your mom probably never said don't burp. She probably said don't burp in public."

He snorted a half laugh. "All right. Whatever. How do I burp her?"

She hoisted herself off the bed and walked over to him. Lifting Bella from his arms, she said, "You have to put her over your shoulder." She arranged the baby on his shoulder and he quickly put one hand beneath her bottom and one hand on her back. Their fingers brushed. Electricity skipped up her arm, reminding her of their kiss, but she ignored it.

"There. See?" She took a step back and quickly turned to walk back to the bed, far too tempted to check his face to see if he'd felt the zing, too. "Now, all you have to do is pat her back until she burps."

He patted and Bella burped loudly. "Well, that's interesting."

"That's actually great. Now, give her the bottle again."

Bella finished her bottle, burped again, then fell asleep.

Matt whispered, "So do I put her in bed?"

"Yes, but expect to get up again soon. She's never slept this much before."

Sympathy for Bella flashed across his face, and Claire looked away. He was far too handsome and she was far too attracted to him to let all the sympathy and empathy she knew he felt sway her. Combining his good looks and her attraction with appreciation for his love for Bella, it wouldn't be long before she found herself genuinely liking him—and they'd already decided they weren't going there.

With Bella in her crib, Matt returned to his room and Claire crawled under the covers on her bed again. She nearly got out her e-reader, expecting Bella to awaken soon and not wanting to fall asleep only to have to wake up again. But she drifted off to sleep and didn't have another thought until the sound of Bella crying caused her to bounce up. Faint light peeked in at the meeting of the drapes. It had to be at least seven!

This time, she lifted Bella from her crib, took her into the bathroom and got her cleaned up for the day without waking Matt. She put her fingers over her lips to silence giggling Bella as they sneaked through Matt's room to the bedroom door.

She was just about done feeding Bella some of the cereal that had been delivered the night before when Matt sleepily entered the kitchen.

"I told you I want to help. You should have gotten me up for this…and when she got up again last night."

He wore the navy blue pajamas he'd worn the night before. A big navy velour robe hung loosely on his shoulders. Untied, the belt dangled to the floor and followed behind him like a thin train.

Still, with his hair sticking out in all directions and his eyes drooping sleepily, he was incredibly sexy. Sort of messed up like a guy who'd spent the morning making love. And much more approachable than the guy in the white shirt and handmade suit.

Knowing her brain had gone in a bad, bad direction, she turned her attention away from him and onto the baby as she answered his question.

"That's just it. Bella didn't get up last night. After her three o'clock feeding she slept until now."

Halfway to the counter, he stopped, faced her. "She did?"

"Yes!" She lifted Bella off her lap and nuzzled noses with her. "Our girl had a good night's sleep. In the four days I had her she barely slept four hours. With you, she's sleeping."

Matt's heart about stopped. "That's good?"

"That's excellent!"

He swallowed the lump of emotion that formed in his throat. He might not be brilliant at parenting. Hell, he might not be ready to parent, but it seemed Bella trusted him. That gave him such an emotional high he could have happily kissed Claire, but everything that had happened between them the day before came tumbling back and his chest tightened.

He didn't want to get involved with her. Worse, he didn't want her to know how tied in knots she had him. So he headed for the counter and pulled out the coffee and filters.

"You still should have woken me when she got up."

"There was no need."

Pouring grounds into the filter, he said, "She's my responsibility and I take my responsibilities seriously."

To his complete surprise, she sniffed a laugh. "No kidding. A guy doesn't get to be where you are by shirking his responsibilities." She paused, glanced around. "Unless you inherited your money."

"No. I didn't."

She only smiled.

"You've never heard of me, have you?"

"Should I have? Are you some kind of celebrity?"

He gaped at her. "Don't you read the financial pages? See the most eligible bachelor section of any Boston magazine? I'm not a movie star but I'm kind of well known in Boston."

"Never heard of you until we were contacted by Ginny's attorney." She lifted Bella and tickled her belly with her nose. "Look, I get it that you're some big-deal financial guy. And that's cool, but I don't keep up on that stuff."

He said, "Whatever," brushing her off, but his heart beat out a strange tattoo. It was the first time since he'd gotten rich that he met someone who didn't know the details of who he was. He might have thought it would be insulting. Instead, it felt strangely liberating.

"I'm going to take her upstairs while I change." Light and happy, Claire's voice drifted over to him. "Now that her tummy's full, she may go down for a nap, which will give us time to call the nanny service."

His stomach plummeted. The nanny service. That explained the happiness. As soon as he officially hired help, she got to go home.

Annoyance zinged through him, making him snippy. She might be glad to be leaving, but she didn't have to be so obvious about it. "I guess I may be doing some apologizing since you hung up on the service I called last night."

She rose with a laugh. "Or we could just call a different service."

"I thought you said that was the best one?"

"That one's the best, but the other two aren't too far behind. We'll decide which to call when I get downstairs."

She left the kitchen and he found a bowl and a box of cereal. By the time she returned, he'd eaten and read the morning paper.

She set the baby monitor on the table. The small screen above the little speaker showed Bella sound asleep in her crib.

"I thought that needed to stay in her room."

"The camera and microphone are in the room. The screen and speaker go where we go." She sighed. "It took me a little longer to get her to sleep than I'd expected."

He set the paper aside, trying to be nonchalant about the fact that the cute jeans she'd changed into had set his heart to humming again and her desire to go home annoyed him. He shouldn't want her to stay. He should be glad she was going. So that's how he acted. Cool. Casual. Unconcerned that she was leaving.

"Give me a minute to get into some clothes and we'll call the nanny service." He headed for the door, but stopped. Just because he was annoyed that didn't give him license to be a bad host.

"Have you eaten?"

"No, but a cup of coffee will be enough."

He frowned. "Really, Ms. Kincaid. A professional like you should know a good breakfast is necessary."

She laughed. "Yeah. I should know. But I'm not much of a breakfast person."

She turned, opened a cupboard, grabbed a mug and poured herself a cup of coffee.

Matt stood watching her, mesmerized. She was so casual around him, and his home, that the place didn't feel so…sterile. Maybe that's why he didn't want her to leave? Even filled with people, his house never felt like a home.

He shook his head. Now where the hell were his thoughts going? He had to stop this.

He turned away from the sight of her sipping her coffee and left the kitchen.

In his closet, ridiculously, he stared at the clothes. She made simple jeans and a T-shirt look good. It wasn't that he felt he needed to one-up her. He didn't even feel he should be trying to entice her. But he had the strangest urge to look really good.

Irritated with himself for thinking such weird things, he grabbed jeans and a T-shirt and put them on. God only knew why this woman made him think like this. But he wasn't falling victim. He refused.

He found her in the kitchen reading the same paper he had read while she was with Bella. "Ready?"

She snagged the baby monitor as she rose. "As ready as I'll ever be."

Finally. A little sadness in her voice. Not that he wanted her to stay. He was sure he and Bella would be fine once they got a nanny. It was simply insulting that she was so eager to bustle away. He knew her sadness probably stemmed from not wanting to leave Bella. But that pleased him more than thinking she didn't want to leave him. Bella was a baby who needed all the love and affection she could get. He was a grown man who could find himself a new sex partner and be happy—

He frowned. Now, why did that suddenly seem tawdry? Unappealing?

She met him at the door. Holding the baby monitor in one hand as she slid the other into the back pocket of her jeans, she looked up at him. "The business cards are still in the den?"

His mouth went dry. Putting her hand behind her back caused her breasts to punch out, just slightly. But enough to bring his gaze there. He followed the path of a neat little pink T-shirt that hugged her trim waist and fell short of meeting the waistband of her low-rise jeans, exposing an enticing strip of pink skin.

"Well?"

His gaze jumped to hers. "Huh?"

"The business cards? Are they in the den?"

"Um. Yes." Praying to God she hadn't seen the direction of his gaze, but knowing she'd have to be blind to have missed it, he pushed on the swinging door and headed down the hall.

In his office, she set the monitor on the desk between them as he picked up the business cards she'd given him the day before.

If it killed him, he intended to get his cool back. "Okay, agency number one is out for now, since you hung up on them."

She sniffed and looked away.

"So we're on to agency two."

He dialed the first three numbers on the landline on his desk and suddenly a squawk came from the monitor. He glanced at the screen and saw Bella pulling herself into a sitting position as she sobbed.

Claire rose. Motioning with her hand, she said, "You keep going. I'll get her. She probably needs a diaper change."

He winced at the thought of changing a diaper, but replaced the receiver back in its cradle. "No. I'm taking advantage of as much time as I can to learn what I need to learn. I'm not sitting on the sidelines. I haven't changed a diaper yet and while you're here I'd like to do that."

"I think that's a great idea."

In Bella's bedroom, she held back while he approached the crib. Bella sobbed, her little arms raised as if begging for someone to hold her.

"I'm here," he said, feeling the full weight of that. He was here. He would care for her. He would do this.

But when he lifted her into his arms, she didn't settle. She wiped her wet face on the shoulder of his shirt, but still screamed as if the hounds of hell were chasing her.

"Shh. Shh. Bella, it's okay," he crooned, taking a few steps, rocking a bit to comfort her, but she kept crying.

Then she saw Claire. She stretched toward her, wailing like a banshee.

Claire caught his gaze. "May I?"

He levered Bella over to her. "Please."

Bella wrapped her arms around Claire's neck as if she'd found a lifeline.

"I guess she didn't wake up because she needed a diaper."

Claire sniffed a laugh. "No. I think she might have had a bad dream." She rubbed her nose against Bella's face. "Hey, sweetie. It's okay. Don't cry. I have you."

Her crying subsided a bit, but she curled into Claire as if trying to get inside her skin. As if she was afraid of being left.

Matt swallowed. She *was* afraid of being left. She'd lost both of her parents five days ago. Then she'd been put into Claire's custody and Claire had become her anchor.

Bella hadn't slept through the night because she trusted Matt or even because she liked her new crib. She'd slept through the night because she was finally growing accustomed to Claire.

And Claire was leaving.

He scrubbed his hand across his mouth, unsure of what

to do. He hated to see Bella cry but he also hated being dependent upon Claire. She had a life. She was leaving.

He stepped forward, took the baby from Claire's arms. "Hey," he said, then—against every male instinct in his body—he sucked in a breath and did what he had to do. He danced her around in a big sweeping waltz step. "There's no need to cry."

As if by magic, Bella stopped crying, but Claire laughed. "You're dancing."

No kidding. Humiliation and embarrassment buffeted him, but he ignored them. "It's not a big deal," he said, though he knew it was. He probably looked like an idiot. "We've done this before."

"You have?"

"Yes. Yesterday, before you got here, I discovered dancing keeps her quiet."

"I discovered it the first night I had her."

A little more comfortable, Matt waltzed her around the room again. "She likes it."

"Maybe her mom danced with her?"

He stopped. Sadness made his stomach plummet. "Maybe she did."

She caught his gaze. "Don't take that the wrong way. It's nice for Bella to have that connection."

"It's good to remind her of her mom?"

"I don't think she thinks of her mom. I think she associates the dancing with love."

His heart froze in his chest. He looked from Claire to Bella and back to Claire again. "Dancing makes her feel loved."

"That's what I'm guessing."

"Then we'll dance."

CHAPTER SEVEN

TEN minutes later, Claire carried Bella to Matt's office, an odd feeling in her stomach. For as much of a big, strong, stubborn guy as Matt Patterson was, he really wanted to do what was right for this baby. He genuinely wanted to be a good daddy. He didn't mind looking a bit silly. And he wanted to learn.

She sat on the chair in front of the desk as Matt dialed the number for the nanny service.

"Hello, this is Matt Patterson. May I speak with Mary Mahoney?"

He sat in silence, waiting to be transferred, while Claire straightened the collar on Bella's pale green one-piece pajama. "You look especially pretty in green."

As if she understood the compliment, Bella grinned at her, but her little blue eyes were red from crying and still watery. Claire's heart twisted. In an hour or so they'd put her down for a nap again, then the temporary nanny would arrive, Claire would leave and Bella would wake up to two people she considered strangers. Plus, there was no guarantee that the nanny would teach Matt. Or even let him spend any quality time with Bella. Or let him dance.

If Matt knew more about babies, he could stand his ground with a stern nanny. But as unconfident as he was now, he'd let a nanny take over. And Bella would lose her daddy.

Suddenly Matt straightened in his chair. "Hello. Yes. Ms. Mahoney. I'm Matt Patterson. I recently got custody—"

She pressed her fingers on the button in the cradle for the phone receiver and disconnected the call.

He gaped at her. "Are you trying to make me look like an idiot?"

"No." She hugged cuddly Bella to her, swept her lips across her downy hair. "But I think it might be premature to leave Bella with a nanny. I think what we need to do is have me stay another day so she can get more adjusted to you."

He slowly replaced the phone receiver in its cradle. "You want to stay?"

Refusing to meet his gaze, she fussed with Bella's pajamas again. "I wouldn't say I *want* to stay, but I think I *need* to stay for Bella's sake."

"I can't say it's a bad idea, but you might want to mention these things to me before I call someone, instead of just hanging up the phone when I'm talking."

She winced. "Sorry." She said it casually, but the full ramifications of what she'd done by hanging up the phone began to sink in. She'd slept in a bedroom next to his the night before. True, she'd closed the door, but she was still in his house. And they'd kissed—because they were attracted. True, they'd talked that out. They weren't suited. So they were avoiding or ignoring that attraction.

But what if something happened that they couldn't? What if they kissed again? What if he wanted to do more than kiss? Could she resist him?

She mentally shook herself. Of course she could resist

him. She'd been resisting men for five years—*men she hadn't been attracted to.*

She peeked up at Matt. Strong shoulders. Handsome face. Sexy eyes.

She'd be spending another whole day with him…sleeping next to his bedroom again—

Oh, boy.

Studying her across the desk, he leaned back in his chair. "So what do we do now?"

The smart thing to do would be to keep them so focused on Bella and so busy she could forget this ridiculous attraction. Especially since he didn't seem to be having the same trepidation about it that she was. "You said you wanted to learn a few more things before a nanny completely takes over. Why don't we spend today doing some of that?"

He sat up. "Okay."

Trying to be nonchalant, she said, "Too bad she doesn't need a diaper change, since you danced instead of changed her diaper the last time she cried."

He sniffed a laugh.

The room got quiet.

The urge to run bubbled up in her, but she gathered her courage. After all, she was doing this for Bella.

"So since she doesn't need a diaper, has already been fed and doesn't want to sleep…maybe we should play."

He glanced over. "Play?"

"Sure." She rose, walked the baby to the thick Oriental rug in front of the sofa and lowered herself and Bella to the floor. "Babies are naturally curious. So sometimes playing can be as simple as setting her on the floor and letting her explore."

He ambled over. "And how do I fit into this equation?"

"You keep her from getting hurt, as you point out things that might be fun for her."

He sat on the floor beside her. "Like what?"

She peered around. There wasn't a damned thing in his house that might interest a baby. Worse, sitting on the floor with him only inches away, sprawled out comfortably, caused weird feelings to ripple through her. This was how he'd be with Bella. A sort of clueless but affable dad. He'd be sweet. Loving.

Great. Adding emotion to her attraction had been real smart.

She popped up off the floor. Seeing him as a good dad upped his likability by about a thousand percent. If she wasn't careful, she wouldn't just be fighting a sexual attraction; she'd be falling for another guy who was all wrong for her.

"Maybe I should go upstairs and get her one of the rattles and her bear."

She walked up the spiral staircase and back the hall to his bedroom, then took a deep breath as she leaned against the closed door.

She was fine. There was nothing to worry about. She'd learned her lesson about falling for self-absorbed men. She wasn't in any danger of losing her heart. Even thinking that was stupid. She'd agreed to stay for Bella. Bella needed a real daddy, not just a guy who paid for a nanny. She needed a daddy who would play with her when he came home from work, tuck her in at night, kiss her forehead. And she could teach him to do all that, if she kept her wits about her. It might be a little uncomfortable for her and she might have to miss work—

Miss work! She hadn't told her boss she would be taking time off!

She raced to her purse and retrieved her cell phone. With one click she speed dialed Joni's number.

"Dysart Adoptions."

"Oh, my gosh! Joni! I'm so sorry! I forgot all about you."

Joni, the owner of the adoption agency, chuckled. "That's okay. I figured you were busy with Bella."

"I was." She winced. "I *am*. Matt Patterson's staff are all on vacation so I volunteered to help him."

"Oh?"

"We were just walking back to the den to contact a nanny service when Bella woke up from her morning nap and she was inconsolable."

"Poor thing!"

"I know. The sweet baby is having so much trouble adjusting. Matt grabbed her out of the crib and it didn't even slow her down. But when she saw me, she reached for me and cuddled in and pretty soon she was calm."

"She's gotten accustomed to you."

"Yes."

"And you're not ready to leave her."

"I can't leave her like this. Plus, once she was calm, Matt took her and danced with her."

"Danced with her?"

"It calms her. I didn't tell him. He figured it out for himself. I can see he has the potential to be a really great dad. In a few days, I could teach him so much and then he would be comfortable around the baby and wouldn't desert her to a nanny when he gets one."

"You think he has the potential to get so accustomed to Bella that he'd spend time with her?"

"Yes. There's just something about the way he deals with her that makes me see he wants this. He *wants* to be a good dad. And if I can help him, I think I should." She paused, bit her bottom lip. "You're okay with me staying the rest of the week? I'll take it as vacation time."

"It's Tuesday. That's four whole days."

"I know…but Bella needs me."

"I think it's kind of cute."

Her breath stuttered out on a long sigh. "I don't know about cute. I just feel awful for her. She's so small and she can't even talk to tell us how she feels. And Matt genuinely wants to be a good dad. Right now, he's waiting for the right moment to learn how to change a diaper."

Joni laughed.

"Okay. I've got to run. I left her on the floor of a den that looks like it could be part of a museum."

Joni's voice perked up. "Oh, interesting. You're getting a sneak peek at his house!"

"Yes. I am. But I wouldn't want to live here. Everything's perfect. And I think that's going to be hard on Bella, too. While I'm here I might just suggest he create a few baby-friendly rooms."

"Well, have fun. And good luck with Bella."

"Thanks."

After disconnecting the call, she removed Bella's bear from the crib and dug through the diaper bag for one of the two rattles. She returned to the den feeling a lot better about her decision to help Matt. Joni didn't see anything wrong with her staying. In fact, she thought it was cute. Because that's the kind of people she and Joni were. They loved kids. Babies especially. They'd dedicated their lives to caring for them. Staying at this house for Bella and teaching Matt to be a good dad wasn't out of line. It was what she did.

As she entered the den, Matt said, "What took you so long?"

"I had to call my boss and arrange for some time off."

He groaned. "Sorry. I forgot about that."

"That's okay. She's fine with me staying a couple more days. In fact, I took the rest of the week off so I can help. We all have Bella's best interests at heart." She glanced around. "By the way…where is she?"

"Under the desk."

"Under the desk!"

"Don't worry. There's nothing under there. And she seems to like it." He smiled briefly. "It reminds me of when my sister Charlotte and I used to sit under my dad's desk and call it a fort."

"A fort?"

"We were always at war with our other sisters." He paused.

Knowing family was a sensitive subject for him and not wanting to get him in another bad mood, she ignored that last comment and went in search of Bella.

After moving the office chair out of the way, she stooped in front of the entry to the desk. "What are you doing?"

Bella screeched happily and patted her chubby thighs.

"Oh, so you do like it under there?"

She squealed with delight.

Claire raised her head until she could see above the desk. Catching Matt's gaze, she said, "Come over. Play with her." She waved the bear. "I have props."

He hoisted himself off the floor and strolled over. "Props?"

"The bear and the rattle. Things that will make playing easier."

He snorted a laugh, but slid the tall-backed chair far enough away from the desk that he could crouch beside Claire. "Hey, Bella."

She gurgled what Claire surmised equaled hello in baby talk.

"So, this is how the tiny half lives."

Bella laughed.

Claire turned a bit to face him. "She likes you. She really does. She just needs to get accustomed to you."

"And that will require me sitting on the floor a lot?"

"Among other things."

He shook his head, once again getting comfortable on the floor, laying out as he had on the Oriental rug in front of the sofa. "You know, I'm glad you don't know me. Because I have no reputation with you, I don't have to worry about ruining it by doing foolish things like sitting on the floor."

She looked away. How would he feel if he knew that the things he considered foolish like laying out on the floor actually made him more attractive to her?

She shifted the conversation back to Bella, the reason she'd stayed. "You also don't have a reputation to ruin with Bella. No matter what you do, this baby will love you." She reached in and tickled Bella's tummy. "Just as you are."

The idea that someone could love him just as he was stopped Matt cold. He peeked under the desk, at the little girl happily gurgling as if she'd found heaven. He scooted a little closer, looked at Bella with new eyes. Not as a baby who needed *his* protection, but as someone who would love *him*.

Just as he was.

Nobody had ever loved him just as he was. Even Ginny wanted him to change. That was why they'd divorced. She'd wanted a more attentive, loving husband. He'd been as closed off as a man could get. And even when he tried to be more honest, more receptive, he couldn't take those final steps.

He peeked at Claire. "No matter what I do…she'll love me?"

Claire smiled. "Yes. As long as you love her."

"I've never really been good at love."

She shrugged. "There is no such thing as good or bad in love. There's just love. If you love this little girl, she will know it and she will respond."

Bella cooed with happiness. He imagined her first birthday, imagined her learning to walk, learning to talk, turning to him for help and guidance and affection. And hugging him. Returning the love and affection he gave her.

Unimaginable warmth filled him. Along with a mountain of regret.

He swallowed hard. "I didn't really love her mom the way she needed to be loved."

"Obviously, you did something right. She left her child in your care."

"What I did right was stay friends with her." He peeked over at Claire. "And her new husband. Oswald was a great guy. A smart guy. But he always just missed the boat when it came to the big deals. So I let him sell me this house." He glanced around at it. "And having both the sale of this house and a sale to me to put on his résumé gave him the leg up he needed. When he…" He swallowed, unable to say *died*. Instead, he said, "This time last week he was one of the biggest real-estate brokers in Boston."

She put a comforting hand on his arm. "That's a great story."

"That's the only reason my ex-wife stayed friends with me. I felt I owed her so I helped her new husband. I con-

sidered the score settled. They felt I'd gone above and beyond the call of duty and made me their new best friend."

Claire shook her head. "You're so down on yourself.
Did you ever stop to think that maybe they liked you?"

"Wall Street's Iceman? The guy who broke Ginny's
heart?" He snorted a laugh. "I doubt it."

"I think you're selling yourself short."

There she was again, seeing the good in him. She didn't
understand how cool and distant he was, even though
she'd said she did after their kiss at her apartment. He
had to remind her she wasn't magically going to find his
nice side, or she would get hurt.

He caught Claire's gaze. "I loved my ex-wife. I truly
did. But being dedicated to work, I ignored her. She had
seen I wasn't capable of real love and she moved on. I
didn't fault her for that. I didn't blame her. But she knew
me. The real me. The me who doesn't love."

Claire ran a finger down Bella's chubby arm, making
the baby giggle. "Look at this sweet child. Do you really
believe your ex-wife would have left her in your care if
she genuinely believed you were incapable of loving her?"

"Maybe she left Bella with me because I have money
enough to get her a good nanny, buy her everything she
needs, see that she gets into a good university."

Claire gasped, clearly offended by his interpretation
of Ginny's motives. "That's not how moms think! More
than money, more than nannies, more than grand houses
and fancy educations, babies need love. Mommies know
that. Ginny wouldn't have left Bella in your care if she
believed you couldn't love her."

Real fear tightened Matt's chest. He could care for this
baby. He could give her affection. Giving her affection
seemed to come naturally. But real love? That wasn't in
the cards. Ginny would have known that.

"Ginny didn't believe I could love. She made me guardian only because she needed a name to put in her will. She never suspected she was going to die. Otherwise, she would have thought this through—found someone better to raise her daughter."

His solid, certain voice could have convinced Claire he was right...except she knew moms. They did not leave their babies with just anyone. They didn't make guardianship decisions lightly. Unfortunately, he wasn't in the mood to hear that, so she didn't reply.

Still, looking at him, reclining on the floor, watching the baby under his desk, waiting for his chance to learn how to change a diaper, she frowned. Very few people probably saw him this relaxed, but his ex-wife would have. She would have been with him in all kinds of situations and would have known him better than anybody ever had.

Ginny had to have seen something in him that nobody else saw.

And if she did see Matt as a man capable of loving a little girl enough to raise her, what would it take to bring out whatever Ginny had seen in him?

She didn't know. But the part of her that loved Bella knew she had to figure that out. She had the rest of the week. Plenty of time to push him a bit. But later. When he'd be a bit more receptive. There were lots of other, less threatening, less personal things they could discuss now to relax him. Get him to trust her. Before she began probing for whatever it was Ginny had seen in him.

"Speaking of big fancy houses not being what babies need, you might want to make a few kid-friendly places for Bella."

He glanced over. "Kid-friendly?"

"I think you'll need a playroom for her. You'll probably want a big family room...somewhere the two of you can play board games or video games and watch TV."

"Maybe foosball? Or ping pong."

"Sure. Whatever you want. Your best conversations with her will happen while you're doing something else."

"Makes sense."

The room got quiet. Bella happily sucked on her rattle. Claire once again searched her brain for something Bella-related to discuss, and realized he'd never made firm plans about his trip the following week. If he would be taking Bella to Texas, then teaching him how to travel with a baby ranked almost as high as demonstrating how to change a diaper.

"So what about the reunion in Texas? You said you might not go."

He sighed. "I have to go. I promised my sisters, Ellie, Charlotte and Alex."

"Ah." So he would need help.

"Don't make too much of that."

"That's okay. I'm not interested in your family as much as I am in helping you plan for the trip. You're probably going to need a baby carrier and lots more clothes."

He shrugged. "The temporary nanny should be able to help me with that, though, right?"

Her cheeks heated. Why did she keep forgetting he'd be replacing her? Was it because she wanted to see him raise Bella on his own—or because she couldn't stand the thought of being replaced?

She glanced at sweet Bella and her heart melted. But when she moved her gaze to Matt, her stomach tumbled. He saw himself as such a terrible person, yet here he lay, on the floor, just to be with Bella. To give her time to get accustomed to him.

How was a woman supposed to resist a guy like that?

"Yes. The nanny will take care of most of that." Fumbling for something to say to get her mind off how irresistible he became every time he was good to Bella, she inadvertently took them back to family again. "I think it will be good for Bella to get out among your family."

"Family is the group who taught me that it's best to never show your soft side."

"Really? I'd love to have a sister or brother." She smiled wistfully. "A sister to confide in. A brother to defend me... or for me to look up to."

"You can have my sister Alex. She's a chatterbox. And I hear I have a half brother Holt. You can have him, too. He's supposedly somebody everybody looks up to."

Her eyes widened. "You don't know if your own brother is somebody everybody looks up to?"

"I don't want to know!"

His shouted words echoed around the room. Embarrassment flooded Claire's entire body. He might be sweet and sexy when he was caring for Bella, but *this* was the real Matt Patterson.

What had he called himself? Iceman?

No matter what Ginny had seen in him, he was an iceman.

She rose. "You know, suddenly I am hungry. I think I'll just go to the kitchen and see if I can scout out something for breakfast."

He blew his breath out on a sigh. "Can you take the baby with you? I have some overseas calls to make."

She smiled politely and said, "Sure," but his request that she take the baby with her was another reminder that he wasn't a sweet guy, grappling with caring for a baby. He was a rich man, accustomed to people doing his bidding. He didn't *like* her. He might be attracted to her, but he saw her as an employee, a servant. He might also want to be a good dad for Bella, but he had a business to run and that was his priority.

She left the room, Bella on her arm. Matt hoisted himself from the floor and plopped down into the tall-backed chair. When Ellie had first told him about this family reunion, he wasn't interested, but when Alex and then Charlotte also started to pester him about it, he agreed to go. Especially for Charlotte. Because he liked her. Because she could persuade him to do things he didn't really want to do. Even when the ramifications of what he'd agreed to do had settled in, he'd decided he could go, be his cool, aloof self and then just come home and forget all about Texas and his real dad and the four half siblings he didn't need.

But now he had Bella. A baby. Because Ginny, the ex-wife who'd become a real friend to him after their divorce, had died. Grief rumbled in his chest, squeezing his heart. It came with a heaviness he couldn't even define or describe. He felt more for the wife who had dumped him than the pack of family he had but really didn't know. It didn't seem right to be off meeting them, as if nothing had happened, when Ginny was dead.

He was sorry he'd yelled at Claire. But she didn't get it. Not having a family, she didn't realize that real families weren't warm and fuzzy. Siblings were competitive. Parents could hold grudges. Hurts could run deep. And getting a baby to raise wasn't a gift from the heavens. It was a responsibility.

He leaned back in his chair, but bounced forward again. The best way to forget about his personal life was to work. He picked up the phone receiver, dialed a number and got his mind where it needed to be. On business.

He talked with two banks and four prospective investors for his latest venture. Twenty minutes later, the office door opened and Claire haltingly stepped inside. "My boss called. I have to go to work. Just for an hour or so to debrief her on some cases she'll need to handle for me tomorrow. But I'll be back."

The fact that she would still stay after he'd yelled at her humbled him. It was no wonder she thought there were good people in the world. She was one of them.

"Okay. Thanks."

She motioned toward the ceiling. "Bella's upstairs in her crib...asleep."

He nodded, wishing she'd just leave because he was feeling weird things about her, too. Wondering why she was so nice to a guy who was nothing but snippy with her. Wondering why she was alone, not married, and remembering the bad relationship in her past that she'd mentioned but not really explained. Wondering why he kept thinking about her, when he shouldn't care. When he should have let her leave that morning.

He said, "Thanks." But a vision of Bella waking, screaming for Claire, filled him, and he remembered why he hadn't let her leave. He couldn't care for Bella. Oh, he knew the basics, he could even dance with her to quiet her, but so far Claire was the one Bella really wanted. And he hadn't yet changed a diaper or fed her. Dancing wouldn't help if her pants were wet and her tummy empty.

He swallowed a lump in his throat that felt very much like his pride. "What do I do if she wakes up?"

She took a few more careful steps into the room. "She should sleep the entire time I'm gone. But if she doesn't, change her diaper, give her a bottle and play with her like we did this morning."

He nodded, but she wouldn't look at him. She kept her gaze focused on the floor.

Heat swamped him. He hadn't meant to be so angry with her. After all, his family wasn't her fault.

"You might want to get Jimmy to help you set up the play yard and swing we bought yesterday afternoon with the crib. She'll love the swing. It will definitely settle her if you can't get her to stop crying."

He said, "Thanks," wishing she'd just meet his gaze, knowing he didn't deserve a smile. But she turned and left the room.

He tossed his pencil to his desk. *This* was why he hated dealing with people, and the truth of why he didn't want to go to Texas. Alone in London, with too much time to think about things, he'd begun to wonder if maybe his problem with his extended family wasn't the fault of his seven siblings but his.

Maybe *he* was the reason the whole damned family couldn't get along. After all, *he* and his twin, Ellie, contributed to the reason his mother had left Texas. At least, that was what Cedric had told him the night of their big fight. Had his mother not gotten pregnant, she might have been able to handle living in Texas. But having twins in a rural county, so far away from her family, had made her run.

Claire left Matt's house, grateful for an hour alone in her car, even if she was fighting traffic.

When she arrived at Dysart Adoptions, she immediately walked back to Joni's office.

"Hey."

Blond-haired, blue-eyed Joni looked up. "Hey! I'm glad you could come in."

She winced. "I'm sorry I dumped everything on you without any notice."

Joni motioned for her to sit. "It's not like we're really

busy. I just hate to see you wasting your vacation on something that's essentially work."

"I know. But Bella's special and in a way so is Matt. He
wants to be a good dad so much that he can't hide it. But
he's more than a bit rough around the edges." She slid to
the seat in front of Joni's desk. "Did you know his nickname on Wall Street is Iceman?"

Joni's face fell. "How awful for Bella."

"Well, that's just it. I'd think how awful for Bella, if
I didn't keep getting glimpses of a nice guy underneath
his Iceman exterior."

Joni laughed, but her laughter quickly died. "Oh. Wait."
She studied Claire for a second, then said, "You're not
falling for him, are you?"

Claire sat up in her chair. "Absolutely not." She'd had
this conversation with herself in the car driving to the
adoption agency. And convinced herself she hadn't gotten angry that he'd yelled at her; she'd gotten angry that
he hadn't learned to control his temper around the baby.
"Number one, he's so far out of my league I'd be crazy
to even consider it. Number two, I'm literally teaching
this guy how to love. He says he hurt his ex-wife so badly
he had to make it up to her by helping her new husband
with a business deal. And he can't understand why Ginny
would leave her daughter in his care when she above everybody else knows he can't love. I'd be *crazy* to get involved with him."

Joni said, "Okay. Good."

"I mean, it's not like the guy doesn't have potential. If
I'm reading the situation right, I think he had a very soft
heart at one time and something happened in his family
that broke it. I'm guessing his Iceman image is a defensive
wall to keep him from getting hurt again. Which is why I
think there's lots of hope for him with Bella."

Joni inclined her head. "That makes sense." She caught Claire's gaze. "As long as you're only working to repair his heart enough to raise a baby, not because you want something to happen between you two."

"I already said I don't want anything to happen between us."

"Because bringing him far enough along that he'd be able to love you—as well as a baby—would be a big job."

"I know."

"And it would probably end up with you getting hurt."

"I know that, too."

"Just checking."

Joni dropped the subject after that and they went to work on quickly reviewing the few cases Claire had on her desk. But when she left Dysart Adoptions, Joni's words rolled around in her head.

She could probably teach Matt enough to care for Bella in a day or two. She hadn't needed to take the whole week off.

Was she subconsciously trying to heal him for herself?

Did she think she could be the woman of his dreams?

CHAPTER EIGHT

WHEN Claire returned, she found Matt in the kitchen, making lunch. Bella sat in the high chair, banging a rattle on the tray. Matt stood at the grill beside the stainless-steel stove.

"Are those grilled cheese sandwiches I smell?"

"Yes."

She shrugged out of her coat. "Really?"

He glanced over, then turned his attention back to his sandwiches. His voice was chilly as the ocean in January when he said, "I can cook. I wasn't always rich."

"Ah."

"My stepfather was rich. And yes, I grew up in the lap of luxury, but I had to put myself through school. I got a job, lived in a rat hole of an apartment and paid enough tuition to put a new wing on the library just to get a basic bachelor's degree."

Unable to stop herself, she laughed. "Why would you want to live in a rat hole of an apartment if your family was rich?"

"I had a falling-out with my stepfather." His voice wavered a bit, as if he didn't want to answer, but he had.

She hung her coat across the back of a chair. Combining the conversation she'd had with Joni to this revelation, she knew it was time to tread lightly. She'd been pushing him to be sweet, to be nice, to be *honest,* for Bella's sake, and it finally dawned on her how hard that might be for him. He was a guy so accustomed to getting his own way that he'd rather pay his tuition himself and live in a rat hole than make up with his stepfather. And here she was forcing him to buckle under for everything she wanted.

Of course, she was doing it for Bella.

She ambled toward the grill. She continually pushed him because Bella needed good care, but she didn't have to be a shrew. She pointed at the sandwiches. "You wouldn't want to share those, would you?"

"If my mother taught me anything, it was to share. I'm a great host."

"I'd set the table as repayment."

"I suppose that could be a deal."

"Great."

She rummaged until she found plates and cups, set the table and made a pot of coffee. He heated soup to go with the sandwiches and they sat at the table to eat, with Bella happily chattering in the high chair beside them.

"So how does a preppy boy survive living in a rat hole?"

He stopped his spoon halfway to his mouth. His lips quirked a bit. "Not easily."

"I can imagine."

"I don't think you can. I'd never actually seen a bug indoors before, so cockroaches scared the hell out of me."

She burst out laughing. "Good grief!"

"The walls of my apartment were paper thin. I froze in the winter and sweltered in the summer." He smiled, almost wistfully. "It certainly taught me a lot about life." He caught her gaze. "Real life. Not the sheltered existence I had as Cedric Patterson's son."

"I'll bet." She cocked her head. If he'd survived that,

learning to care for Bella should be a piece of cake. But now wasn't the time to remind him of that. They were making up after their argument and she would do her part. She would share a little about herself, too, so he wouldn't feel he was always the one giving. "I actually did about the same thing."

He frowned. "Really? You left the lap of luxury for a rat hole?"

"Maybe not the lap of luxury, but a very comfortable home. I was angry with my dad because he just never seemed to want me around, so I refused to take his money for tuition." She shook her head. "Actually, that's not totally true. I never asked him for money for tuition to see if he'd remember that I needed it. He didn't. All the deadlines passed and suddenly I had a twenty-thousand-dollar tuition bill that needed to be paid immediately and no money. And I was too angry to ask my dad to please remember he had a daughter."

Matt's face softened as he said, "What did you do?"

"I went to the bank and withdrew my savings and paid it."

"Ouch."

"At least I had savings. I had the first semester's tuition and enough for a good bit of the second semester, but I was furious. He never even considered that I'd need money. I was getting an allowance, but it wasn't enough for tuition and books and the dorm. Just basics like one meal a day and shampoo. And I realized he didn't even care enough about me to ask." She swallowed back the wave of emotion that clogged her throat. "So I decided the hell with him and I went job hunting."

"That's when you became a nanny."

"Yep. Changed my classes to night classes and lived in

with the families I worked for so I didn't have to worry about the dorm. And became my own woman."

His brow furrowed. "So, we're sort of alike."

"A little, but my story doesn't end as happily as yours."

He sent her a look, encouraging her to explain. Unsure if she should, she sucked in a breath. But in the end, she decided that if she intended to push him past his boundaries, the least she could do was be honest with him.

"My dad died my third year at university. All the money he made, all the money that kept him from me, meant nothing. He had a heart attack when he was alone and, with no one to help him or even call an ambulance, he died."

Matt reached across the table and covered her hand with his. "I'm so sorry."

"If he'd paid one whit of attention to me, I would have been there. He wouldn't have died. But he'd treated me like an afterthought and I genuinely believed he didn't want me around." Bottled up feelings began to pop free, making her voice shaky and her eyes water. "But do you want to know the real punch line of this story? All his money came to me. All that money that kept him from me." She paused to take a cleansing breath. "I didn't want it. But I wasn't so foolish as to flush it down a toilet."

He barked a short laugh, one of acknowledgment, but with very little humor.

"I bought a new car and my condo and gave the rest to charity."

He studied her from across the table. "You gave your inheritance to charity?"

"I didn't want it. I took enough for a decent start on life, then let it go. I didn't want the money that had stolen my dad from me."

"And that's why you're not impressed with money."

She inclined her head, not able to speak. Now she wasn't just remembering her time at university. Memories of her lonely years as a little girl had also floated to the surface. Memories of how much she'd wanted her father's love, and how stubborn she'd gotten as a teenager, staying out of the house on weekends that she'd known he'd be home because she feared he'd only spend his time working and ignore her. And she couldn't handle the pain of his silent rejection anymore.

Tears filled her eyes and the lump of emotion came back to her throat. She missed her dad. But, then again, it seemed she'd spent her whole life missing her dad.

"That's why you want me to be a good dad for Bella." She nodded.

He pulled his hand away and scrubbed it down his face. "I'm sorry."

"I'm sorry, too." Her voice broke. They were finally genuinely getting to know each other. He wasn't apologizing for bringing up a sensitive subject any more than she was apologizing for getting hurt over his sniping at her. Their apologies were for their misconceptions about each other up to this point. All the same, it was the first time she'd spoken about her dad with anyone and emotions she hadn't expected overwhelmed her.

"Sometimes I look back on the years I was in school being stubborn and headstrong over my dad's 'slights' and I realize that if I'd pushed for his attention things might have been very different."

To her embarrassment, her tears spilled over. She'd cried about her dad before, but never so honestly and certainly never with another person. But she could talk about this with Matt because she knew he understood. He hadn't gotten along with his stepfather any better than she'd gotten along with her father. But that didn't make it hurt any less. It also didn't take away the guilt. She'd been twenty-one when her dad died. Surely, she could have been mature enough to go to his house and say, "Let's have dinner?"

Fresh tears erupted at that and she rose from the table to get something to wipe her eyes. After a few seconds of searching for tissues, her frustration with looking collided with her frustration with her life and her tears became full-scale sobbing. "Is there a box of tissues in this room that seems to have everything but tissues?"

Panicked by her tears, he bounced off his seat. "That's a good question." He roamed around the room, fruitlessly seeking tissues, and in the end ripped a paper towel off the roll by the sink.

But when he reached her, she wouldn't look at him again, reminding him of how she wouldn't look at him after he'd yelled about not wanting to know his family. Regret filled him, along with intense longing to be kind to this woman who'd had a childhood far more difficult than his.

Rather than hand the paper towel to her, he rolled it in a ball and lightly dabbed it along the tracks of her tears.

That brought her gaze to his and he swallowed. She was so beautiful, but right in that moment it wasn't her beauty that called to him. It was something more, something deeper, something so important he didn't dare let himself examine it.

But he also couldn't ignore it. With their gazes locked and tears welling in her eyes again, that "something deeper" inside him wouldn't let this moment slide away. He lowered his head, watching her eyes darken. With fear? With curiosity? He couldn't tell. He only knew that if he didn't kiss her right this second, he would be sorry.

Softly, slowly, he let his lips graze hers, telling her with his actions that he understood and wanted to comfort her.

And every bit as slowly her lips rose to meet his, answering him, accepting his comfort.

The kiss grew as they experimented with the feel and taste of each other's lips. Arousal surged through him, along with the knowledge that she wasn't like any other woman he'd ever known. Not even Ginny, a pampered princess who might have had to fight alongside her second husband for success, but who didn't understand suffering. Sadness. The feeling of not quite living up to the expectations of the person who meant the most to you.

Claire understood. She was a real person. A real woman. Someone with problems and goals, who knew life didn't always turn out the way you hoped.

She suddenly pulled away from him. "What are you doing?"

She stepped back, gaping at him as if he were crazy. "You told me you're a mean, coldhearted playboy. Somebody I should stay away from. Why the hell would you kiss me like that?"

Like that. She hadn't spelled it out, but he knew what she meant. Why had he kissed her like he meant it? Like he had feelings for her. Like they had connected.

His breath caught in his chest and seemed to knot there. What the hell was he doing?

"I need to wash my face." She took another step back, then turned and raced out of the kitchen.

He rubbed his hand across the back of his neck as he sat at the table again. Vibrating with confusion, he stared at his soup. He couldn't argue her logic. Didn't want to apologize. How could he? What would he say? *Hey, we connected. Why not kiss?* He wasn't like that. He didn't want to be like that! He wanted to be left alone.

Yet she needed him. He more than sensed it. And something inside of him surged with longing to be the one to fix whatever was wrong.

It was absurd. Not just because he'd never wanted to be a great "fixer" of people. He was an iceman. But also because he didn't know how to fix anybody. Hell, he couldn't even fix himself.

Racing up the stairs to the makeshift nursery, Claire just wanted to roll up in a ball and die. She didn't know what was worse, exposing her secrets to a virtual stranger, or accepting his comfort when she knew deep down inside he didn't mean it.

Oh, for a few seconds she thought he had. The sweet, sensitive way he'd kissed her made her believe her story had touched him. And maybe it had, but it didn't mean anything. He was who he was. And by God, she'd promised herself and Joni she wasn't going to try to change him.

Yet, the second his lips touched hers, her common sense fled out the window!

What the hell was she thinking? They might have a lot of things from their pasts in common, but how long had she known this guy? Twenty-four hours? Only an idiot didn't learn from her mistakes. And she'd made a huge mistake at university with Ben, a professor she barely knew. She would not make that mistake again. Especially not with a guy nicknamed Iceman.

She stepped into his bedroom and closed the door with a sigh. They had a huge house at their disposal yet they were virtually sleeping in the same room. Sharing a bathroom. Spending twenty-four hours a day together. Telling secrets they hadn't told another soul. Was it any wonder they were acting out of character?

She splashed water on her face and looked at her reflection in the mirror around the waterfall. This was the danger Joni had warned her about and she'd fluffed off thinking she was strong enough to resist him.

Well, maybe she wasn't.

Loneliness made her vulnerable; longing for a family had made her take a foolish risk with Ben. Being with Matt seemed to bring out her loneliness and her longing and wish for things in him that absolutely weren't there.

Unless she wanted to make another mistake, they had to stop having personal conversations. She had to take this time together and make it all about baby lessons again. No more watching his feelings. No more friendly overtures. Nothing but baby lessons.

When she returned downstairs, he was happily playing with Bella, who still sat in the high chair. As she entered the kitchen, his eyes clouded with regret, which only made her feel worse. If she hadn't blubbered on about her dad, he probably wouldn't have kissed her.

"You're back."

"I told you I just needed to wash my face."

"Look, I'm sorry—"

She stopped him with a wave of her hand. "We're fine. Talking about my dad upset me and I took it out on you."

His eyebrows rose. "Took it out on me?"

"I normally don't freak out when someone kisses me." She drew a breath. "But…" She waited until he met her gaze before she said, "Our circumstances are unusual. We're virtually sleeping in the same room. We're playing house with a baby. I think we need to use a little common sense and not do things like talk about our lives and kiss."

Looking incredibly relieved, he nodded.

They fed Bella as if nothing had happened and carried her back to the nursery. Focusing on the baby, Claire's calm, confident demeanor returned. As Matt went to the dresser for clean pj's, Claire opened Bella's little jeans and stifled a laugh over the sight he'd made of her diaper.

"I should have given you a diaper lesson before I left."

He sniffed. "Maybe."

The tightness in her chest loosened a bit. This was what they needed to do. Focus on Bella. Forget about kissing. Forget about talking. Stop trying to be friends.

She considered offering to give him diaper lessons now, but didn't feel comfortable with them standing so close when they were only a few minutes off a kiss and an argument. Instead, she let him go downstairs for a fresh bottle.

A few minutes later, with Bella asleep in the crib, Matt led her into the office/den. Walking to his desk, he peered back at her. "While you were at your office, I took the liberty of calling a nanny service."

She could have been insulted, thinking he was trying to get rid of her. But after that kiss she wanted to leave.

"Not giving me a chance to hang up on them this time?"

He smiled. "Exactly."

As he sat in the chair behind the desk, she sat on the one in front of it. "So?"

"So…since you're here, I thought I might skip the temporary nanny and I talked with them about hiring someone permanently. They emailed a bunch of résumés and I printed them out."

He reached behind to the printer on the credenza, pulled out a stack of papers and handed them to her. "I'm giving you first right of refusal. Knowing me the way you do, and also knowing Bella, you probably understand better than anyone who won't fit with us."

She took the résumés. "I can weed out the prospective

nannies I think won't work." She glanced up at him. "But you can't choose a nanny from a résumé."

"I'd intended to interview them."

She nodded. "Good."

He pointed across the desk at the papers she held. "You pick the ones I should interview."

She looked down at the résumés. Now that their relationship had returned to something more businesslike, her goal for being here—making sure Bella got the best care—guided her again. "If you want, I can help you with the interviews."

"That would be great."

She began reading the résumés, looking specifically for nannies with experience with babies. They called the agency and set up interviews with six of the candidates for Friday.

"So if all goes well," Claire said, rising from her seat. "You should have somebody on Saturday."

Matt tossed his pen to his desk. "Yeah." And then she would go. And then he could stop feeling these odd things he always felt around her.

That was good.

Very good.

Very good for *both* of them.

She made a few marks on the résumés, and he remained in his seat, not really sure if he should stay or go. Luckily, Bella's little voice tumbled from the baby monitor.

He bounced off his seat. "I'll get her."

Claire rose, too. "I'll help. I think it's time for the diaper lesson."

A laugh bubbled up, but he stopped it before it could escape. Even when she was mad at him, she could be funny. And he liked that—a lot more than he cared to admit. But she'd had a rough childhood, and she deserved a good life with a nice guy. He didn't fit that bill. So he had to stop responding to her. Stop laughing. Stop telling her things. In fact, maybe it was time to let her go. He knew a lot about caring for Bella and he wasn't an idiot. Now that he was comfortable with the baby, he could figure out a lot of the rest of it himself. And she'd chosen the best candidates for his nanny. He'd interviewed people before. Surely, he could hire his own nanny.

They walked up the stairs and entered the nursery to find Bella sitting up, her face tearstained, her lips turned down in an angry pout.

"Oh, sweetie," Claire said, lifting Bella from the crib. "You're all right."

Bella nuzzled into Claire's neck, and clung to her, causing Matt's heart to somersault. For as much as he wished he could let Claire leave so he could stop having these "feelings" about her, Bella needed her.

Still, he had to get Bella beyond this. She was his child to raise and he would step up.

He walked over, took Bella from Claire. "Hey—" He almost said *kid,* but wondered if the reason Bella was so slow to bond with him was his direct manner with her. So he said, "Sweetie," as Claire did. "How about if Daddy changes your pants this time?"

She sniffed and turned to Claire, reaching for her, but Claire stepped back as if she understood Matt's intention to spend more time with Bella and speed up the bonding process. "I'm right here. But Daddy's going to change you."

Bella yelped. Matt just kept going. He walked to the bed and set Bella down.

Claire said, "We should have ordered a changing table."

He peeked back. "What's that?"

"It looks like a chest of drawers for a baby but the top

is made in such a way that you can change her on it. It's higher so changing her is easier."

"Sounds like we should order one when we get back downstairs."

She nodded.

Remembering more of the things he'd seen Claire do, Matt tickled Bella's tummy. "So did you have a good nap?"

She yelped again.

"Not much of a happy riser, are you?"

He unsnapped the crotch of her pajamas, undid her diaper and froze. "Damn."

Standing behind him, her lips pressed together to keep from smiling, Claire only raised her eyebrows when he peeked at her.

"Can you get me a diaper?"

"Yes. I was going to get one before you asked, but decided it was important for you to realize lesson one of diaper changing. Get the clean diaper before you take off the dirty one."

Once again, he had to stifle a laugh. He turned his attention to Bella. "While we wait for the diaper, anything you want to talk about?"

She giggled.

"You know, once you get past that grumpy, first-waking-up stage, you're actually a very happy kid."

Claire handed him the clean diaper. "It's taking less and less time for her to respond to you."

He slid the diaper beneath her and pulled the sides together.

Leaning over his shoulder, Claire said, "You should wipe her bottom with one of these cloths," she offered him a container of baby wipes and he took one. "As you clean her, check to make sure her bottom's not red."

"What do I do if it's red?"

She showed him some creams and ointments in the diaper bag and explained about diaper rash. They pronounced her bottom fine and she took the used wipe from him, tossed it in the trash and turned his attention back to the diaper.

"Attach the strips tighter this time. That prevents accidents, but it's also more comfortable for her not to have her diaper sliding around every time she moves."

He pulled the tabs tighter. "Got it."

Finished, he snapped her sleeper and lifted her from the bed. "Playtime?"

Claire nodded and headed for the door. "First, though, we'll order the changing table." She paused and smiled at him. His heart did the weird thing again, part squeeze, part roll. He loved it when she smiled. But he also knew they were bad for each other and she hadn't meant anything by the smile, except her intention to get along with him while she taught him.

"And a few toys. Things that require a little more of her attention than the bear and the rattles. Things that can actually keep her busy or give you something to do while you play with her."

"Okay."

In only a few minutes on the internet they'd found and ordered the changing table and some interesting toys.

"I like the cone," he said, referring to the toy with the multicolored rings that fit on a cone. "It's simple, but I can see how it will keep her busy."

"And showing her how to play with the rings will give you something to do with her."

Holding Bella, who chewed on her rattle, Matt rose from his seat behind the desk. He didn't get two steps away before his phone rang.

He stopped and Claire stepped forward to get Bella. "I'll take her."

He reached for the phone. "Thanks. I don't get a lot of calls here so this has to be important."

Claire took Bella to the rug in front of the sofa, sat her on the floor and lowered herself beside her. After a few seconds of peekaboo, she crawled to the left of the sofa, hiding from the baby, only to pop out every few seconds and say, "Boo."

There was a voice on the other end of the line, "Mr. Patterson? Are you there?"

Realizing he'd been so preoccupied with Claire that he hadn't even said hello, Matt responded, "Um, sorry. I'm here."

"It's Rafe from Hansen's Department Store. The baby carrier you ordered doesn't come in that shade of pink. We can order one, but we already have it in blue or green."

"I want the pink," he said absently, watching Claire play with Bella. She was a natural with kids and her game reminded him of hot summer days spent at Cedric's beach house, when he and his siblings played hide-and-seek. Though his mother had never joined in, he could see Claire joining her children. He could see her climbing sand mounds at the beach or peeking out from behind trees in the lush yard behind his house. *His* house. *This estate.*

"Also some of the toys will have to be ordered."

He shook his head, bringing himself back to the present. "That's fine."

"Great. We'll deliver what we have in stock this afternoon. And the rest we should have by Thursday."

"Thanks."

But when he hung up the phone, he didn't go over to Bella. Instead, he walked to the front of the desk and sat on the edge. He knew he was supposed to be watching Claire to get the gist of how to play with Bella, but he couldn't stop picturing her with lots of kids. Playing, but always with a mother's eye on them.

And he suddenly realized why he couldn't stop watching her. The picture appealed to him. Her, with kids, and a house that would be a real home. He wouldn't be an interloper being passed off as someone's son. He'd be Daddy.

A squeak erupted from his throat. Now, what was he doing? Trying to make up for his past with a woman he hardly knew…and wanting kids?

That was just wrong.

Bella's giggling brought him back to the present. Claire crawled over to her and tickled her tummy. Then she scooped her up with her as she rose.

"You're such a funny little girl."

Bella squealed with delight.

"You love to play."

She cuddled Bella to her and the baby nestled in. Just about to turn away before he started spinning odd fantasies again, Matt stopped himself.

Maybe he wasn't so much envisioning himself with a family, but Claire. After their discussions today, he'd be an idiot not to realize this was a woman who longed for a family.

He frowned, watching her.

Maybe that's what drew him? They hadn't known each other long enough to really like each other. Yet he couldn't deny being drawn to her. So did he want a family…or did he simply want help with Bella? Real help. Not just a nanny to care for his baby, but someone to love her in ways Matt wasn't sure he could?

CHAPTER NINE

WITH his new questions about Claire confusing him, Matt spent Wednesday trying to avoid her. But how could he when caring for Bella together put them in the same room all the time? When she finally went to bed, he got a few minutes of peace and quiet, but when he entered his bedroom, he could smell her. Her scent wasn't just in the bathroom anymore. No. It was everywhere.

Thursday morning, Bella seemed to have learned that spitting out her food could be entertaining, so Matt found himself stationed by the high chair, wiping spit food off the tray, putting himself directly in line with Claire's scent.

After breakfast, they rolled a ball back and forth for an hour, keeping Claire's scent around him and emphasizing the fact that they didn't talk.

They couldn't. Every time they talked, they got to know each other. And when he got to know her, he liked her. But when they didn't talk, he thought about her. Wondered how a little girl got along without a mom when she had a distant dad. Wondered why she wasn't bitter, as he was about his family. Wondered how she'd stayed so sweet.

Though he needed to learn everything he could while he had Claire with him, by Thursday afternoon he knew there had to be a better way to handle this. They had to find something to do while they cared for the baby. Something that would occupy their minds enough that he could stop thinking.

He wanted twenty minutes of not thinking. Not about his family, not about Bella and especially not his unwanted attraction to Claire.

He pushed himself away from the desk. "You know what? I think we should spend the rest of the afternoon cooking dinner."

Claire glanced over. "Cooking dinner?"

"Yeah. I'm getting a little tired of takeout. But we also have to spend time with the baby. So I thought we could put her in the high chair and chitchat with her as we put a roast in the oven."

She walked the baby over to him. "That's a great idea. We'll get dinner, but you'll also learn how to multitask with a baby."

"How is that different from regular multitasking?"

"No matter what you're doing, if Bella needs tending to, she becomes the priority. This is a great way to start seeing that."

Matt shook his head, unable to stop the laugh that escaped. "Seriously? You think I'm that stupid?"

He expected her to have some kind of funny comeback. Instead, she froze. "You laughed."

"What you said was either insulting or funny. I chose funny."

"Okay…" She bit her lip. "It's just that—" She stopped again.

"What?"

"When we met you never laughed. You smiled a bit, but sort of craftily like you were trying to figure me out. Then you started 'kind of' laughing. But not really laughing, more like chuckling. You just really laughed. A genuine laugh. As if you're happy."

He headed for the door. "I'm not happy." He stopped, raked his fingers through his hair, as that damned confusion overwhelmed him again. Technically, he was happy. He liked who he was and what he did. "That's not to say I'm unhappy. Things are working out with Bella." He stopped again. What the hell was going on with him? Why did he feel he had to explain himself to her? He strode to the door. "Could we please drop it?"

She raced after him. "Why? I think it's cute. You like Bella. Or maybe you like the idea of being a dad." She smiled dreamily. "It's cute."

He walked out of the office and toward the kitchen. "It's not cute. I'm confused." Realizing he was talking to her again, admitting things he shouldn't, he stopped abruptly and she almost plowed into his back. "Could we just forget it?"

"Okay. Sure. I'm certainly not trying to talk about personal things. But I think Bella makes you happy. That's all I want to say. You don't have to answer, explain or refute it. It's just an observation."

But as they worked together seasoning the roast, peeling potatoes, preparing vegetables to make a salad when the roast was done, she continued to wear that ridiculously dreamy smile. A smile that said she was thrilled all this was working out for Bella.

Bella sat in her high chair, cheerfully banging a rattle on the tray. Claire chopped veggies, dreamily thinking thoughts Matt was absolutely positive he didn't want to know. And he organized everything, getting rid of his pent-up energy and doing what needed to be done. Like the man of the house.

Damn. There he went again. Thinking about things, his

life, in ways that were foreign. He wasn't a family man. He didn't want a family.

But he had one.

And he had to admit that with Bella settling in and him growing accustomed to her he did feel…happy.

All these years he'd thought his successes and toys made had him happy. But the new feeling bubbling through him told him they only made him feel successful.

Claire or Bella or maybe Claire and Bella made him happy.

And it scared the snot out of him.

The buzzer for the gate rang and he walked to the intercom. The screen above the row of buttons showed a truck with the Hansen's Department Store logo on the door.

"Yes."

"I have a delivery for Matt Patterson."

"Gate is opening. Come to the front entrance."

Without looking at Claire, he said, "I'll take care of this," and left the room.

After lighting the burner under the potatoes to cook them for mashed potatoes, Claire fell to the chair near the high chair. "Your daddy is the first person I've ever met who didn't want to be happy."

Bella gurgled.

"You're right. Let's hope he gets accustomed to it." She ruffled Bella's soft tuft of hair. "What am I thinking? *You'll* get him accustomed to it."

She would. Because Bella had the rest of her life to worm her way into his heart.

Which was a very good reminder to Claire. With everything Matt did, she liked him more. Try as he might to be grouchy and sullen, he was growing accustomed to Bella and enjoying being a dad. And that was very attractive. But, though he'd accommodated a baby in his life, this wasn't a guy who would fall head over heels in love with a woman. She'd be lucky if he remembered her name after she left. She wasn't here to make him happy, worm her way into his heart or fall in love. She was here for the baby. And *she'd* do well to remember that.

Claire stayed in the kitchen with Bella and finished the mashed potatoes. When the delivery man left, she unwrapped the additional toys that had arrived that afternoon. She showed Matt how to dump the colored rings from the cone onto the floor and help Bella rearrange them on the cone again. With all the playing, Bella grew tired more quickly than usual and Claire and Matt just barely got her bathed before she fell asleep at seven.

They walked into the kitchen silently. Both of them probably as tired as Bella, and both of them lost in thought.

Matt went directly to the oven. "With her going to bed this early, is she going to sleep tonight?"

Claire shrugged. "Hard to say. But when a baby is falling asleep on your arm, you can't really keep her awake."

He set the roast on the stove. The delicious aroma floated over to Claire and her stomach growled. She set the table as he carved the roast. She got the salad from the refrigerator and put the mashed potatoes into the microwave for a quick reheat.

They sat down to eat as silent as they'd been while putting together their meal.

After a minute of quiet, Matt rose. He pressed a few buttons on the panel containing the intercom and video feed from the gate, and soft music filled the kitchen.

"No reason for us to be completely uncivilized," he said as he returned to his seat.

"Right." She sucked in a breath. Obviously, the quiet in the room got to him, too. But they'd made a promise not to talk about personal things, and neither one of them wanted to risk it. Of course, his job was probably a safe subject.

"Do you do a lot of traveling for your business?"

"Only because I want to. If you're worried about me leaving Bella, I can arrange my schedule so I don't have to." He smiled. "People will come to me."

She nodded, but the urge to tease him rose up in her, so strong and so natural, it nearly stole her breath. Since that kiss, they'd focused on Bella. Hadn't teased. Hadn't meandered into personal territory. And that had worked out very well. No yelling. No hurt feelings. She would not overstep those boundaries.

"Good point."

"So what about you? Have they done okay without you at Dysart Adoptions this week?"

"Easily. Joni and I are basically the only two caseworkers, but with our receptionist we're enough. We go through a lot of slow seasons. We're in one now."

"Me, too." He dug into his mashed potatoes. "I love what I do, though."

"What *exactly* do you do?"

"Buy and sell things. Stocks. Companies."

Comfortable with their safe topic, they talked about his business dealings through the remainder of dinner. She learned he'd gotten his nickname "Iceman" because he could be totally heartless about firing upper management.

Which made her laugh. "Seriously. Who gets all upset about a guy being asked to leave a big corporation when he goes with a golden parachute?"

"You're forgetting who gave me the nickname... Other CEOs. The very people I fire." He frowned. "And we forgot dessert." He glanced over at her. "We don't have dessert."

"You have pudding cups."

"That's right! I do."

He walked to the refrigerator, pulled out two pudding cups and ambled back. "Vanilla or chocolate?"

"Chocolate."

"Great. Vanilla's actually my favorite."

He handed her the pudding cup and took his seat again.

She peeled off the lid, took a bite and groaned in ecstasy. "These are great."

"No point in having a secret vice if it isn't great."

She laughed. "I never thought of that."

They finished their pudding and she automatically got up to clear the table. "You go make your calls or whatever you need to do." The baby monitor had stayed silent. Bella was okay. And she could wash a few dishes.

But he shook his head. "I'm not going to leave you to clean up alone. You're helping me enough."

Warmth spiraled through her. She'd always known he appreciated her help, but it never hurt to hear the words.

After gathering the dishes, she walked them to the sink.

His eyebrows rose. "You're not using the dishwasher?"

"For a couple dishes? We can have these done in five minutes. The dishwasher will take forty and tons more water."

As she filled a sink, he found a dishtowel, slung it over his shoulder, then finished clearing the table.

When the sink was filled to capacity with dirty dishes and sparkling bubbles, she washed a plate, rinsed it and put it in the dish drainer. "Somebody must wash dishes in here. Otherwise, there wouldn't be a drainer."

"I think my cook prefers to wash the pots."

She peeked at him through her peripheral vision. "Really?"

"She's very fussy about her pots."

"Makes sense, I guess. I don't cook much." She glanced at him again. "Not much reason to cook for one."

"Unless you're hungry."

"I eat a big lunch."

"Oh, so in other words if you ever got married and had someone to cook for, you'd start eating supper and get as round as Bella?"

She gaped at him. "Did you just call Bella fat?"

"She's not fat. She's healthy."

Her eyebrow rose. "And I'm not?"

His mouth fell open. "I didn't say that!"

She caught a handful of soap bubbles in her cupped hand and flung them at him. She'd intended to hit his T-shirt. Instead, she got his nose.

The expression on his face was priceless. But shock quickly morphed into challenge. "You wanna go?"

She eeked. "No! You're the one who called me fat."

"I called Bella fat and you unhealthy. According to you." He reached down, scooped out some bubbles and flipped them into her face.

She gasped and, without thought, got more bubbles and flung them at him. "You said what you said."

"You misinterpreted what I said." He grabbed a bigger handful of suds. With a quick twist of his wrist, he got her hair.

"Hey!" Her eyes narrowed. "Don't mess up my hair!"

"You weren't worried about my nose."

"Okay. Fine. If that's how you want it, this is war!"

"Ha! You think you can beat me! I know every corner of this kitchen. And my sister Charlotte and I were very adept at avoiding our other sisters when we were younger." He filled an available cup with water and darted around the table, behind a chair. "Bring it."

"You wouldn't throw an entire cup of water at me!"

"Guess again."

"And who's going to clean up the mess?"

He shrugged. "Us. When we're done with our war."

Her face contorted. "Why throw the water when you end up having to clean it up?"

"For the fun of the war." He walked from behind the table. "You really didn't have much of a childhood."

She shrugged. "Looks like I didn't."

"Great." He dribbled some water on her head.

Expecting his sympathy and getting a shower, she jumped back sputtering. "What are you doing!"

"We're at war, remember? If I were you, I'd get a cup."

Her eyes narrowed, but he only grinned. Knowing he wouldn't stay passive long, she raced to the sink and got a cup of water, but she paused. "This is ridiculous."

She watched his face sort of deflate. Cup in hand, he walked to the sink, clearly disappointed that he'd failed in getting her to play. When he was close enough, she sloshed the water out of her cup and onto his shirt.

He gasped and jumped back. "You tricked me."

She refilled her cup and scampered away. "All is fair in love and war."

"Oh, this is so on."

She ran to the kitchen island, shielding herself behind it and the rows of pots that hung above it.

"You have to come out sometime."

"Not really. I think I can safely protect myself behind this island for the rest of the war."

She bounced out for one quick slosh toward him, the way an Old West gunfighter bounces from behind a tree just long enough to shoot, then was back behind her island again.

He bent away from the spray. "You missed me."

"I'll get you next time."

He nudged his chin in the direction of her cup. "Not without water." He glanced around. "Let's see. I have a whole cup of water and I stand between you and the sink." He smiled evilly. "Who's winning now?"

She said, "Eek!" and dodged to the right.

When she got to the open space in the overhead pots, he flung his water at her and got her on the chest, soaking her T-shirt.

She glanced down at it in amazement. Then up at him. Then burst out laughing. "All right. One of us has to call a truce."

He walked to the sink. Refilled his cup. Displayed it for her to see. "Or one of us has to surrender."

"Okay. Now you're just being childish."

"And throwing cups of water wasn't? We're just having fun…and I think you're trying to talk your way out of losing the war."

"I'm trying to talk us back to adulthood."

"Why?" He glanced around. "No one's here. No one cares."

But she cared. When he behaved like a silly, fun guy, strange feelings of warmth and happiness danced through her. And fantasies began to spin in her head. She'd never wanted a stuffy, formal family. She wanted a happy family. With a happy dad. And right now he was behaving as if he could be one.

But he couldn't. He was Wall Street's Iceman. This little thing they were doing with the water had to be an aberration.

She raised her hands in surrender. "All right. I surrender."

A look of disappointment flitted across his face, but he didn't put his cup down. Like the town sheriff arresting the bad guy, he brandished it like a gun. "Walk your cup to the sink."

She laughed. "This is ridiculous."

"No, this is how a smart man ends a war, especially when his opponent has already duped him once."

She giggled. "Really? Seriously? I have to walk my cup to the sink."

"And dump out the contents."

As she ambled to the sink, he edged around, so he could see her every move.

She laughed again.

"Now dump it out."

She poured the remaining water from her cup into the empty sink.

"And put the cup into the dishwater in the other sink."

Pressing her lips together to stop another giggle, she put the cup in the water.

"Now step away from the sink."

"You really get into this role playing, don't you?"

"Charlotte and I rarely lost a water battle."

"Sounds like your childhood was fun."

He said, "It was. But I'm still watching you. Put both hands up and step away from the sink."

This time she let the gale of laughter roll out of her. She walked far enough away from the sink to appease him. "That was fun. That was *really* fun."

Watching her warily, he set his cup on the sink. "Yeah, it was."

She glanced down at herself. "Except I'm soaked."

Following the line of her vision, he saw that her sodden T-shirt had molded to her, outlining her perfect breasts. The wonderful feeling of joy enveloping them suddenly shifted. It was clear she'd never had an ounce of fun as a kid and something inside him wanted to show her all of that. Show her how to have fun.

Him. The Iceman. He wanted to show somebody how to have fun.

He hadn't thought about fun in twenty years.

Yet she made him want to have fun again.

And if that wasn't confusing enough, looking at her, dripping wet and incredibly sexy, his definition of fun had morphed from water battles to adult games in his amazing shower. He wanted to make love but not in a serious, purely physical way. In a fun, joyful way.

He stepped back, cleared his throat. "You are wet. Why don't you go upstairs first and get a shower? I'll be up in a minute."

She smiled like a happy child. "Yeah. Guess I should."

She turned without another thought for the dishes or cleaning up the water they'd tossed at each other. But as Matt grabbed a mop—from a closet he found after searching around awhile—he told himself he didn't mind cleaning up after their water battle.

He needed to be away from her for a few minutes. Not only had she awakened urges in him he hadn't felt... well, ever. But also, water fighting with her reminded him of happier times. Magnificently simple times when he'd thought his sisters were his sisters. When there were no half anythings. And everybody loved a good water battle in the pool, the ocean or the bathroom.

He grinned stupidly. They were bad kids, but he'd loved that part of his childhood.

His grin faded. He missed his sisters. Not the adult versions, but the kids he used to play with.

A great ache filled his chest.

He missed being happy.

But when he finished cleaning the kitchen he went to

his room and absently ambled into the bathroom; he forgot he had a guest. He found Claire brushing her teeth in front of one of the bowls of his double-bowl sinks and his thoughts swung back in the other direction.

In her pretty pink pajamas, with her little pink toes sticking out and her big brown eyes still shining with laughter, she was the epitome of that perfect mom he'd suspected she'd be. Happy. Filled with joy. Waiting for her husband to come to bed. So they could—

He jumped back. Not out of embarrassment that he'd walked in on her in the bathroom. But because that vision scared him. After Ginny, he always pictured himself alone—believed he deserved to be alone. Now in a few days one little slip of a woman had him thinking about family, kids, fun…and sex filled with emotion. Not just physical pleasure, but physical pleasure wrapped in a blanket of happiness.

This woman scared him.

"I'll just go back out and wait until you're finished."

She spit in the sink. That alone should have had him running. Instead, it felt very natural, very normal.

"No. No. I'm just about done. You can come in."

He hesitated, then walked in. This was ridiculous. How could one person change what you felt about everything? In four days? From Monday to Thursday? And could he really count Monday, since he hadn't gotten to Dysart Adoptions until after four? It was ridiculous.

He ambled to the sink, got his toothbrush and rolled some paste on it.

Towel-drying her hair, she said, "So tomorrow, we interview nannies."

He nodded.

"That should be easy. Especially after the water battle."

She caught his gaze in the mirror and smiled at him.

"Now, we both know you're looking for someone fun. Someone who can play with Bella."

Yeah, *her*. He was looking for her. She might not have played games as a child, but she knew how to play with Bella and she'd happily played with him. She longed to play. And he longed to teach her to play. To be happy. To be part of a family.

His eyes locked on hers in the mirror. He felt a thousand longings spring up, a thousand possibilities and a thousand things he never in a million years believed he'd feel.

It was everything he could do not to run out of the bathroom.

CHAPTER TEN

THE next morning, Matt barely looked at Claire when they woke up with Bella. He silently changed the baby's diaper and carried her downstairs.

Claire's heart stuttered a bit. She'd fallen asleep foolishly happy. They'd had fun in the water battle. And she'd seen that playful, wonderful side of him again. Having him withdraw stung, even if it did remind her to watch herself. She wasn't supposed to like him too much. He was wrong for her. The bits and pieces of Happy Matt that she saw came and went. They were too fleeting to be dependable. And he didn't want her, either. Otherwise, he'd have been happy this morning. Flirty as he was the night before. Not sullen, as if he regretted everything they'd done.

She prepared Bella's cereal and, again, Matt insisted he be the one to feed her.

She gave him the spoon and sat on the chair across the table from them.

"Here you are, sweetie," he crooned, sliding the bite of cereal into the baby's mouth. Bella smiled sleepily before opening her mouth wide to take it.

Matt laughed. "You make this easy, Miss Bella."

Claire smiled, too. It might not be wise for her to get involved with him, but when he wasn't being Wall Street's

Iceman, he was definitely nicer than he believed himself to be.

She frowned. This was another thing Ginny had probably seen while married to him. Buried deep down inside of Matt there really was a nice guy.

But if he was always working, how could Ginny have seen that? When had she seen nice Matt? When they met? Had they gone to school together?

"How'd you meet Bella's mom?"

Preoccupied with feeding Bella, Matt said, "We took the same train to work."

She frowned. That didn't give Ginny much chance to see him as a nice guy. "Really? You rode a train?"

"Subway. I lived in New York City back then."

"It's still hard to see you on a train."

"I told you. I learned all about good money management while attending university. Just because I'd gotten a great job, I wasn't about to throw my money lessons out the window. I lived conservatively and was never poor again."

"So how'd you meet? Did you sit beside each other?"

He smiled. "Actually, I'd noticed her on the train for weeks before we spoke. It wasn't until I gave a pregnant woman my seat and ended up standing beside her that I talked to her."

His smile grew. "She was beautiful. Every guy in the train had talked to her, but she'd blown them off." He turned and met Claire's gaze briefly. "Until we suddenly found ourselves holding the same pole. Then I said something goofy and she laughed. After that, we sat beside each other every day. Saved each other seats." He paused, his head tilted. "We talked. A lot. Before I could screw up the courage to ask her out."

He peeked over his shoulder at her again. "You could make coffee."

"Good idea." She rose from the chair and walked to the counter. But considering everything he'd just told her—how he and Ginny had met, how they'd stayed friends even after their divorce and how Ginny had given Bella to Matt to raise, she spun around again.

Ginny hadn't given him a second look until he relinquished his seat to a pregnant woman. Then she'd talked to him. And it wasn't until they'd talked several times—on their train rides—that she'd gone out with him. She hadn't just believed Matt to be a nice guy. She'd tested him. She'd seen him do a good deed, then quizzed him. That's why she'd believed him to be honorable and good, and strong enough to raise her child. She'd gotten to know the real Matt before she even agreed to go out with him.

And that was why Claire kept falling for him. Just like Ginny, she'd been given a space of time to see the real Matt Patterson. Had they met any other way she'd have met the Iceman. Cool. Calculating. Watching him with Bella, she was getting to know his good side.

No. That wasn't true, either. It was more like being stuck together for days, twenty-four hours each day, they were getting to know the real people they were underneath.

And underneath all his bluster, Matt Patterson was a genuinely nice guy.

After the coffee brewed, she poured two cups and walked back to the table.

Claire set his coffee in front of him. "Our first nanny interview isn't until nine. We can take a few minutes, drink our coffee and chat with her."

Matt took a sip from his coffee, then glanced at Bella. "So what do you want to talk about today?"

Bella giggled.

But strange thoughts went through Claire's brain. He was getting so good with Bella. Not merely competent. But loving. Treating her as his own child. Making the two of them a family without even realizing it.

She didn't know why she was surprised. She'd seen hints, even before Monday was over, that he had what it took to be a great dad.

The question was…

Did he have what it took to be a great husband?

And did she have what it took to hang around long enough for him to realize they belonged together?

The thought made her freeze in place. When had she decided they belonged together?

She thought about the night before, having fun, talking normally, just genuinely liking each other, and she realized she and Happy Matt were incredibly compatible. That was the guy she liked. The guy she might even be falling in love with. The guy she could easily see herself spending the rest of her life with.

Iceman Matt was another story. And Iceman Matt seemed to be around more often than not.

Still… What she wouldn't give for a chance, a real chance, to be with Happy Matt.

Maybe if she just continued to make him laugh, to treat him normally, as if life was supposed to be fun, he'd come out and stay out.

The first nanny arrived at nine and Matt led her to the den. She took a seat in front of his desk and Claire sat on the chair beside her.

"So…" He glanced at her résumé, then quickly looked up at her. "Peaches?"

"Yes. My mother apparently had terrible cravings when

she was pregnant with me." She pointed at her head. "The red hair was just a happy accident."

He laughed. Then caught himself. He could count on one hand the times he generally laughed in one week, but lately everything seemed to strike him as funny.

He knew why. Claire was bringing emotions out in him that he'd repressed for years. But he'd repressed them for good reason. He didn't get along with his family. He didn't make a good husband. So, it hurt him to miss his sisters. It hurt to see himself as a family man—when he knew he wasn't a family man. He was a strong, determined businessman who would literally have to squeeze a baby into his life. He had to get himself back to normal. And the best way to get himself back to normal would be to hire a nanny and get Claire out of his house.

Though the thought of her leaving hurt, too, that was actually the point. She made him want things he couldn't have. And he would feel these odd things until she left. But once she was gone, he'd be fine.

He looked at Peaches's résumé again. He asked her a few questions about her employment, but no matter how hard he tried to poke holes in her experience he couldn't. Peaches—however odd her name—was a candidate for Bella's nanny.

He ushered her to the front door, and when he returned to the den, Claire grinned at him. A responding grin rose up in him but he squelched it.

"I liked her."

He walked to his desk. "I did, too. But I have to admit, I was hoping for someone more conservative."

She laughed. "Conservative? After our water battle?"

His gaze dipped to the desk. "That water battle was stupid."

"That water battle was fun."

He knew it was. But the crazy urges it brought out in

him were wrong. He'd spent the past twelve years on his own, even when he was married to Ginny, becoming successful by keeping his nose to the grindstone. That's who he was. He needed to remember that.

"Oh, surely you're not regretting our water battle?"

Thoughts of sloshing water on her made him want to laugh again and brought his longings to life. He shouldn't want to be playful and silly. But more important, he didn't have the right to risk Claire's heart by dragging her into fantasies that had no place for him. Fantasies that would dissolve like dust as soon as he got back to work. If he didn't settle this right now, she'd get her hopes up and they'd have a real mess on their hands.

"Actually, I am."

"But—"

"No buts. I'm a single man with a conglomerate that takes most, if not all, of my time, trying to fit a baby into my life. I should be taking this more seriously."

"I think you're doing exactly—"

"Stop! I know you think I need to change and I know you're leading me in that direction. But I am who I am. I promise you I will raise Bella well. You can stop worrying and stop trying to change me."

She pressed her lips together as if he'd mortally embarrassed her and Matt's heart compressed into a tiny ball. Or maybe it went back to the shape it always had been— a tiny, tiny ball.

A tiny ball that would barely be able to handle loving a baby let alone adding a sweet, wonderful woman to the list.

The doorbell rang. She bounced out of her seat. "I'll bring this nanny back."

Pretending great interest in the résumé for the next nanny, he let her go.

* * *

The remainder of the interviews went smoothly. They chose three great candidates, any one of whom would make a great nanny, and Matt was suddenly extremely happy.

But Claire knew why. Once he got a nanny, she would leave. No wonder his mood had lifted. No more being pushed about Bella or how he should behave or what he should do.

Well, okay. She got the message. He did not want to be pushed into being the guy she got along with, the guy she liked.

She swallowed down the sadness that filled her. Not just for herself but for him. She wasn't a stranger to loneliness and she recognized all the signs in Matt. But he didn't want her help. And she—

Well, she was tired of being rejected. After their water battle she'd thought something had changed between them, but Matt regretted it. He regretted laughing with her. He regretted having fun with her.

And she was really tired of being someone's regret. First her dad's. Then Ben's. Now Matt's?

She didn't think so.

It was time to distance herself. Really distance herself. Tomorrow he would conduct second interviews. By tomorrow night he could have a nanny and she could go home. Protect her heart. Never be somebody's regret again.

But as she turned to leave the room, regret rose up in *her*. Regret that she hadn't been able to reach him, to make him want her enough to forget all the things that tied him down. All the reasons he wanted to stay lonely.

When Bella woke from her nap, Claire lifted her from her crib and immediately handed her to Matt. When the baby wouldn't settle, Claire drifted away, hoping that being out of sight would put her out of the baby's mind.

No such luck.

Matt might not be a total stranger to her, but fresh from a nap when Bella was disoriented and in need of the familiar, Matt wasn't the person she wanted to hug.

Finally, she walked over, took Bella from Matt and said, "She needs her things."

"Whatever she wants we can buy."

"No. I didn't say that she *wanted* her things. I said she *needs* her things. *Her* things." If her voice was a little snippy, she didn't care. This baby needed some comfort. And it seemed they were always catering to Matt. What he wanted. How he wanted things done. That stopped here. That stopped now. "She needs the things that make her relax. Things that make her happy. We need to go to her house, get her special stuffed animal, see if she had a particular blanket she slept with, find her favorite snuggly pajamas."

"She'll get accustomed to—"

"Hey!" Her temper boiled over. She was coming to like a guy who obviously didn't want to like her, while caring for a baby she was going to miss. She needed to get this job done and get away before she got any more emotionally involved. The time for diplomacy had passed. "In almost four days she hasn't grown accustomed to you. Why the hell should she suddenly fall in love with a strange bear?"

Matt's eyebrows rose.

Claire stiffened. That had been stupid. She never, ever vented like that. But he had her so frustrated. The whole situation did. Why was she upset over losing a man she barely knew? Especially one who was now sorry they'd had a water battle that had made her laugh like nothing in her entire life had ever made her laugh. They'd had so much fun and now he regretted it.

Why did he want to be a grouchy man when he had such a wonderful man inside him?

She headed for the nursery door. "Come with me or stay behind. But Bella and I are going to her former house to get the things that will make her comfortable."

As she left the room, she heard Matt's annoyed breath, but by the time she got Bella into a little jacket and found her own coat, he was behind her, walking toward the limo with her.

Realizing she hadn't called Jimmy, she stopped.

He nudged her to keep going. "I called him."

It didn't amaze her that it seemed he'd read her mind. He hadn't. He'd thought of Jimmy because when he needed to go somewhere he always called Jimmy. She refused to make a big deal out of him knowing what she was thinking. This whole situation was a mess. A setup for disaster. Them playing house. Her already in love with Bella and falling for the nice guy Matt showed her when he let his guard down. Him being sweet one minute, grouchy the next.

What woman wouldn't be confused?

They drove to a beautiful estate not far from Matt's and also not as big or elaborate. About half the size of Matt's, the two-story brick house sat on a green lawn.

He unbuckled Bella, told Jimmy they'd only be about ten minutes and led her up the walk.

She glanced around with a gasp. "I never thought about security. How are we going to get in?"

He pulled a key from his pocket. "We're covered."

Of course, if Ginny trusted him enough to give him her baby, she'd certainly trust him with a key to her house.

After punching numbers into a pad by the door, he used the key and let them inside.

Silent and eerie, the front hall greeted them. Walking into the home of people she didn't know—especially considering those two people were dead—filled her with trepidation. But when Bella squealed with delight, sadness quickly replaced Claire's fears. Sorrow seeped into her soul. This was Bella's home. The last time she'd been here she'd been with her mommy and daddy.

Matt, however, didn't pause. He walked up the curving stairway, led Claire to a room in the back and opened the door on a nursery.

Claire whispered. "How did you know where it was?"

"I am her godfather. It was mandatory that I peek in on her occasionally."

"You make it sound like you'd only looked at her as a favor to her parents."

He cocked his head. "I guess that *was* all I did it for."

Disappointed in him, she said, "Oh," and followed him into the nursery. A well-worn pink blanket lay in the crib. As soon as she saw it, Bella screeched.

Claire scooped it up and Bella grabbed it. Pressing her face into the soft material, she cooed with delight.

"I think we've found her blanket."

Matt stood off to the side, stiff, erect. "What else does she need?"

Claire looked around. "Let's let her decide." She smiled at Bella. "What else, sweetie?"

Blanket over her arm, Bella stretched toward the crib again. Claire walked over and saw the big-eared stuffed dog. She pulled it out.

Bella squawked, hugging the dog like a lifeline.

"Two things down. I don't know how many more to go."

"How many does she need? Seriously. We've got her dog and her blanket. Isn't that enough?"

Hearing the annoyance in his voice, Claire nearly turned on him again. If this was the Iceman, she was glad he hadn't put in too many appearances. "I don't know. We should probably get some of her clothes. Especially pajamas. Then we can go."

"Great." He walked to her. "I'll hold Bella. You pack a bag for her."

Claire found a big diaper bag and as quickly as she could she filled it with baby clothes. Not the beautiful, obviously expensive things she found in the closet, though she chose a few of those. What she was most interested in were the worn jeans, scruffy pajamas, soft T-shirts. The things she suspected Bella probably wore all the time. The things that would make Bella comfortable.

Without her.

She was being replaced by worn pajamas, a soft blanket and a big-eared scruffy dog.

Her eyes filled with tears, but anger soon dried them. All Matt would have to do would be to say one word and she would visit Bella. Regularly. But no. He didn't want to play. He didn't want to be soft. He wouldn't trust. And she wouldn't put herself out there only to be rejected again.

When the diaper bag was full, she walked to the door. Matt followed silently behind her.

But at the bottom of the stairs, he stopped. He sucked in a breath and squeezed his eyes shut.

"What?"

He swallowed. "This was the house Ginny and I had lived in. I gave it to her in the divorce. She liked it enough that she kept it."

Damn.

Remorse for all her nasty thoughts about his mood filled her. Not sure what to say, she stayed silent.

He shook his head. "We really did have a happy beginning to our marriage."

"Most beginnings are happy."

"And then work got in the way."

At the sadness in his voice, pain pierced her heart. He and Ginny might have divorced but they'd obviously loved each other.

She glanced around, suddenly understanding something else about Matt Patterson. He wasn't just struggling with the idea of his life changing drastically because of getting Bella after Ginny's death. He'd lost a woman he'd once loved and he was grieving. "You really loved her."

He peeked over at her, as if reluctant to admit any more personal things to her. But finally he said, "Yes. But the deals always took me away."

"You were trying to prove yourself to your stepfather."

He barked a laugh. "If nothing else, I know you pay attention when I talk."

Had that been an insult or a compliment? "Am I wrong?"

He shifted Bella on his arm. "No. You're not wrong. My need to prove myself was stronger than my need to keep her." He paused, swallowed. "The thing is, I always believed she'd stay. I believed if she loved me she'd want what I wanted."

"But she didn't."

"No."

An odd sensation enveloped her. As if she understood the sadness Ginny had felt when she'd divorced him. The disappointment that she'd lost the man she'd married, the man she'd loved.

Still, she said nothing. She felt for Matt, but she also

understood Ginny. She'd barely come up on her father's radar because of his work. It would be a hundred times sadder to lose the man you adored, the man you knew still lived somewhere deep down inside your husband.

She hoisted the diaper bag to her shoulder. "Let's go."

"Okay." He followed her to the front door. But before stepping out, he took one final survey of the front foyer.

Her heart broke for him, but she couldn't say anything comforting or soothing. He didn't want her to, but she also knew this was something he'd have to come to terms with himself.

There were no words of comfort for someone who was guilty as charged.

CHAPTER ELEVEN

CLAIRE tossed the diaper bag into the car and slid in. Matt climbed in and strapped Bella into the car seat. As Jimmy started the limo, Matt leaned back. Seeing Ginny's house, seeing how Bella had reacted to her blanket and well-worn dog, he'd figured out some things. Ginny had turned the house they'd lived in into a home. A real home. Even without people, it hadn't seemed empty.

From the second he'd walked in the door, he'd seen signs of her and Oswald everywhere. A pipe in an ashtray. Vacation pictures. Comfortable sofas in the living room beside the foyer. Throw rugs to catch dirt from shoes. Colorful afghans on chairs for chilly winter nights. People lived in that house and it showed.

While his house was big and cold and certainly not kid-friendly.

Most of that he could fix with a remodel. But he couldn't change the fact that his house was sterile, unless he brought more people into his life. His first thought was Claire. She'd be the perfect mother for Bella. She'd brighten the house more than any remodel possibly could. And he wanted her. He'd sleep with her in a heartbeat and she'd sleep with him. He knew she had feelings for him. Strong feelings. She couldn't keep them out of her eyes, her voice. She wasn't just attracted to him. She liked him.

But she wanted a real home, not the shell she'd have with a man too repressed to feel emotions. Forget about expressing them.

Driving away from the house he'd shared with the last woman he'd hurt, he knew he couldn't draw Claire into a relationship. It wouldn't be fair.

Which took him to his family.

Since the water battle with Claire, he'd been thinking about his sisters. Charlotte was now married and had a child. *A baby.* Maybe having another baby around was what Bella needed?

His heart lifted. Charlotte was the closest of his siblings. He could see Bella playing with her baby. But Charlotte lived in Italy now. Though her visits would be special, they would be few and far between. He needed more. Bella needed more. People to come and go. People who populated pictures on his mantel, pictures he'd take at picnics and on vacations with aunts, uncles, cousins.

A family.

He needed to make more of an effort with his sisters. He'd been cold. He'd been distant. Because he'd been hurt by Cedric. But punishing his sisters for things Cedric had said had been wrong. Plus, Cedric was sick now. It was time to let go of the past.

Still, he needed to vet this with someone. See if it really was the good idea he thought it was. And Claire, like always, was available. "I've been thinking a lot about my family."

Claire faced him, but her voice was cool when she said, "Because of the reunion?"

"And Bella." He cautiously caught her gaze. "And the water fight. I know this is going to sound weird, but I miss my sisters as kids. I'd like to bring them back into my life so Bella would have family. A big family. Lots of family."

"That sounds very nice."

He put his head back. "Problem is I don't know them as adults. I was the oldest. I left for school at eighteen. Didn't even visit. I told my mom I needed my weekends and holidays to work." He peeked over at her. "And that wasn't a lie. I did need to work."

"But you actually stayed away because you were angry with your stepdad?"

"And I took it out on everybody."

"So you've barely seen them."

He nodded. "I've attended a function here and there. But that's it."

"So maybe this reunion would be a great chance to catch up?"

"It would." He reached over and ran his finger across the tiny hand Bella had resting on the bumper pad that kept her in the car seat. She caught it and cooed. "I want Bella to have family."

"That's really good!"

He frowned. He knew that news would make her happy. But after her being nothing but cool in this conversation, her overly bright response was out of place. It was as if she'd noticed he hadn't included her in the equation. If it hurt her, she wouldn't show it. But by not arguing or asking why she wasn't included, it also proved she accepted it. He was shoving her out of his life because that's what he always did. He wouldn't commit to another woman. The visit to Ginny's house should have shown her why she should be glad to get away while she could.

When they reached his house, she quickly undid Bella and carried her inside. Walking up the stairway, she told him she didn't want his help putting the baby to bed.

He wasn't surprised. She was cutting ties. The way

they should be. So he didn't press to join her and Bella in the nursery. He walked back to the den.

Even before he reached his desk, the phone rang.

"Matt Patterson."

"Hey, big brother!"

"Charlotte?"

"Yep. Look, I know you're going to hate this, but I promised I'd call you and tell you so I'm just going to spit it out."

Fearing the worst, he fell to his chair. "So spit."

"Holt's called a family meeting for tomorrow. He wants us all on the same page before the Larkville festivities start next Wednesday."

Holt. The man who would be the family patriarch had Matt not been born a few months earlier. His first reaction was to want to dig in his heels and refuse to come. But after his thoughts that day, he sat back on his seat, considered a different path.

"Will Alex and Ellie be there?" he asked, referring to his and Charlotte's other two sisters.

"They're already here."

He squeezed his eyes shut. It was now or never. Swallow his pride and do what had to be done, or worry that Bella would grow up alone, as isolated as he was. He glanced around his quiet, quiet den. Even knowing Claire and Bella were upstairs, the house was hollow, empty. Missing something that could only be filled by people. Family.

He blew out his breath. "Okay, count me in. I can't be there until afternoon, but I'll be there."

He heard the surprise in her voice as she said, "Family meeting's at six. Let me know when you arrive and I'll pick you up at the airstrip."

He hung up the phone with butterflies in his stomach.

He didn't know how he was supposed to blend into this family, when technically he should be the leader. But if he demanded his place as leader, he'd undoubtedly alienate everyone.

Sighing, he rose from his chair. He'd figure something out.

Upstairs with Bella, Claire couldn't shake a huge case of guilt. After the cool way she'd treated Matt at Ginny's, and the even cooler way she'd reacted when he tried to talk to her about his family, it just didn't feel right to be leaving the next day. Yes, there was no defense for his ignoring Ginny in favor of proving himself to his stepdad, but she could have said something consoling. Maybe even said that the way he worked to become a real father to Bella proved he wasn't the same guy who'd constantly deserted Ginny. He was changing.

But that was the whole point, wasn't it? He was changing. Slowly. But still, he was changing. And when he'd finally talked about Ginny, she'd given him the cold shoulder, wouldn't console him. She'd let him stew.

When he'd most needed her, she'd emotionally deserted him.

She rocked Bella on the rocker, let her snuggle with her dog and blanket and listened to the happy baby murmurs of a little girl finally reunited with a few things that brought her comfort. Though one kind of peace settled over her, it only shined a light on how uneasy she felt about Matt.

It had been so wrong not to comfort him, but he'd told her to butt out of his life. So she had. She had for her own self-protection as much as to comply with his order. She already worried that she was falling in love with him.

And he didn't want to reciprocate those feelings. She'd be crazy to think otherwise.

Still…he needed her. She knew he needed her. Getting back with his family, making amends, wouldn't be easy. He'd need somebody in his corner.

And this time tomorrow she'd be gone.

Matt called the nanny service and canceled the interviews scheduled for the following day. Then he talked to his pilot and called Charlotte back with an arrival time. As he hung up the phone from talking to his sister, Claire walked into the room.

"How's Bella?"

"Sleeping like an angel, happily hugging her blanket and dog."

Finally, finally, things were working out. Now he just had to tell Claire that as of tomorrow, at about noon, her services would no longer be required.

His heart squeezed at that, but he ignored it. She deserved a good man. He was not a good man. The fun they'd had in the water battle was an aberration. Being so comfortable in his bathroom, a mistake. He needed to let her go.

"Would you mind taking a seat?"

She hesitated, then pasted on a smile. He could tell she knew what was coming. Even if he hadn't decided to go to Larkville, she would have been able to go home tomorrow after the nanny came on the job. A smart woman, she would understand it was time to discuss her leaving.

"I just got a call from my sister. It seems my half brother Holt has called a family meeting for tomorrow."

"A family meeting?"

"Our Calhoun/Patterson reunion is tied up with a community festival. They'll be honoring my biological father at a big party next Saturday."

"Oh."

"I don't know Holt, but if he's smart he's probably getting us all there early to give us time to talk through the fact that the man being honored actually has twins he didn't know."

She frowned.

"Ellie and I were conceived in my mother and Clay's very short marriage. He never knew about us because his soon-to-be new wife hid the letter my mother sent informing him of her pregnancy."

Her eyes widened. "You're a twin?"

He almost smiled. She didn't bat an eye at the scandal surrounding Clay Calhoun never knowing his kids. But she was agog over the fact that he was a twin. "Yes. My sister's name is Ellie."

She gaped at him. "How can you have a twin and not talk about her?"

"I told you. I haven't really spoken to most of my family in a decade. But that's over now and I've decided to go to the family meeting. Which means I leave tomorrow."

"Well, I guess that's great. You know...for your family and all."

"It is and it isn't. Because I'm leaving early, I had to cancel the nanny interviews...."

She frowned. "So who'll be staying with Bella?"

"I'm taking her with me."

"By yourself?"

He'd planned on getting help from his sisters once they were in Texas but he'd forgotten about the plane ride itself. And from the expression on Claire's face he guessed it wasn't a good idea for him to travel with a baby alone.

Before he could say anything, she looked away.

He didn't blame her. After the distant way he'd behaved since their discussion of the water battle, she wasn't going to volunteer. But, of course, after the way he'd behaved, asking her to accompany him now would not be construed as anything other than the favor it would be. So maybe it was a blessing they'd had their spat?

"I know it's an imposition to ask, but could you come with us?"

She said nothing.

"I wouldn't ask, but it's important for me to go to that meeting tomorrow." He leaned back in his chair. "Technically, I'm the oldest. Holt's the oldest of his family, but I'm our father's first son. I should be family patriarch."

Her gaze snapped to his. "You're not going down there to start a fight, are you?"

He laughed. "No, I am not going down there to fight."

"Then why is it suddenly so important?"

"I told you. Not only is Holt apparently staving off potentially embarrassing scenes, but also I came to some conclusions today. I want Bella to have a family. I'm willing to do more than compromise."

She studied him. "Really?"

He sucked in a breath. "Yeah. I just don't know yet what I'm going to do or how I'm going to do it, but I want at least my sisters in Bella's life. If I have to swallow my pride to do it, I will."

Laughing, she shook her head. "Well, I'll be damned."

"Don't make fun. This isn't going to be easy for me."

Slowly, she brought her gaze to meet his. "It might not be easy but it's the right thing. I'm not making fun of you. I'm proud of you."

Warmth spiraled through him at her praise. The truth was he was a tad proud of himself for being willing to make the first moves to get his family back. And not for himself. For Bella. In the past few days he'd done all kinds of good things. He'd been changing with leaps and bounds, genuinely understanding the right things for Bella, and he had Claire to thank for that.

He cleared his throat. Now was not the time to be thinking good thoughts about Claire. He'd finally resolved their situation in his mind. He didn't want those strange feelings he had for her bubbling up again, confusing things. Especially since he needed her again.

Before he could say anything, she did. "I'll go with you."

"You will?"

"Yes. You're going to make a good daddy, Matt Patterson. And if my spending a few more days with you and Bella helps that along, then I'll go to Texas." She laughed and rose from her seat. "I better do some laundry, get my jeans and shirts washed since that's all the clothes I have."

She left the room and Matt stared after her. No ranting or raving about clothes. No telling him what *she* needed. She was doing this only for Bella and him. Getting nothing out of it for herself. Yet, she just left the room to do some laundry as if favors were an everyday occurrence for her.

She was definitely too good for him.

The next morning, Claire called Joni.

"We're taking the baby to Texas."

"And you're calling because you don't think you'll be back on Monday?"

"I have no idea when we'll get back." She winced. "Matt actually talked about a banquet next Saturday night. I'm going to need another week off."

"Okay. As your boss, I'm fine with another week off.

As you're friend, my reaction is… What the hell are you thinking?"

She laughed. "He took everything to another level yesterday. He isn't just determined to be a good dad for Bella. He's also reuniting with his family. He hasn't really been involved in his family in years and, because of Bella, he's taking steps to be in their lives again."

"Seriously? Claire. This is not your problem. There's always going to be one more thing with this guy and before you know it you're going to have been his temporary nanny for a year…or two…with no pay!"

"I'm helping a friend." She paused, wincing, knowing how bad this sounded, but convinced she was doing the right thing. "Matt's a good guy. Bella's a sweet baby. None of this has been easy for him, but I know my being around has helped him and I can't desert him now."

She didn't mention that she'd left him to flounder on the trip to Ginny's house and still felt bad about that. She didn't mention the funny catch in her heart when she thought about how hard he'd worked and how far he'd come. She also didn't mention that she worried that she was falling in love with him, because that didn't count. She knew the compromises he was making for Bella and his family were difficult enough. There wasn't any room in his head or his heart for a romance. No matter how much she liked him or how much she wanted it, he didn't. She *would* remember that.

"And I promise, once we get back from Texas, that will be it. I will walk away."

"I hope so."

"I will."

She disconnected the call and fed Bella some cereal. A few minutes later, Matt stumbled into the kitchen. Wearing his navy striped pajamas without a robe, he looked sleepy and sexy and, oh, so huggable.

She wanted to swoon, but didn't. If she was going to behave as she'd told Joni she would, and keep her heart intact, then this was a business trip for her. She might see a good side of him. She might desperately want to help him. She might even be more attracted to him than she'd ever been to another man, but he'd warned her off several times. She would handle this trip like a professional.

"What time are we leaving for Texas?"

"What time do you want to go?"

"Well, I washed my jeans and my few tops last night, so I'm as ready as I'll ever be."

He turned. "You don't want to go home and get more clothes?"

She shrugged. Unable to think of anything she'd like to take with her, she said, "I have no idea what the weather will be like or how the locals will dress. I'd like to wait and see what everyone else wears. Then I can pick up a few things while I'm there."

He said, "Okay," and faced the coffeepot again.

He played with Bella as he drank his coffee, cementing her belief that he was a nice guy who deserved her help.

While he packed a bag for himself, she packed a bag for Bella. Jimmy drove them to the airport.

When she saw Matt's plane, her eyebrows rose in surprise. "It's kinda small."

"I have no need for a bigger plane."

"Just thought you'd want to be a little fancy."

Carrying Bella, while Jimmy handed their luggage to the eager flight crew, Matt said, "Wait until you see the inside."

The inside was white leather. Soft-cushioned seats that looked like recliners greeted them. He showed her a big-screen TV along a back wall that they could watch in-flight because their seats completely turned around.

The plane taxied and was airborne in a few minutes. Bella fell asleep immediately and Matt showed Claire how to work the TV before he pulled some papers from a brief-case. A comfortable silence settled over them.

She smiled and relaxed against the seat, pleased that everything was calm and content. She had nothing to worry about. They were friends.

A tug on her heart reminded her that she wanted to be more than friends, but she ignored it.

He didn't want her. She wouldn't want him.

When they landed at the small airstrip in front of a hangar at the back of the ranch, Matt unbuckled his seat belt and immediately reached for the one securing Bella's safety seat. He unclicked a few buckles, unsnapped a few snaps and lifted her out of the seat.

"Hey, sleepyhead."

She squinted, trying to open her eyes but not quite succeeding.

He laughed and grabbed the diaper bag.

Claire reached out to help him. "Let me take her."

"No. I've got her." He did. He had this baby who had been entrusted to his care. He'd never desert her. He'd do whatever needed to be done for her. He was officially a daddy.

As he walked down the plane's stairs, he noticed a big white SUV about thirty feet away. Leaning against the back door was his sister Charlotte. Tall and lanky, with shoulder-length brown hair, she didn't look one bit out of place wearing jeans and a Stetson...and were those cowboy boots?

He burst out laughing and nudged his head in her direction. "Would you believe that's my rebellious little sister Charlotte?"

Claire laughed.

Charlotte shoved away from the car and opened her arms to him as he approached. "What? You've never seen a cowboy hat?"

"I like your boots."

"Yeah, well, I like your baby." She took Bella from him and glanced at Claire. "I'm Charlotte, by the way. Matt's sister."

Claire reached out and shook the hand she extended. "I'm Claire. I'm helping him with Bella, the baby."

She peeked at Matt. "Where did you get a baby?"

He winced. "She's Ginny's little girl."

Her face softened. "Oh, Matt. I'm so sorry."

"So was I." Sadness rose up in him again, but only the sadness of a man who had lost a good friend, not the sadness of a man who had lost the love of his life. For the first time since he'd heard of Ginny's death, he felt at peace with it. "We're more concerned with getting Bella past it."

"Well, it looks like you're doing a good job." Charlotte bounced the baby playfully. "You're such a sweetie!"

Bella squealed happily.

Charlotte handed Bella to Matt, then opened the passenger door of the SUV with a wince. "Sorry. Since I didn't know you had a baby, I didn't bring a car seat. But it's a short ride. You can hold her."

"As long as it's a short ride."

"Very short."

Claire said, "Let me hold her in the back."

"That's probably a good idea." He handed the baby to Claire and stepped up into the SUV. Unexpectedly plush seats greeted him, but everything also seemed to have a longhorn motif. One of Matt's eyebrows rose.

Charlotte laughed. "Things are a little different here in Texas. Laid-back. Lucio had a bit of a time getting adjusted when we arrived, but he's fine now."

"Lucio? Your husband?"

"Love of my life."

"And where's Maria?" Matt asked, referring to her baby.

"She's back at the ranch, waiting to meet her uncle."

"So where's everybody else?"

She started the SUV and pulled away from the airstrip. "Everybody's at the ranch house." She peeked over at him. "Waiting to meet you."

A shiver of apprehension ran through him. It was the first time in his life he'd so desperately wanted something—not for himself—but for someone else. And he knew his past behavior might prevent him from getting it. That he'd disappoint and deprive Bella went through him like a knife.

Still, he ignored the fears rumbling through him. He wasn't just the Iceman on Wall Street. He'd survived getting a baby. Meeting a few half siblings would not throw him for a loop.

In only a few minutes, they were at the white clapboard ranch house. Simple and functional, it still somehow projected an air of stability and power. Corrals and outbuildings dotted the property. Horses grazed lazily behind the split-rail fence. Cattle roamed the pastures.

Everything was spit and polished, as if prepped for the big celebration the following week.

Wonder swept through him. An odd tingling. This is what he came from. These were his real roots.

After they exited the SUV, Charlotte took Bella from Matt and led him up the wood plank porch in back of the house. They entered through the door that led to a large kitchen. Men and women sat in the chairs around the cozy table. Others leaned against the cabinets. Matt's mouth fell at the sheer number of them.

His pretty blonde twin, Ellie, laughed, rose from the table and raced over. "It's so good to see you." She hugged him briefly and he closed his eyes as wave upon wave of emotion pummeled him. He didn't realize how much he'd missed his twin until this very second.

He had to clear his throat before he could say, "It's good to see you, too."

"And who's this?" Ellie said with a laugh as she reached for Bella.

Charlotte said, "Matt's baby." She pointed at Claire. "And that's Claire."

Everybody glanced at Matt expectantly.

He smiled. "Claire's helping me with Bella. Ginny and Oswald left custody of Bella to me."

A hush fell over the room, then everyone began to volunteer to help him with the baby. Bella was passed from hand to hand.

Charlotte continued with introductions. Ellie was with the town sheriff, Jed Jackson. Alex was there with a tall Australian named Jack. Megan Calhoun, one of Matt's half sisters, was "promised" to Adam somebody-or-another. There was a Nate and Sarah. A Jess and John. And Lucio holding Charlotte's new baby, Maria.

For the first time in his life, Matt wasn't afraid to take a newborn, examine her, pronounce her beautiful.

Everybody laughed.

Then a tall, dark-haired cowboy entered the kitchen. All talking stopped. A pretty blonde stepped up beside him, and Matt realized she hadn't been introduced when Charlotte was reciting couples.

Charlotte carefully said, "And that's Holt and Kathryn."

Matt's eyes met Holt's. The guy looked like he wrestled cattle for a living and given that he was the operator of this ranch Matt supposed he did.

"So you're the great Iceman."

CHAPTER TWELVE

LOOKING at Holt Calhoun, Matt swallowed. He had a choice. Assert his rights as oldest or simply say hello, extend his hand, create the bridge that would make all these people family.

He held out his hand.

"It's nice to meet you."

Holt stepped away from Kathryn. Took the hand Matt had extended. Shook once.

"Maybe we should reserve judgment on that." He pointed at the door. "How about a tour of the town?"

Matt glanced at Claire. She gave him a brief smile. They both knew this was Holt's way of getting Matt away for the discussion everybody knew they needed to have.

Yet it didn't feel right to leave Claire behind with so many strangers. "I'd love a tour of the town, if Claire and Bella can come."

"Oh, no!" Ellie said, taking Bella. "This little cutie stays. She's got cousins to meet and aunts to play with."

Holt glanced at Claire. "How about you, Claire? Do you want to stay?"

"Actually, I wouldn't mind a trip to town to get something a little lighter to wear." She tugged at the collar of her shirt. "It's hot down here."

Holt laughed. "Texas is probably hotter than Boston in October."

"So you guys go," Charlotte said. "We'll take care of Bella. Claire can shop for some cooler clothes." She smiled craftily. "And Holt can have his talk with Matt."

They piled into Holt's truck, which, luckily, had a backseat for Claire. As much as she wanted some shorts and lightweight T-shirts, Charlotte's comment sort of frightened her about the upcoming conversation. She didn't really want to be part of a fight between the two oldest Calhoun sons…even if one was named Patterson.

She settled back on her seat as Holt said, "So what do you think?"

Matt said, "About what?"

Holt pointed out the windshield. "Everything you see is Calhoun land."

Claire couldn't stop her eyebrows from rising. That was a lot of land.

"I think our dad was a hell of an entrepreneur."

"And a good guy, too." Holt shifted on his seat. "At the banquet you'll hear stories of how he helped people." He glanced at Matt. "When I stepped into his shoes on the ranch the 'helping people' thing just sort of seemed to come with the territory."

Matt said nothing. Claire held her breath.

"I wanted to get you away from the rest of the family because I wanted to tell you that I recognize you are oldest. There's nothing in the will that gives me the ranch. Nothing that puts me in charge. I just did what needed to be done."

Matt glanced back at Claire and her heart stumbled in her chest. It was almost as if he was acknowledging her part in what he was about to say.

He looked at Holt again. "And you'll keep doing it.

I might be the oldest, but you're the best person to run things here in Texas." He grinned. "Now, if you'd like a little investment advice for profits and reserves, that might be something we could talk about."

Holt barked a laugh. And, to Claire's surprise, the conversation became cordial. Like a man proud of his heritage, Holt pointed out things of interest as they drove into town. Like a man curious about his heritage, Matt listened with rapt attention.

They passed Gracie May's Diner, the SmartMart, Gus's Fillin' Station and Hal's Drug and Photo store.

"The festival concerts will be held there," Holt said, pointing to a stage being built in what looked to be a park as he slid his truck into a space along Main Street. He jumped out and Matt took Claire's hand to help her out.

As he released her hand, she smiled at him and he returned her smile, as if he knew she would be proud of him. And by God, she was. This time last week, he would have grabbed his rights as oldest, just because they were his. After Bella—after *her*—he wanted to get along.

No. He wanted to do the right thing.

"Dad's banquet will be held in the Cattleman's Association Hall," Holt said when Claire and Matt rounded the truck and met him on the sidewalk. "I can show you that as we're driving home." He slapped Matt's back. "So while Claire's shopping, big brother, you have a choice. Coffee at Gracie's or a beer at the Saddle Up bar."

"Think I'll go for the beer." He faced Claire. "Will you be okay on your own?"

She grinned. After almost a week with Matt and Bella, it felt good to be on her own. "Yeah. I think I might explore a bit."

Holt laughed. "Not much to explore."

She chuckled and headed off in search of shorts and some tank tops.

An hour later, arms loaded with packages, not just clothes but souvenirs for Joni, she found the guys at Saddle Up, deep in conversation. As soon as they saw her, both rose. They were so different. Holt with his jeans and work shirt and a body built by hard work and Matt in his jeans and T-shirt and a whipcord lean, sexy body. Yet, they looked the same. It was clear they shared a bloodline. Even if Matt was better looking.

Of course, she was prejudiced. And happy. As if being in Texas brought out the best in him, Matt was chatty and solicitous. Immediately upon their return to the ranch house, he asked Kathryn which rooms they could use, saying he was sure Claire was eager to get into something cooler.

Because she was. As Holt had said, Texas heat was very different from Boston heat and she was drenched in sweat.

In the shower she tried not to make too much of Matt's behavior. But when she came downstairs, dressed in her shorts and tank top, and his eyes drank her in like a vintage wine, it was impossible not to notice that Happy Matt was here.

He sucked in a breath. "You look great."

She laughed. "It's only shorts and a T-shirt!"

"I know, but you have great legs. You should wear shorts all the time."

She laughed again. Not sure how to take his sudden, unexpected interest in her. She'd always known he was attracted to her. Hell, she was attracted to him. It seemed that in Texas he couldn't control it. Or maybe he couldn't control it because he was relaxed, happy. Letting himself do things he was too restrained to do in Boston.

"I don't think our climate would really support me wearing shorts all the time."

"Too bad." He caught her gaze. "Wanna check on Bella with me?"

"Yes, actually, I would."

They walked upstairs to the room where Bella and Izzy, Kathryn's daughter, had been sleeping, expecting to find two babies sitting up in the crib. But when they opened the door, they found four women, three babies—Bella, Izzy and Charlotte's baby, Maria—and Brady.

Walking into the fray, they began to separate. Matt took her hand. "We're looking for Bella."

Obviously having heard his voice, she squealed. Following the sound of the squeal, Claire found Bella sitting on Alex's lap. She walked over, taking Matt with her.

"How's our girl?" she said, then held back a gasp, realizing she'd more or less included herself into the group of Matt and Bella.

But Matt said, "Looks like our baby is fine."

Warmth filled her heart. He'd included her, too.

He let go of her hand and plucked Bella from Alex's lap. "What do you say, kid? Want some time outside with the old folks."

Bella squealed with delight. Not just because she wanted to go outside. From the way she reached for Claire, it was clear she was happy to see people she knew again.

Filled with love, Claire said, "Stay with your daddy."

Though Bella appeared a bit perturbed, she looked into Matt's face and cooed.

He laughed and carried Bella out of the room and downstairs, but everywhere they went a crowd of people had gathered. He caught Claire's hand again and led them outside.

She told herself it was nothing but a necessity, a way of

keeping them together. But she couldn't stop the hopeful swelling of her heart. What if having everything straightened out with his family had been the final piece of the puzzle he'd needed to be able to accept himself and move on. And what if she was part of that moving on?

After dinner—barbecue on a big outside grill, served on picnic tables with red-and-white-checkered tablecloths—the Calhouns and Pattersons talked about the ranch, their heritage and what they would be doing with the land, ranch profits and the other family holdings. Though half the people involved were neither Calhouns nor Pattersons, in-laws weren't just invited to sit in on the conversation, their opinions were respected and heard. Even Claire sat beside Matt, listening, participating when asked.

When the meeting was concluded, Ellie came over and sat on the bench seat next to Matt. She nudged her shoulder into his. "I have something to tell you."

"Me?"

"Yes. Jed and I are married."

"That's normally what people who are engaged do."

Claire stifled a laugh at his fun comment. Happy Matt, the man who loved to tease, was definitely here.

Ellie playfully punched his arm. "Be happy for me!"

He smiled warmly and little tingles danced up Claire's spine. She'd never seen him like this. Warm. Open.

Ellie grinned, then she drew in a slow breath, waiting for his answer.

In reply, he laughed—really laughed—and slid his arm around Claire's shoulders, as if drawing her into the intimate conversation. "I'm very happy for you."

Emotion flooded Claire.

Tears pricked at her eyelids. With Matt's arm around her shoulders and so much happy family stuff happening around her, she felt a part of things, too. And a rightness. As if this was exactly where she was supposed to be. That these people were her family, too.

Knowing that was dangerous thinking, she shifted to get out from under Matt's hold, but he held her fast, drawing her back when she would have moved away, as if silently telling her this was where she belonged.

Her chest tightened. She'd never felt so much love in a crowd of people before. Most of them might have only met this past year, but they were family. Solid. Dependable. There for one another.

And it seemed Matt wanted her to be part of that.

She couldn't even describe the emotions that bubbled up in her at that. After being alone most of her life, with a few friends and lots of scars from her failed relationship, she finally had a place where she belonged.

Around nine o'clock, everyone began to gather up their plates and serving dishes and head for home. Kathryn and Claire took the babies, Izzy and Bella, upstairs to bathe them. Holt left to go to the barn to talk with the ranch foreman. When the babies were in bed, Kathryn left to take a shower and Claire went in search of Matt.

Perfect peace settled over the ranch and caught Claire in its liquid warmth. With Matt behaving as if she belonged with him, it was hard not to spin fantasies. As much as she told herself not to, pictures of them together, forever, a part of this family easily formed.

She walked through the silent downstairs and found him on the front porch.

When he saw her, he rose from a wicker chair. "Want to go for a walk? Maybe see a little bit of the ranch?"

She glanced at him with a smile. "It's dark." And there weren't any streetlights as there were in Boston. Dark in Texas meant dark!

Matt shrugged. "Paths are lit."

She glanced over at the two paths. One led to a barn and was lit by light from the barn. The other led to the corral. That one was lit by light coming from the house. Still, it wasn't as if they had to worry about bumping into anything in the empty land. Plus, they hadn't had two minutes by themselves. With everything that was going on, he might have put his arm around her shoulders, held her hand and even included her in things with Bella, but he hadn't had a chance to tell her how he was feeling. The way he felt about her had changed—she could sense it in his touch—but she needed to hear.

"Sure. I'd love a walk."

They headed down the well-worn path. Claire looked up, amazed at the number of stars in the sky. "Look at all the stars."

"There's no city light blocking them out," Matt said as they walked down the trail. "What I can't get over is the quiet."

"Yeah." It was perfect. Everybody liked Matt. He liked them. And he liked her. Everyone had accepted her as if she fit, too. The peace of the ranch was like icing on a cake.

When Matt caught her hand, her heart swelled. This was it. She wasn't wrong. He liked her and she liked him. And though things weren't happening fast on this trip, she was glad. They'd connected so quickly in Boston that they could have made a mess of things. But here in Larkville, where time passed slowly and people moved slowly, they were regaining their equilibrium.

"Okay, so I was thinking," Matt said as he pulled her to a stop under a huge leafy tree. "I fit a little better than I'd imagined."

She laughed and stepped close to him. For once it felt right to act on what she was feeling. "You belong here."

"I think I do." He glanced around. "I also think I'm going to like being part of this family." He brought his gaze back to hers and smiled. "That's why I'm giving you your freedom."

She frowned. The words felt heavy, cold. Like stones that had been outside in winter. Out of place on this warm Texas night. "What?"

"Things fell into place perfectly here. And I have all kinds of sisterly help with Bella. It was an inconvenience for you to come here. So…" He smiled at her. "I'm letting you go home."

Her heart stopped as her brain tried to catch up with what was going on. "You're kicking me out?"

He laughed. "No. I'm letting you go home."

"But—" She stopped, unable to put what she was feeling into words. "You put your arm around me!"

Okay. That sounded stupid and maybe even childish, but it was the gist of what she felt. He'd made overtures all day. Done subtle, affectionate things. She'd thought they were connecting. For real. On a deep, intimate level.

She combed her fingers through her hair. She *hadn't* misinterpreted.

By the time she looked at him again, his eyes were narrowed, as if he'd been thinking through what she'd said about putting his arm around her. "You mean when Ellie told me she was married?"

"Yes." Oh, God. A horrible thought came to her. Had she misinterpreted his simple gestures because she liked him so much? Loved him, really. She'd been sitting on the edge of it for days and now she was here. Firmly in love with a guy who didn't want her.

Exactly what she'd promised Joni she would avoid.

She stepped back. "Okay. Yeah. You're right. I need to go home." She swallowed back a boatload of tears. Not just because she was losing something she really wanted, but also because she'd made a fool of herself. She didn't even have any pride left to save her. She turned and sprinted away.

"Claire! Claire, wait!"

But Holt picked that second to come out of the barn. "We have a bit of a problem."

Matt turned. "Problem?"

"I've got some numbers you need to see."

The "numbers" turned out to be the report of an investment that had gone south. The amount of money the family lost had been substantial, but a quick look at the rest of the portfolio put Matt's mind at ease. He explained to Holt that with a shift of a few investments they could make that money back and more.

He was glad he'd been able to help Holt, alleviate his concerns so he wouldn't have to go to sleep worried. But by the time they got back to the house, Kathryn was waiting for them in the kitchen.

"Did you tell Claire to go?"

Matt winced. This was the part of families that most men hated. Having to answer for things that should be private. Still, Kathryn was a wonderful woman. Someone Matt instinctively liked. He knew she wasn't prying, but concerned.

"I think Claire and I had a difference of opinion about her leaving. She's been helping me all week. I thought she'd be glad to go. But I think she wanted to stay. If she does, that's fine. She can stay. I'll talk to her in the morning."

"She's gone."

"What?" He shook his head. "She can't go. I didn't call the pilot."

"I think she flew commercial."

"Flew?"

"She was lucky to catch a flight that was leaving to-night." She frowned. "You do realize you've been in that barn for three hours."

"Oh." Matt sat.

Holt said, "Everything okay?"

He sucked in a breath. "Claire and I have sort of liked each other since we met at the adoption agency keeping Bella for me. I think her feelings went a little faster and a little further than mine." He smiled at Holt. "Her leaving is for the best. It would be a mess if she'd stayed. For both of us. But especially her. She needs to get back to work."

Holt nodded. "Okay, then."

But when Matt walked up the stairs to his bedroom and sank to his bed, alone, which he always was, his stomach flip-flopped. His feelings had been moving as fast as Claire's, and those gestures he'd been making all day—he hadn't been able to stop them. He liked her so much he couldn't stop touching her, wanting her. It was so easy to feel close to her, but he should have stopped his need to touch. Not just because he was afraid of something that happened so fast, but because she deserved better.

Much better. She might not realize it now, but his let-ting her leave was a gift to her.

CHAPTER THIRTEEN

MONDAY morning, Claire forced herself out of bed and into the shower. She washed her hair, put on makeup and slipped into her favorite red dress. Yes, Sunday had been a disaster of weeping and berating herself for falling for someone who didn't want her. But it was time to stop brooding over a man she'd known a week. She was stronger and smarter than that.

She knew Bella was safe and well cared for. She knew Matt didn't want her, hadn't seen her as anything but a helpmate. So feeling bad about it was only self-pity. And she didn't do self-pity. She picked herself up, dusted herself off and went on with life.

But even after that pep talk, by the time she got to the office, she was in tears.

Margaret, the receptionist, rose as Claire pushed open the Dysart Adoptions door. "Are you okay?"

"I'm fine," she said through a fresh round of sobbing.

Joni Dysart, the tall, thin blonde who owned Dysart Adoptions, came shuffling out. She put her arm around Claire, led her into her office and shut the door. "Oh, shoot. What happened to you going to Texas?"

"Oh, I went." She snatched a tissue from the box on the credenza, then fell to the seat in front of Joni's desk, as Joni sat on the tall-backed chair behind it. "And everything just kind of fell into place. With his family, he turned into the nice guy I'd been seeing glimpses of and suddenly he was doing things like holding my hand and putting his arm around me. I took it as a sign that we were feeling the same things." She peeked up and caught Joni's gaze. "But Saturday night, he told me I could go home."

"Simpleton!" Joni said with relish. "I could slap him! Don't pin this one on yourself. He doesn't want any woman. At least, not permanently." Joni handed the box of tissues from the credenza to Claire. "I told you he had a reputation."

"But we were different. We bonded over Bella."

Joni sighed. "What's the one thing we know better than anybody else?"

"That babies don't fix bad marriages or create relationships."

"Exactly."

"But he was just so different around her."

"Because he had a responsibility to be a good dad, and if there's one thing Iceman Patterson respects, it's responsibility."

"Oh, shoot. I know that. I always knew that. I just stopped reminding myself." Getting ahold of herself, she sniffed back the next round of tears. "What's wrong with me?"

"Nothing. You fell for a good-looking guy who was showing you his nice side because of the baby. And apparently the way he behaved with his family."

"Why didn't I see that?"

"Because you loved Bella. You wanted to see the best in him for her sake."

"I guess."

"Any woman would have fallen—"

"Being in love with someone after a few days isn't falling. It's leaping. I leaped into love with him—just as I did with Ben—except this time I knew it was wrong." She blew her nose. "I'm such an idiot."

"You're not an idiot."

"You're right. I'm not an idiot. So that only leaves desperate. His family made me feel so at home. A part of them. Like I finally belonged somewhere." She blew her nose again. "I'm a desperate woman who does stupid things."

Joni groaned. "You're not desperate, either. His family sounds very nice and he… Well, he's a great-looking guy. It would be hard not to be infatuated with him."

"And he truly loves Bella." She swallowed. "Okay. I get it. He was putting together a little family with Bella. And I…" She sighed. "I've always wanted a family. I guess it was hard to watch someone making one without trying to be involved."

"Look, I'm not the person to tell you your business, but maybe an actual vacation would be a good idea?"

"Vacation?"

"You were planning to take the week off, anyway. Why not go somewhere like a cruise…or maybe…Fiji…or Africa. Somewhere you'll be so busy you won't have time to think of Matt."

The thought of getting away for a few days lifted her spirits. "Maybe."

"Definitely. You fell too fast for the wrong guy. You need to clear your head."

Claire swallowed. Though she did agree she needed to clear her head, she didn't agree that Matt was the wrong guy. He might appear to be self-centered and cold to the rest of the world, but she'd met the real Matt Patterson. And he was wonderful. Everything she wanted. The problem was he didn't want her.

He might have been her right guy, but she hadn't been his right woman.

By Monday night, Matt thought his world had ended. No matter how many happy people were around him. No matter how many great things he saw, how many Larkville residents told him about his wonderful dad. No matter how much he loved seeing Bella with the other kids…

He missed Claire.

"You should just go and get her."

He faced Charlotte. "That transparent, huh?"

"Yes. We're all talking about it. We're just not doing it in front of you."

Normally, that would have made him mad. Knowing these woman usually talked out of love, not gossip, he laughed. "You don't understand. She's a wonderful woman. She deserves better than me."

Charlotte frowned. "Really?" She motioned for him to grab a bowl of macaroni salad and follow her out to the picnic tables they were setting for an impromptu supper. "It seems to me it's you she wants."

"And I'm not sure why."

"Seriously?" Charlotte laughed. "Could it be because you're handsome and smart and fun?"

"I'm not…" He almost said *fun,* then he remembered their water battle. He remembered laughing with her over Bella. He remembered teasing her and letting her tease him. He remembered putting his arm around her shoulders, as if bringing her into his family when Ellie told him she was married. Being with her made him fun.

They did love each other.

Charlotte stopped him halfway to the table, before they were in earshot of his other brothers and sisters and their mates. "Look, I don't want to be the one to tell you your business, but are you trying to repeat history?"

He gave her a puzzled look.

"Clay and Finella. Each lived without the love of his or her life. All because she wanted Clay to come after her and he didn't."

She paused, sucked in a breath. "Of course, we know now that he didn't get the letter she'd sent him, telling him she wanted another chance. But we also both know that though Mom was happy, there was always something missing from her life. Is that how you want to live?"

Matt looked away, thinking about his mother, knowing as Charlotte had said that there was always something missing from her life. Always a rim of sadness around an otherwise perfect existence.

"Clay didn't have a chance to get back the love of his life. But all you have to do is believe in yourself…believe in Claire…get in your plane and bring her back."

Standing in front of her closet, Claire whipped through the items hanging there, unable to find anything suitable for a vacation. Her clothes were old, and, worse, everything she owned was dowdy.

Was this how she'd seen herself in the years since Ben? Old? Uninteresting? Undesirable?

Tears filled her eyes. It was. She knew it was.

Until she met Matt. What she saw reflected in his eyes had made her feel like a woman again. A desirable woman. She'd been attracted to him because he was gorgeous. She'd begun to feel good about herself because it was clear he found her attractive. But she'd fallen in love because he was good, kind, bighearted, even if he didn't give himself credit for being any of those things.

She'd longed to be the person to show him how good he was, the same way he'd been the person to make her feel good about herself again.

But he didn't want that.

He didn't want her.

She whipped another shirt across the closet pole—a shirt she'd never worn because it was a dull, ugly purple. Why had she bought these things?

She finally found a sleeveless red top that might—and she stressed *might*—be okay for the flight down. But the sad truth was, she was probably going to have to buy a whole new wardrobe in St. Thomas.

She frowned. Would that be so bad? She had money. She needed clothes. She needed a whole new life.

Her doorbell rang. She tossed the red shirt to her bed and raced to answer, assuming it was Joni, here to make sure she didn't chicken out at the last minute and decide not to go.

Well, Joni didn't have to worry about that. Only a desperate woman fell in love in a few days…and with a man who kept telling her he didn't want her.

She *needed* a vacation!

As she reached the door, her heart protested. She didn't need a vacation. She needed love. She needed a man who challenged her and made her feel beautiful. A man who could be painfully honest. A man who understood her troubles because he'd lived something similar.

She needed Matt.

Telling herself she wasn't going to get him, she yanked open the door—

And there he stood.

Her mouth fell open. "Matt?"

"Hey." He shoved his hands into his jeans pockets. "Can I come in?"

Confused, she stepped back without thinking, motioning for him to enter. "I thought you were in Texas."

"I was. But after you left I realized I needed you."

He *needed* her? If it was possible for a heart to explode, hers definitely might.

With a shrug, he caught her gaze. "And Bella needs you."

Oh.

Her heart stuttered to a stop. She got it. He didn't need her the way she thought. He wanted a babysitter. Everybody he expected to be able to help him with Bella was probably busy with the festival or their own kids.

She held on to her poise by the merest thread. "You shouldn't have gone to Texas without hiring a nanny."

He chuckled—that wonderful chuckle that had taken him so long to let loose now seemed second nature, as if he was finally happy. Another arrow pierced her heart. He was happy without her. He needed a nanny, saw her as an employee.

"Bella needs more than a nanny. She needs you."

Drowning in the insult of him coming to her only for help with the baby and fearing she'd burst into tears, she turned away and headed for her bedroom, her head high, her shoulders back.

Insult and anger radiating through every muscle and bone in her body, she stiffly said, "I'm sorry but I'm booked on a flight to St. Thomas."

He scrambled after her. "St. Thomas? You're going on vacation?"

"I don't see what business that is of yours."

"It's all kinds of business of mine!"

She whipped around. "Really? Why? Because you need a nanny and everything you want comes first?"

Hurt registered on his face first, then incredulity. As if he couldn't believe she'd said that. He took a step back, swiped his hand across his mouth. "Is that how you see me?"

Unexpected fear rippled through her. She didn't know what she was risking, but she suddenly knew if she answered his question wrong, she'd regret it for the rest of her life.

She blew her breath out on a long stream. Even forgetting the potential regret, her innate fairness wouldn't let her lay a guilt trip on him. He hadn't ever been anything but honest with her. He'd also warned her that if she got involved with him, she'd get hurt. They'd also only known each other a few days.

She had no right to be angry, or hurt, or even slightly insulted. She'd volunteered to help him.

"Okay, look. I had time to help you with Bella last week." She peeked up at him, then regretted it. His intense green eyes focused on her like two laser beams, reminding her of the day they'd met, when he'd truly needed her and she hadn't been able to resist coming to his aid.

She sucked in a breath. "But now I can't help you. I need a week away. A week for myself."

He tilted his head. "Why?"

"I'm tired?"

He laughed. "Yeah. Babies can be tiring. But you already had yesterday to rest. You should be fine... Why aren't you?"

Because you broke my heart?

Man, she wanted to say that! She wanted to say, "Look, you scoundrel. You broke my heart! And you can afford a nanny. So get lost."

But standing two feet away from him, so close she could touch him, something inside her shattered. He was the only person she'd ever really told about her dad. He was the only man who'd ever so honestly confided in her, trusted her with his most painful secrets. He was the first person she felt happy and beautiful with.

Her lips trembled.

"I didn't come here because I want you to be my nanny. I came here because I think I love you."

Her gaze flew to his.

"It's crazy. It's not wise. My sister told me that I should come here and ask you for a date, not ask you to marry me...but my gut says ask you to marry me."

She stared at him. "You're asking me to marry you?"

He nodded.

"Oh, my God."

"That's not a yes."

Unsure her legs could support her, she leaned against the wall.

He caught her by the elbows and pulled her to him. "It's crazy. It's weird. But I spent yesterday without you thinking I'd done the right thing because I didn't deserve you. Then I saw my brothers and sisters all happy and I thought, why not me? When Charlotte reminded me that my mom had left Clay Calhoun, the real love of her life and was never happy again, I knew I didn't want that to be me. When you're not with me, I feel like a part of me is missing."

She gazed up at him, whispered, "I've felt that, too."

"You don't have to marry me tomorrow. You don't

have to marry me next week or next month. We could still date."

She shook her head. "No." A laugh escaped. "Well, maybe for a while… Would you kiss me already?"

He yanked her to him and kissed her so fast, so powerfully, that her breath caught. His lips swooped over hers claiming her possessively, but she kissed him back, every bit as eager to seal this union and giddy with the knowledge that he loved her. This strong, smart, determined man had chosen her.

"What do you say we take this to the bedroom?"

She winced. "My bed's covered in clothes."

"Clothes?"

"I need new ones."

His eyes narrowed. "Now?"

She plucked at the front of his shirt. "Actually, I still have the clothes I bought in Texas and they'd be good for the festivities down there. But I need to buy something better for the banquet, if you're serious about marrying me."

He answered without hesitation. "You're the love of my life. I don't know how I know it, but what I feel for you is so strong I can't deny it."

"Then I think we'd better hit a store for a new banquet dress before we head back to Texas and Bella. I don't like both of us leaving her for too long. Besides—" She plucked at his shirt again. "I sort of thought we'd save making love."

He frowned. "Save it? Are you talking about waiting for marriage?"

She laughed. "No. But I would like to wait until we know it's right. Special."

He glanced around. "And taking you in your hallway wouldn't be special?"

She laughed again. "You can really be silly."

He grinned. "I know. I love it."

She rose to her tiptoes and brushed a kiss across his lips. "And I love you, too."

"So we wait?"

"Until we know that it's time."

"Honey. We have plenty of time. If I have anything to say about it, we have the rest of our lives."

EPILOGUE

Cowboy boots and tuxedos. If Matt had thought it strange to have the banquet in honor of Clay Calhoun in the wood-frame Cattleman's Association Hall, the cowboy boots and tuxedos topped that.

Prominent members of the community sat at the main banquet table, including Holt.

He resisted the urge to scowl at his brother. Holt had assumed that since he and Claire had returned to Texas "engaged," they were sleeping together so he'd put them in the same room.

Matt had secretly hoped that having only one bed would push the issue of making love, but Claire wanted their first time to be special, and for days he'd kept his promise. Luckily, going to the festival and getting to know his siblings had been so time-consuming that they'd fallen into bed exhausted.

They'd slept together but hadn't made love.

And that morning when he'd awakened beside her, he suddenly understood why she'd wanted to wait. With her hair spread out over her pillow and her prim pink paja-mas giving her skin a soft glow he realized how beauti-ful she was—how special. In all the hustle and bustle of realizing they were in love, then returning to Texas, and taking care of Bella, they'd never really had ten true romantic minutes.

But tonight he intended to rectify that. He'd bought a bottle of champagne, arranged to have their bedroom filled with roses and Kathryn had agreed to keep Bella with Izzy all night so he and Claire would have time alone.

He just had to get through this banquet.

One by one the speakers rose, talking about Clay Calhoun. His dad. His real dad.

Matt's chest tightened. His heart expanded. He didn't have to wonder who he was anymore, where he'd come from. He knew. The speakers told story after story of Clay Calhoun's kindness, generosity and love for the land.

He listened to stories of how his real father was a great man, and felt the seeds of that kind of strength living inside him.

Claire squeezed his hand. "You get that from him. The goodness you always tried to suppress. That's Clay Calhoun's impact on you." She smiled. "Good genes."

He laughed.

When Holt rose to speak, the entire room got quiet. He took the podium slowly, tapped on the mic, making it screech, and cleared his throat.

"My father," he said, "truly was a great man. Not because he did a few great things, but because he did a thousand small things greatly. He gave advice when needed, a helping hand when advice wasn't enough. I don't expect to fill his boots."

He met Matt's gaze from across the room. Matt nodded once, encouraging him to go on. He was proud of his brother. As proud as a man could be. And so happy to have finally found not just a family, but real love.

"So I can't fill his boots, but most of you know I'm there if you need me."

A general round of agreement rippled through the crowd.

"But the town's bigger than it used to be and one man probably couldn't help as many people as my dad could. Which is why we're glad there's a troop of us now. There are enough Calhouns and Pattersons that if one of us can't help you, another of us can. Just in case you don't know who we are, I'll introduce everybody."

He motioned to the long table filled with Calhouns and Pattersons. Family, Matt thought, once again overwhelmed by the importance of it.

"There's my sister Jess, her husband, Johnny, and their son, Brady." Tall, blonde Jessica and dark-haired Johnny rose, but adorable five-year-old Brady stole the show, waving to the crowd and causing a short burst of laughter to fill the room.

"Right beside them is Ellie Patterson, my half sister from Dad's first marriage and her husband, Jed. You'll know him better as Sheriff Jackson," he said, reminding everybody that Ellie's husband was the town sheriff. Holding Jed's hand, Matt's twin rose.

Something fierce began to build inside Matt. Pride and a connection so strong and so sweet it almost took his breath.

"Then there's Alex and Jack. They'll be back and forth from Australia, but they know they always have a home here." He motioned to the couple beyond Alex and Jack. "My sister Megan and her beau, Adam."

Because Holt was making introductions by going down the line of people sitting at the banquet table, Charlotte and Lucio, the next in line, rose automatically.

Holt smiled. "And that's Charlotte, her husband, Lucio, and their little girl, Maria." Charlotte fondly smiled down at Maria.

"After them, that's my brother Nate and you all already know Sarah." The couple rose and accepted a smattering of applause.

Then Holt stopped. He caught Matt's gaze again. Keeping with the spirit of the introductions, Matt took Claire's hand and stood.

Holt smiled stupidly. "And that guy who just rose? That's *my* big brother. Matt. Now most of you know, I like to be the one in charge but over the past few days I've learned my big brother knows a lot, and even though I'm the one in Texas, the one who will run the ranch and its holdings, Matt's the head of the family." He grinned again. "My big brother."

The crowd laughed. Matt shook his head and laughed, too. Claire squeezed his hand.

"If we can talk this guy into visiting Larkville a time or two every year, I have a feeling he could help us with everything from finances and start-up businesses to making hotcakes. His fiancée, Claire, happened to mention he's very good in the kitchen."

Everybody laughed again.

"Why don't you come up here and take your place, big brother? Say a few words."

Matt shook his head. He hadn't prepared anything to say. Wasn't sure what to say. Holt would still shoulder the burden of the family holdings. Matt was more or less a figurehead.

"Come on. Come up and say something. This is where you belong."

Where he belonged. It all suddenly clicked. This *was* where he belonged. It was where they all belonged.

Matt glanced at Claire. "Come with me."

She pressed her hand to her chest. "Me?"

"We're a team now."

She smiled and took the hand he extended. He led Claire to the podium, feeling odd, but also knowing that he'd come home. Maybe, just maybe, he really was supposed to head this family.

And when they got back to the ranch, he'd claim his woman, the love of his life, a woman he probably wouldn't have met if he'd been raised in Texas.

So maybe things did work out the way they were supposed to, after all?

* * * * *

THE NANNY
BOMBSHELL

BY
MICHELLE CELMER

Bestselling author **Michelle Celmer** lives in south-eastern Michigan with her husband, their three children, two dogs and two cats. When she's not writing or busy being a mum, you can find her in the garden or curled up with a romance novel. And if you twist her arm really hard, you can usually persuade her into a day of power shopping.

Michelle loves to hear from readers. Visit her website, www.michellecelmer.com, or write to her at PO Box 300, Clawson, MI 48017, USA.

To my granddaughter, Aubrey Helen Ann

One

This was not good.

As a former defensive center, MVP and team captain for the New York Scorpions, Cooper Landon was one of the city's most beloved sports heroes. His hockey career had never been anything but an asset.

Until today.

He looked out the conference room window in the Manhattan office of his attorney, where he had been parked for the past ninety minutes, hands wedged in the pockets of his jeans, watching the late afternoon traffic crawl along Park Avenue. The early June sun reflected with a blinding intensity off the windows of the building across the street and the sidewalks were clogged with people going about their daily routine. Businessmen catching cabs, mothers pushing strollers. Three weeks ago he'd been one of them, walking through life oblivious to how quickly his world could be turned completely upside down.

One senseless accident had robbed him of the only family he had. Now his brother, Ash, and sister-in-law, Susan, were dead, and his twin infant nieces were orphans.

He clenched his fists, fighting back the anger and injustice of it, when what he wanted to do was slam them through the tinted glass.

He still had his nieces, he reminded himself. Though they had been adopted, Ash and Susan couldn't have loved them more if they were their own flesh and blood. Now they were Coop's responsibility, and he was determined to do right by them, give them the sort of life his brother wanted them to have. He owed Ash.

"So, what did you think of that last one?" Ben Hearst, his attorney, asked him. He sat at the conference table sorting through the applications and taking notes on the nanny candidates they had seen that afternoon.

Coop turned to him, unable to mask his frustration. "I wouldn't trust her to watch a hamster."

Like the three other women they had interviewed that day, the latest applicant had been more interested in his hockey career than talking about the twins. He'd met her type a million times before. In her short skirt and low-cut blouse, she was looking to land herself a famous husband. Though in the past he would have enjoyed the attention and, yeah, he probably would have taken advantage of it, now he found it annoying. He wasn't seen as the guardian of two precious girls who lost their parents, but as a piece of meat. He'd lost his brother two weeks ago and not a single nanny candidate had thought to offer their condolences.

After two days and a dozen equally unproductive interviews, he was beginning to think he would never find the right nanny.

His housekeeper, who had been grudgingly helping him with the twins and was about twenty years past her child-rearing prime, had threatened to quit if he didn't find someone else to care for them.

"I'm really sorry," Ben said. "I guess we should have anticipated this happening."

Maybe Coop should have taken Ben's advice and used a service. He just didn't feel that a bunch of strangers would be qualified to choose the person who would be best to care for the twins.

"I think you're going to like this next one," Ben told him.

"Is she qualified?"

"Overqualified, actually." He handed Coop the file. "You could say that I was saving the best for last."

Sierra Evans, twenty-six. She had graduated from college with a degree in nursing, and it listed her current occupation as a pediatric nurse. Coop blinked, then looked at Ben. "Is this right?"

He smiled and nodded. "I was surprised, too."

She was single and childless with a clean record. She didn't have so much as a parking ticket. On paper she looked perfect. Although in his experience, if something seemed too good to be true, it usually was. "What's the catch?"

Ben shrugged. "Maybe there isn't one. She's waiting in the lobby. You ready to meet her?"

"Let's do it," he said, feeling hopeful for the first time since this whole mess started. Maybe this one would be as good as she sounded.

Using the intercom, Ben asked the receptionist, "Would you send Miss Evans in please?"

A minute later the door opened and a woman walked in. Immediately Coop could see that she was different from the others. She was dressed in scrubs—dark-blue pants and a white top with Sesame Street characters all over it—and comfortable-looking shoes. Not typical attire for a job interview but a decided improvement over the clingy, revealing choices of her predecessors. She was average height, average build…very unremarkable. But her face, that was anything but average.

Her eyes were so dark brown they looked black and a slight tilt in the corners gave her an Asian appearance. Her mouth was wide, lips full and sensual, and though she didn't wear a stitch of makeup, she didn't need any. Her black hair was long and glossy and pulled back in a slightly lopsided ponytail.

One thing was clear. This woman was no groupie.

"Miss Evans," Ben said, rising to shake her hand. "I'm Ben Hearst, and this is Cooper Landon."

Coop gave her a nod but stayed put in his place by the window.

"I apologize for the scrubs," she said in a voice that was on the husky side. "I came straight from work."

"It's not a problem," Ben assured her, gesturing to a chair. "Please, have a seat."

She sat, placing her purse—a nondesigner bag that had seen better days—on the table beside her and folded her hands in her lap. Coop stood silently observing as Ben launched into the litany of questions he'd asked every candidate. She dutifully answered every one of them, darting glances Coop's way every so often but keeping her attention on Ben. The others had asked Coop questions, tried to engage him in conversation.

But from Miss Evans there was no starry-eyed gazing, no flirting or innuendo. No smoldering smiles and suggestions that she would do *anything* for the job. In fact, she avoided his gaze, as if his presence made her nervous.

"You understand that this is a live-in position. You will be responsible for the twins 24/7. 11:00 a.m. to 4:00 p.m. on Sundays, and every fourth weekend from Saturday at 8:00 a.m. to Sunday at 8:00 p.m., is yours to spend as you wish," Ben said.

She nodded. "I understand."

Ben turned to Coop. "Do you have anything to add?"

"Yeah, I do." He addressed Miss Evans directly. "Why would you give up a job as a pediatric nurse to be a nanny?"

"I love working with kids…obviously," she said with a shy smile—a pretty smile. "But working in the neonatal intensive care unit is a very high-stress job. It's emotionally draining. I need a change of pace. And I can't deny that the live-in situation is alluring."

A red flag began to wave furiously. "Why is that?"

"My dad is ill and unable to care for himself. The salary you're offering, along with not having to pay rent, would make it possible for me to put him in a top-notch facility. In fact, there's a place in Jersey that has a spot opening up this week, so the timing would be perfect."

That was the last thing he had expected her to say, and for a second he was speechless. He didn't know of many people, especially someone in her tax bracket, who would sacrifice such a large chunk of their salary for the care of a parent. Even Ben looked a little surprised.

He shot Coop a look that asked, *What do you think?*

As things stood, Coop couldn't come up with a single reason not to hire her on the spot, but he didn't want to act rashly. This was about the girls, not his personal convenience.

"I'd like you to come by and meet my nieces tomorrow," he told her.

She regarded him hopefully. "Does that mean I have the job?"

"I'd like to see you interact with them before I make the final decision, but I'll be honest, you're by far the most qualified candidate we've seen so far."

"Tomorrow is my day off so I can come anytime."

"Why don't we say 1:00 p.m., after the girls' lunch. I'm a novice at this parenting thing, so it usually takes me until then to get them bathed, dressed and fed."

She smiled. "One is fine."

"I'm on the Upper East Side. Ben will give you the address."

Ben jotted down Coop's address and handed it to her. She took the slip of paper and tucked it into her purse.

Ben stood, and Miss Evans rose to her feet. She grabbed her purse and slung it over her shoulder.

"One more thing, Miss Evans," Coop said. "Are you a hockey fan?"

She hesitated. "Um…is it a prerequisite for the job?"

He felt a smile tugging at the corner of his mouth. "Of course not."

"Then, no, not really. I've never much been into sports. Although I was in a bowling league in college. Until recently my dad was a pretty big hockey fan, though."

"So you know who I am?"

"Is there anyone in New York who doesn't?"

Probably not, and only recently had that fact become a liability. "That isn't going to be an issue?"

She cocked her head slightly. "I'm not sure what you mean."

Her confusion made him feel like an idiot for even asking. Was he so used to women fawning over him that he'd come to expect it? Maybe he wasn't her type, or maybe she had a boyfriend. "Never mind."

She turned to leave, then paused and turned back to him.

"I wanted to say, I was so sorry to hear about your brother and his wife. I know how hard it is to lose someone you love."

The sympathy in her dark eyes made him want to squirm, and that familiar knot lodged somewhere in the vicinity of his Adam's apple. It annoyed him when the others hadn't mentioned it, but when she did, it made him uncomfortable. Maybe because she seemed as though she really meant it.

"Thank you," he said. He'd certainly had his share of loss. First his parents when he was twelve, and now Ash and Susan. Maybe that was the price he had to pay for fame and success.

He would give it all up, sell his soul if that was what it took to get his brother back.

After she left Ben asked him, "So, you really think she's the one?"

"She's definitely qualified, and it sounds as though she needs the job. As long as the girls like her, I'll offer her the position."

"Easy on the eyes, too."

He shot Ben a look. "If I manage to find a nanny worth hiring, do you honestly think I would risk screwing it up by getting physically involved?"

Ben smirked. "Honestly?"

Okay, a month ago…maybe. But everything had changed since then.

"I prefer blondes," he told Ben. "The kind with no expectations and questionable morals."

Besides, taking care of the girls, seeing that they were raised in the manner Ash and Susan would want, was his top priority. Coop owed his brother that much. When their parents died, Ash had only been eighteen, but he'd put his own life on hold to raise Coop. And Coop hadn't made it easy at first. He'd been hurt and confused and had lashed out. He was out of control and fast on his way to becoming a full-fledged juvenile delinquent when the school psychologist told Ash that Coop needed a constructive outlet for his anger. She suggested a physical sport, so Ash had signed him up for hockey.

Coop had never been very athletic or interested in sports, but he took to the game instantly, and though he was on a team with kids who had been playing since they were old enough to balance on skates, he rapidly surpassed their skills. Within two years he was playing in a travel league and became the star player. At nineteen he was picked up by the New York Scorpions.

A knee injury two years ago had cut his career short, but smart investments—again thanks to the urging of his brother—had left him wealthy beyond his wildest dreams. Without Ash, and the sacrifices he made, it never would have been possible. Now Coop had the chance to repay him. But he couldn't do it alone. He was ill-equipped. He knew nothing about caring for an infant, much less two at once. Hell, until two weeks ago he'd never so much as changed a diaper. Without his housekeeper to help, he would be lost.

If Miss Evans turned out to be the right person for the job—and he had the feeling she was—he would never risk screwing it up by sleeping with her.

She was off-limits.

Sierra Evans rode the elevator down to the lobby of the attorney's office building, sagging with relief against the paneled wall. That had gone much better than she could have hoped and she was almost positive that the job was as good as hers. It was a good thing, too, because the situation was far worse than she could have imagined.

Clearly Cooper Landon had better things to do than care for his twin nieces. He was probably too busy traipsing around like the playboy of the Western world. She wasn't one to listen to gossip, but in his case, his actions and reputation as a womanizing partier painted a disturbing picture. That was not the kind of atmosphere in which she wanted her daughters raised.

Her daughters. Only recently had she begun thinking of them as hers again.

With Ash and Susan gone, it seemed wrong that the twins would be so carelessly pawned off on someone like Cooper. But she would save them. She would take care of them and love them. It was all that mattered now.

The doors slid open and she stepped out. She crossed the swanky lobby and pushed out the door into the sunshine, heading down Park Avenue in the direction of the subway, feeling hopeful for the first time in two weeks.

Giving the twins up had been the hardest thing she'd ever done in her life, but she knew it was for the best. Between her student loans and exorbitant rent, not to mention her dad's failing health and mounting medical bills, she was in no position financially or emotionally to care for infant twins. She knew that Ash and Susan, the girls' adoptive parents, would give her babies everything that she couldn't.

But in the blink of an eye they were gone. She had been standing in front of the television, flipping through the channels when she paused on the news report about the plane crash. When she realized it was Ash and Susan they were talking about, her knees had buckled and she'd dropped to the nubby, threadbare shag carpet. In a panic she had flipped through the channels, desperate for more details, terrified to the depths of her soul that the girls had been on the flight with them. She'd sat up all night, alternating between the television and her laptop, gripped by a fear and a soul-wrenching grief that had been all-consuming.

At 7:00 a.m. the following morning the early news confirmed that the girls had in fact been left with Susan's family and were not in the crash. Sierra had been so relieved she wept. But then the reality of the situation hit hard. Who would take the girls? Would they go to Susan's family permanently or, God forbid, be dropped into the foster-care system?

She had contacted her lawyer immediately, and after a few calls he had learned what to her was unthinkable. Cooper would be their guardian. What the hell had Ash been thinking, choosing him? What possible interest could a womanizing, life of the party, ex-hockey player have in two infant babies?

She'd asked her lawyer to contact him on her behalf using no names, assuming that he would be more than happy to give the girls back to their natural mother. She would find a way to make it work. But Cooper had refused to give them up.

Her lawyer said she could try to fight him for custody, but the odds weren't in her favor. She had severed her parental rights, and getting them back would take a lengthy and expensive legal battle. But knowing Cooper would undoubtedly need help, and would probably be thrilled with someone of her qualifications, she'd managed to get herself an interview for the nanny position.

Sierra boarded the subway at Lexington and took the F Train to Queens. Normally she visited her dad on Wednesdays, but she had the appointment at Cooper's apartment tomorrow so she had to rearrange her schedule. With any luck he would offer her the job on the spot, and she could go home and start packing immediately.

She took a cab from the station to the dumpy, third-rate nursing home where her dad had spent the past fourteen months. As she passed the nursing station she said hi to the nurse seated there and received a grunt of annoyance in return. She would think that being in the same profession there would be some semblance of professional courtesy, but the opposite was true. The nurses seemed to resent her presence.

She hated that her dad had to stay in this horrible place where the employees were apathetic and the care was borderline criminal, but this was all that Medicare would cover and home care at this late stage of the disease was just too expensive. His body had lost the ability to perform anything but the most basic functions. He couldn't speak, barely reacted to stimuli and had to be fed through a tube. His heart was still beating, his lungs still pulling in air, but eventually his body would forget how to do that, too. It could be weeks, or months. He might even linger on for a year or more. There was just no way to know. If she could get him into the place in Jersey it would be harder to visit, but at least he would be well cared for.

"Hi, Lenny." She greeted her dad's roommate, a ninety-one-year-old war vet who had lost his right foot and his left arm in the battle at Normandy.

"Hey there, Sierra," he said cheerfully from his wheelchair. He was dressed in dark brown pants and a Kelly-green cardigan sweater that were as old and tattered as their wearer.

"How is Dad today?" she asked, dropping her purse in the chair and walking to his bedside. It broke her heart to see him so shriveled and lifeless. Nothing more than a shell of the man he used to be—the loving dad who single-handedly raised Sierra and her little sister Joy. Now he was wasting away.

"It's been a good day," Lenny said.

"Hi, Daddy," she said, pressing a kiss to his papery cheek. He was awake, but he didn't acknowledge her. On a good day he lay quietly, either sleeping or staring at the dappled sunshine through the dusty vertical blinds. On a bad day, he moaned. A low, tortured, unearthly sound. They didn't know if he was in pain, or if it was just some random involuntary function. But on those days he was sedated.

"How is that little boy of yours?" Lenny asked. "Must be reaching about school age by now."

She sighed softly to herself. Lenny's memory wasn't the best. He somehow managed to remember that she'd been pregnant, but he forgot the dozen or so times when she had explained that she'd given the girls up for adoption. And clearly he was confusing her with other people in his life because sometimes he thought she had an older boy and other times it was a baby girl. And rather than explain yet again, she just went with it.

"Growing like a weed," she told him, and before he could ask more questions they announced over the intercom that it was time for bingo in the community room.

"Gotta go!" Lenny said, wheeling himself toward the door. "Can I bring you back a cookie?"

"No thanks, Lenny."

When he was gone she sat on the edge of her dad's bed and took his hand. It was cold and contracted into a stiff fist. "I had my job interview today," she told him, even though she doubted his brain could process the sounds he was hearing as anything but gibberish. "It went really well, and I get to see the girls tomorrow. If the other applicants looked anything like the bimbo who interviewed right before me, I'm a shoo-in."

She brushed a few silvery strands of hair back from his forehead. "I know you're probably thinking that I should stay out of this and trust Ash and Susan's judgment, but I just can't. The man is a train wreck just waiting to happen. I have to make sure the girls are okay. If I can't do that as their mother, I can at least do it as their nanny."

And if that meant sacrificing her freedom and working for Cooper Landon until the girls no longer needed her, that was what she was prepared to do.

Two

The next afternoon at six minutes after one, Sierra knocked on the door of Cooper's penthouse apartment, brimming with nervous excitement, her heart in her throat. She had barely slept last night in anticipation of this very moment. Though she had known that when she signed away her parental rights she might never see the girls again, she had still hoped. She just hadn't expected it to happen until they were teenagers and old enough to make the decision to meet their birth mother. But here she was, barely five months later, just seconds away from the big moment.

The door was opened by a woman. Sierra assumed it was the housekeeper, judging by the maid's uniform. She was tall and lanky with a pinched face and steel-gray hair that was pulled back severely and twisted into a bun. Sierra placed her in her mid to late sixties.

"Can I *help* you?" the woman asked in a gravely clipped tone.

"I have an appointment with Mr. Landon."

"Are you Miss Evans?"

"Yes, I am." Which she must have already known, considering the doorman had called up to announce her about a minute ago.

She looked Sierra up and down with scrutiny, pursed her lips and said, "I'm Ms. Densmore, Mr. Landon's housekeeper. You're late."

"Sorry. I had trouble getting a cab."

"I should warn you that if you do get the job, tardiness will not be tolerated."

Sierra failed to see how she could be tardy for a job she was at 24/7, but she didn't push the issue. "It won't happen again."

Ms. Densmore gave a resentful sniff and said, "Follow me."

Even the housekeeper's chilly greeting wasn't enough to smother Sierra's excitement. Her hands trembled as she followed her through the foyer into an ultra-modern, open-concept living space. Near a row of ceiling-high windows that boasted a panoramic view of Central Park, with the afternoon sunshine washing over them like gold dust, were the twins. They sat side by side in identical ExerSaucers, babbling and swatting at the colorful toys.

They were so big! And they had changed more than she could have imagined possible. If she had seen them on the street, she probably wouldn't have recognized them. She was hit by a sense of longing so keen she had to bite down on her lip to keep from bursting into tears. She forced her feet to remain rooted to the deeply polished mahogany floor while she was announced, when what she wanted to do was fling herself into the room, drop down to her knees and gather her children in her arms.

"The one on the left is Fern," Ms. Densmore said, with not a hint of affection in her tone. "She's the loud, demanding one. The other is Ivy. She's the quiet, sneaky one."

Sneaky? At five months old? It sounded as if Ms. Densmore just didn't like children. She was probably a spinster. She sure looked like one.

Not only would Sierra have to deal with a partying, egomaniac athlete, but also an overbearing and critical housekeeper. How fun. And it frosted her that Cooper let this pinched, frigid, nasty old bat who clearly didn't like children anywhere near the girls.

"I'll go get Mr. Landon," she said, striding down a hall that Sierra assumed led to the bedrooms.

Alone with her girls for the first time since their birth, she crossed the room and knelt down in front of them. "Look how big you are, and how beautiful," she whispered.

They gazed back at her with wide, inquisitive blue eyes. Though they weren't identical, they looked very much alike. They both had her thick, pin-straight black hair and high cheekbones, but any other traces of the Chinese traits that had come from her great-grandmother on her mother's side had skipped them. They had eyes just like their father and his long, slender fingers.

Fern let out a squeal and reached for her. Sierra wanted so badly to hold her, but she wasn't sure if she should wait for Cooper. Tears stinging her eyes, she took one of Fern's chubby little hands in hers and held it. She had missed them so much, and the guilt she felt for leaving them, for putting them in this situation, sat like a stone in her belly. But she was here now, and she would never leave them again. She would see that they were raised properly.

"She wants you to pick her up."

Sierra turned to see Cooper standing several feet behind her, big and burly, in bare feet with his slightly wrinkled shirt untucked and his hands wedged in the pockets of a pair of threadbare jeans. His dirty-blond hair was damp and a little messy, as if he'd towel-dried it and hadn't bothered with a brush. No one could deny that he was attractive with his pale blue eyes and dimpled smile. The slightly crooked nose was even a little charming. Maybe it was his total lack of self-consciousness that was so appealing right now, but athletes had never been her thing. She preferred studious men. Professional types. The kind who didn't make a living swinging a big stick and beating the crap out of other people.

"Do you mind?" she asked.

"Of course not. That's what this interview is about."

Sierra lifted Fern out of the seat and set the infant in her lap. She smelled like baby shampoo and powder. Fern fixated on the gold chain hanging down the front of her blouse and grabbed for it, so Sierra tucked it under her collar. "She's so big."

"Around fifteen pounds I think. I remember my sister-in-law saying that they were average size for their age. I'm not sure what they weighed when they were born. I think there's a baby book still packed away somewhere with all that information in it."

They had been just over six pounds each, but she couldn't tell him that or that the baby book he referred to had been started by her and given to Ash and Susan as a gift when they took the girls home. She had documented her entire pregnancy—when she felt the first kick, when she had her sonogram—so the adoptive parents would feel more involved and they could show the girls when they got older. And although she had included photos of her belly in various stages of development, there were no shots of her face. There was nothing anywhere that identified her as being the birth mother.

Ivy began to fuss—probably jealous that her sister was getting all the attention. Sierra was debating the logistics of how to extract her from the seat while still holding Fern when, without prompting, Cooper reached for Ivy and plucked her out. He lifted her high over his head, making her gasp and giggle, and plunked her down in his arms.

Sierra must have looked concerned because he laughed and said, "Don't let her mild manner fool you. She's a mini daredevil."

As he sat on the floor across from her and set Ivy in his lap, Sierra caught the scent of some sort of masculine soap. Fern reached for him and tried to wiggle her way out of Sierra's arms. She hadn't expected the girls to be so at ease with him, so attached. Not this quickly. And she expected him to be much more inept and disinterested.

"You work with younger babies?" Cooper asked.

"Newborns usually. But before the NICU I worked in the pediatric ward."

"I'm going to the market," Ms. Densmore announced from the kitchen. Sierra had been so focused on the girls she hadn't noticed that it was big and open with natural wood and frosted glass cupboard doors and yards of glossy granite countertops. Modern, yet functional—not that she ever spent much time in one. Cooking—or at least, cooking *well*—had never been one of her great accomplishments.

Ms. Densmore wore a light spring jacket, which was totally unnecessary considering it was at least seventy-five degrees outside, and clutched an old-lady-style black handbag. "Do you need anything?" she asked Cooper.

"Diapers and formula," he told her. "And those little jars of fruit the girls like." He paused, then added, "And the dried cereal, too. The flaky kind in the blue box. I think we're running low."

Looking annoyed, Ms. Densmore left out of what must have been the service entrance behind the kitchen. Sierra couldn't help but wonder how Coop would know the cereal was low and why he would even bother to look.

"The girls are eating solid foods?" she asked him.

"Cereal and fruit. And of course formula. It's astounding how much they can put away. I feel as if I'm constantly making bottles."

He made the bottles? She had a hard time picturing that. Surely Ms. Cranky-Pants must have been doing most of the work.

"Are they sleeping through the night?" she asked him.

"Not yet. It's getting better, though. At first, they woke up constantly." He smiled down at Ivy affectionately, and a little sadly, brushing a wisp of hair off her forehead. "I think they just really missed their parents. But last night they only woke up twice, and they both went back to their cribs. Half the time they end up in my bed with me. I'll admit that I'm looking forward to a good night's sleep. Alone."

"*You* get up with them?" she asked, not meaning to sound quite so incredulous.

Rather than look offended, he smiled. "Yeah, and I'll warn you right now that they're both bed hogs. I have no idea how a person so small could take up so much room."

The idea of him, such a big, burly, rough-around-the-edges guy, snuggled up in bed with two infants, was too adorable for words.

"Out of curiosity, who did you think would get up with them?" he asked.

"I just assumed… I mean, doesn't Ms. Densmore take care of them?"

"She occasionally watches them while I work, but only because I'm desperate. After raising six kids of her own and two of her grandchildren, she says she's finished taking care of babies."

So much for Sierra's spinster theory.

"Is she always so…" She struggled for a kind way to say *nasty,* but Cooper seemed to read her mind.

"Cranky? Incorrigible?" he suggested, with a slightly crooked smile that she hated to admit made her heart beat the tiniest bit faster.

She couldn't help smiling back.

"She won't be winning any congeniality awards, I know, but she's a good housekeeper, and one hel…" he grinned and shook his head. "I mean *heck* of a fantastic cook. Sorry, I'm not used to having to censor my language."

At least he was making an effort. He would be thankful for that in a year or so when the twins started repeating everything he said verbatim.

"Ms. Densmore isn't crazy about the bad language,

either," he said. "Of course, sometimes I do it just to annoy her."

"I don't think she likes me much," Sierra said.

"It really doesn't matter what she thinks. She's not hiring you. I am. And I happen to think you're perfect for the job." He paused then added, "I'm assuming, since you're here now, that you're still interested."

Her heart skipped a beat. "Absolutely. Does that mean you're officially offering it to me?"

"Under one condition—I need your word that you'll stick around. That you're invested in the position. I can't tell you how tough that first week was, right after…" He closed his eyes, took a deep breath and blew it out. "Things have just begun to settle down, and I've got the girls in something that resembles a routine. They need consistency—or at least that's what the social worker told me. The worst thing for them would be a string of nannies bouncing in and out of their lives."

He would never have to worry about that with her. "I won't let them down."

"You're *sure?* Because these two are a handful. It's a lot of work. More than I ever imagined possible. Professional hockey was a cakewalk compared to this. I need to be sure that you're committed."

"I'm giving up my apartment and putting my dad in a home that I can't begin to afford without this salary. I'm definitely committed."

He looked relieved. "In that case, the job is yours. And the sooner you can start, the better."

Her own relief was so keen she could have sobbed. She hugged Fern closer. Her little girls would be okay. She would be there to take care of them, to nurture them. And maybe someday, when they were old enough to understand, she would be able to tell them who she really was and explain why she had let them go. Maybe she could be a real mother to them.

"Miss Evans?" Coop was watching her expectantly, waiting for a reply.

"It's Sierra," she told him. "And I can start right away if that works for you. I just need a day to pack and move my things in."

He looked surprised. "What about your apartment? Your furniture? Don't you need time to—"

"I'll sublet. A friend from work is interested in taking my place and she'll be using all my furniture." Her dad's furniture, actually. By the time Sierra started making enough money to afford her own place, he was too sick to live alone, so she had stayed with him instead, on the pull-out couch of the dinky one-bedroom apartment he'd had to take when he went on disability. She had never really had a place of her own. And from the looks of it, she wouldn't for a very long time. But if that meant the girls would be happy and well taken care of, it was a sacrifice she was happy to make.

"I just need to pack my clothes and a few personal items," she told him. "I can do that today and move everything over tomorrow."

"And work? You don't need to give them notice?"

She shook her head. She was taking a chance burning that bridge, but being with the girls as soon as possible took precedence. As long as they needed her, she wouldn't be going back to nursing anyway.

"I'll have Ben, my lawyer, draw up the contract this afternoon," he said. "Considering my former profession there are privacy issues."

"I understand."

"And of course you're welcome to have your own lawyer look at it before you sign."

"I'll call him today."

"Great. Why don't I show you the girls' room, and where you'll be staying?"

"Okay."

They got up from the floor and he led her down the hall, Ivy in his arms and Sierra holding Fern, who seemed perfectly content despite Sierra being a relative stranger. Was it possible that she sensed the mother-daughter connection? Or was she just a friendly, outgoing baby?

"This is the nursery," he said, indicating a door on the left and gesturing her inside. It was by far the largest and prettiest little girls' room she had ever laid eyes on. The color scheme was pale pink and pastel green. The walls, bedding, curtains and even the carpet looked fluffy and soft, like cotton candy. Matching white cribs perched side by side, and a white rocking chair sat in the corner next to the window. She could just imagine herself holding the girls close, singing them a lullaby and rocking them to sleep.

This room was exactly what she would have wanted for them but never could have afforded. With her they wouldn't have had more than a tiny corner of her bedroom.

"It's beautiful, Cooper."

"It's Coop," he said and flashed that easy grin. "No one but my mom called me Cooper, and that was usually when she was angry about something. And as for the room, I can't take credit. It's an exact reproduction of their room at Ash and Susan's. I thought it might make the transition easier for them."

Once again he had surprised her. Maybe he wasn't quite as self-centered as she first imagined. Or maybe he was only playing the role of responsible uncle out of necessity. Maybe once he had her there to take care of the girls for him, he would live up to his party reputation, including the supposedly revolving bedroom door.

Time would tell.

"They have their own bathroom and a walk-in closet over there," he said, gesturing to a closed door across the room.

She walked over and opened it. The closet was huge! Toys lined either side of the floor—things they had used and some still in the original boxes. Seeing them, Fern shifted restlessly in Sierra's arms, clearly wanting to get down and play.

From the bars hung a wardrobe big enough for a dozen infants. Dresses and jumpers and tiny pairs of jeans and shirts—all designer labels and many with the tags still attached, and all in duplicate. In her wildest dreams Sierra never could have afforded even close to this many clothes, and certainly not this quality. They were neatly organized by style, color and size—all spelled out on sticky notes on the shelf above the bar.

Sierra had never seen anything like it. "Wow. Did you do this?"

"God, no," Coop said. "This is Ms. Densmore's thing. She's a little fanatical about organization."

"Just a little." She would have a coronary if she looked in Sierra's closet. Besides being just a fraction the size, it was so piled with junk she could barely close the door. Neatness had never been one of her strong suits. That had been okay living with her dad, who was never tidy himself, but here she would have to make an effort to be more organized.

"The bathroom is through there," Coop said, walking past her to open the door, filling the air with the delicious scent of soap and man. The guy really did smell great, and though it was silly, he looked even more attractive holding the baby, which made no sense at all. Or maybe it was just that she'd always been a sucker for a man who was good with kids—because in her profession she had seen too many who weren't. Deadbeat dads who couldn't even be bothered to visit their sick child in the hospital. And of course there were the abusive dads who put their kids in the hospital. Those were the really heartbreaking cases and one of the reasons she had transferred from pediatrics to the NICU.

But having an easy way with an infant didn't make a man a good father, she reminded herself. Neither did giving them a big beautiful bedroom or an enormous closet filled with toys and designer clothes. The twins needed nurturing, they needed to know that even though their parents were gone, someone still loved them and cared about them.

She held Fern closer and rubbed her back, and the infant laid her head on Sierra's shoulder, her thumb tucked in her mouth.

"I'll show you your room," Coop said, and she followed him to the bedroom across the hall. It was even larger than the girls' room, with the added bonus of a cozy sitting area by the window. With the bedroom, walk-in closet and private bath, it was larger than her entire apartment. All that was missing was the tiny, galley-style kitchen, but she had a gourmet kitchen just a few rooms away at her disposal.

The furnishings and decor weren't exactly her style. The black, white and gray color scheme was too modern and cold and the steel and glass furnishings were a bit masculine, but bringing some of her own things in would liven it up a little. She could learn to live with it.

"That bad, huh?"

Startled by the comment, Sierra looked over at Coop. He was frowning. "I didn't say that."

"You didn't have to. It's written all over your face. You hate it."

"I don't *hate* it."

One brow tipped up. "Now you're lying."

"It's not what I would have chosen, but it's very… stylish."

He laughed. "You are *so* lying. You think it's terrible."

She bit her lip to keep from smiling, but the corners of her mouth tipped up regardless. "I'll get used to it."

"I'll call my decorator. You can fix it however you like. Paint, furniture, the works."

She opened her mouth to tell him that wouldn't be necessary, and he held up one ridiculously large palm to shush her. "Do you really think I'm going to let you stay in a room you despise? This is going to be your home. I want you to be comfortable here."

She wondered if he was always this nice, or if he was just so desperate for a reliable nanny he would do anything to convince her to take the job. If that was the case, she could probably negotiate a higher salary, but it wasn't about the money. She just wanted to be with her girls.

"If you're sure it's not a problem, I wouldn't mind adding a few feminine touches," she told him.

"You can sleep in the nursery until it's finished, or if you'd prefer more privacy, there's a fold-out love seat in my office."

"The nursery is fine." She didn't care about privacy, and she liked the idea of sleeping near her girls.

He nodded to Fern and said, "I think we should lay them down. It's afternoon nap time."

Sierra looked down at Fern and realized that she had fallen asleep, her thumb still wedged in her mouth, and Ivy, who had laid her head on Coop's enormously wide shoulder, was looking drowsy, too.

They carried the girls back to the nursery and laid them in their beds—Fern on the right side and Ivy on the left—then they stepped quietly out and Coop shut the door behind them.

"How long will they sleep?" Sierra asked.

"On a good day, two hours. But they slept in until eight this morning, so maybe less." He paused in the hall and asked, "Before we call my attorney, would you like something to drink? We have juice and soda...baby formula."

She smiled. "I'm good, thanks."

"Okay, if you're having any second thoughts, this is your last chance to change your mind."

That would never happen. He was stuck with her. "No second thoughts."

"Great, let's go to my office and call Ben," Coop said with a grin. "Let's get this show on the road."

Three

Coop stood outside Sierra's bedroom door, hoping she hadn't already gone to sleep for the night. It was barely nine-thirty, but today had been her first official day watching the girls, so he was guessing that she was probably pretty exhausted. God knows they wore him out.

She had signed the contract the afternoon of her second interview, then spent most of the next day moving her things and unpacking. He had offered to pay a service to do the moving for her, but she had insisted she had it covered, showing up in the early afternoon with a slew of boxes and two youngish male friends—orderlies from the hospital, she'd told him—who had been openly thrilled to meet the great Coop Landon.

Though Coop had tried to pay them for the help, they refused to take any cash. Instead he offered them each a beer, and while Sierra unpacked and the twins napped, he and the guys sat out on the rooftop patio. They asked him about his career and the upcoming season draft picks, leaving a couple of hours later with autographed pucks.

Coop had hoped to be around today to help Sierra and the twins make the transition, but he'd been trapped in meetings with the marketing team for his new sports equipment line all morning, and in the afternoon he'd met with the owner of his former team. If things went as planned, Coop would own the team before the start of the next season in October. Owning the New York Scorpions had been his dream since he started playing for the team. For twenty-two years, until his bad knee took him off the ice, he lived and breathed hockey. He loved everything about the game. Buying a team was the natural next step, and he had the players' blessing.

After the meetings Coop had enjoyed his first dinner out with friends in weeks. Well, he hadn't actually *enjoyed* it. Though he had been counting the days until he was free again, throughout the entire meal his mind kept wandering back to Fern and Ivy and how they were doing with Sierra. Should he have canceled his meetings and spent that first day with them? Was it irresponsible of him to have left them with a stranger? Not that he didn't trust Sierra—he just wanted to be sure that he was doing the right thing. They had already lost their parents—he didn't want them to think that he was abandoning them, too.

When the rest of the party had moved on to a local bar for after-dinner drinks, dancing and skirt chasing, to the surprise of his friends, Coop had called it a night. On a typical evening he closed out the bar, moved on to a party and usually didn't go home alone. But the ribbing he endured from his buddies was mild. Hell, it had been less than a month since he lost his brother. It was going to take him a little time to get back into his normal routine. And right now the twins needed him. He would try to work from home the rest of the week, so he could spend more time with them. After more than two weeks of being together almost constantly, he had gotten used to having them around.

He rapped lightly on Sierra's bedroom door, and after several seconds it opened a crack and she peeked out. He could see that she had already changed into her pajamas—a short, pink, babydoll-style nightgown. His eyes automatically drifted lower, to her bare legs. They weren't particularly long, or slender, so the impulse to touch her, to slide his palm up the inside of one creamy thigh and under the hem of her gown—and the resulting pull of lust it created—caught him completely off guard. He had to make an effort to keep his gaze above her neck and on her eyes, which were dark and inquisitive, with that exotic tilt. Her hair, which he'd only ever seen up in a ponytail, hung in a long, silky black sheet over her shoulders, and he itched to run his fingers through it. Instead he shoved his hands in the pockets of his slacks.

You can look, but you can't touch, he reminded himself, and not for the first time since she'd come by to meet the girls. She was absolutely nothing like the sort of woman he would typically be attracted to. Maybe that alone was what he found so appealing. She was different. A novelty. But her position as the twins' nanny was just too crucial to put in jeopardy.

Maybe hiring such an attractive woman had been a bad idea, even if she was the most qualified. Maybe he should have held out and interviewed a few more people, made an effort to find someone older or, better yet, a guy.

"Did you want something?" she asked, and he realized that he was just standing there staring at her.

Way to make yourself look like an idiot, Coop. He was usually pretty smooth when it came to women. He had no idea why he was acting like such a dope.

"I hope I didn't wake you," he said.

"No, I was still up."

"I just wanted to check in, see how it went today."

"It went really well. It'll take some time to get into a routine, but I'm following their lead."

"I'm sorry I wasn't here to help out."

She looked confused. "I didn't expect you to help."

He felt his eyes drifting lower, to the cleavage at the neckline of her gown. She wasn't large-busted, but she wasn't what he would consider small, either. She was… average. So why couldn't he seem to look away?

She noticed him noticing but made no move to cover herself. And why should she? It was her room. He was the intruder.

And he was making a complete ass of himself.

"Was there anything else?" she asked.

He forced his gaze back to her face. "I thought we could just talk for a while. We haven't had a chance to go over the girls' schedules. I thought you might have questions."

She looked hesitant, and he thought her answer was going to be no. And could he blame her? He was behaving like a first-rate pervert. But after several seconds, she said, "Okay, I'll be out in just a minute."

She snapped the door closed and he walked to the kitchen, mentally knocking himself in the head. What the hell was wrong with him? He was acting as if he'd never seen an attractive woman before. One of his dining companions that evening had worn a form-fitting dress that was shorter and lower cut than Sierra's nightgown and he hadn't felt even a twinge of interest. He needed to quit eyeballing her, or she was going to think he was some sort of deviant. The last thing he wanted was for her to be uncomfortable in his home.

Coop opened the wine refrigerator and fished out an open bottle of pinot grigio. Unlike his teammates, he preferred a quality wine to beer or liquor. He'd never been one to enjoy getting drunk. Not since his wild days anyway, when he'd taken pretty much anything that gave him a buzz because at the time it meant taking his pain away.

He took two glasses from the cupboard and set them on the island countertop. Sierra walked in as he was pouring. She had changed into a pair of black leggings and an oversize, faded yellow T-shirt. He found his gaze drawn to her legs again. He typically dated women who were supermodel skinny—and a few of those women had actually been supermodels—but not necessarily because that was what he preferred. That just seemed to be the type of woman who gravitated toward him. He liked that Sierra had some meat on her bones. She was not heavy by any stretch of the imagination. She just looked…healthy. Although he was sure that most women would take that as an insult.

He quickly reminded himself that it didn't matter what she looked like because she was off-limits.

"Have a seat," he said, and she slid onto one of the bar stools across the island from him. He corked the wine and slid one of the glasses toward her. "I hope you like white."

"Oh…um…" She hesitated, a frown causing an

adorable little wrinkle between her brows. "Maybe I shouldn't."

He put the bottle back in the fridge. Maybe she thought he was trying to get her drunk so he could take advantage of her. "One glass," he said. "Unless you don't drink."

"No, I do. I'm just not sure if it's a good idea."

"Are you underage?"

She flashed him a cute smile. "You know I'm not. I'm just worried that one of the girls might wake up. In fact, I'd say it's a strong possibility, so I need to stay sharp."

"You think one little glass of wine will impair you?" He folded his arms. "You must be quite the light-weight."

Her chin lifted a notch. "I can hold my own. I just don't want to make a bad impression."

"If you drank an entire bottle, that might worry me, but one glass? Do you think I would offer if I thought it was a bad idea?"

"I guess not."

"Let's put it this way: If the twins were your daughters, and you wanted to wind down after a busy day, would you feel comfortable allowing yourself a glass of wine?"

"Yes."

He slid the wine closer. "So, stop worrying about what I think, and enjoy."

She took it.

"A toast, to your first day," he said, clinking his glass against hers.

She sipped, nodded and said, "Nice. I wouldn't have imagined you as the wine-drinking type."

"I'm sure there are a lot of things about me that

would surprise you." He rested his hip against the edge of the countertop. "But tell me about you."

"I thought we were going to talk about the girls."

"We will, but I'd like to know a little bit about you first."

She sipped again, then set her glass down. "You read my file."

"Yeah, but that was just the basics. I'd like to know more about you as a person. Like, what made you get into nursing?"

"My mom, actually."

"She was a nurse?

"No, she was a homemaker. She got breast cancer when I was a kid. The nurses were so wonderful to her and to me and my dad and sister. Especially when she was in hospice. I decided then, that's what I wanted to do."

"She passed away?"

Sierra nodded. "When I was fourteen."

"That's a tough age for a girl to lose her mother."

"It was harder for my sister, I think. She was only ten."

He circled the counter and sat on the stool beside hers. "Is there a good age to lose a parent? I was twelve when my mom and dad died. It was really rough."

"My sister used to be this sweet, happy-go-lucky kid, but after she got really moody and brooding."

"I was angry," he said. "I went from being a pretty decent kid to the class bully."

"It's not uncommon, in that situation, for a boy to pick on someone smaller and weaker. It probably gave you a feeling of power in an otherwise powerless situation."

"Except I went after kids who were bigger than me.

Because I was so big for my age, that usually meant I was fighting boys who were older than me. And I got the snot kicked out of me a couple of times, but usually I won. And you're right, it did make me feel powerful. I felt like it was the only thing I had any control over."

"My sister never picked on anyone, but she was into drugs for a while. Thankfully she cleaned herself up, but when my dad got sick she just couldn't handle it. When she turned eighteen she took off for L.A. She's an actress, or trying to be. She's done a couple of commercials and a few walk-on parts. Mostly she's a waitress."

"What is it that your dad has?" he asked, hoping he wasn't being too nosy.

"He's in the final stages of Alzheimer's."

"How old is he?"

"Fifty."

Damn. "That's really young for Alzheimer's, isn't it?"

She nodded. "It's rare, but it happens. He started getting symptoms when he was forty-six, and the disease progressed much faster than it would in someone older. They tried every drug out there to slow the progression, but nothing seemed to work. It's not likely he'll live out the year."

"I'm so sorry."

She shrugged, eyes lowered, running her thumb around the rim of her glass. "The truth is, he died months ago, at least in all the ways that matter. He's just a shell. A functioning body. I know he hates living this way."

She looked so sad. He wanted to hug her, or rub her shoulder, or do something to comfort her, but it didn't seem appropriate to be touching her. So his only choice was to comfort her with words and shared experiences. Because when it came to losing a parent, he knew just how deeply painful and traumatic it could be.

"When my parents got in the car accident, my dad died instantly. My mom survived the crash, but she was in a coma and brain-dead. My brother, Ash, was eighteen, and he had to make the decision to take her off life support."

"What a horrible thing for him to have to go through. No one should have to make that decision. Not at any age."

"I was too young to really grasp what was happening. I thought he did it because he was mad at her or didn't love her. Only when I got older did I understand that there was no hope."

"I signed a Do Not Resuscitate order for my dad. It was so hard, but I know it's what he wants. Working in the NICU, I've seen parents have to make impossible choices. It was heartbreaking. You have to hold it together at work, be strong for the parents, but I can't tell you how many times I went home and cried my eyes out. Parents of healthy kids just don't realize how lucky they are."

"I can understand how you would burn out in a job like that."

"Don't get me wrong, I really love nursing. I liked that I was helping people. But it can be emotionally draining."

"Do you think you'll miss it?"

She smiled. "With the twins to take care of, I doubt I'll have time."

He hoped she wouldn't eventually burn out, the way she had with nursing. Maybe giving her so little time off had been a bad idea. He knew firsthand how tough it was caring for the twins nonstop. A few hours off on a Sunday and one weekend a month weren't much time. Maybe he should have considered hiring two nannies, one for during the week, and one for the weekends. "You're sure it's not going to be too much?"

"Watching the twins?"

"By taking this job, you're pretty much giving up your social life."

"I gave that up when my dad got too sick to care for himself. He couldn't be alone, so we had a caregiver while I worked, then I took over when I got home."

"Every day? That sounds expensive."

She nodded. "It was. We blew through his savings in just a few months. But I didn't want him to have to go in a nursing home. I kept him with me as long as I could. But eventually it got to the point where I just couldn't provide the best care for him."

"When did you go out? Have fun?"

"I've always been more of a homebody."

"What about dating?"

The sudden tuck between her brows said her love life was a touchy subject. And really it was none of his business. Or maybe she thought it was some sort of cheesy pickup line.

"You can tell me to mind my own business," he said.

"It's okay. Things are just a little complicated right now. I'm not in a good place emotionally to be getting into a relationship." She glanced over at him. "That's probably tough for someone like you to understand."

"Someone so morally vacant?"

Her eyes widened. "No, I didn't mean—"

"It's okay," he said with a laugh. "A few weeks ago, I probably wouldn't have understood."

Dating and being out with other people had been

such an intrinsic part of who he was, he probably wouldn't have been able to grasp the concept of leading a quiet, domesticated life. Since the crash that had taken his brother, his attitude and his perception about what was really important had been altered. Like tonight for instance. Why go out barhopping to meet a woman for what would ultimately be a meaningless and quite frankly unsatisfying encounter when the twins needed him at home?

"Priorities change," he said.

She nodded. "Yes they do. You see things a certain way, then suddenly it's not about what you want anymore."

He wondered if she was talking about her dad. "I know exactly what you mean."

"You really love them," she said.

"The twins?" he found himself grinning. "Yeah, I do. What's not to love? This was obviously not a part of my plans, but I want to do right by them. I owe Ash that much. He sacrificed a lot to raise me. He worked two jobs and put college off for years to be there for me, and believe me, I was a handful. Some people thought that because the twins aren't Ash's biological kids it somehow absolved me of all responsibility. Even their birth mother seemed to think so."

"What do you mean?"

"Her lawyer contacted my lawyer. Apparently she saw on the news that Ash and Susan had died and she wanted the girls back. I can only assume that she thought I would be a failure as a dad."

"And you didn't consider it?"

"Not for a second. And even if I didn't think I could handle taking care of the girls myself, why would I give them to someone who didn't want them to begin with?"

That tuck was back between her brows. "Maybe she wanted them but just couldn't keep them. Maybe she thought giving them up was the best thing for the twins."

"And that changed in five months? She thinks she can give the girls more than I can? With me they'll never want for a thing. They'll have the best of everything. Clothes, education, you name it. Could she do that?"

"So you assume that because she isn't rich she wouldn't be a good parent?" she asked in a sharp tone.

For someone who didn't even know the birth mother she was acting awfully defensive. "The truth is, I don't know why she gave them up, but it doesn't matter. My brother adopted the twins and loved them like his own flesh and blood. He wanted the girls raised by me, and I'm honoring his wishes."

Her expression softened. "I'm sorry, I didn't mean to snap. In my line of work, I've seen young mothers harshly misjudged. It's a natural instinct to defend them."

"Not to mention that you've no doubt heard about my reputation and question my ability to properly raise the girls."

She shook her head. "I didn't say—"

"You didn't have to." It was amazing the people who had strong opinions about his ability to be a good father. Some of his closest friends—the single ones—thought he was crazy for taking on the responsibility. And the friends with families—not that he had many of those—openly doubted his capabilities as a parent.

He intended to prove them all wrong.

"Like I said before," he told Sierra firmly, meaning every word, "priorities change. For me, the girls come first, and they always will."

Four

Sierra could hardly believe how snippy she had gotten with Coop last night.

She replayed the conversation in her head as she got the girls ready for their afternoon nap, cringing inwardly as she placed Ivy on her belly on the carpet with a toy while she wrestled a wiggling Fern out of her jumper and into a fresh diaper.

Antagonize your boss. Way to go Sierra. Was she *trying* to get fired? Or even worse, give him any reason to doubt that she was just the twin's nanny? But all that garbage about him changing his priorities had really ruffled her feathers, and she didn't believe it for a minute, not after the way he was ogling her when she opened the bedroom door in her nightgown. And if he thought she would be interested in a man like him, he was dreaming.

Although she couldn't deny that in a very small and

completely depraved way it had been just the tiniest bit exciting. And to his credit Coop had looked conflicted, like he knew it was wrong, but he just couldn't help himself. Which she was sure summed him up in a nutshell. He would try to change, try to be a good father to the twins, but in the end he would fail because that was just the sort of man he was.

But it had been an awfully long time since someone had looked at her in a sexual way, and what woman wouldn't feel at least the tiniest bit special to be noticed by a rich, gorgeous guy who was known for dating actresses and supermodels? She also didn't let herself forget that he was a womanizer, and she was one of hundreds of women he had looked at in that very same way.

She laid Fern in her crib and turned to pick up Ivy, but she had rolled all the way across the room and wound up by the closet door.

"Come back here, you little sneak," she said, scooping her up and nibbling the ticklish spot on her neck. Ivy giggled and squirmed, but when Sierra laid her on the changing table she didn't put up a fuss. She was definitely the milder mannered of the two, but she had a curious nature. Sierra was sure that left to her own devices, Ivy could get herself into trouble. There was no doubt that Ivy was more like her, and Fern seemed to take after their birth father's side of the family. Sierra was having such a blast getting to know them, learning all their little personality quirks. She realized how fortunate she was to have this opportunity and she wouldn't take it for granted. And if being with her daughters meant putting up with an occasional inappropriate glance, it was worth it.

Speaking of Mr. Inappropriate, Sierra heard the deep

timbre of Coop's voice from his office down the hall. He was on the phone again. He was working from home today, or so he said. Exactly what he was doing in there, or what that so-called "work" entailed, she wasn't sure. Polishing his various trophies? Giving interviews?

Other than basking in the glow of his former fame, she wasn't sure what he did with his time.

She laid Ivy in her crib and blew each of the girls a kiss good-night, then she closed the curtain to smother the light and stepped out of the room…colliding with Coop, who was on his way in. He said, "Whoa!" looking just as surprised to see her as she was to see him. She instinctively held her hands up to soften the inevitable collision and wound up with her palms pressed against the hard wall of his chest, breathing in the warm and clean aroma of his skin. He wore the scent of soap and shampoo the way other men wore three-hundred dollar cologne. And though it was completely irrational, the urge to slide her hands up around his neck, to plaster herself against him, hit her swift and hard.

Touching Coop was clearly a bad idea.

She pulled away so fast her upper back and head hit the door frame with a thud.

Coop winced. "You okay?"

She grimaced and rubbed her head. "Fine."

"You sure? You hit that pretty hard." He reached behind her and cupped the back of her head in one enormous palm, but his touch was gentle as he probed for an injury, his fingers slipping through her hair beneath the root of her ponytail, spreading warmth against her scalp. "I don't feel a bump."

But, oh man, did it feel nice.

Nice? Ugh! This was insane. Knowing the sort of man he was, his touch should have repulsed her.

She ducked away from his hand. "I'm fine, really. You just startled me."

He frowned, tucking his hands in the pockets of his jeans, as if maybe he realized that touching her wasn't appropriate. Or maybe he liked it as much as she did. "Sorry. Where are the girls?"

"I just put them down for their nap."

"Why didn't you tell me? I'd like to say good-night."

Honestly, she hadn't thought it would matter to him. "I thought I heard you on the phone and I didn't want to disturb you."

"Well, next time let me know," he said, sounding irritated. "If I'm here, the girls come first."

"Okay. I'm sorry. They're still awake if you want to see them."

His expression softened. "Just for a second."

He disappeared into their room and Sierra walked to the kitchen to clean up the girls' lunch dishes. Coop really was taking this "being there for the girls" business pretty seriously. But how long would that last? It was probably a novelty, being the caring uncle. She was sure it wouldn't be long before he slipped back into his old ways and wouldn't have the time or the inclination to say good-night to the twins.

"What is this?" Ms. Densmore snipped, holding up the empty bottles from the girls' lunch as Sierra walked into the kitchen.

Was this some sort of trick question? "Um…bottles?"

She flung daggers with her eyes. "And why were they on the kitchen counter and not in the dishwasher?"

"Because I didn't put them there yet."

"Anything you use in the kitchen must be put in the

dishwasher or washed by *you*. And any messes you and the children make are yours to clean."

"I'm aware of that," Sierra said, and only because Ms. Densmore had given her this identical lecture *three* times now. "I planned to clean up after I put the twins down for their nap. Their *care* is my priority."

"I also noticed a basket of your clothes in the laundry room. I'd like to remind you that you are responsible for your own laundry. That includes clothing, towels and bedding. I work for Mr. Landon. Not you or anyone else. Is that clear?"

Sienna gritted her teeth. She was sure it bugged the hell out of the housekeeper that she was forced to feed Sierra, although Coop was right about her being an excellent cook. "The washer was already running so I set them there temporarily."

Sierra had done absolutely nothing to offend her, so she had no clue why Ms. Densmore was so cranky, so inclined to dislike her.

"As I have said to Mr. Landon on numerous occasions, I took this job because there were no children. I am not a nanny or a babysitter. Do not ask me to hold, change, feed or play with the twins. They are *your* responsibility, and yours alone."

As if she'd want her girls anywhere near this nasty old bitch. "I'm pretty clear on that, thanks."

Ms. Densmore shoved the bottles at her and Sierra took them. Then, her pointy, beak nose in the air, Ms. Densmore stalked away to the laundry room behind the kitchen. And though it was petty and immature, Sierra gestured rudely to her retreating back.

"That wasn't very ladylike."

She spun around to find Coop watching her, a wry grin on his face.

He folded his arms across his ridiculously wide chest and said, "I'm glad the girls weren't here to see that."

She bit her lip and hooked her hands behind her back. "Um…sorry?"

Coop laughed. "I'm kidding. I would have done exactly the same thing. And you're right, the girls are your first priority. The dishwasher can wait."

"I have no idea why she dislikes me so much."

"Don't take it personally. She doesn't like me, either, but she's one hell of an awesome housekeeper."

"You would think she would be happy to have me here. Now she doesn't have to deal with the twins."

"I'll have a talk with her."

That could be a really bad idea. "Maybe you shouldn't. I don't want her to think I tattled on her. It will just make things worse."

"Don't worry, I'll take care of it."

Coop walked to the laundry room and over the sound of the washer and dryer she heard the door snap closed behind him. Tempted as she was to sneak back there and press her ear to the door to listen, she put the lunch dishes in the dishwasher instead. Coop was back a couple of minutes later, a satisfied smile on his face.

"She won't hassle you anymore," he said. "If you need me, I'll be in my office."

Whatever he'd said to Ms. Densmore, it had worked. She came out of the laundry room several minutes later, red faced with either embarrassment or anger, and didn't say a word or even look at Sierra. She maintained her tight-lipped silence until dinnertime when she served a Mexican dish that was so delicious Sierra had two helpings.

Sierra was surprised when Coop invited her to eat in the dining room with him. She had just assumed that she would be treated like any other hired help and eat in the kitchen with the girls. Because surely he wouldn't want two infants around making a fuss and disrupting his meal. But he actually insisted on it. While Sierra sat at one end of the table, Ivy in her high chair next to her, he sat with Fern, alternately feeding her then himself. When Fern started to fuss and Sierra offered to take over, he refused. He wiped applesauce from her face and hands with a washcloth, plucked her from her high chair and sat her in his lap while he finished his meal, dodging her grasping hands as she tried to intercept his fork. After their talk last night, maybe he felt he had to prove some sort of point.

When they were done with dinner he switched on the enormous flat-screen television in the living room and tuned it to ESPN. Then he stretched out on the floor and played with the girls while she sat on the couch feeling a little like an outsider.

The girls obviously adored him and it scared the hell out of her. Not because she thought they would love him more. She'd reconciled her position in the girls' lives. She just hated to see the girls become attached to him, only to have him grow bored with parenting. They were a novelty, but his fascination with them would fade. He was still reeling from his brother's death, but that would only last so long. Eventually he would go back to his womanizing, partying ways. And when he did, *she* would be there to offer the stability they needed. She was the person the twins would learn to depend on.

The worst part was that he had flat-out admitted he thought that he could buy their affection by giving them "the best money could buy," but what they really needed, his love and emotional support, he wasn't capable of giving. Not for any extended length of time.

When it was time for the twins to go to bed Coop helped her wrestle them into their pajamas. He gave them each a kiss good-night, then he and Sierra laid them in their cribs.

On their way out of the room Sierra grabbed their soiled clothes from the day and switched off the light. "I'm going to go throw these in the wash."

"You don't have to do the girls' laundry," Coop said, following her down the hall. "Leave it for Ms. Densmore."

"It's okay. I wanted to do a few of my own things, too. Unless you'd prefer I wash the twins' clothes separately."

He looked confused. "Why would I care about that?"

Sierra shrugged. "Some people are picky about the way their kids' clothes are washed."

"Well, not me."

Somehow she didn't imagine he would be. And he probably wouldn't care that she had every intention of washing their "hand wash only" dresses on Delicate in the machine.

Sierra dumped the clothes in the washing machine, noting that the room was tidy to point of fanaticism. There wasn't so much as a speck of dust on the floor or a stitch of clothing anywhere. Ms. Densmore must have been as anal about keeping the laundry done as she was with keeping the house clean.

Sierra opened the cabinet to find the detergents, stain removers and fabric softeners organized neatly by function and perfectly aligned so the labels were facing out. She grabbed the liquid detergent, measured out a cupful and poured it into the machine. She put the cap back on, ignoring the small bit that sloshed over the side of the bottle, then, smiling serenely, stuck it back on the shelf crooked. She did the same with the fabric softener, then gave the stain removers a quick jostle just for fun before she started the machine.

She walked back out into the kitchen and found Coop sitting at the island on a barstool, two glasses of red wine on the counter.

"Take a load off," he said, nudging the other stool with his foot. "I was in the mood for red tonight. It's a Malbec. I hope that's okay."

She wasn't picky. However, she had just assumed that last night's shared wine had been a one-time thing. "You don't have to serve me wine every night."

"I know I don't."

Did he plan to make a habit of this because she wasn't sure if she was comfortable with that. Not that she minded relaxing with a glass of wine at the end of the day. It was the company that made her a little nervous. Especially when he sat so darned close to her. Last night she'd sat beside him feeling edgy, as if she were waiting for him to pounce. Which he didn't, of course. He had been a perfect gentleman. Yet he still made her nervous.

"Maybe we could sit in the living room," she suggested. Far, far away from each other.

Coop shrugged. "Sure."

What she would rather do is take the glass to her room and curl up in bed with the mystery novel she'd been reading, but she didn't want to be rude.

He sprawled in the chair by the window, his long, muscular legs stretched out in front of him, and Sierra sat with her legs tucked underneath her on the corner of the couch. He was yards away from her, so why the tension lingering in the air? And why could she not stop looking at him? Yes, he was easy on the eyes, but she didn't even like him.

Coop sipped his wine, then rested the glass on his stomach—which was no doubt totally ripped and as perfect as the rest of him—his fingers laced together and cupping the bowl. "What do you think of the wine?"

She took a sip, letting it roll around her tongue. She didn't know much about wines, but it tasted pretty good to her. Very bold and fruity. A huge step up from the cheap brands she could afford. "I like it. It tastes expensive."

"It is. But what's the point of having all this money if I can't enjoy the finer things? Which reminds me, I talked to my decorator today. He's tied up with another project and won't be available to meet with you for at least three weeks. If that's not soon enough for you, we can find someone who's available now."

"Three weeks is fine. There's no rush."

"You're sure?"

"Positive. I really appreciate that you want me to be comfortable, though." The truth was, she hadn't been spending much time in there anyway. The twins kept her busy all day, and when she was in her room, she was usually asleep.

"I meant to ask you yesterday—what's going on with your dad? You mentioned moving him to a different place."

"They're taking him by ambulance to the new nursing home Saturday morning."

"Do you need to be there?"

Even if she did, she had a responsibility to the girls. "He's in good hands. I'll be visiting him Sunday during my time off. I can get him settled in then."

"You know, you don't have to wait until Sundays to see him. You can go anytime you'd like. I don't mind if you take the girls with you."

"He's going to be all the way out in Jersey. I don't own a car and taking the twins on the train or the bus would be a logistical nightmare."

He shrugged. "So take my car."

"I can't."

"It's okay, really."

"No, I mean I *really* can't. I don't know how."

His brows rose. "You never learned to drive?"

"I've always lived in the city. I never needed to. And gas prices being what they are, public transportation just makes more sense."

"Well then, why don't I take you? We could go Saturday when he's transferred."

Huh? Why would he want to take time out of his day to haul her to Jersey? Surely he had something better to do. "You really don't have to do that."

"I want to."

She didn't know what to say. Why was he being so nice to her? Why did he even care if she saw her dad? He was her employer, not her pal.

"You're looking at me really weirdly right now," Coop said. "Either you're not used to people doing nice things for you, or you're seriously questioning my motives."

A little bit of both actually, and it was creepy how he seemed to always know what she was thinking. "I'm sure you have other things—"

"No, I don't. My schedule is totally free this weekend." He paused, then added, "And for the record, I have no ulterior motives."

She had a hard time buying that. "You're sure it's no trouble?"

"None at all. And I'll bet the girls would like to get out of the house."

Sierra was going to remind him that she'd taken them for a long walk in the park that morning, but it seemed like a moot point. He obviously wasn't going to take no for an answer, and she really would like to be there when they moved her dad, not only to make certain he was handled respectfully, but also to see that none of his very few possessions were left behind. The pictures and keepsakes. Not that he would know either way. Maybe, she thought sadly, it would be best if she just held on to them now.

"I'll call the nursing home tomorrow and find out when the ambulance will be there. Maybe we could be there a half an hour or so beforehand, then follow them over to the new facility."

"Just let me know when and I'll be ready."

"Thanks."

He narrowed his eyes slightly. "But…you're still wondering why I'm doing this for you. You apparently have this preconceived notion about the kind of person that I am."

She couldn't deny it. He would be surprised by how much she actually did know about him. The real stuff, not the rumors and conjecture. But she couldn't tell him that.

"Believe it or not, I'm a pretty decent guy." He paused then added, "And an above-average dancer."

She would have to take his word on that. "I clearly have trust issues," she said. Fool me once, shame on you, and all of that. Maybe he didn't have ulterior motives, but that was not usually the case. And under normal circumstances she would have told him no on principle alone, but just this one time she would make an exception.

"I guess it will just take time for you to believe that I'm not a bad guy," he said.

Honestly, she didn't understand why he cared what she thought of him. Was he this personable with all of his employees? Granted she had only worked for him a couple of days, but she had never seen him offer Ms. Densmore a glass of wine or heard him offer to drive her anywhere. She was sure it had a lot to do with Sierra being young and, yes, she was what most men considered attractive. Not a raving beauty but not too shabby, either. Then again, she was nowhere near as glamorous as the women she had seen him linked to in the past. But Coop hadn't been born wealthy. Who was to say he didn't enjoy slumming it occasionally?

Well, if he thought doing nice things for her was a direct route into her pants, that just because he was rich and famous and above average in the looks department she would go all gooey, he was in for a rude awakening.

Five

Sierra stood in her dad's new room, resisting the natural instinct to step in and help as the ambulance attendants worked with the nursing home staff to get her dad moved from the gurney to his bed, where he would most likely spend the rest of his life. At least in this new facility the staff was friendly and helpful and she could rest easy knowing that her dad would be well cared for. Unfortunately the ambulance had been an hour late to pick him up and the paperwork had taken an eternity.

Coop had been incredibly patient, taking over with the twins, but that patience had to be wearing thin by now. He was sitting in the rec room with them, and though she had fed them their lunch in the car on the way over, they were about an hour and a half past their nap time and last time she checked were getting fussy. She was thankful to have been around for the transfer, but she felt the crushing weight of guilt for making Coop—her employer—wait around for her.

She would have to make this visit a short one.

Once they got him situated in bed, everyone cleared out of the room. The nurse must have mistaken her guilt for conflicted feelings about her dad because she rubbed Sierra's arm, smiled warmly and said, "Don't worry, honey, we'll take good care of him."

When she was gone Sierra walked over to the bed. The curtain between him and his roommate was drawn, but according to the nurse, the man in the next bed was also comatose. "I can't stay, Dad, but I'll come back to-morrow, I promise."

She kissed his cheek, feeling guilty for cutting her visit so short, and headed to the rec room where Coop and the girls were waiting for her. To look at him, no one would guess that he was a multi-millionaire celeb-rity. In jeans, a T-shirt and worn tennis shoes, pacing the floor, looking completely at ease with one restless twin in each arm, he looked like just a regular guy. Albeit most "regular" guys weren't six-three with the physique of an Adonis.

She would be lying if she denied it was an adorable sight, the way he bounced the girls patiently. For some-one who hadn't anticipated being a dad, and had the duty thrust on him unexpectedly, he had done amaz-ingly well. She couldn't help but wonder if she had been unfairly harsh on him. In the five days she'd worked for him she had seen no hint of the womanizing party animal. So why couldn't she shake the feeling that he was destined to let the girls down?

It was all very confusing.

"I'm so sorry it's taken this long," she told him, plucking a wiggling Ivy from him.

"It's okay," Coop said, looking as though he genu-inely meant it. "Is he all settled in?"

"Finally." Ivy squirmed in her arms, so Sierra transferred her to the opposite hip. "Let's get out of here. These two are way past their nap time."

"You don't want to stay and visit a little longer?"

She figured by now he would have been exasperated with the girls' fussing and would be gunning to get back on the road for home. To his credit, though, he hadn't once complained. Not while they sat at the other nursing home waiting for the transport, or when they sat stuck in weekend traffic. But as much as she would love to stay for just a little while longer, to make sure the trip had no adverse effects on her dad physically, she had already taken up way too much of Coop's personal time.

"I'll come by tomorrow on my time off," she told Coop, grabbing the packed-to-the-gills designer label diaper bag and slinging it over her shoulder. Coop commandeered the double umbrella stroller—top-of-the-line, of course, because when it came to the twins Ash and Susan had spared no expense—and they walked out of the building and through the parking lot to his vehicle. Earlier that morning, as she waited on the sidewalk outside his building for him to bring the car around, she'd expected either some flashy little sports car—which logistically she knew wouldn't work with two infants—or at the opposite end of the excess spectrum, a Hummer. Instead he had pulled up in a low-key silver SUV, proving once again that the man she thought she had pegged and the real Cooper were two very different people.

She and Coop each buckled a twin into her car seat, and within five minutes of exiting the lot, both girls were out cold.

"So, where to now?" Coop asked.

Sierra just assumed they would head back into the city. "Home, I guess."

"But it's a gorgeous summer afternoon. We should do something. I don't know about you, but I'm starving. Why don't we grab a bite to eat?"

"The girls just fell asleep. If we wake them up now and drag them into a restaurant, I don't anticipate it being a pleasant experience."

"Good point."

"Besides, don't you need to get home? It's Saturday. You must have plans for later."

"Nope, no plans tonight," Coop said.

He hadn't gone out the night before, either. The four of them had eaten dinner together, then Coop wrestled and played with the twins until their bedtime. After they were tucked into bed, Sierra thought for sure that he would go out, but when she emerged from the laundry room after putting in her daily load of soiled clothes, Coop had been sitting in the living room with two glasses of wine. And though she had planned on reading for a while then going to sleep early, it seemed rude to turn him down after he had gone through the trouble of actually pouring the wine.

One quick glass, she had promised herself, and she would be in bed before nine-thirty. But one glass turned into two, and she and Coop got to talking about his hockey playing days—a subject that even she had to admit was pretty interesting—and before she knew it, it was nearly midnight. Though he did still make her a little nervous and the idea of a friendship with him made her slightly uncomfortable, he was so easygoing and charming she couldn't help but like him.

"On our way in we passed a deli and a small park,"

he said. "We could pick up sandwiches, eat in the car, then go for a drive while the twins sleep."

That actually wasn't a bad idea. If they took the twins home now, the minute they took them out of their car seats they would probably wake up, cutting their nap short by at least an hour, which would probably make them crabby for the rest of the day. But the idea of spending so much time in such close quarters with Coop made her nervous. Not that she was worried he would act inappropriately. If he had wanted to try something, he would have done it by now, and aside from ogling her in her nightie the other evening—which admittedly was her own fault for not putting on a robe— he'd been a perfect gentleman. These feelings of unease were her own doing.

Illogical and inappropriate as it was, she was attracted to Coop, and clearly the feeling was mutual. The air felt electrically charged whenever he was near, and then there was that unwelcome little zap of energy that passed between them whenever they touched, even if it was something as innocent as their fingers brushing when he handed her a jar of baby food. And even though she had no intention whatsoever of expanding the dynamics of their relationship to include intimacy, she couldn't shake the feeling that they were crossing some line of morality.

But what the heck, it was just a sandwich. And it really was the best thing for the girls, and that was what mattered, right?

"I could eat," she said.

"Great." He flashed her one of those adorable grins. The dimpled kind that made her heart go all wonky.

God, she was pathetic.

Though she offered to go inside the deli and order

the food while he waited with the girls, he insisted on going himself and refused the money she tried to give him to cover the expense of her food.

"You shouldn't have to pay for my lunch," she told him.

"If we were at home you would be eating food that I paid for, so what's the difference?"

It was tough to argue with logic like that. Besides, he was out of the car before she could utter another word.

He was in and back out of the deli in five minutes with his grilled Reuben and her turkey on whole grain. He also got coleslaw, a bag of potato chips, bottled water and sodas. They found the park a few blocks away and parked in a spot facing the playground under the shade of a tree. Sierra worried the girls might wake up when he shut the engine off, but they were both out cold.

They spread their lunch out on the console and started eating.

"Can I ask you a question?" she said.

"Sure."

"Besides being a celebrity, what do you do now? For a living, I mean. Do you work?"

Her question seemed to amuse him. "I work really hard actually. I have my own line of hockey equipment coming out, and I started a chain of sports centers a few years ago and they've taken off. We're opening six more by next January."

"What kind of sports centers?"

"Ice rinks and indoor playing fields. Kids sports are big business these days. On top of that I own a couple dozen vacation properties around the world that I rent out. Also very lucrative."

Wow, so much for her theory that he sat around basking in his former fame. It sounded as if he kept himself really busy.

"Where are the vacation homes?" she asked him.

He named off the different cities, and then described the sorts of properties he owned. The list was an impressive one. Clearly he was a very sharp businessman.

"I never realized there was such a market for rental vacation homes."

"Most people aren't in a financial position to drop the money on a home they may only use a couple of times a year, so they rent. Not only is it a lot cheaper, but also you're not locked into one city or country."

She reached into the bag of chips for her third handful.

"I guess you were hungry," Coop teased.

She shot him a look. "Be careful, or you'll give me a complex."

"Are you kidding? I think it's great that you eat like a normal human being. I've taken women to some of the finest restaurants in the city and they order a side salad and seltzer water, or, even worse, they order a huge expensive meal and eat three bites."

"Maybe this is a dumb question, but if it bothers you so much, why do you always date super-skinny women? I mean, doesn't that sort of come with the territory?"

"Convenience, I guess."

Her brows rose. *"Convenience?"*

"They just happen to be the kind of women who hang around the people I hang around with."

"You mean, the kind who throw themselves at you."

He shrugged. "More or less."

"Have you ever had to actually pursue a woman you wanted to date?"

He thought about that for a second, then shook his head and said, "No, not really. In fact, never."

"Seriously? Not once? Not even in high school?"

"Since I was old enough to take an interest in girls I was the team star. Girls flocked to me."

She shook her head in disbelief. "Wow. That's just... *wow.*"

"Can you blame them? I mean, look at me. I'm rich, good-looking, a famous athlete. Who wouldn't want me? I'm completely irresistible."

She couldn't tell if he was serious or just teasing her. Could he honestly be *that* arrogant? "I wouldn't."

That seemed to amuse him. "You already do. You try to pretend you don't, but I can sense it."

"I think you've been hit in the head with a hockey stick a few too many times because I do *not* want you. You aren't even my type."

"But that's what makes it so exciting. You know you shouldn't like me, you know it's wrong because you work for me, but you just can't stop thinking about me."

How did he do that? How did he always seem to know what was going on inside her head? It was probably the third or fourth time he'd done this to her. It couldn't just be a lucky guess.

It was disturbing and...fascinating. And no way in *hell* could she ever let him know just how right he was. "So what you're saying is, all that stuff about you being a nice guy was bull. Everything nice that you've done is because you've been trying to get into my pants?"

"No, I am a nice guy. And for the record, if all I wanted was to get into your pants, I'd have been there by now."

Her eyes went wide. "Oh, really?"

"You're not nearly as tough as you think you are. If I tried to kiss you right now, you wouldn't stop me."

The thought of him leaning over the console and pressing his lips to hers made her heart flutter and her stomach bottom out. But she squared her shoulders and said, "If you tried to kiss me, you would be wearing the family jewels for earrings."

He threw his head back and laughed.

"You don't think I would do it?"

"No, you probably would, just to prove how tough you are. Then you would give in and let me kiss you anyway."

"The depth of your arrogance is truly remarkable."

"It's one of my most charming qualities," he said, but his grin said that he was definitely teasing her this time.

Maybe the confidence was a smoke screen, or this was his way of testing the waters or teasing her. Maybe he really liked her, but being so used to women throwing themselves at him, the possibility of being rejected scared him.

Weirdly enough, the idea that under the tough-guy exterior there could be a vulnerable man made him that much more appealing.

Ugh. What was *wrong* with her?

"Even if I did want you," she said, "which, despite what you believe, I really don't, I would never risk it. I can't even imagine putting my father back in that hellhole we just got him out of. And without this job I can't even come close to affording the new place. So I have every reason *not* to want you."

Before Coop had time to process that, Ivy began to stir in the backseat.

"Uh-oh," he said, glancing back at her. "We better get moving before she wakes up."

He balled up the paper wrapper from his sandwich and shoved it back in the bag, then started the engine. She thought once they got moving, he might segue back into the conversation, but he turned the radio on instead, and she breathed a silent sigh of relief. She hoped she had made her point, he would drop the subject forever and the sexual tension that had been a constant companion in their relationship would magically disappear. Then they could have a normal employee/employer relationship. Because she feared Coop was right. If he kissed her, she wasn't sure she would be able to tell him no.

And she had the sinking feeling that this conversation, inappropriate as it was, was nowhere close to over.

Six

Sierra didn't hear from her sister very often. She would go months at a time without a single word. Sierra would call and leave messages that Joy wouldn't return, send cards that would come back as undeliverable. Then out of the blue Joy would call and always with the same feeble excuses. She was crazy-busy, or had moved, or her phone had been disconnected because she couldn't pay the bill. But the reality was that Joy was fragile. Watching their mother slowly waste away had damaged her. She simply didn't have the emotional capacity to handle the hopelessness of their dad's illness and dealt with it by moving a couple thousand miles away and cutting off all contact.

Sierra hadn't even been able to reach her when she learned about Ash and Susan's death, and frankly she could have used a bit of emotional support. Which was why Sierra was surprised to see her name on her caller

ID that night after she and Coop put the twins to bed. She had just stepped out of the room and was closing the door when her phone started to ring.

She considered not answering, giving Joy a taste of her own medicine for a change. Sometimes she got tired of being the responsible sister. But after two rings guilt got the best of her. Suppose it was something important? And what if Joy didn't call again for months? Besides their dad and the twins, Sierra had no one else. Not to mention that it was an awesome excuse to skip the post-bedtime glass of wine with Coop. And after what had happened this afternoon, the less time she spent with him the better.

"It's my sister. I have to take this," she said, slipping into her bedroom and shutting the door, pretending she didn't see the brief flash of disappointment that passed across his face.

"Guess who!" Joy chirped when Sierra answered.

"Hey, sis." She sat on the edge of her bed. "What's it been, three months?"

That earned a long-suffering sigh from her sister. "I know, I know, I should call more often. But what I've got to say now will make up for it."

"Oh, yeah?" Somehow she doubted that.

"I'm coming home!"

"You're moving back to New York?"

Sierra's heart lifted, then swiftly plunged when her sister laughed and said, "God, no! Are you kidding? Los Angeles is too fabulous to leave. I'm staying at a friend's Malibu beachfront home and it's totally amazing. In fact, I'm sitting in the sand, watching the tide move in as we speak."

She could just picture Joy in one of her flowing peasant skirts and gauzy blouses, her long, tanned legs folded beneath her, her waist-length, wavy black hair blowing in the salty breeze. She would be holding a designer beer in her hand with one of those skinny cigarettes she liked to smoke dangling between two fingers. She had always been so much cooler than Sierra, so much more self-confident. Yet so tortured. And she was sure that the friend Joy was staying with was a man and that she was also sharing his bedroom.

"Then why did you say you're coming home?" Sierra asked.

"Because I'm flying in for a visit."

"When?"

"A week from this coming Wednesday. They're holding auditions for an independent film that's supposed to start filming this August and my agent thinks I'm a shoo-in for the lead roll. I'll be in town a week just in case I get a callback."

"That sounds promising." Although according to Joy, her agent thought she was a shoo-in for every role he set her up for, or so it seemed.

"I know what you're thinking," Joy said.

"I didn't say a word."

"You didn't have to. I can feel your skepticism over the phone line. But this is different. My new agent has some really awesome connections."

"New agent? What happened to the old one?"

"I didn't tell you about that? We parted ways about two months ago."

And Sierra hadn't talked to her in three months. "Why? I thought he was some sort of super-agent."

"His wife sort of caught us going at it in his office."

"You *slept* with your *married* agent?" Why did that not surprise her?

"A girl does what she can to get ahead, and it was

no hardship, believe me. Besides, you're not exactly in a position to pass judgment."

Technically the twins' father was a married man, but it was a totally different situation. "He and his wife were separated, and it was only that one night."

By the time she realized she was pregnant, he and his wife had reconciled. Not that she would have wanted to marry him. He was a nice guy, but they both knew right after it happened that it had been a mistake.

"So, you said you're coming to visit?" Sierra said, changing the subject.

"For a week. And needless to say, I'll be staying with my favorite sister."

"Oh." That was going to be a problem.

"What do you mean, 'oh'? I thought you would be happy to see me."

"I am. It's just that staying with me is going to be a problem."

"Why? Don't tell me you're living with someone. And even if you are, he damned well better let your baby sister stay for a couple of nights."

"I actually am living with someone, but not in the way that you think. I mean, we're not a couple. I work for him."

"As a nurse?"

"As a nanny."

"A *nanny?* You gave the girls up, what, six months ago? Isn't that, like, a painful reminder?"

"Joy, hold on a minute, I have to check something." She walked to her door and opened it a crack. If she was going to tell Joy what was going on, she didn't want to risk Coop overhearing. From the living room she could hear the television and knew he was probably in his favorite chair, engrossed in whatever sporting event he was watching. She closed her door and walked back to the bed. "Did you get any of my messages about the twins' adoptive parents?"

"I did, yeah. I wanted to call, but…you know…"

She was sorry, but she couldn't deal with it. Same old story. "Well, the girls went to their uncle, Ash's brother."

"Isn't he like some famous athlete or something?"

"A former hockey player. A womanizing party animal. Not exactly the sort of person I wanted raising my girls."

"Oh, Si, I'm so sorry. Have you talked to your lawyer? Is there anything he can do? Can you claim he's unfit and get the girls back?"

She fidgeted with the edge of the pillowcase, knowing this next part was not going to go over well. "My lawyer talked to his lawyer, but he refused to give them up. There's nothing I can do. So I took matters into my own hands."

Joy gasped. "You *kidnapped* them?"

Sierra laughed. "Of course not! I would never do something like that. But I needed to be there for them, to know that they were okay, so when I heard that he was looking for a nanny…"

Another gasp. "Are you saying that *you're* the twins' nanny?"

"You should see them, Joy. They're so beautiful and so sweet. And I get to be with them 24/7."

"And this guy, their uncle, he knows you're their mother?"

"God, no! And he can never know."

"Sierra, that's *crazy*. What are you going to do, just take care of the girls for the rest of your life, with them never knowing that you're their birth mother?"

"I'll stay with them as long as they need me. And maybe some day I can tell them the truth."

"What about your life? What about men and marriage and having more kids? You're just going to give that all up."

"Not forever. I figure once they're in school full-time they won't need me nearly as much. As long as I'm here in the mornings and when they get home after school, they won't really need me to spend the night."

"It sounds as if you have it all figured out."

"I do."

"And this uncle…"

"Coop. Coop Landon."

"Is he really awful?"

In a way she wished he was. It would make this a lot less confusing. "Actually, he seems like a good guy. So far. Not at all what I expected." Almost too good, *too* nice. "He's really committed to taking care of the twins. For now anyway. That doesn't mean he won't eventually revert back to his old ways. That's why it's so important that I'm here for the girls. To see that they're raised properly."

"Suppose he finds out who you are? What then?"

"He won't. The original birth certificate is sealed, and obviously Ash and Susan never told him. There's no possible way that he could find out."

"Famous last words."

She brushed off her sister's concerns. "Just be happy for me, okay? This is what I want."

"Oh, honey, I am happy for you. I just don't want to see you hurt."

"I won't be. It's foolproof." As long as she didn't do something stupid, like fall for Coop. "So anyway, that's why you can't stay with me. I'm living in his Upper East Side penthouse apartment."

"Sounds…roomy."

Not that roomy. "Joy, you can't stay here."

"Why not? You said this Coop is a good guy. I'm sure he wouldn't mind."

"Joy—"

"You could at least ask. Because frankly I have no-where else to go. My credit cards are maxed out and I have three dollars in my checking account. My agent had to lend me the money for the ticket, which of course is nonrefundable. If I can't stay with you, I'm crashing on a park bench."

She would pay for a hotel for her sister if she could, but there wasn't a decent place within thirty blocks that was less that one-fifty a night. The expense of moving their dad had taken up all of Sierra's cash, and like Joy, her credit cards were maxed out. It was going to take her months to catch up. And though she hated the idea of taking advantage of Coop's hospitality, this could be the perfect opportunity for a dose of emotional black-mail. "I'll ask him on one condition."

"Anything."

"You have to swear that when you're here you'll come with me to see Dad."

She sighed heavily. "Si, you know how I feel about those places. They creep me out."

"Just recently I was able to move him into a really nice place in Jersey. It's not creepy at all."

"It's just the idea of all those old, sick people…ugh."

She fought the urge to tell her sister to grow up. "This is Dad we're talking about. The man who raised you, remember?"

"According to what you told me the last time we

talked, he's not even going to know I'm there. So what's the point?"

"We don't know that for sure. And he probably doesn't have much time left. This could be the last time you see him alive."

"Do you really think that's how I want to remember him?"

And did she think Sierra enjoyed bearing the brunt of his illness alone? Both emotionally and financially. "I'm sorry, but this is nonnegotiable. Either you promise, or it's the park bench for you."

Joy was quiet for several seconds, then she sighed again and said, "Fine, I'll go see him."

"And I'll ask Coop if you can stay." He had already done so much for her, had been so accommodating, she didn't want him to think that she was taking advantage of his hospitality. Yet she had little doubt that he would say yes. He seemed to like to keep up the "good guy" persona. On the bright side, Joy wouldn't be coming in for another week and a half, so Sierra could wait at least another week to ask him. Surely by then she would have worked off the last favor. She couldn't think of anything worse than being indebted to a man like Coop. There might just come a day when he called in the debt and demanded payment.

She would do this one thing for her sister's sake, but after that she would never ask Coop for a favor again.

"Dude, they're Russian models," Vlad said, but with his thick accent, *dude* came out sounding more like *dute*. "These babes are *super hot*. You can't say no."

As Coop had explained to his other former teammate, Niko, who had called him last night, he had turned over a new leaf. His days of staying out all night partying and bringing home women—even if they were *super hot*—were over. Vlad's call suggested that either he hadn't talked to Niko or he didn't think Coop had been serious.

"Sorry dude, you're going to have to count me out. Like I told Niko, I'm a family man now."

"But you find nanny, yes?"

"Yes, but I'm still responsible for the twins. They need me around."

Vlad grumbled a bit and gave him a serious ribbing for "losing his touch," but it didn't bother Coop. He said goodbye and reached down to pick up the toy Ivy had flung onto the sidewalk from the stroller and gave it back to her. The warm morning breeze rustled the newspapers on the table beside them on the café patio, and as he caught a glimpse of Sierra through the front window, standing in line, waiting to order them a cappuccino, Coop felt utterly content.

Besides, if the deal went through and he bought the team, the entire dynamic of his relationship with his former teammates would change. He would go from being their teammate and partner in crime to their boss. But he was ready to make that change.

He stuck his phone back in his shorts pocket and adjusted the stroller so that the twins were shaded from the morning sun. It would be another scorching day as July quickly approached, but at nine-thirty the temperature was an ideal seventy-five degrees. Most days, before the twins, he wouldn't have even been out of bed yet. In his twenties he could have easily spent the entire night out, slept a few hours, then arrived to practice on time and given a stellar performance. Recently though, the late nights out had been taking their toll. Parties and barhopping until 5:00 a.m. usually meant sleeping half the day away.

These days he was in bed before midnight—sometimes even earlier—and up with the sun. He had always been more of a night owl and had figured that the radical change to his schedule would be jarring, but he found that he actually liked getting up early. This morning he had woken before dawn, made coffee and sat on the rooftop terrace to watch the sun rise. He came back down with his empty cup a while later to find Sierra, still in her nightgown, fixing the twins their morning bottles.

She had jumped out of her skin when he said good morning, clearly surprised to find that he was already up. And though he'd tried to be a gentleman and not ogle her, he found himself staring at her cleavage again. And her legs. A woman as attractive as Sierra couldn't walk around half-naked with a man in the house and expect him to look the other way. And the fact that she hadn't tried to cover herself, nor did she set any speed records mixing the formula and filling the bottle, told him that maybe she liked him looking.

He glanced through the front window of the café and saw that she had inched ahead several feet in line and was only a few customers away from the counter. It had been his idea to stop for coffee and also his idea to come with her and the girls for their morning walk. He had just gotten back from jogging in the park as she was walking out the door. And it was an intrusion on her routine that had Sierra's panties in a serious twist. No big surprise considering the way she had been avoiding him the past week. He was sure it had everything to do with their conversation the day they moved her dad into the new nursing home. She could pretend all she liked, but she wasn't fooling him. She wanted him just as much as he wanted her.

A shadow passed over him and he looked up expecting Sierra, surprised to find an unfamiliar young woman in athletic attire standing by the table clutching a bottled water.

"Mr. Landon," she gushed, sounding a little out of breath. "Hi. I just wanted to say, I'm a *huge* fan."

Her long blond hair was pulled back in a ponytail and a sheen of sweat glazed her forehead. She must have been jogging past and noticed him sitting there. He wasn't really in the mood to deal with a fan, but he turned on the charm and said, "Thank you, Miss…"

"It's Amber. Amber Radcliff."

"It's nice to meet you, Amber."

Short and petite, she could have easily passed for seventeen, but he had the feeling she was closer to twenty-five. Just the right age. She was also very attractive, not to mention slender and toned. In fact, she was exactly the sort of woman he would normally be attracted to, yet when she smiled down at him, he didn't feel so much as a twinge of interest. She didn't even seem to notice that there was a stroller beside him with two infants inside.

"I've been a hockey fan, like, my *whole* life," she said, slipping uninvited into the empty seat across from him. "My dad has season tickets and we never missed a home game. I know you probably hear this all the time, but I am truly your number-one fan."

Her and a couple hundred thousand other fans. "Well, then I'm glad you stopped to say hi."

"The team just hasn't been the same since you retired. Last season was such a disappointment. I mean, they didn't even make the championships."

"I'm sure things will turn around next season." Because he would be in charge. Negotiations were currently at a standstill, but he was confident the current owner would come around and accept Coop's very reasonable offer.

Sierra appeared at the table, holding two cappuccinos and looking annoyed, not that he blamed her with some strange woman sitting in her chair. "Excuse me."

Amber looked up, gave Sierra a quick once-over, flashed her an oh-no-you-didn't look and said, "Excuse *me,* but I saw him first."

Seven

Sierra's brows rose, and Coop stifled a laugh. It was like that sometimes with fans. They figured just because they'd shelled out the cash to watch him bang a puck around the ice, they had some sort of claim on his personal time.

"Sierra," he said, "this is Amber. She's my biggest fan."

Sierra set the drinks down on the table with a clunk. "Charmed to meet you, Amber, but you're in my seat."

"Oh…sorry." Amber flushed a vivid shade of pink and awkwardly stood. "I didn't realize…"

"It's all good," Coop said, smiling up at her. "Give my best to your dad, and tell him I said thanks for being such a loyal fan. And don't give up on the team. They'll come back strong next season, I guarantee it."

She mumbled a goodbye, tripping on the wheel of the stroller in her haste to get away.

"Well, that was interesting," Sierra said, sliding into her seat.

"It's the price you pay as a celebrity, I guess."

"Are all your fans that rude?"

"Some are a bit more aggressive than others, but no harm done. Besides, without the fans, I wouldn't have had a job. There wouldn't be a league, and I would have no team to buy." He took a sip of his cappuccino. "Delicious. Thanks."

"Were the twins okay?"

"Fine. Although Ivy keeps tossing her toy on the ground."

"Because she knows you'll pick it back up again."

"They do have me wrapped," he admitted, smiling down at them. And he would no doubt continue to spoil them until they were all grown up.

Sierra was quiet for a minute, a furrow in her brow as she gazed absently at her cup, running her thumb around the edge. She had seemed distracted all morning, as if there was something on her mind. Something bothering her. He would like to know if it was something he had done.

"Penny for your thoughts," he said.

She looked up. "You don't want to know."

Whatever it was, it looked as if it wasn't pleasant. If she was about to tell him she was quitting, after so adamantly vowing her dedication to the girls, he was going to be seriously pissed off. "Is there a problem?"

"Not exactly, no."

"Then what is it exactly?"

"I need a favor. A really big one. And I want you to know that you are under absolutely no obligation to say yes. But I promised I would at least ask."

"So ask me."

Ivy started to fuss, so Sierra reached into the diaper bag for a bottle of juice and handed it to her, and when Fern saw it and began to fuss, she gave her one, too. "The thing is, my sister has an audition in New York so she's coming to visit."

"Do you need time off?"

She shook her head. "No. Anything we do together we can take the girls with us. The thing is, she would normally crash at my place. Unfortunately, I hadn't actually gotten around to telling her about my new job, so she just assumed she could stay with me. I guess she had to borrow money from her agent for the plane ticket, which is nonrefundable of course, and she doesn't have money for a hotel."

"So you want to know if she can stay with us."

"I wouldn't even ask, but Joy is a master at making me feel guilty. She threatened to sleep on a park bench."

"When? And how long?"

"She's flying in around noon tomorrow and staying a week. Which I know is a really long time."

He shrugged and said, "That's fine."

"You're sure you don't mind? Because you shouldn't be expected to invite complete strangers into your home."

"But she's not a stranger. She's your sister. And for the record, it's not a very big favor. If you asked me for a kidney, or a lung, that would be a big deal."

"But she's a stranger to you, and I feel like a dork for putting you on the spot."

He drew in a breath and sighed. Would she ever learn that he wasn't the ogre she seemed to have pegged him for? "Because we both know that deep down I'm a big fat jerk who would never do something nice for someone if not forced."

She shot him a look. "You know that isn't what I mean."

Sometimes she made him feel that way, as if she always expected the worst from him, despite the fact that in the two weeks he had known her, he had been nothing but courteous and accommodating and he hadn't once complained about anything. Someone must have done a serious number on her to make her so wary of trusting him. And trusting her own instincts.

"She's welcome to stay. And I'm not saying that because I feel obligated or because I'm trying to get into your pants."

Sierra bit her lip and lowered her eyes. "I didn't think that."

Not that he didn't want to. Get into her pants, that is. But not at the expense of losing her as the twins' nanny, and certainly not if she felt she owed him out of some sense of duty or repayment.

Ivy tossed her bottle this time, so far that it hit the chair leg of the elderly woman sitting at the next table. She leaned down to pick it up, carefully wiped it off with her napkin, then gave it back to Ivy, who squealed happily.

"What beautiful little girls," the woman said with a smile. "They look just like their mommy, but they have their daddy's eyes."

There didn't seem any point in trying to explain the situation, so Coop just smiled and thanked the woman. When he turned back to Sierra, she looked troubled. Did the idea that someone might mistake the twins for their children disturb her so much? There were an awful lot of women out there who would be happy to earn that distinction. Clearly she was not one of them.

She leaned in and whispered, "You don't think they look like me, do you?"

"I can see why someone might think you're their mother."

"What do you mean?"

"You have similar skin tone and dark hair. But do you actually look alike?" He shrugged. "I don't really see it. And other than the fact that they have two eyes, the similarities between them and me pretty much stop there." He paused then said, "However, to see you with the twins, one would naturally assume they are yours."

She cocked her head slightly. "Why is that?"

"Because you treat them like a mother would treat her own children."

"I'm not sure what you mean. How else am I supposed to treat them?"

"Susan once told me that before she and Ash adopted the girls, she would sit at the park on her lunch break and watch the kids on the playground, hoping that some day she could watch her own kids playing there. She said she could always tell which of the adults were parents and which were nannies or au pairs. The parents interacted with their kids. She said you could just tell that they wanted to be there, that they cared. The caregivers, however, stood around in packs basically ignoring the kids and talking amongst themselves, occasionally shouting out a reprimand. She said that she made her mind up then that if she ever was blessed with a baby, she would quit working and stay home. And she did."

"It sounds like she was a really good mom," Sierra said softly.

"She was. So I'm sure you can imagine how I must have felt, knowing I had to hire a nanny, when Susan was so against the idea. Knowing that there was no way I could manage it alone, be both a mom and a dad to them. Feeling as if I was letting them down, as if I had failed them somehow. But then you came along, and in two weeks time you have surpassed my expectations by leaps and bounds. I can rest easy knowing that even when I can't be around, the twins are loved and well cared for. And even though they don't have a mom, they have someone who gives them all the love and affection a real mom would."

Sierra bit her lip, and her eyes welled up. He hadn't meant to make her cry. He just wanted her to know what an important part of their lives she had become and how much he appreciated it. And that it had nothing to do with wanting to get into her pants.

He reached across the table and wrapped his hand around hers, half expecting her to pull away. "So when I do something nice for you, it's because I want you to know how much we appreciate having you around. And I want you to be as happy with us as we are with you. I want you to feel like you're a part of our family. Unconventional as it is."

She swiped at her eyes with her free hand. "Thank you."

Ivy shrieked and threw her bottle again, and this time Fern followed suit. Coop let go of Sierra's hand to pick them up. "I think the natives are getting restless."

She sniffled and swiped at her eyes again. "Yeah, we should probably get moving."

Leaving their barely touched cappuccinos behind, they gathered their things and left the café. Coop had the overwhelming desire to link his fingers through hers, but with both her hands clutching the stroller handle he couldn't have anyway.

It defied logic, this irrational need to be close to her. To do things like skip meetings and ignore his friends just to spend time with her and the twins. He could have practically any other woman that he wanted. Women who showered him with flattery and clawed over each other for his attention. Women willing to be whatever and whoever he wanted just to make him happy.

Didn't it just figure that he had to fall for the one woman who didn't want him?

While the girls napped Sierra did laundry, wishing that this morning at the coffee shop had never happened.

Did Coop have to be so darned nice all the time? That stuff about her taking care of the girls was hands down the sweetest and kindest thing anyone had ever said to her. He was making it really hard for her to not like him. In fact, when he'd taken her hand in his… oh, my God. His hand was big and strong and had a roughness that should have been unpleasant, yet all she could think about was him rubbing it all over her. If they hadn't been in a public place, she might have done something completely insane like fling the table aside, plant herself in his lap and kiss him senseless. And then she would have divested him of the tank top and running shorts and put *her* hands all over *him*. The fact that he was still sweaty, unshaven and disheveled from his run should have been a turnoff, yet when she imagined touching his slick skin, feeling the rasp of his beard against her cheek, tasting the salty tang of his lips, she'd gone into hormone overload. She didn't even like sweaty, disheveled, unshaven men.

Why was she even thinking about this?

As good as it would be—and she *knew* it would be

good—it would be a mistake. She still wasn't sure why he was attracted to her in the first place. Was it convenience—because he said himself that was how he normally chose his women? And what could be more convenient than a woman living right under his roof? Or was it the thrill of the chase fueling his interest? And if she let him catch her, just how long would it take before he got bored?

Probably not very long. And after he dumped her, she would find herself heartbroken, out of a job, homeless, and, worst of all, ripped away from her children. She simply had too much to lose. She had to do what was best for them.

The spin cycle ended and she tossed the damp linens into the dryer along with a dryer sheet and set it on High, then she dumped hers and the girls' dirty clothes in the washing machine.

She poured a scoop of detergent over the clothes, then realized she was still wearing the shirt that Fern had flung a glob of pureed carrots all over at lunch. Ms. Densmore was at the market and Coop had left an hour ago for a meeting that he said would drag on until at least dinnertime, so figuring she could make it from the laundry room to her bedroom undetected in her bra, she pulled the shirt over her head, spritzed the spot with stain remover and tossed it in, too.

She shut the lid, started the machine and headed out of the laundry room...stopping dead in her tracks when she realized that Coop was in the kitchen.

For a second she thought that her mind must be playing tricks on her. No one's luck could be *that* bad.

She blinked. Then she blinked again.

Nope, that was definitely Coop, his hip wedged against the island countertop, his eyes lowered as he sorted through the mail he must have picked up on his way in. And any second now he was going to look up and see her standing there in her bra.

She could make a run for her bedroom, but she couldn't imagine doing anything so undignified, nor would she run back to the laundry room. Besides, Coop must have sensed her there because he looked up. And *he* blinked. Then he blinked again. Then his eyes settled on her breasts and he said, "You're not wearing a shirt."

She could have at least covered herself with her hands or grabbed the dish towel hanging on the oven door, but for some weird reason she just stood there, as if, deep down she *wanted* him to see her half-naked. Which she was pretty sure she didn't.

"Ms. Densmore is at the market, and I didn't think you would be home so soon," she said.

"My lawyer had to cut the meeting short," he explained, his gaze still fixed below her neck. "For which I plan to thank him *profusely* the next time I see him."

The heat in his eyes was so intense she actually thought her bra might ignite. "That explains it then."

"Out of curiosity, do you always walk around in your bra when no one is home?"

"My shirt had carrots on it from the girls' lunch. I threw it in the washing machine." When he didn't respond she said, "You could be a gentleman and look the other way."

He tossed the mail on the counter, but it hit the edge, slid off and landed on the floor instead. "I could. And I would if I thought for a second that you didn't like me looking at you."

There he went, reading her mind again. She really wished he would stop doing that. "Who says I like it?"

"If you didn't you would have made some attempt to cover yourself or leave the room. And your heart wouldn't be racing."

Right again.

"Not to mention you're giving off enough phero-mones right now to take down an entire professional hockey team. And you know what that means."

She didn't have a clue, but the idea of what it might be made her knees weak. "What does it mean?"

"It means that I *have* to kiss you."

Eight

"Coop, that would be a really bad idea," Sierra said, but her voice was trembling.

Maybe it was, but right now, Coop didn't care. He crossed the room toward her and she held her breath. "All you have to do is tell me no."

"I just did."

He stopped a few inches from her and he could actually feel the heat radiating from her bare skin. "You said it would be a bad idea, but you didn't actually say don't do it."

"But that was what I meant."

"So say it."

She opened her mouth and closed it again.

Oh, yeah, she wanted him. He reached up and ran the pad of his thumb up her arm, from elbow to shoulder, then back down again. Sierra shivered.

"Tell me to stop," he said, and when she didn't say

a word, when she just gazed up at him with lust-filled eyes, her cheeks flush with excitement, he knew she was as good as his.

He cupped her cheek in his palm, stroked with his thumb, and he could feel her melting, giving in. "Last chance," he said.

She blew out an exasperated breath. "Oh, for heaven's sake just shut up and *kiss* me already!"

He was smiling as he lowered his head, slanting his mouth over hers. When their lips touched, and her tongue slid against his, desire slammed him from every direction at once.

Holy hell.

Never in his life had he felt such an intense connection to a woman just from kissing her. Of course, he'd never met a woman quite like her. And he knew without a doubt that a kiss was never going to be enough. He wanted more…*needed* it in a way he had never needed anything before.

She slid her arms around his neck, trying to get closer, but his arm was in the way. She broke the kiss and looked down at his crotch, which he was cupping in his free hand, then she looked up at him questioningly.

"Just in case I was wrong and you followed through on your threat."

"Threat?"

"You said that if I tried to kiss you I would be wearing the family jewels for earrings."

She laughed and shook her head. "You do realize, the fact that you thought I might actually do it makes you about a million times more appealing."

He grinned. "I told you, I'm irresistible."

"Coop, this is so wrong," she said.

He slid his hands across her bare back. Sierra sighed and her eyes drifted closed. "Nothing that feels this good could be wrong."

She must have agreed because she wrapped her arms around his neck, pulled his head down and kissed him. He might have taken her right there in the kitchen—he sure wanted to—but Sierra deserved better than sex on the counter or up against the refrigerator. She wasn't some woman he'd picked up in a bar or at a party. She was special. She wasn't in it for the cheap thrill of being with a celebrity. This would mean something to her, something profound. She deserved tenderness and romance, and when he did make love to her—which he would do, there was no longer any doubt about that— he wanted to take his time. He didn't want to have to worry about things like the twins waking up from their nap, which they were likely to do pretty soon. And though he could be content to stand there kissing and touching her until they did, Ms. Densmore could walk in at any moment. Not that he gave a crap what *she* thought, but he didn't want Sierra to feel embarrassed or uncomfortable. He really *cared* about her, which was just too damned weird.

Could he possibly be falling in love with her?

He didn't *do* love. Hell, he usually didn't do next week. To him women were nothing more than a way to pass the time. And not because of some psychological wound or fear of commitment. He hadn't been profoundly wounded by his parents' death or dumped by his one true love. He hadn't been double-crossed or cheated on. He had just been too focused on his career to make the time for a long-term relationship. He also hadn't met anyone he'd cared so deeply for that he couldn't live without them. But it was bound to happen eventually, wasn't it? What was the saying? There was someone for everyone? Maybe Sierra was his someone.

It took every bit of restraint he possessed to break the kiss, when there was really no guarantee she would ever let him kiss her again. He was giving her time to rethink this, to change her mind. But that was just a chance he had to take.

He took her hands, pulled them from around his neck and cradled them against his chest. "We should stop before we get too carried away."

She looked surprised and disappointed and maybe a little relieved, too. "The girls will be up soon."

"Exactly. And unless you want Ms. Densmore to see you half-naked, you might want to put a shirt on."

She looked down, as though she had completely forgotten she wasn't wearing one. "It might almost be worth it to see the look on her face."

From behind the kitchen they heard the service-entrance door open. If she wanted to see the look on Ms. Densmore's face, this was her chance. Instead she turned tail and darted from the room, ponytail swishing.

He chuckled at her retreating back. Not so tough, was she?

Ms. Densmore appeared with two canvas shopping bags full of groceries. He'd told her a million times that she could just order the groceries and have them delivered, but she insisted on walking to the market and carrying the bags back herself nearly every day.

When she saw him standing there she said, "I didn't expect you home so soon."

She looked tired, so he took the bags from her and set them up on the countertop. "Meeting ended early."

While she put her purse away he poked through

the bags, finding a variety of fresh vegetables, several jars of baby food and a package of boneless, skinless chicken breasts. "Chicken for dinner tonight?"

"Chicken parmesan," she said, looking curiously at the mail on the floor and stooping to pick it up. "We need to talk."

He could see by her expression, which was more troubled than sour, that there was a problem. "What's up?"

She put the chicken in the fridge, closed the door and turned to him. "I'm afraid I can't work for you any longer."

He knew she wasn't thrilled with having the twins around, but he didn't think she was miserable enough to quit. She may not have been a very nice person, but she was a good housekeeper and he hated to lose her. "Is there a specific problem? And if so, is there anything I can do to fix it?"

"I took this job because it fit certain criteria. First, there were no children and not likely to ever be any, and second, you were rarely here. I like to be alone and left to my own devices. Since you brought the twins here everything has changed. I have to cook all the time and I hate cooking." She paused and said bitterly, "Not to mention that your nanny has been *tormenting* me."

He couldn't help laughing, which only made her glare at him. "I'm sorry, but *Sierra?* She's not exactly the tormenting type."

"She plays tricks on me."

"What kind of tricks?"

"She moves things around just to irritate me. She takes the milk off the door and puts it on the shelf and she rearranges things in the laundry room. She's petty and childish."

"I'll have a talk with her."

"It's too late for that. Besides, as long as the twins are around I won't ever be happy working here again."

He was sorry she felt that way, but neither did he want an unhappy employee. Or one who couldn't appreciate two sweet and beautiful infants. "So is this your two-week notice?"

"I got a new job and they need me to start immediately, so today is my last day."

"Today?" He couldn't believe she would leave him in a lurch that way.

"Let's not pretend that you wouldn't have eventually fired me. *She* would have insisted."

"Sierra? That's not her call."

"When she becomes the lady of the house it will be, and you know that will be the eventual outcome."

Coop had no idea that his feelings for Sierra were so obvious. And she was right. If he and Sierra did ever get married, she would insist that he get rid of Ms. Densmore, and of course he would because he would do practically anything she asked to make her happy.

"Don't worry," Ms. Densmore said. "You'll call a service and have a replacement before the week is out."

She was right. He just hated the idea of training someone new. "Do you mind my asking who you're going to be working for?"

"A diplomat and his wife. Their children are grown and they spend three weeks out of every month traveling. I'll pretty much be left alone to do my job."

"That sounds perfect for you."

"With the exception of the past month, it really has been a pleasure working for you, Mr. Landon. I just can't be happy here any longer. I'm too old and set in my ways to change."

"I understand."

"I'm sure Sierra can handle things until you find someone new."

He'd seen Sierra's bedroom. Housekeeping was a concept that seemed to escape her completely. Besides, with two infants to care for, she wouldn't have time to cook and clean, too. He needed someone within the next few days at the latest.

"Dinner will be ready at six-thirty," she said. "And I'm making a double recipe so there will be some left over. You can warm it for dinner later this week."

"Thanks."

She turned and busied herself starting dinner as Coop went to look for Sierra, to tell her what he was sure she would consider very good news. The nursery door was closed, meaning the girls were still asleep, so he knocked on Sierra's bedroom door instead. She opened it after a few seconds, and he was sorry to see that she had changed into a clean shirt.

"Have you got a minute?" he asked.

"Of course." She stepped aside and let him in. The bed was unmade, there was a bath towel draped over the chair, the desk was piled with papers and junk, and there was a pile of books and magazines on the floor next to the bed.

"Excuse the mess," she said. "I just can't ever seem to find the time to straighten up. After being with the girls all day I'm usually too exhausted to do much of anything."

Which meant doubling as housekeeper would be out of the question. "It's your room. If you want to keep it messy, that's your choice."

"I know it drives Ms. Densmore crazy, but she won't set foot in my room."

"Funny you should mention her. She's the reason I came to talk to you."

A worry line bisected Sierra's brow. "She didn't see me without my shirt on, did she?"

"Nope. But the way I hear it, you've been tormenting my housekeeper."

Uh-oh. Someone had tattled on her.

Sierra put on her best innocent look and asked, "What do you mean?"

Coop folded his arms, and though he was trying to look tough, there was humor in his eyes. "Don't even try to pretend that you don't know what I'm talking about. You know I can always tell when you're lying."

It was that mind-reading thing that he did. *So* annoying. "To call it 'torment' is an exaggeration. They were just...*pranks*. And you can't tell me that she didn't deserve it. She's so *mean*."

"She just quit."

She gasped and slapped a hand over her heart. "She didn't!"

"She did, just now in the kitchen. This is her last day."

"Oh my gosh, Coop. I'm so sorry. I wanted to annoy her, not make her leave. This is all my fault. Do you want me to talk to her? Promise to behave from now on?"

He grinned and shook his head. "You may have accelerated the process, but she would have left eventually anyway. She said she's been unhappy since the girls moved in. It wasn't what she signed on for. I hired her five years ago, when I was still playing hockey and barely ever here. She liked it that way."

"I still feel bad."

"Don't," he said, and gestured to a framed photo on the dresser. "Is that your mom?"

She smiled and nodded. It was Sierra's favorite shot of her. It was taken in the park, on a sunny spring afternoon. Her mom was sitting cross-legged in the grass on the old patchwork quilt they always used for picnics or at the beach, and she was looking up at the camera, smiling. "Wasn't she beautiful?"

He walked over and picked it up. "Very beautiful."

"She was always smiling, always happy. And it was infectious. You could not be in the same room and not feel like smiling. And she loved hugs, loved to snuggle. She and I would curl up on the love seat together every Sunday and read books or do crossword puzzles all day long. She was so much fun, always thinking up new adventures, trying new things. And my dad loved her so much. He never remarried. He didn't even date very often. I don't think he ever got over losing her. They never fought, never bickered. They had the perfect marriage."

"She was Asian?" Coop asked.

She nodded. "Her grandmother was Chinese. I used to wish that I looked more like her."

"You do look like her."

"I actually favor my dad more. Joy looks more like she did."

"You really miss her."

She nodded. "Every day."

He walked over to where she stood, took her hand and tugged her to him. She didn't put up a fight when he pulled her close and looped his arms around her, and it felt so *good* to lay her head on his chest, to listen to the beat of his heart. He was so big and strong and he smelled so yummy. And kissing him…oh, my. It was a little slice of heaven. And now it was just going to be the two of them, alone in the house—with the girls, too, of course. The idea made her both excited and nervous. She knew that kissing Coop had been a bad idea and that letting it go any further would be a mistake of epic proportions. But couldn't she pretend, just for a little while, that they actually had a chance? That an affair with Coop wouldn't ruin everything?

No, because for whatever reason, and though it defied logic, he seemed to genuinely like her. If all he cared about was getting her between the sheets, that's where they would be right now. And if she believed for a second that his feelings for her were anything but a passing phase, she wouldn't hesitate to drag him there herself. Unfortunately, she and Coop were just too different. It would never work.

She untangled herself from his arms and backed away. "We need to talk."

"Why do I get the feeling that I'm not going to like this?"

"What happened earlier, it was really, *really* nice."

"But…?"

"You and I both know that it's not going to work."

"We don't know that."

"I don't want to have an affair."

"I don't, either. I know this will be hard for you to believe, but I want more this time. I'm ready."

If only that were true. "How can you know that? You've known me what? Two weeks?"

"I can't explain it. All I know is that I've never wanted anyone the way I want you. It just…feels right."

His expression was so earnest, she didn't doubt he believed every word he said, and oh how she wished she could throw caution to the wind and believe him, too. But there was too much at stake. "I want you, too, Coop. And I don't doubt that it will be really, really good for a while, but eventually something will go wrong. You'll be unhappy, and I'll be unhappy, then things will get awkward, and though you'll hate to have to do it, you'll fire me because it will be what's for the best."

"I wouldn't do that."

"Yes, you would. You wouldn't have any other choice. Because think about it—what are you going to do? Dump me, then bring other women home right in front of me?"

"You're assuming it won't work. But what if it does? We could be really good together."

"That isn't a chance I'm willing to take." And there was no way to make him understand why without telling him the truth. And if she was looking for a way to get fired, that was it.

"So, the job is more important than your feelings for me?" he asked.

"The girls need me more than you do. And, if I lose this job, my father goes back into that hellhole he was in. I won't do that to him."

She could tell by his frown that he knew she was right, he just didn't want to accept it.

"I could fire you now," he said. "Then you would be free to date me."

She raised her brows at him. "So what you're saying is, if I don't sleep with you, you'll fire me?"

His frown deepened, and he rubbed a hand across his jaw. "When you say it like that it sounds really sleazy."

"That's because it *is* sleazy. It's also sexual harassment." Not that she believed his threat was anything but an empty one. He just wasn't used to not getting his way, but he would have to *get* used to it.

In her jeans pocket, the cell phone started to ring and she pulled it out to check the display. When she saw the number of the nursing home her heart skipped like a stone on a very deep, cold lake. That always happened when someone called about her dad because her first thought was inevitably that he had passed away. But they had lots of other reasons for calling her. So why, this time, did she have an especially bad feeling?

"I have to take this," she told Coop. "It's the nursing home."

She answered the phone, pulse pounding, her heart in her throat.

"Miss Evans, this is Meg Douglas, administrator of Heartland Nursing Center."

"Hi, Meg, what can I do for you?" she asked, hoping she said something simple, like there was a form that needed to be signed or a treatment they needed authorization for.

"I'm so sorry to have to inform you that your father passed away."

Nine

Coop changed the twins' diapers, wrestled them into their pajamas, then sat in the rocking chair with them, one on each arm, but neither made it even halfway through their bottle before they were sound asleep. It had been a busy afternoon of going first to the nursing home so Sierra could see her dad one last time, then to the funeral home to make the final arrangements. By the time they finally got home it was well past the twins' bedtime.

Ms. Densmore had left dinner warming in the oven and, in a show of kindness that surprised both him and Sierra, a note on the refrigerator expressing her sympathy for Sierra's loss. She wasn't so sorry that she offered to stay on a few days longer, though. Not that he expected her to.

He got up and carried the twins' limp little bodies to their cribs, kissed them and tucked them in. For a minute he stood there, watching them sleep, feeling so…peaceful. At first he'd believed that once he hired someone to care for the twins, life would go back to the way it had been before he got the girls. Two months ago, if someone had told him he would enjoy being a parent and be content as a family man, he would have laughed in their face. He figured he would be happy playing the role of the fun and cool uncle, showering them with gifts and seeing that they were financially set while someone else dealt with the day-to-day issues. The feedings and the diapers and all the messy emotional stuff that would later come with hormonal teenaged girls. He realized now that they deserved better than that. They deserved a real, conventional family.

Shutting the nursery door softly behind him, he took the half-finished bottles to the kitchen and stuck them in the fridge, just in case one or both of the girls woke up hungry in the middle of the night. His and Sierra's dinner dishes were still in the sink, so he rinsed them, stuck them in the dishwasher and set it to run, recalling the days when he and his brother hadn't even been able to afford a dishwasher, and doing them by hand had been Coop's responsibility. He'd had to do his own laundry and cook three days a week, too. Maybe he was spoiled now, but he had no desire to return to those days, even temporarily. And with caring for the twins, her sister's visit and planning her dad's memorial service, Sierra definitely wouldn't have time to clean and cook. He didn't even know if she *could* cook.

He made a mental note to call a service first thing tomorrow and set up interviews for a new housekeeper as soon as humanly possible.

Though he normally drank wine in the evenings, a cold beer had a nice ring to it tonight, so he grabbed two from the fridge. He switched out the kitchen light, hooked the baby monitor to his belt and walked to the rooftop terrace where he'd sent Sierra while he got the twins settled for bed. She'd balked, of course, and gave him the usual line about how he had done enough already and she needed to do her job, but with a little persuasion she'd caved. It was strange, but lately he'd begun thinking of her as not so much a nanny, but the two of them as partners in raising the girls. And he liked it that way.

The sun had nearly set, so he hit the switch and turned on the party lights that hung around the perimeter of the terrace.

Sierra looked up from the lounge chair where she sat, her knees tucked up under her chin. When they got home she had changed into shorts and a tank top, and her feet were bare. He half expected her to be crying, but her eyes were dry. The only time she had cried today was when she'd gone into her dad's room.

"Are the twins in bed?" she asked.

"Out cold before their heads hit the mattress," he said, holding up one of the two beers. "Can I interest you in a cold one?"

"That actually sounds really good, thanks."

He twisted the tops off and handed her one of the bottles, then stretched out in the chair beside hers.

She took a long, deep pull on her drink, sighed contentedly and said, "That hits the spot. Thank you for helping me with the twins today and for driving me all over the place. I'm not sure how I would have managed without you."

"It was my pleasure," he told her, as he had the dozen other times she had thanked him during the day. He took a drink of his beer and cradled the bottle in his lap between his thighs. "How are you doing?"

"You know, I'm okay. I'm not nearly as upset as I thought I would be. I mean, I'm sad and I'm going to miss him, but the man who was my dad has been gone for a while now. No one should have to live that way. For his sake I'm relieved that it's over, that he's at peace." She looked over at Coop. "Does that make me a terrible person?"

"Not at all."

"I'm worried about Joy, though."

"She didn't take the news well?"

"No, she took it a little too well. She hasn't actually seen our father in almost four years. That's why I thought it was so important she see him when she was here. Now she'll never get the chance. I'm worried that she's going to regret it for the rest of her life. I asked if she wanted them to hold off on cremating him, so she could at least see him, but she said no. She doesn't want to remember him like that."

"It's her decision."

"I know." She took another swallow of beer and set the bottle on the ground beside her.

"Is there anything I can do? Do you need anything for the memorial? I know money is tight for you and your sister."

"I'm not letting you pay for my dad's memorial, so don't even suggest it."

"So what will you do?"

She shrugged. "I haven't quite figured that out yet."

"Is there insurance? If you don't mind my asking."

"There's a small policy. But after the medical bills and the funeral costs, there won't be much left. It's going to be at least a couple of weeks before I get a check."

"How about I give you an advance on next week's salary? Or more if you need it."

She hesitated, chewing her lip.

"I don't mind," he said. "And I'm pretty sure I can trust you to stick around."

She hesitated, picking at the label on her beer bottle. He didn't get why she was so wary of accepting his help. Isn't that what friendship was about? And he definitely considered her a friend. He would like to consider her much more than that if she would let him.

"You're sure it's not an imposition?" she asked.

"If it was, I wouldn't have offered."

"In that case, I would really appreciate it."

"I'll have the money wired into your account first thing in the morning."

"Thank you."

She was quiet for several minutes, so he said, "Penny for your thoughts."

"I was just thinking about the twins and how sad it is that they won't remember their parents. At least I got fourteen years with my mom. I have enough wonderful memories to keep her alive in my mind forever. Or maybe, if the girls had to lose their mother and father, it was better now than, say, five or ten years from now. That way they don't know what they've missed. There was no emotional connection. Or maybe I'm totally wrong." She shrugged. "Who knows really."

"Losing Ash and Susan doesn't mean they won't have two loving parents."

She looked confused. "What do you mean?"

"The twins shouldn't be raised by an uncle. It's

not good enough for them, either. They deserve a real family."

Her face paled. "Are you saying you plan to give them up?"

"No, of course not. I love them. I'm ready to settle down and be a family man. So I've decided to adopt them."

Sierra bit down hard on her lip, blinking back the tears that were welling in her eyes. She had wanted to believe that Coop had changed, that he would be a good father, but until just now she hadn't been sure. It felt as if an enormous weight had been lifted off her shoulders, as if she could breathe for the first time since she heard the horrible news of the crash. She was confident that no matter what happened between her and Coop, the twins would be okay. He loved them and wanted to be their father.

She looked over at Coop and realized he was watching her, worry creasing his brow. "I hope those are happy tears you're fighting," he said. "That you aren't thinking what a terrible parent I'll be and how sorry you feel for the girls."

More like tears of relief. "Actually, I was thinking how lucky they are to have someone like you." She reached for his hand and he folded it around hers. "And how proud Ash and Susan would be and how grateful."

"Come here," he said, tugging on her arm, pulling her out of her chair and into his lap. She curled up against his chest and he wrapped his arms around her, holding her so tight it was a little hard to breathe. And though she couldn't see his face, when he spoke he sounded a little choked up. "Thank you, Sierra. You have no idea how much that means coming from you."

She tucked her face in the crook of his neck, breathed in the scent of his skin. Why did he have to be so wonderful?

"You know the girls are going to need a mother," he said, stroking her hair. "Someone who loves them as much as I do. We could be a family."

"You hardly know me."

"I know how happy I've been since you came into our lives. And how much the twins love you." His hand slipped down to caress her cheek. "I know how crazy you make me and how much I want you."

Did he really want her, or was it that she was convenient? She fit into his new "family plan." And did it really matter? They could be a family. That was what the girls needed, and isn't that was this was about? "And if it doesn't work?"

He tipped her chin up so he could see her face. "Isn't it worth it to at least try?"

Yes, she realized, it was. They were doing it for the girls.

She turned in Coop's lap so she was straddling his thighs, then she cupped his face in her palms and kissed him. And he was right about one thing. Anything that felt this good couldn't be wrong.

She circled her arms around his neck, sliding her fingers through the softness of his hair, and as she did she could feel the stress leaching from her bones, the empty place in her heart being filled again. After what had been a long, stressful and pretty lousy day, he'd made her feel happy. In fact, she couldn't recall a time in her life when she had been as happy and content as she was with Coop and the twins. That had to mean something, didn't it? She had been trying so hard not to fall for him, maybe it was time to relax and let it happen, let nature take its course. Besides, how could she say no to a man who kissed the way he did? In no time his soft lips, the warm slide of his tongue, had her feeling all restless and achy.

Although she couldn't help noticing that kissing was *all* they were doing. She was practically crawling out of her skin for more, and he seemed perfectly content to run his fingers through her hair and caress her cheeks, but not much else. And when she tried to move things forward, tried to touch him, he took her hands and curled them against his chest.

Now that he had her where he wanted her, had he suddenly developed cold feet? Had he decided that he didn't want her after all? He was aroused, that much was obvious, so why wasn't he moving things forward?

She stopped kissing him. "Okay, what's the deal?"

He looked confused. "Deal?"

"You do know how to do this, right? I mean, it's not your first time or anything?"

One brow arched. "Is that a rhetorical question?"

"You're not doing anything," she said.

"Sure I am. I'm kissing you." He grinned that slightly crooked smile. "And for the record I'm thoroughly enjoying it. Is there something wrong with taking things slow? I want you to be sure about this."

Could she really blame him for being cautious? She was sending some pretty major mixed signals. Coop, though, had been pretty clear about what he wanted from the get-go.

"I want this, Coop," she told him. "I'm ready."

"Ready for what, that's the question," he said. "Am I going to get to second base? Third base? Am I going to knock it out of the park?"

She couldn't resist smiling. Were they really using

sports euphemisms? "You can't hit a home run if you don't step up to the plate."

He grinned. "In that case, maybe we should move this party to my bedroom."

Ten

Watching Coop undress—and taking off her own clothes in front of him—was one of the most erotic and terrifying experiences of Sierra's entire life. He had insisted on keeping the bedside lamp on, and she couldn't help but worry that he wouldn't like what he saw. But if he noticed the faint stretch marks on her hips and the side of her belly, or that her tummy wasn't quite as firm as it had been before the twins, he didn't let it show. She was sure that he'd been with women who were thinner and larger busted and all around prettier than she was, yet he looked at her as though she was the most beautiful woman in the world.

Coop seemed completely comfortable in his nudity. And why wouldn't he? He was simply *perfect.* From his rumpled hair to his long, slender feet, and every inch in between. She'd never been crazy about hairy men, so the sprinkling of dark-blond hair across his pecks and the thin trail bisecting his abs was ideal. And all those muscles…wow.

"I've never been with anyone so big," she said.

One brow arched up as he glanced down at his crotch. "I always thought I was sort of average."

She laughed. "I meant muscular."

He grinned. "Oh, *that*."

But he wasn't *average* anywhere. "I just want to touch you all over."

"I think we can arrange that." He pulled back the blankets, climbed into bed and laid down, then patted the mattress beside him. "Hop in."

Feeling nervous and excited all at once, she slid in beside him. And though she wanted this more than he would ever know, as he pulled her close and started kissing her, she found she couldn't relax. Not that it didn't feel good. But he'd been with a lot of women, and she was willing to bet that compared to most of them she was, at best, a novice. Her experiences with her high school boyfriend had been more awkward than satisfying, and the handful of encounters she'd had while she was in nursing school hadn't exactly been earth-shattering. Her last sexual experience sixteen months ago with the twins' father had at most been a drunken *wham, bam, thank you ma'am* that they both regretted the minute it was over.

She wanted sex to be fun and satisfying. She wanted to feel that spark, that…*connection.* The sensation of being intrinsically linked—if such a thing really existed. Yet every new experience left her feeling disappointed and empty, faking her orgasms just to be polite, wondering if it was something she was doing wrong. What if the same thing happened with Coop? What if she couldn't satisfy him, either? What if she didn't live up to his expectations?

She had herself in such a state that when he cupped a hand over her breast, instead of letting herself enjoy it, she tensed up. He stopped kissing her, pushed himself up on one elbow and gazed down at her. "Now who's just lying there?"

Her cheeks flushed with embarrassment. She was naked, in bed with a gorgeous, sexy man and she was completely blowing it. "I'm sorry."

"Maybe we should stop."

She shook her head. "No. I don't want to stop."

"You have done this before, right?" he teased. "I mean, it's not your first time or anything."

If he wasn't so adorable, she might have slugged him. Instead she found herself smiling. "Yes, I've done this before. But probably not even close to as many times as you have."

He stroked her cheek, a frown settling into the crease between his brows. "And that bothers you?"

"No, of course not. I'm just worried that I won't measure up. That I'm going to disappoint you."

"Sierra, you won't. Trust me."

"But I *could*."

"Or I could disappoint you. Have you considered that? Maybe I've been with so many women because I'm such a lousy lay no one would sleep with me twice."

She couldn't help it, she laughed. "That is the dumbest thing I've ever heard."

"And for the record, I haven't slept with *that* many women. And not because I haven't had the opportunity. I'm just very selective about who I hop into bed with."

His idea of *not that many* could be three hundred for all she knew. And maybe that should have bothered her, but it didn't. Because she knew it was different this time. He was different. This actually meant something to him.

"What can I do to make you more comfortable?" he asked. "To assure you that your disappointing me isn't even a remote possibility."

"Maybe you could give me some pointers, you know, tell me what you like."

"You could kiss me. I like that. And you mentioned something about touching me all over. That sounds pretty good, too." He took her hand and cradled it against his chest, brushed his lips against hers so sweetly. "We'll take it slow, okay?"

She nodded, feeling more relaxed already. He had a way of putting her at ease. And good to his word he was diligent about telling her exactly what he wanted and where he liked to be touched—which was pretty much everywhere and involved using her hands and her mouth. And after a while of his patient tutoring, she gained the confidence to experiment all on her own, which he seemed to like even more. And Coop was anything but a disappointment. The man knew his way around a woman's body. He made her feel sexy and beautiful.

By the time he reached into the night table drawer for a condom, she was so ready to take that next step, she could barely wait for him to cover himself. He pressed her thighs apart, and she held her breath, but then he just looked at her.

"You're so beautiful," he said.

"Coop, please," she pleaded.

"What, Sierra? What do you want?"

Him. She just wanted him.

But he already knew because he lowered himself

over her, and the look of pure ecstasy as he eased himself inside of her almost did her in. He groaned and ran his fingers though her hair, his eyes rolling closed, and she finally felt it, that connection. And it was even more intense, more extraordinary than she ever imagined. This was it. This was what making love was supposed to feel like. And whatever happened between them, as long as she lived, she would never forget this moment.

Everything after that was a blur of skin against skin, mingling breath and soft moans and intense pleasure that kept building and building. She wasn't sure who came first, who set whom off, but it was the closest thing to heaven on earth that she had even known. Afterward they lay wrapped in each other's arms, legs intertwined, breathing hard. And all she wanted was to be closer. They could melt together, become one person, and she didn't think that would be close enough.

In that instant the reality of the situation hit her like a punch to the belly. She hadn't planned it, hadn't expected it, not in a million years, but now there was no denying it. She was in love with Coop.

Coop was a disgrace to the male gender.

In his entire life he had never come first. Not once. He prided himself on being completely in control at all times. Until last night.

Watching Sierra writhe beneath him, hearing her moans and whimpers, had pushed him so far past the point of no return, a nuclear explosion wouldn't have been able to stop him. She made him feel things he hadn't realized he was even capable of feeling. For the first time in his life, sex actually meant something. He had reached a level of intimacy that until last night he hadn't even known existed. It should have scared the hell out of him, but he had never felt more content in his entire life.

"She's grabbing her suitcase right now," Sierra said from the passenger's seat, dropping her phone back in her purse. "She said to meet her outside of Terminal C."

Joy's flight had been a few minutes late, so they had been driving around in circles while Joy deplaned and collected her luggage.

"I'm glad I fed the twins their lunch early today," Sierra said, looking back at them, sitting contentedly in their car seats. "And thank you again for picking Joy up. She could have taken the bus."

"It's no problem." He reached over and took her hand, twining his fingers through hers. "Besides, I owe you for last night."

She blew out an exasperated breath and rolled her eyes. "I don't know why you're making such a big deal out of this. It couldn't have been more than a few seconds before me."

That was a few seconds too long as far as he was concerned. "I don't lose control like that."

"I didn't even *notice*. I wouldn't have even known if you hadn't said something."

"Well, it's not going to happen again." And it hadn't. Not the second or third time last night, or this morning in bed, or in the shower. Not that there hadn't been a couple of close calls.

She shook her head, as if he were hopeless. "Men and their egos. Besides, I sort of like knowing that I make you lose control."

"That reminds me, we need to stop at the pharmacy on the way home. We blew through my entire supply of condoms."

"We don't have to use them if you don't want to."

He glanced over at her. "You take birth control pills?"

"IUD."

Sex without a condom…interesting idea.

From the time he reached puberty Ash had drilled into Coop the importance of always using protection. Years before Coop became sexually active, Ash had bought him a box of condoms and ordered him to keep one in his wallet at all times, just in case. A thing for which Coop was eternally grateful, ever since one fateful night his junior year of high school when Missy Noble's parents were out for the evening and she jumped him on the den couch right in the middle of some chick movie whose title escaped him now.

Being the stickler for safety that Coop was, not to mention the very real likelihood of being trapped into a relationship with an *accidental* pregnancy, he'd actually never had sex without one. But the idea was an intriguing one.

"I've been told that it feels better for the man that way," she said.

"Who told you that?"

"The men who tried to get me to do it without one, so I'm not sure if it's actually true or not. But logistically you would think so."

He looked over at her and grinned. "I guess we'll have to put that theory to the test, won't we? Just so you know, I get tested regularly."

"As a nurse I have to," she said.

"How's tonight looking for you?" he asked.

"With my sister here?"

"What we do in the privacy of our bedroom is our business."

"*Our* bedroom?"

"She's going to be sleeping in your room, so it just makes sense that you sleep in mine. And continue to sleep there when she's gone."

"You don't think we should take things a little bit slower?"

"You didn't seem to want to go slow last night."

"Having sex and me moving into your bedroom are two very different things."

"We're living together, Sierra. Where you sleep at this point is just logistics." He gave her hand a squeeze. "We're together. I want you to sleep with me."

She hesitated for a second, then nodded and said, "Okay."

Coop steered the SUV up to the C terminal and spotted Joy immediately. She was a taller, slimmer version of her big sister, with the same dark hair, though Joy's was wavier and hung clear down to her waist. Gauging by her long gauzy skirt, tie-dye tank, leather sandals and beaded necklaces, she was the free-spirit type. A total contrast to Sierra, who couldn't be more practical and conservative.

"There she is!" Sierra said excitedly.

Coop pulled up beside her and before he could even come to a complete stop Sierra was out the door.

He turned to the twins and said, "I'll be right back, you two," then hopped out to grab Joy's bag. By the time he made it around the vehicle the sisters were locked in a firm embrace, and when they finally parted they were both misty-eyed.

Sierra turned to him. "Coop, this is my sister, Joy. Joy, this is Coop, my...boss."

Joy offered him a finely boned hand to shake, but her grip was firm. "I can't thank you enough for giving me a place to stay while I'm here. And for picking me up."

"I hope you don't mind squeezing in between the girls," he said.

"It beats takin' the bus."

He opened the door for Joy, and when both women were inside he grabbed the suitcase, heaved it into the back, then got back in the driver's side. Sierra was introducing her sister to the twins.

"That's Fern on the right and Ivy on the left," she said.

Joy shook each one of their tiny hands, which the twins seemed to love. "Nice to meet you, girls. And it's a pleasure to meet the man who my sister can't seem to stop talking about. Are you two a couple yet or what?"

"Joy!" Sierra said, reaching back to whack her sister in the leg. Then she told Coop, "You'll have to excuse my sister. She has no filter."

Joy just laughed and said, "Love you, sis."

Coop had known Joy all of about two minutes, but he had the distinct feeling that he was going to like Sierra's sister, and he didn't doubt that her visit would be an interesting one.

"You're sleeping with him," Joy said when the twins were down for a nap and they were finally alone in Sierra's bedroom…or Joy's bedroom as the case happened to be now.

"Yeah," she admitted. "As of last night."

"I kinda figured. There was a vibe." Joy heaved her suitcase onto the bed and unzipped it. "I knew he had to be hot for you to let your sister crash here."

"You don't pack light," Sierra said as she emptied the contents of her case onto the duvet.

"The guy I've been staying with is getting his place

fumigated while I'm gone, so it just made sense to bring it all. Have you got a few extra hangers?"

Sierra pointed to the closet door. "In there."

Joy crossed the room and pulled the door open. "Holy mother of God, this closet is *huge*."

"I know. It's twenty times the size of the dinky closet in my apartment."

"I didn't realize that hockey players made so much money," she called from inside the closet, emerging with a dozen or so hangers.

"He's also a successful businessman. And he does tons of charity work. He sponsors teams in low-income areas and donates his time to hold workshops for young players. For someone who had no interest in having kids of his own, he sure does a lot for them." She took note of the hippie-style clothing in a host of bright colors piled on the bed and asked Joy, "Did you bring something to wear to the memorial?"

Joy made a face. "I don't do black."

Sierra sighed, watching her hang her clothes and lay them neatly on the bed to be put in the closet. "It doesn't have to be black. Just not so…bright. If I don't have anything that fits you, we can go shopping tomorrow after your audition."

"You know I don't have any money."

"But I do. Coop advanced me a month's pay so I could pay for the memorial service."

"That was nice of him." She paused then said with a grin, "I suppose it had nothing to do with the fact that you put out."

She glared at her sister. "Not that it's any of your business, but he offered it *before* I slept with him. And only because I refused to let him pay for the memorial himself. He's always trying to do things like that for me."

"Wow, that must be rough. I know I would hate having a rich, sexy man try to take care of me. How can you stand it?"

Sierra leaned close to give her sister a playful swat on the behind. "I almost forgot what a smart ass you are."

Joy smiled. "I've been told it's one of my most charming qualities."

It could be. But then there were the times when it was just plain annoying.

"You know I like to take care of myself," Sierra said, and now that she no longer had to pay for their father's care, she could build herself a nice nest egg.

But how would that work exactly? Now that she and Coop were a couple, would he keep paying her, or would he expect her to care for the girls for free?

It was just one of many things that they would have to discuss. Like how far he wanted to take this relationship. Would she be his perpetual live-in girlfriend, or was he open to the idea of marriage some day? Would he want more kids, or were the twins going to be it for him? And if being with the twins meant sacrificing a little, wasn't it worth it?

She still wasn't one-hundred percent sure that moving into his bedroom at this early stage in their relationship was a good idea. Yes, technically they were living together, but sleeping in the same room after being lovers for less than twenty-four hours seemed to be pushing the boundaries of respectability.

"You know you're going to have to tell him the truth," Joy said.

And there lay her other problem—telling Coop she

was the twins' birth mother. But what would be even more difficult would be telling him about the birth father. "I'll tell him when the time is right."

"Honestly, I'm surprised he hasn't figured it out on his own. They look just like you."

"We were at a café yesterday morning and the woman at the next table assumed we were the twins' parents. She said they looked just like me, but have their daddy's eyes."

"What did Coop say?"

"He doesn't see it, I guess."

"If you want this thing with Coop to go anywhere, you have to be honest with him."

"I'm in love with him."

Joy looped an arm around her shoulder. "Si, you can't start a relationship based on lies. Trust me. I know this from personal experience."

She laid her head on her sister's shoulder. "How did I get myself into this mess?"

"He'll understand."

"Will he?"

"If he loves you he will."

The trouble was, she didn't know if he loved her or not. He hadn't said he did, but of course, neither had she. It was one thing to feel it, but to actually put it out there, to leave herself so vulnerable…it scared her half to death. Especially when she was pretty sure that for him, his affection for her was in part motivated by his desire to do right by the twins. Was it her that he cared about, or was it the idea of what their relationship symbolized? His mental image of the perfect family.

If she did tell him the truth—*when* she told him—would his feelings for her be strong enough to take such a direct blow? And what if she didn't tell him? Would it really be so bad? What if knowing the truth changed his perception of his relationship to the girls? What if it did more damage than good? There was no way that he could ever find out on his own.

Joy took her hand and grasped it firmly, and as if she were reading Sierra's mind said, "Si, you have to tell him."

"I will." Probably. Maybe.

"When?"

"When the time is right." If it ever was.

Eleven

Sierra and Coop had just gotten the girls settled for the night and into bed, and he had slipped into his office to answer the phone, when Joy exploded through the front door of the apartment in a whirl of color and exuberance and announced at the top of her lungs, "I got it!"

She'd had her audition that morning and had been waiting all day for a callback, pacing the apartment like a restless panther, whining all through dinner that if she hadn't heard something by now, she wasn't going to and that her career as an actress was over. When Sierra couldn't take it a minute longer, she'd given her money and sent her out to find a dress for the memorial. Apparently she'd found one.

"That was fast," she said, setting the girls' empty bottles in the kitchen sink. "Let's see it."

"See it?" Joy said, looking confused.

"The dress." She turned to her sister, realizing that Joy wasn't holding a bag.

"I didn't get a dress. I got the *role*."

Confused, she said, "I thought if they were interested, they would have you in for a second audition."

"Normally they would, but they were so impressed with my performance and thought I was so perfect for the role, they offered me the part!"

"Oh my gosh!" Her baby sister was going to play the leading role in a movie! "Joy, that is so awesome!"

She threw her arms around her sister and hugged her, and that's how Coop found them a second later when he came out of his office.

"I heard shouting," he said.

"Joy got the part," Sierra said.

"Hey, that's great!" Coop said, looking genuinely happy for her. "I hope you'll remember us little guys when you're a big Hollywood star."

Joy laughed. "Let's not get ahead of ourselves. Although this could open some major doors for me. And honestly, I'm just thrilled to have a job. I had to give up my waitressing job to come here. If it wasn't for my friend Jerry letting me stay at his place, I would be out on the streets until filming starts."

"When is that?" Sierra asked.

"Early August in Vancouver, and we wrap in September."

"I've played in Vancouver," Coop said. "You'll love it there."

"Oh, my God!" Joy said, practically vibrating with excitement. "I can't believe I actually got it!"

Joy was usually so negative and brooding, it was nice to see her happy for a change. Sierra was about to suggest they celebrate when the doorbell rang.

"That's Vlad and Niko," Coop said, heading for the

door. "Former teammates. They called to say they were stopping by."

He pulled the door open and on the other side stood two very large, sharply dressed Russian men. One looked to be around Coop's age and the other was younger. Early twenties maybe. Both men smelled as if they had bathed in cologne.

Sierra heard Joy suck in a quiet breath and say, "Yum."

"Ladies, this is Vlad," Coop said, gesturing to the older man, "And this is Niko. Guys, this is my girlfriend, Sierra, and her sister, Joy."

Neither man could mask his surprise. Sierra was assuming that men like Coop didn't usually have "girlfriends."

"Is good to meet you," Vlad said with a thick accent, addressing Sierra, but Niko's eyes were pinned on Joy, and she was looking back at him as if he were a juicy steak she would like to sink her teeth into. If she weren't a vegetarian, that is.

"You come out with us," Vlad told Coop. "Big party at the Web's place. You bring girlfriend. And sister, too."

"The Web?" Sierra asked.

"Jimmy Webster," Coop told her. "The Scorpions goalie. He's known for his wild parties. And thanks for the invitation, guys, but I'm going to have to pass."

"You must come," Vlad said. "I don't take no for answer."

Coop shrugged. "I have to be here for the twins."

"But you have nanny for twins," Vlad said.

"Actually, I'm the nanny," Sierra said, which got her a curious look from both men. She could just imagine what they were thinking. How cliché it must have appeared. The starry-eyed nanny falls for the famous athlete.

Sierra turned to Coop. "You go. I'll stay here and watch the girls."

"See," Vlad said. "Is okay. You come with us."

Instead of darting off to change, Coop looped an arm around her shoulder and said, "No can do. Sorry."

Sierra wasn't exactly crazy about the idea of him going to a party where there would be women more beautiful and desirable than her lobbying to be his next conquest, but it was something she would just have to get used to. She couldn't expect him to give up his friends and his social life just because she lacked the party mentality. "It's really okay. Go be with your friends."

"Web's parties are really only good for two things—getting wasted and picking up women. I'm well past my partying days, and the only woman I want is standing next to me."

If he was just saying that to keep from hurting her feelings, she couldn't tell. He looked as though he meant it, and it made her feel all warm and fuzzy inside.

"How about you?" Niko said, his gaze still pinned on Joy. "You come to party."

It was more of a demand than a question, which would have annoyed Sierra, but Joy smiled a catlike grin and said, "I'll go grab my purse."

"Do you think she'll be okay?" Sierra asked after they left, Joy draped on the younger player's arm. Not that she didn't think Joy could hold her own, but she didn't know the Russian guys, and she was still Sierra's baby sister. She would always feel responsible for her.

"Those guys are harmless," Coop assured her. "It

looks as though she already has Niko wrapped around her finger."

"Men have always been helpless to resist her beauty." And usually got way more than they bargained for. Joy was beautiful and sexy, but she was also moody and temperamental. It would take a special kind of man to put up with her antics. In the long term, that is.

"Why don't you come sit down?" Coop said, nudging her toward the couch.

"Let me finish up in the kitchen real quick." She had been doing her best to keep things tidy until Coop found a new housekeeper, but she'd been tied up a good part of the day finalizing the details for the memorial, and already clutter was beginning to form on every flat surface and the furniture had developed a very fine layer of dust.

"Leave it for tomorrow," he said, trying to steer her toward the couch, but she ducked under his arm. She already had a full day tomorrow.

"Five minutes," she said, heading into the kitchen.

Coop stretched out in his chair and turned on ESPN as she finished loading the dishwasher and wiped down the countertops. Ms. Densmore had kept them polished to a gleaming shine, but under Sierra's care they were looking dull and hazy. She poked through the cleaning closet for something to polish them, but after reading the label decided it was too much work to start tonight. She fished out one of those disposable duster thingies instead, but as she started to dust the living room furniture Coop looked up from the sports show he was watching and said, "What are you doing? Come sit down and relax."

"The apartment is filthy," she said.

"And we'll have a new housekeeper in a few days."

He reached over and linked his hand around her wrist, pulling her down into his lap. He took the duster and flung it behind him onto the floor, creating an even bigger mess of the room. Then he pressed a soft kiss to her lips. "This should be our alone time."

And she still felt guilty for making him stay home or making him feel as though he had to. "Are you sure you're not upset about missing the party? Because you can still go."

"I didn't want to go. If it had been one of the married guys having a party, then sure, but only if we got a sitter and you came with me."

"I'm really not the party type."

"You wouldn't like a party where the couples are all married and instead of getting hammered and hooking up, they talk about preschools and which diapers are the most absorbent?"

"They do not."

"They do, seriously. I used to think they were totally insane. What could be more boring? Now I totally get it."

"I guess I wouldn't mind a party like that," she said.

"The married guys on the team are very family oriented, and I think you would like the wives. They're very down-to-earth and friendly. Everyone gets together for barbecues during the summer. We should go sometime."

That actually sounded like fun. There was only one problem. "You said it's the players and their wives, but I'm not your wife."

"Not yet. But there are girlfriends, too. The point is, it's not a meat market."

Sierra's breath backed up in her chest. Did he really just say "not yet," as in, someday she would be? Was he actually suggesting that he intended to make her an honest woman?

"We don't have to go," Coop said.

"No, I'd like to."

"Are you sure? Because you just had a really funny look on your face."

"It wasn't that. I just didn't know… I didn't realize how you felt about that. About us."

His brow wrinkled. "I'm not sure what you mean."

"I said 'I'm not your wife,' and you said 'not yet.'"

His frown deepened. "Are you saying that you wouldn't want to be my wife?"

"No! Of course not. I just didn't know that you would *want* me to be. That you ever wanted to get married. You strike me as the perpetual bachelor type."

"It's not as if at some point I decided that I would never get married. To be honest, I was jealous as hell of Ash. He found the perfect partner for himself, and they were so happy. I just haven't had any luck finding the right one for me. I may not be ready for a trip down the aisle right now, but eventually, sure. Isn't that what everyone wants?"

The question was: Did he want to take that trip with her? That was definitely what he was implying, right? And how long was eventually? Months? A year? Ten years? She'd never been in a relationship serious enough to even consider marriage, so how long did it take to get to the wedding? Or the proposal? After he got down on one knee, how long before they said *I do?*

"You know," he said, nuzzling her cheek, nibbling her ear, sending a delicious little shiver of pleasure up her spine. "You came to bed so late last night we never got to test out that condom theory."

She and Joy had sat up until almost three last night

talking, and Coop had been sound asleep by the time she slipped into bed beside him. "But we have the place all to ourselves now," she said, turning in his lap so she was straddling him. She reached down and tugged at the hem of his T-shirt, pulling it up over his head. He was so beautiful, it was still a little hard to believe that a man like him would want someone like her. But she could feel by the hard ridge between her thighs that he did.

She pulled her shirt up over her head and tossed it on the floor with his. He made a rumbly sound in his throat and wrapped his big, warm hands over her hips.

"You are the sexiest woman on the planet," he said, sliding his hands upward, skimming her bra cups with his thumbs. He sure made her feel as if she were. So why did she have the nagging feeling that it wasn't destined to last, that she was a novelty, and at some point the shine would wear thin? That he was going to miss the parties and the running around.

Either way, it was too late now. She was hooked. She loved him, and maybe someday he would learn to love her, too. They could make this work. She would be such a good wife, and keep him so happy, he wouldn't ever want to let her go.

For the twins' sake she had to at least try.

Holy freaking hell.

Coop lay spread-eagled on his back in bed, the covers tangled around his ankles, sweat beading his brow, still quaking with aftershocks from what was hands down the most intense orgasm he'd ever had. Making love to Sierra without the barrier of latex, to really feel her for the first time, was the hottest, most erotic experience of his life.

"So is it true?" Sierra asked, grinning down at him, still straddling his lap, her skin rosy with the afterglow of her own pleasure. Looking smug as hell. "Is it better without a condom?"

He tried to scowl at her, but he felt so good, so relaxed, he couldn't muster the energy. "You're evil," he said instead, and her smile widened. He should have known, when she insisted on being on top, that she was up to something. That she intended to humiliate him again. But even he couldn't deny it was the most pleasurable humiliation he'd ever had to endure.

"You beat me by what, five seconds?" she said.

No thanks to her. He had obviously been having trouble holding it together, but instead of giving him a few seconds to get a grip, she had to go and do that thing with his nipples, which of course had instantly set him off.

For someone who claimed not to have much experience with men, she sure knew which buttons to push.

"It's the principle of the thing," he told her. "The man should never come first."

"That's just dumb."

"Yeah, well, as soon as I can breathe again, you're in trouble." He wrapped his arms around her and pulled her down against his chest, kissing the smirk off her face. Sierra slid down beside him, curling up against his side. It felt as if that was exactly where she belonged. Beside him. It was astounding to him what adding an emotional connection could do to crank up the level of intimacy. He had never felt as close to anyone, as connected to another person. He had no doubt that she would be the perfect wife. A good mother, a good friend and an exceptional lover. And he knew that once she met his friends, and trusted them enough to drop her guard a little, she would fit right in.

Yeah, she wasn't much of a housekeeper, and her expertise in the kitchen was pretty much limited to things she could heat in the microwave, but he could hire people to do that. In all the ways that counted, she was exactly the sort of woman he would want as a companion. She was predictable and uncomplicated…what you see is what you get. And she was as devoted to the twins, to taking care of them, as he was. Never had he imagined finding someone so completely perfect. He'd never been one to believe in cosmic forces, but he was honestly beginning to think that fate had brought them together. She had been thrust into some pretty rotten circumstances, and like him she had come out swinging. In fact, in a lot of ways they were very much alike.

So why couldn't he shake the feeling that she was holding something back? That she didn't completely trust him. He was sure it had more to do with her own insecurities than anything he had done. She just needed time. Time to trust him and believe him when he said that he wanted to make this work. That he wanted them to be a family.

But as her hand slid south down his stomach, he decided that he had plenty of time to worry about that later.

Twelve

When Sierra got back from her morning walk with the twins the next day, Joy was awake—a surprise considering she didn't wander in until after 4:00 a.m.—and she was dusting the living room dressed in yoga pants and a sport bra. And she somehow made it look glamorous.

"You don't have to do that," Sierra told her, taking the twins from the stroller and sitting them in their ExerSaucers.

"Someone has to do it."

"I'll get around to it."

Joy shot her a look. "No you won't. You hate cleaning."

She couldn't deny it. People would naturally think that Joy, being such a free spirit, would be the one with the aversion to cleaning, and Sierra, the responsible one, would be neat as a pin, but the opposite was true.

"If you decide to have anyone come back here after the memorial tomorrow, it should at least be tidy," Joy said.

"Well, thank you. I'm sure Coop will appreciate it."

"Consider it payment for letting me stay here. And introducing me to Niko. He's too adorable for words."

"How was the party?"

"Wild. Those hockey dudes really know how to have a good time."

Sierra walked into the kitchen to fix the twins' bottles and nearly gasped when she realized that it was spotless and the granite had been polished to a gleaming shine. "Oh my gosh! It looks amazing in here!"

Joy shrugged, like it was no big deal. "I like cleaning. It relieves stress."

She took after their dad in that respect. And Sierra was like their mom, who was more interested in curling up with a book or taking a long, leisurely walk in the park or working in the local community garden. Their home had been messy but happy. Even when they found the cancer, it hadn't knocked her spirits down, or if it had, she never let it show. Not even when she had been too sick from the chemo to eat or when the pain must have been excruciating. She had taken it in stride up until the very end.

It would be twelve years in September, and though the pain of losing her had dulled, Sierra still missed her as keenly as she had that first year. She missed her warm hugs, and her gentle voice. Her playful nature. Why sit inside cleaning bedrooms and doing homework when there was a world full of adventures to explore? Sierra only hoped that she would be as good a mother, as good a wife as her mom had been.

She poured juice into bottles and carried them to the

living room for the twins. "Do you still miss her?" she asked Joy.

"Miss who?" she asked, though Sierra had the feeling she knew exactly who she meant.

"Mom. It'll be twelve years this fall."

Joy shrugged. "I guess."

"You *guess?*" How could she *not* miss her?

"You were always closer with her than I was."

"What are you talking about? Of course I wasn't."

Joy stopped dusting and turned to her. "Si, come on. Half the time she didn't even know we were there, and the other half she spent doting on you. You two were just alike, she used to say."

"Yes, she and I were more alike, but she didn't love you any less."

"Didn't it ever bother you that the entire world seemed to revolve around her? Dad ran himself ragged working two jobs, and half the time she wouldn't even have dinner fixed when he got home. We would end up eating sandwiches or fast food."

"Not everyone is a good cook," Sierra said.

"But she didn't even try. And the apartment was always a mess. It was as if she was allergic to cleaning or something. Dad got one day a week off, and he would have to spend it vacuuming and picking up all the junk she and you left all over."

Sierra couldn't believe she would talk about their mom like that, that she even felt that way. "She was a good wife and mother. Dad adored her."

"She was a flake, and dad was miserable. My bed was right next to the wall and I could hear them fighting when they thought we were asleep."

"All couples fight sometimes."

"Sure, but with them it was a nightly thing."

Sierra shook her head. "No, they were happy."

"Look, believe me or don't believe me, I really don't care. I know what I heard. I don't doubt that Dad loved her, but he *wasn't* happy."

Maybe their mom could be a little self-centered at times, but she loved her family, all of them equally, despite what Joy believed. She did her best. If that wasn't good enough for Joy, that was *her* problem.

Joy's cell phone, which was sitting on the coffee table, started to ring and she dashed over to grab it.

"It's Jerry!" she said excitedly, who Sierra remembered was the "friend" she had been staying with. "Did you get my message? I got the part!" She flopped down on the couch and propped her feet on the coffee table. "I know! Isn't it awesome… No, not until August. Maybe you can come visit me there."

There was a pause, and Joy's smile began to disintegrate. "No, I don't have anyone else I can stay with until then. Why?" Joy sat up as outrage crept over her features. "What do you mean she's moving back in? You told me that you're getting divorced!"

Another married boyfriend? What was Joy's fixation with unavailable men? Why couldn't she find a nice, single guy? One who wouldn't screw her over and break her heart.

Joy jerked to her feet, shouting into the phone, "You sleazy-ass son of a bitch. You've been planning this since before I left, haven't you? You were never going to fumigate. You just wanted my stuff out so you could move her back in. I could have had a totally hot Russian guy last night, but I was being faithful to you, you big jerk! He was young and hot and I'll bet he doesn't have any of your *performance* problems."

Whoa. Maybe this was a conversation best kept private. Not that she thought Joy gave a damn if Sierra heard. She liked that element of drama. *Clearly.*

Joy listened, looking angrier by the second, then growled, "Take your apologies and shove them, you heartless bastard." She disconnected the call, blew out a frustrated breath and said, "Well, *crap.*"

"You okay?" Sierra asked.

Joy collapsed back onto the couch. "It's official, I'm homeless."

"I meant about Jerry. You were dating him?"

She shrugged. "I don't know if you would actually call it dating. He gave me a place to stay and I kept him company."

Sierra could just imagine what that entailed.

"I mean, I liked him, but it's not as if we had some sort of future. He's kind of old to be thinking long term."

"How old?"

"Fifty-two."

Sierra's jaw dropped. "He's *thirty* years older than you?"

"Like I said, I didn't want to marry the guy. It was just…convenient."

Sierra raised a brow.

"For *both* of us. He liked having a much younger companion to flaunt, and I liked having a roof over my head."

"You liked him enough to be faithful to him," Sierra said.

Joy shrugged. "He was a nice guy. Or so I thought."

Sierra had the feeling Joy cared about him more than she wanted to admit. "So, what are you going to do?"

"I have no idea. I gave up my waitressing job for this trip and the film doesn't start shooting until the end of

August. Even if I could find another job it would be a month before I could afford first and last months' rent."

"Can't you get some sort of signing bonus?"

She shook her head. "It's very low budget. My salary will barely cover living expenses."

"So what are you going to do? Stay with another friend?"

"When you mooch off everyone you know, eventually you run out of people to mooch off. But don't worry," she said, pushing herself back up off the couch and grabbing the duster. "I'll figure something out. I always do."

Sierra was a little surprised that Joy hadn't asked if she could stay with her and Coop. Maybe she knew Sierra would say no. It was one thing to have her stay for a short visit, but for more than a month? If she had her own place, no problem, but she would never ask Coop for that kind of favor.

Joy was a big girl. She was going to have to figure this one out on her own.

Coop sat at the conference table in his lawyer's office, fisting his hands in his lap, struggling to keep his cool, to keep his expression passive.

"We agreed on a price," he told his former boss, Mike Norris, the current owner of the New York Scorpions. A price that had been a couple million less than what he wanted today.

The arrogant bastard sat back in his chair, an unlit cigar clamped between his teeth, wearing a smug smile. Flanking him were his business manager and his lawyer, both of whom were as overweight, out of shape and devoid of human decency as Mike.

"My team, my terms," Mike said. "Take it or leave it."

He knew how badly Coop wanted it, and he was trying to use it to his advantage. The paperwork had been drawn up and Coop came here thinking that they would be signing to lock in the terms. But Mike had gotten greedy. Coop should have seen this coming, he should have known the son of a bitch would pull something at the last minute.

At the price they had agreed on last week, buying the team would have had its risks, but it was still what he considered a sound investment. At the price Mike was demanding now, Coop would be putting too much on the line. His conservative nature with money was responsible for his healthy portfolio. If it were just his financial future hanging in the balance, he might say what the hell and go for it, but he had the twins to consider now. Sierra, too, although he doubted his money was a motivating factor in her feelings toward him. In fact, he was pretty sure she was intimidated by it. It was one of her most appealing qualities.

"Why the hesitation, Landon?" Mike said. "You know you want it, and we all know you can afford it. If you're hesitating because you think I'm going to back down, it ain't gonna happen." He leaned in toward the table, his belly flab preventing him from getting very close. "Just say yes and we've got a deal."

Even if he had planned to say yes, to give Mike what he wanted, that would have killed the deal.

He wanted that team, wanted it more than anything in his life, and giving it up would be one of the hardest things he would ever have to do, but it would be for the best. He glanced over at Ben, whose expression seemed to say that he knew what was coming, then Coop pushed back from the table and stood. "Sorry, gentleman, but I'm going to have to pass."

He started for the door and Mike called after him, sounding a little less smug now. "This deal is only good this afternoon. After today the price goes up again."

Mike thought Coop was bluffing. He wasn't. And though Coop wanted to tell him to shove his threat where the sun don't shine, he restrained himself. He was dying to see Mike's expression as he left, but he resisted the urge to turn and look as he walked out the conference room door and down the hall to Ben's office.

He sat down, taking long, deep breaths, fisting his hands in his lap when what he wanted to do was wrap them around that smug bastard's throat.

Ben walked in the office several minutes later, presumably after seeing the other men out.

"Coop, I'm sorry. I had no idea they were going to pull that."

Coop shrugged. "It's not your fault."

"You have every right to be furious. I know how much you wanted this."

It wasn't just about owning the team and the money that it would bring in. He cared about those guys. Mike was an old-school businessman who, until he bought the team five years ago, had never even been to a hockey game. For him it was nothing more than an investment. He knew nothing about the game and had been running the team into the ground since he took over. He didn't care about the players—his only goal was to pad his pockets. And the players knew it. They also knew that when Coop was at the helm, things would change. They would be back on top.

He felt as if he was letting them down.

"I don't know what I'm going to tell the guys."

"You're going to tell them exactly what happened.

Norris screwed you. But don't consider this over. Not yet. You should have seen Norris's face when you walked out. He really thought he had you. I wouldn't be too surprised if we get a call from him in a day or two backing down on his price."

"If he does, make it clear that I'm not paying him a penny over what we originally agreed on."

"There's something else we need to talk about," Ben said, and the furrow in his brow made Coop think that whatever it was, it wasn't good. "I didn't want to say anything before we signed the deal, and now probably isn't the best time after what happened in there…"

Whatever it was, it couldn't be much worse than what he'd just gone through. "Just tell me."

"A source at the National Transportation Safety Board has informed me that the official report on the plane crash is going to be released Monday."

Coop's heart clenched in his chest, then climbed up into his throat. "Did this source tell you what's in the report."

"They're calling it pilot error."

"No way!" Coop shot up from his seat. "No way it was pilot error. Your source must have it wrong."

"According to the report there were narcotics recovered from the scene."

"Which wouldn't surprise me in the least. Susan hurt her back a week before the trip. She ruptured a disc. It was so painful she couldn't even pick the twins up. I'm sure her doctor can confirm that. And she wasn't flying the plane."

"He said they found narcotics and marijuana in both Susan and Ash's systems."

No way. He knew that Ash and Susan smoked occasionally, but Ash would *never* take anything and then operate a plane. "I don't believe it. I know my brother, Ben. Ash would never take drugs and fly."

"We'll know more when we get a copy of the report, but if it's true, all hell is going to break loose and the vultures are going to descend. You might even want to get out of town for a few days, or even a week or two. Until things die down."

With the deal falling through he had nothing pressing to keep him in town, and frankly, he could use a vacation. "We have the memorial for Sierra's dad tomorrow, but after that there's nothing keeping me in the city. I think a trip to my place in Cabo might be in order."

"How is it working out with Sierra?"

Coop scrubbed a hand across his jaw. "Um…well, better than I anticipated, actually."

Ben narrowed his eyes. "Oh, yeah, how much better?"

A smile tugged at the corners of his mouth. "She moved into my bedroom two nights ago."

"I distinctly recall you telling me that you weren't going to sleep with her."

"It wasn't something I planned. But she's just so… extraordinary."

"So it's serious?"

"Yeah, I think so. She's everything I didn't realize that I wanted in a woman."

Ben grinned and shook his head. "I had no idea you were such a romantic, Coop. You should needlepoint that on a pillow."

"Who'd have thought, right? But she's smart and funny and beautiful, and the twins love her. And she doesn't seem to give a damn about my money."

"Should I start drafting the prenup?"

"Let's not get ahead of ourselves." Besides, he couldn't imagine making Sierra sign one of those. It would be the same as saying that he didn't trust her. He was a pretty good judge of character and as far as he could tell, she didn't have a deceitful bone in her body.

Ben eyed him warily. "You do plan to have a prenup, right? Assuming that you're going to marry her eventually."

"I'm definitely going to marry her. Eventually. But as far as a prenup…I don't think that's going to be necessary. She's not after my money."

"Not now, maybe…"

"I trust her, Ben."

"It's not about trust. It's about protecting you both in the case of a divorce."

"That would never happen. She's it for me. I know she is."

"One of my partners specializes in divorce, and the horror stories he could tell you—"

"That wouldn't happen to me and Sierra. We both come from very stable, loving homes. We aren't products of divorce. Her parents were happily married and so were mine. Whatever problems we might have, we would work them out."

"You're rationalizing."

"I'm being realistic."

"So am I."

"To even ask would feel like a betrayal. It would be like saying that I don't trust her."

"If the two of you have such a great relationship, I would think she would understand. The least you could do is ask. If she balks, I might reconsider my position on the matter."

"She won't."

"Promise me that you'll at least consider it."

"I will. And like I said, we have no immediate plans to get hitched. I haven't even proposed yet."

"Just keep it in mind when you do."

In a way Coop wished he hadn't said anything to Ben about marrying her. What with the sour deal, the accident report and Ben's prenup lecture, Coop left his office feeling downright depressed.

But on the bright side, things couldn't get much worse.

Thirteen

Coop caught a cab back home, getting out a block early so he could pick up a bouquet of flowers for Sierra from a street vendor. Remembering that they had never really had a chance to celebrate Joy's new job, he got her one, too. He walked the rest of the way home, the sun's heat beating down on his shoulders and back, melting the tension that had settled into his bones. Which made a week or two in a sunny locale sound even more appealing. If they left Sunday, they would be long gone before the backlash from the NTSB report hit the media.

The doorman greeted Coop as he headed inside and he had the elevator all to himself on the ride up. He opened the apartment door and the scent of something delicious tantalized his senses. Something that smelled too good to have come from a microwave. He dropped his keys on the entryway table and walked into the living room, realizing that not only was someone cooking, but also someone had cleaned. The apartment was spotless.

Sierra appeared from the hallway, jerking with surprise when she saw him standing there. "Hey! Hi, I didn't hear you come in."

At the sight of her, his heart instantly lifted, a smile tugged at his lips and all the crap that happened today, all the rotten news, didn't seem so terrible any longer. "I just got here."

"I just put the girls down for a nap." Her eyes settled on the bouquets he was carrying. "Nice flowers."

"One for you," he said, handing her the larger of the two.

"Thank you!" She pushed up on her toes and kissed him. "I can't even remember the last time someone gave me flowers."

"This one is for Joy," he said of the second bouquet. "To say congratulations. Is she here?"

"She ran down to the market. She should be back soon. In the meantime why don't I put them in water? They look like they're starting to wilt."

"It's hot as blazes out."

"I know. It was pretty warm and sticky when we took our walk this morning. Do you have a vase?"

He shrugged. "I recall Ms. Densmore setting out fresh flowers, but if there is a vase I have no idea where it would be."

He followed her to the kitchen, where she began to search for something to put the flowers in.

"Whatever you're making, it smells delicious."

"It's some sort of Mexican casserole, but I can't take credit. Joy said she was tired of carryout. But I'll warn you that it's vegetarian."

He didn't care, as long as it tasted good. Because

frankly, he was tired of carryout, too. He'd been spoiled by Ms. Densmore's home-cooked meals and the five-star dinning that he'd grown used to.

He opened the fridge and grabbed a beer, noticing that someone had even cleaned out the food that had begun to spoil. "The apartment looks great, by the way."

"Also thanks to Joy," she said, rising up on her toes to peer in the cabinet above the refrigerator. "She went through here like a maniac this morning."

He twisted the cap off his beer and took a long pull. "She doesn't strike me as the type who would like to clean."

"You wouldn't think it to look at her, but Joy is far more domestically gifted than I am," she said, going through another cupboard with no luck. "She says it relieves stress. And she was pretty stressed out today."

"Is she nervous about the film role?"

"No, apparently the much older guy that she was living with decided to move his wife back in, so she's got nowhere to live and no job when she goes back to L.A."

"What is she going to do?"

Sierra shrugged. "Joy is twenty-two. It's time she started taking responsibility for herself. She can't be the reckless kid any longer."

Joy may have been a bit irresponsible, but she was still family. He knew from personal experience that pursuing dreams took sacrifice, and it sounded as if this film role was the break she had been working toward. He knew Sierra wasn't in a position to help her out, and though he knew she would never ask him to help Joy, he could. In fact, he had a pretty good idea how he could do it, without actually appearing to do it.

Sierra finally found the vases in the very back of one of the lower cabinets and pulled out two. "These should work."

She set them on the countertop, then turned to him. "I almost forgot, how did your meeting go?"

"The deal fell through."

"What! What happened?"

He told her how Norris had raised his price and that he had turned him down. "Ben seems to think that he'll come around, but I'm not holding my breath."

"I'm so sorry, Coop. I know how much you wanted this."

"I'm more concerned about the guys on the team. Since Norris took over he's been running the team into the ground. They were counting on me to turn things around."

"They're your friends. They respect you. I'm sure they'll understand."

"I hope so."

As she was filling the vases with water the front door opened and Joy stepped inside, weighed down with more plastic grocery bags than one person should carry. Coop set his beer down and rushed over to help her. "I hope Sierra gave you money out of the house account for all this," he said, carrying several bags to the kitchen.

"Since I'm broke and my shoplifting days are over—" she set her bags down on the granite with a thunk "—she had no choice."

"Look what Coop got you," Sierra said, dropping Joy's bouquet into a vase.

"Well, damn, wasn't that sweet of you." Joy leaned close and inhaled the scent of the blooms. "They're lovely. Thanks."

"Originally I bought them to say congratulations, but I think they work better as a thank-you for cleaning the apartment and cooking dinner."

"It's the least I can do. Besides," she added, shooting Sierra a wry smile, "you've probably noticed my sister isn't much of a housekeeper. Or a cook."

Sierra gave her a playful jab in the arm. "And let's see you balance a checkbook or pay your rent on time."

"Gotta find a place to live before I can pay rent, don't I?"

She had just given him the perfect segue. "Sierra mentioned that your living arrangements have changed, and I wondered if that meant you might not be going back to L.A."

She collapsed on one of the stools, looking thoroughly frustrated. "Honestly, I'm not sure what I'm going to do. I want to go back to L.A., but I might have a better chance finding a job here."

"Can I offer a third option?"

She shrugged. "I'm open to pretty much anything at this point."

"Then how do you feel about Mexico?"

"You think you're pretty sneaky, don't you?" Sierra called to Coop from bed later that night when they were in their room with the door closed. It was still a little strange to think of it as *their* room, but she was feeling more comfortable there. It was decorated in warmer colors than the spare room, with traditionally styled cherrywood furniture, including a king-size bed so huge she could get lost in it. Though there wasn't much chance of that happening, considering that Coop was a cuddler. She was used to sleeping alone, so sharing a bed would take a bit of getting used to, but she couldn't deny the pleasures of waking spooned with a warm, naked and aroused man.

Coop stuck his head out of the bathroom, a toothbrush wedged in his mouth. "If brushing one's teeth can be considered sneaky," he said around a mouthful of toothpaste.

She shot him a look. "Two weeks in Mexico?"

He grinned. "Oh, *that*."

He was gone again, and she heard the water running, then he walked out of the bathroom.

"You knew Joy didn't have anywhere to go," she said. "And rather than making her figure this out on her own—"

"In my defense, I had already planned to take the trip, and I would have invited her to come with us even if she did have a place in L.A. to go back to." He sat on the edge of the mattress to untie his shoes. "But yes, I'm trying to help her. Is there something wrong with that?"

"I just worry that she's never going to learn to be responsible, to take care of herself."

"She seems to have done okay until now. And following your dream takes sacrifice. That I know from personal experience."

Maybe he had a point. Besides, this way she would get to spend a little more time with Joy because who knew when she would talk to her again?

He kicked his shoes off, peeled off his socks, then stood and pulled his shirt over his head. His jeans went next, then his boxers.

Nice.

He looked so good naked, it was a shame he couldn't walk around like that all the time.

He gathered his clothes and dropped them in the

hamper, then he pulled the covers back and slipped into bed beside her. But instead of pulling her into his arms and kissing her, like he normally would, he rolled onto his side facing her, wearing a troubled expression. He'd been unusually quiet all night, and she had a pretty good idea what was on his mind. He'd mentioned the accident report being released and what his lawyer's source had said it contained. And though he had clearly been disturbed, he'd seemed hesitant to discuss it. Maybe because Joy had been there, or maybe he just hadn't been ready to deal with it. But maybe now he was.

She rolled onto her side facing him and asked, "Are you thinking about Ash and Susan?"

He drew in a deep breath and blew it out. "I just keep thinking, there has to be some sort of mistake."

She hated to believe that the people she had entrusted her children to could be so irresponsible, but facts were facts. If the report said there were drugs in their systems, then there probably were.

"I *know* Ash," Coop said. "He just wouldn't do something like that."

And she knew for a fact that he didn't know everything about Ash. Everyone had secrets and did things that they weren't proud of. Everyone made mistakes.

"If it had been faulty equipment or turbulent weather…" He shook his head. "But pilot error? It just seems so senseless. How could he do that to Susan and the girls?"

"And you?"

"*Yes,* and me. After all we went through losing our parents, why would he put me through that again? I'm just so damned…*angry.*"

"I felt the same way about my mom."

"But she got sick. She couldn't help that."

"Actually, she could have. Joy doesn't know this, and I don't ever want her to know, but I overheard my dad talking to his sister a few months after the funeral. My mom had a cyst in her breast a couple of years earlier but it turned out to be benign. So when she found another lump, she assumed it was a cyst again."

"But it wasn't."

She shook her head. "By the time she went to the doctor, it had already metastasized. It was in her lungs and her bones. There really wasn't much they could do."

"And if she had gone in as soon as she found the lump?"

"Statistically, there's a seventy-three-percent chance she would be alive today. I was *so* angry at her, but being mad wouldn't bring her back. It just made me really miserable." She reached over and touched Coop's arm. "I'm sure your brother didn't get into that plane thinking that something like this would happen. People make mistakes."

"Come here," he said. She scooted closer and he wrapped his arms around her, pulling her against him chest to chest, bare skin against bare skin. Nice.

She closed her eyes and laid her head in the crook of his neck.

"I just want this to be over, so I can get on with my life," he said.

"It doesn't always work that way."

"I miss him."

"I know."

He buried his face against her hair, holding on so tight it was hard to breathe. "He was all I had left."

"You have the twins. They need you."

"And I need them. I never realized how much having

a child could change a man. I'm a better person because of them."

She pulled back so she could see his face. "You said before that you were worried you would let Susan and Ash down, but you've done such an awesome job with the twins. They would be so proud of you." She couldn't imagine being separated from the girls, but if that ever happened, she felt confident that they would be well taken care of. Coop would be a good dad. All the more reason for him not to know the truth. She didn't want to risk changing the way he felt about the girls. And yes, her, too.

"This is probably a really weird time to ask this," he said. "But what are your feelings on prenuptial agreements?"

The timing was a little weird. And it was the second time that week that he'd brought up the subject of marriage. "I haven't really given it much thought," she said. "I've never come close to getting married, and even if I had, the men I date aren't exactly rolling in money."

"But if someone asked you to sign one?"

He looked conflicted, as if he didn't really want to be talking about this. He had seen his attorney that morning, so she could only assume the subject had come up. Which meant he was discussing marrying her with other people now. That had to be a good sign, right?

She hadn't wanted to let herself believe it could really happen. She didn't want to get her hopes up only to have them crushed. But it was looking as though he was seriously planning to marry her. Why discuss a prenup with his attorney if he wasn't?

"I guess it would depend on who was asking," she said.

"What if *I* was asking?"

She shrugged. "I would say sure."

"You wouldn't be upset or hurt?"

"Considering what you're worth, I would think you were a moron if you didn't ask for one. I know you would be fair. And maybe you haven't noticed, but I'm not interested in your money."

A slow smile crept across his face. "Have I ever mentioned what an amazing woman you are?"

If he knew the truth, he may not think she was all that amazing. Learning that his brother may have been under the influence of drugs while flying would be nothing compared to the bombshell she could drop on him. And in this case, what he didn't know really couldn't hurt him. So what was the harm in keeping a secret that he had no chance in ever learning? Why, when things were so good, would she risk rocking the boat?

And if she was so sure it was okay, why did she feel so guilty? Would she ever be able to completely relax with Coop, or would she always feel the nagging feeling of something unsettled between them?

But then Coop pulled her closer, trailed kisses from her lips to her throat and down to her breasts, awakening a passion that she'd felt with no one before him. Like he said before, nothing that felt this good could be wrong. And some things were better left unsaid.

The last month had been the most blissful, most relaxing of Sierra's life. Coop's beachfront condo in Cabo San Lucas was like an oasis. And being out of the States and away from the media seemed to soften the blow of the NTSB report, which was just as bad as Ben's source had predicted.

She and Coop spent their days walking along the

beach or lounging by the pool, and the twins were like little mermaids in their matching swimsuits and floating rings. They *loved* the water, howling pitifully whenever she and Coop took them out. But with all the sun and activity, they were so exhausted by evening, they began to sleep peacefully through the night, leaving the adults plenty of alone time.

They spent their evenings out on the patio sipping wine and snacking on the local fare, and after dark they built bonfires. A few days after they arrived they met a young couple from Amsterdam, Joe and Trina, who were renting a neighboring condo and had a son close to the twins' age. For the next week both the kids and the parents became inseparable. Coop and Joe went golfing together while Sierra and Trina played with the kids by the pool or took them into the village to shop. The week flew by, and everyone was disappointed when Joe and Trina had to leave.

Sierra had hoped that the trip would mean spending some quality time with her sister, but Joy being Joy, she met a man and spent a considerable part of her time with him at his condo about a quarter of a mile down the shore.

When their two weeks were drawing to an end, no one felt ready to leave, and because Coop had no pressing business back in New York, he suggested they stay a third week. Then three weeks became four, and by the time they flew home—with Joy remaining in Mexico until she had to leave for Vancouver—July was practically over.

Everyone missed the sun and the beach and especially the pool. The twins were so despondent at first that Coop suggested they consider looking for a home upstate. Maybe something on a lake with a huge yard for the girls to play in and of course a pool. Sierra hadn't been sure if he was completely serious, but then he disappeared into his office and came out an hour later with a stack of real estate listings that he had printed out.

Life with Coop was more perfect than she could have imagined, and she was happier and more content than she'd ever been. But as close as she and Coop had become, she knew that deep inside she was holding something back. She loved Coop, but she still hadn't said the words. Of course, he hadn't said them, either, or brought up the subject of marriage again, but he'd shown his affection for her in a million other ways. She couldn't expect a man like Coop, who had never even had a steady relationship, to go all gooey and lovesick in his first few months out of the gate. These things took time. Maybe she was holding back because she didn't want to rush him, didn't want to make him feel as though he had to commit to feelings he wasn't quite ready to express. Or maybe she was holding back because of the secrets she couldn't bring herself to tell him.

"What do you think of this one?" Coop asked the week after they returned from their trip. The twins were down for their nap and Coop had called her into his office. He pulled her down into his lap so she could see the listing on his ginormous computer monitor.

"It just went on the market yesterday, and the Realtor thinks it's a great price for the area and probably won't be available for long."

The house itself was gorgeous. Big and beautiful and modern, with all the amenities they were looking for, and when she saw the listing price she practically swallowed her own tongue. "It's so expensive."

He shrugged. "It's half of what this place cost me. And after we settle into the house I'll put this place on the market. So technically I'll actually make money. The Realtor can take us through this afternoon. Maybe Lita can watch the kids for a couple of hours and we can go just the two of us.

Lita was the housekeeper Coop had hired right before they left for Cabo. She had taken care of the apartment while they were gone, and since they returned the twins had taken an immediate shine to her. Even better, she absolutely adored them. Her English wasn't the best, but she kept the apartment spotless, she was a decent cook, and most important, she had a very pleasant disposition. And having raised six kids of her own, she was also an experienced babysitter.

"Unless you don't like the house," Coop said, "In which case we'll keep looking."

"It looks really nice, but what I think doesn't really matter. You're buying it, not me."

"No, *we're* buying it. It's going to be your house as much as mine."

She wished that were true, but until they were married, it was his dime. No community property, no alimony if it didn't work out.

Coop shook his head and rubbed a hand across his jaw. "You don't believe me."

"It has nothing to do with me believing you."

"Then you don't trust me."

"It's not about that, either. We're living together, but technically we're still just dating. If you buy a house, it's going to be *your* house."

"Because we're not married."

She nodded.

"Well, maybe we should get married."

It took a second to process the meaning of his words. Had he really just asked her to marry him? She opened her mouth to reply, but no sound came out. She didn't know what to say. Was he seriously asking, or just throwing out suggestions?

"Is that a no?"

Oh, my God, he was asking, and he expected an answer. "Of course it isn't, I just—"

"Look," he said, turning her in his lap so he could look into her eyes, taking her hands in his and holding them gently. "I know this is hard for you. I know you have trust issues, and I've been trying really hard to give you space, to not overwhelm you, but I'm getting tired of holding back. I love you, Sierra. I know it's only been two months, but it's been the happiest two months of my life. I want to marry you and spend the rest of my life with you. I want us to adopt the girls together and be a real family. If it happens next week, or next year, I don't care. I just need to know that we're on the same page, that you want that, too."

More than he could imagine. "I do want that, and I had no idea you felt that way. I fell in love with you the first time you kissed me. I just didn't say anything because I didn't want to overwhelm *you*. I might have trust issues but not with you."

He grinned, sliding his arms around her. "Sounds like we had a slight breakdown of communication."

She looped her arms around his neck. "I guess we did."

"Let's promise that from now on, we tell each other exactly what we're feeling, that we don't hold anything back."

"I think that's a good idea."

He gave her a soft, sweet kiss. "So, if your answer isn't no…"

"Yes, I'll marry you."

He pulled her close and held her tight.

She loved Coop, and she wanted this, more than anything in her life. She thought about what Joy said, that they couldn't base this relationship on lies. But the truth could tear them apart forever.

Fourteen

Things were moving fast, but Coop liked it that way.

He rolled over in bed and reached for Sierra, but her side of the bed was cold. He squinted at the clock and was surprised to see that it was almost nine, which meant Sierra and the twins were probably taking their morning walk. And he needed to get his butt out of bed. They had a long, busy day ahead of them. After a week of negotiating, they would find out this morning if the sellers of the house they wanted had come back with a reasonable offer. After lunch they had a meeting planned with a wedding coordinator—one who came highly recommended from several of the players' wives—and after that Coop and Sierra were going ring shopping. They had been scouring the Internet for a week, trying to find the perfect one with no luck. She decided that if she was actually seeing them in person, putting them on her finger, something might click. They had a list of a dozen or so places in the city to look, including Cartier, Verdura and of course Tiffany's.

Coop pushed himself out of bed, showered and dressed, then wandered out to the kitchen, surprised to find Lita sitting on the living room floor playing with the twins.

"Good morning, Lita. Where is Miss Evans?"

"Morning, Mr. Landon. She have appointment. She say she leave note for you, on your desk."

"Thanks."

He gave the twins each a kiss on the tops of their heads, then poured himself a cup of coffee and carried it to his office.

He found Sierra's note on his desk by the phone. It said that Ben had called and needed him to call back ASAP. He had been drafting a prenup, even though Coop was still opposed to the idea, but Sierra had insisted.

He sat at his desk and dialed Ben's number.

"Are you sitting down?" Ben asked.

"Actually, yeah, why?"

"I got a call from Mike Norris's lawyer this morning. He wants to talk deal."

Coop's heart stalled in his chest. "You told him I won't budge on price?"

"He knows. Apparently Mike just wants to sell. It would seem that the players have been giving him a bit of a hard time lately."

Coop smiled. He had been worried that they would be angry, but instead they had rallied around him. They knew exactly what Norris was doing and they were pissed.

"When do they want to meet?" Coop asked.

"Tomorrow at three."

"Make it eleven—that way, when the deal is locked in, you and I can go out for lunch to celebrate."

"I'll let him know. Maybe you can come a little early and look over the final draft of the prenup. We made all the changes you asked for, although I still think you're being a little too generous."

"I know what I'm doing."

"I hope so."

He hung up wearing a grin. He had a hunch that Norris would come around, but until just now he hadn't let himself get his hopes up. He still didn't want to count his chickens, but it did sound as if Norris was ready to accept his offer. Everything was falling into place. Personally and professionally. It was almost too good to be true.

He glanced over at the boxes lining one wall of his office. Susan's mother had sent them over after she packed up Ash and Susan's belongings. Things she thought Coop would want. He hadn't been ready to deal with what he would find inside them, especially after reading the NTSB report. But Sierra had been right—being angry at Ash was irrational and counter-productive.

He walked over, grabbed one of the boxes and carried it to his desk. He took a slow, deep breath, telling himself it's like a Band-Aid. You just have to rip it off.

He grabbed the edge of the packing tape and ripped. He opened the flaps, and inside he found a stack of wrapped photo frames. One by one he pulled them from the box and extracted them from the packing. He found photos of Ash and Susan and the girls together. Photos of Ash and Coop with their parents from holidays and vacations, and a 5x7 of Ash and Coop at Coop's high school graduation—Coop in his cap and gown and Ash standing beside him, beaming like a proud parent.

Swallowing back an acute sting of sorrow, he set the photo aside to hang on his office wall.

At the very bottom of the box he found the twins' baby book. Smiling, he lifted it out and flipped through the pages. At the front there were pages and pages of prebirth information, filled in, he was assuming, by the birth mother. Then there was a section recording the events of the girls' first few months, and that was in Susan's handwriting. It contained their growth charts, their sleep and eating schedules, the date of their first smile and the first time eating cereal. A couple of months ago he would have seen keeping such details as a silly waste of time, but now he found himself engrossed.

He sat at his desk sipping his coffee and reading the pages Susan had filled in, which ended abruptly after the girls turned five months. He was assaulted by guilt for not continuing on the tradition, realizing that some day the twins would probably want to look back at it, maybe even show it to their children.

He vowed that, starting today, he would go back and fill in as much information as possible from those missed months, then keep the book up to date from now on. He was sure Sierra would help him. She would remember the finer details he'd forgotten or overlooked.

Curious about the woman who gave birth to the girls, he flipped back to the beginning. He couldn't find her name, which was no surprise, and though there were a few photos of her pregnant belly, they were all from the chest down. Yet as he thumbed through the pages, reading the pregnancy milestones, he was overwhelmed with an eerie sense of déjà vu. He was sure he'd read this before. It just looked so...familiar. He racked his memory, wondering if maybe he'd seen the baby book at Ash and Susan's place. But he was sure he hadn't. Even if it had been sitting right in front of him he wouldn't have thought to pick it up. So why did it look so familiar?

Realization hit him like a stick check to the gut, knocking the air from his lungs. No way. It wasn't possible.

He snatched the note Sierra had left him from the trash beside his desk and compared it to the writing in the baby book, and the coffee he'd just swallowed threatened to rise back up his throat. It was identical. Completely and totally identical.

Sierra, the woman he loved and planned to marry, was the girls' birth mother.

Sierra opened the apartment door, her hair clinging to her damp forehead. It was a hot, sticky morning headed toward a blistering hot afternoon. She went right to the kitchen, poured herself a glass of cold water from the fridge and guzzled it down. Then she went down the hall in search of Lita and the girls. She found them in the nursery in the middle of a diaper change.

"I'm back, Lita. Is Mr. Landon still here?"

"He in his office," she said, concern furrowing her brow. "I go to talk to him, but he look angry."

Which probably meant that their offer on the house had been turned down. Well, shoot. They had seen a dozen different places in the past week, but that was by far their favorite. Coop was going to be so disappointed.

The past week, since she said she would marry him, had been a bit of a whirlwind. He seemed determined to get them married and settled into a house as fast as humanly possible. As if he were trying to make it official before she had a chance to get away. He had even mentioned that if they were going to have more children, he wanted to do it soon, so they would be close in age. She already had her hands pretty full with the twins, but he seemed to want it so badly she didn't have the heart to say she wanted to wait a while.

She felt a little like she was on a speeding train, and even if she wanted off, it was moving too fast to jump.

Sierra walked to Coop's office. The door was closed so she rapped lightly.

"Come in."

She opened the door and stepped inside. Coop was standing by the window, looking out, hands wedged in the pockets of his jeans.

"Hey, is everything okay? Lita said you looked angry."

"Close the door," he said, not looking at her.

Something definitely was wrong. She snapped the door shut and asked, "Coop, what's the matter? Did the Realtor call? Did they turn down our offer?"

"They didn't call yet. I finally started going through one of the boxes of Ash's things."

No wonder he was upset. "Oh, Coop. That must have been really hard."

"I found a whole bunch of photos, and the twins' baby book. It's on my desk."

She walked over to his desk. A stack of framed photographs sat on one corner, and next to it, the baby book she hadn't seen in almost seven months.

"I bookmarked my favorite page. Have a look."

She picked it up and thumbed through it until she found the page, marked with the note she'd written him this morning. She saw the writing on the note and the writing on the page, and her stomach bottomed out. Side by side they were clearly identical. Her knees went so limp she had to sink down into the chair.

She looked up to see that Coop had turned and was glaring down at her, his eyes so cold she nearly shivered.

"That's your handwriting. You're the twins' birth mother."

She closed her eyes and drew in a shaky breath. Joy was right. She should have told him.

"Nothing to say?" he asked, and the anger simmering just below the surface made her heart skip.

"I can explain."

"Don't bother. Here's what I think happened. You wanted them back, but I refused to give them up and you knew you didn't have a shot in hell in court. So instead you decided to infiltrate my home, to prove me unfit."

"No, Coop—"

"But then you looked around and realized what a sweet life you could have as my wife, so you seduced me instead."

"It wasn't like that at all. I just needed to know that they were okay. Your reputation… I didn't know what kind of parent you would be. I was scared. I thought they needed me. I swear, I never intended to act as anything but their nanny. And I never wanted anything from you. You know that."

"Did you ever plan to tell me the truth?"

She could tell him she did, that she was waiting for the right time, but that would be a lie. "I was afraid to."

"Because you thought I would be angry? And feel betrayed? Well, you were right."

"It wasn't that. At least, not entirely. I was afraid

it would change the way you felt about the twins. You're so good with them, and you love them so much. I thought it might change your feelings toward them. And yes, toward me."

"So you just planned to lie to me, what, for the rest of our lives?"

"You'll never know how hard it's been keeping the truth from you. And if I thought for a second that you would understand, I would have told you that very first day. But look at it from my point of view. I didn't know you. All I knew is what I read in the papers and heard on the news. I didn't even know that you had any interest in taking care of twins who you believed you weren't technically related to."

His eyes narrowed. "What do you mean, who I *believed* I wasn't related to?"

Damn it. Had she really just said that?

"Sierra?"

Damn, damn, *damn*.

It was one thing not to tell him and another to lie about it. Besides, he was bound to ask about the birth father some day, and not telling him would be another lie. "Coop, you're the girls' uncle."

"I know that."

"No, I mean that you are the girls' *biological* uncle. Ash wasn't just Fern and Ivy's adoptive dad. He was their birth dad."

The room seemed to tilt on its axis and Coop clutched the edge of the desk for support. "You *slept* with my brother."

"Yes, but it's not what you're thinking."

"You have *no idea* what I'm thinking."

"Please," she said, looking desperate, "give me a chance to explain."

Nothing she could say could take away the sick feeling in his stomach, in his soul. Ash had cheated on Susan. On top of being responsible for killing himself and his wife, Ash, who Coop had considered beyond reproach, had committed adultery. It was as if everything he knew about his brother was a lie.

"I met Ash in a bar."

"Ash didn't hang out in bars."

"And neither did I, but I had just put my father in a nursing home and I felt horrible, and I didn't feel like sitting home alone, so I stopped in for a drink. I just happened to sit beside him at the bar, and we were both drinking vodka tonics, and we got to talking. He said he was there because he and his wife were separating. He told me that they had been having fertility issues for years and after another failed IVF attempt, it was just too much."

Coop knew they had been trying to get pregnant for a while, but Ash never said anything about any negative effects on his marriage. If he and Susan had been separating, he would have said something to Coop. "I don't believe you."

"It's the truth."

"So why didn't he tell me?"

She shrugged. "I don't know. Maybe he was embarrassed? Maybe it was easier to talk to a stranger? All I know is that he had come from his lawyer's office, and they were going to sign papers the next morning. If you don't believe me, I'm sure his lawyer could confirm it. I'm sure with them gone he would waive privilege."

He would be sure to check that. "So you met in a bar…"

"We talked for a long time and had a few drinks too many, and we ended up back at my place. It was a mistake. We both knew it right afterward. He called me the next day to apologize and to tell me that what happened between us had knocked some sense into him. He and Susan had talked and were going to try to work things out. He begged me not to say anything to her, and of course I wouldn't. He was a great guy, and I was really happy for him. But a couple of weeks later I found out I was pregnant. I called him, and of course he was stunned and heartbroken. He wanted a child so badly, but to be in the baby's life he would have to admit to Susan what he'd done, and that would ruin his marriage."

"He would never do that. He would never refuse to take responsibility for his own child."

"He wanted to, but how would he explain the missing money? He said that Susan handled all of their finances. Things were already really tight. The fertility treatments were draining them financially."

If things were that bad, why hadn't he asked Coop for help? Coop *owed* him. He could have been the one to pay the support. Ash had made a mistake, and he should have owned up to it.

"It was a really terrible time for me to be having a baby. I was barely scraping by as it was, and I would have had to put the baby in day care while I worked seventy hours a week. I started to think about adoption, and when I found out I was having twins, I knew I couldn't keep them. I couldn't give them the sort of life they deserved. But I knew who could. I figured if the twins couldn't be with their mother, they could at least be with their dad."

"So why did Ash have to adopt his own kids?"

"He came up with the adoption idea so Susan wouldn't know about the affair. He was so afraid of losing her."

"And you just went along with this. You just gave up your babies to save a virtual stranger's marriage."

"I didn't have a choice. It was an impossible situation. Without his help, I couldn't keep them, and he couldn't give me any financial help without ruining his marriage. Giving them up was the hardest thing I ever had to do, but I did it because it was best for them."

"You must have been pretty happy when you heard about the crash, knowing you would get the chance to be with them again."

Tears welled in her eyes. "That's a terrible thing to say. And it's not true. If I didn't think they would have a good life with Ash and Susan, I never would have suggested the adoption. I would have given them to some other family who was desperate for children."

"You know what I find ironic? All this time I knew something wasn't right. I chocked it up to you having trust issues, when all along you were the one lying, the one who couldn't be trusted."

"I know it was wrong to lie to you, but I didn't have a choice. I didn't expect to fall in love with you. It's not something I planned, and I fought it. You know I did."

"Or that's what you wanted me to believe."

"It's the truth."

"What difference does it make now? It's over. I won't ever be able to trust you again."

She lowered her eyes, wringing her hands in her lap. "I know. And I'm sorry."

"And to think I was willing to marry you without a prenup. That's the last time I question my lawyer's advice." And he didn't doubt for a second that her insistence in signing one was all a part of her scheme. And what if he had married her? What if they'd had a child? The thought made his stomach ache.

"You didn't deserve this," she said. "And I know you won't believe this, but I do love you."

"You're right. I don't believe you."

She rose to her feet, her face pale, looking like she might either be sick or lose consciousness. "I'll go pack."

He laughed. "You don't seriously think I'm going to let you off that easy, let you leave your daughters?"

She blinked, confusion in her eyes. "But…I thought…"

"I may think that you're a miserable human being, but they need you. Do you really think I would rip them away from the only mother they have? But don't think for a second that you are anything but an employee."

"You want me to stay? *Here?*"

"Obviously you're moving back into your bedroom. And I'm going to treat you like the servant that you are. And you're going to take a substantial pay cut."

"You don't think it will be awkward, me staying here?"

"Oh, I'm counting on it. It's going to be that nightmare scenario you mentioned when you were telling me all the supposed reasons why you didn't want to get involved. You are going to live here, day in, day out, watching me get on with my life. Watching me exercise that revolving bedroom door."

"And if I say no? If I quit?"

"You never see the twins again. And you have to live with knowing you abandoned them twice."

She swallowed, tears welling in her eyes again, but he couldn't feel sorry for her. He flat out refused. She'd made him suffer, and now he was going to return the favor.

"Well then," she said, squaring her shoulders, trying to be strong. "I guess I have no choice but to stay."

Fifteen

Coop had given it considerable thought and had come to the conclusion that he was an idiot.

He sat in his office, staring out the window at nothing, without the motivation to do anything but feel sorry for himself. The past two weeks had been the longest and most miserable of his life. If he thought making Sierra suffer would bring him some sort of satisfaction, he'd been dead wrong. He just wanted her to feel as miserable and betrayed and as *hurt* as he was. But knowing that she was unhappy and hurting was only making him feel worse.

He couldn't concentrate, couldn't sleep. When he was out with friends he wanted to be home, but when he was home he felt as restless as a caged animal. He didn't want to upend the twins' lives, but living in the same house with Sierra, seeing day to day how guilty and unhappy she felt, was killing him.

The worst part was that this was just as much his fault as hers. Probably more.

Deep down he had known there was something wrong, that something was just slightly…off. And instead of bothering to try to identify its real source, he'd passed it off as her shortcoming and left it at that, thinking that as soon as she accepted how wonderful he was she would be the perfect companion. When, in reality, he was the one with the bigger problem. He had lousy vision. He saw only what he wanted to see. He had pursued her with a single-minded determination that was almost manic. She'd resisted, and he'd ignored her. She pushed back, he insisted. He hadn't *let* her tell him no.

Looking back, he couldn't help but wonder what the hell he'd been thinking. Moving her into his bedroom after two weeks and planning a wedding six weeks after that. If she'd been pregnant he maybe could have understood the urgency. And speaking of that, the stretch marks should have tipped him off that there might be something she wasn't telling him. He had just assumed that she had been a little overweight at some point and they were the result. It wasn't the sort of thing a man could ask a woman. Not without getting slugged. Or so he wanted to believe. He never really asked her about her past. The truth was, he didn't want to know. It had been easier just to pretend that she was perfect, that her life didn't really begin until she met him.

What a selfish, arrogant jerk he'd been.

Though it had taken a little time to realize it, it wasn't even Sierra who was making him so angry. How could Ash, who had drilled into Coop the virtues of being a responsible adult and a good man, be so careless and self-centered? He should have supported

Sierra, his marriage be damned. He should have owned up to the responsibility, so she could keep the babies, so they could be with their mother, where they belonged. Instead he had ripped them from her arms and taken them for himself. Coop didn't think he would ever understand it or ever be able to forgive him for what he'd done.

Yes, Sierra had lied to him but only because she thought she was doing what was best for her children. They were her number-one priority, as they should be. She was a good mother. She'd made more sacrifices for those girls than most women would ever consider. And he intended to make sure they knew it.

Ironically, now that he knew who Sierra was, warts and all, he loved her more than he had two weeks ago when he had her built up in his mind as the perfect mate. But after the way he'd treated her, why would she ever want him back? He told her that he loved her, that he wanted to spend the rest of his life with her, and at the first sign of trouble, he'd bailed on her. How could she love someone who had failed her so completely? And how could she ever trust that he wouldn't do it again?

He had really hoped by now that she would have come crawling to him on her knees begging for forgiveness, in which case he wouldn't have to admit what an utter jerk he'd been. Clearly that wasn't going to happen. He needed her a whole lot more than she needed him. Or maybe she just believed it was hopeless and didn't want to risk being rejected again.

He heard the doorbell ring and knew that it was Vlad, Niko and a few other guys from the team. Coop had met with Norris, who after some balking had agreed to their original terms. The deal was in place, and in just a few weeks Coop would officially be the new owner, so the guys wanted to celebrate. This deal had been all he could think about for months, yet now that he'd gotten what he wanted, he couldn't work up the will to be excited about it. It was as if losing Sierra had sucked the life right out of him.

Lita poked her head in his office. "Your guests is here, sir."

"Serve them drinks and I'll be right there."

She nodded and backed out.

He had no choice but to go out there and pretend as if everything was fine. But it wasn't, and wouldn't be, until Sierra was his again. And she would be. He would get her back. He just didn't have a clue how to go about it.

Sierra ignored the doorbell and read the girls their bedtime story. She had overheard Coop telling Lita— who seemed hopelessly confused by Sierra's abrupt switch from lady of the house to employee—that he was having a few guys from the team over. Was this him finally getting on with his life? Because she had been waiting, and other than a night out with friends in which he came home alone at an unimpressive nine-thirty and a couple of business meetings, he'd spent most of the past two weeks holed up in his office.

When it came to dishing out revenge, he wasn't very good at it.

That didn't mean she wasn't miserable and unhappy, and she missed him so much every cell in her body ached with it. Yet she couldn't deny the feeling that some enormous, cloying weight had been lifted from her, and for the first time in months she could actually breathe again. She realized now that if she had married

Coop with that secret between them, she never would have been able to relax. She would have forever felt as though she didn't deserve him because everything that he knew about her was essentially a lie.

Unfortunately, the one thing that could have saved their relationship, *the truth,* had been the thing that killed it. Just like her pregnancy, it had been a lose-lose situation from the start, and she had been a fool for letting herself believe that it would work. For thinking that he wouldn't eventually learn the truth. And that it would end in anything but total disaster.

If he could ever find a way to forgive her, she would never lie to him again. But it seemed unlikely that would ever happen. He hated her, and that really sucked, but at least he knew the truth.

From the other room she heard men's voices. No doubt they would go up on the roof, drink and talk about what a waste of time she had been and the compromising position he had managed to trap her into.

Because she was in no mood for a confrontation with Coop's pals, she read the twins a second then a third book, realizing halfway through that they were out cold. She laid them in bed, grabbed their empty bottles and walked to the kitchen. Lita had already left for the night, and the dishwasher was running, so she dropped the bottles in the sink and washed them by hand.

She was setting them on a towel to dry when she heard the sound of footsteps behind her, but the cloying scent of aftershave tipped her off to the source. She turned to find Niko standing behind her.

"I need beer," he said, setting an empty beer bottle on the counter.

Was he just stating fact, or was he expecting her to

wait on him? She was the nanny, not Coop's hostess. His friends could serve themselves, which Niko did.

"Coop tell us it's over," he said, walking past her to the fridge and pulling out a beer. Normally she didn't feel threatened by the younger Russian, but there was something in the way he looked at her tonight. His eyes roamed over her in a way that made her feel dirty.

"That's right," she said.

He stepped closer. "I like sister, maybe I like you, too."

Oh, yuck. "I'm not interested."

She turned to the sink and felt a very large palm settle on her butt. Repulsion roiled her stomach. And she couldn't help wondering if Coop had put him up to this, if that was part of her humiliation. But before she could turn and slap his hand away, it was gone. She spun around to see Coop pulling the Russian away from her, then he drew his arm back and punched him square in the jaw. Actually *punched* him.

Niko's head snapped back and he lost his balance, landing on his ass on the ceramic tile floor.

If he put Niko up to it, then why punch him?

Niko muttered something in Russian that Sierra was guessing was a curse and rubbed his jaw. He looked more annoyed than angry.

"What the hell is wrong with you?" Coop said.

"You say you and her is finished. So I think, why not?"

Coop glared at the Russian, then looked over at Sierra and said, "Are you okay?"

"Fine." Just mildly disgusted.

Coop turned back to Niko, jaw tight, and said, "I'm only going to say this once, so listen clearly and spread the word. The only man who's going to be touching this woman's ass is *me*."

Niko shrugged and pulled himself to his feet. "Okay, fine, jeez. I look but I don't touch."

"No, you don't get to look, either. Or *think* about looking."

Sierra planted her hands on her hips. "Excuse me, but do I have any say in this, since it is *my* ass we're talking about."

He pointed to Niko. "You, back to the terrace." He turned to Sierra. "You, bedroom, *now*."

What did he think, he could just order her around? And if he couldn't, why, as he stomped down the hall to his bedroom, was she following him? Maybe because the fact that he would punch someone to defend her honor was just a tiny bit flattering. But what she didn't appreciate was the part about him basically owning her. He'd lost that right when he dumped her.

He opened the bedroom door and gestured her inside, and she dumbly complied, but she wasn't a total pushover.

"Look. I don't know who you think you—"

That was as far as she got before Coop spun her around, slanted his mouth over hers and kissed away whatever she'd been about to say. His arms went around her, pulling her hard against him, and instead of fighting it and asking what the heck he thought he was doing, it felt so amazingly wonderful, and she had missed him *so* much, she couldn't help but kiss him back.

So much for not being a pushover.

He kicked the door closed.

"I have been such a jerk," he said. "A miserable excuse for a man. I am so sorry."

She tucked her face against his chest, breathed in deep the scent of him, knowing that she was home. Any reservations that she had been feeling before their fight were gone. "I deserved it."

"No you didn't. And when I saw him touch you…" He squeezed her so hard it was difficult to breathe. "Tell me you didn't like it."

"God, no! It was revolting."

"I don't want another man to ever touch you again. Only me, for the rest of our lives."

She cupped his face in her hands. "You're the only man I want, Coop. The only man I'll ever want. And I am so sorry for what I did. It was killing me having to lie to you. I should have told you the truth from the beginning."

"Sierra, it's okay."

"It's not. I should have come to your door, told you I was the twins' mother and asked you if I could be a part of their lives."

"You never would have made it to my door. The doorman would have to let you up, and he wouldn't have done that without permission from me, and I wouldn't have let you near the twins."

"So you're saying it was okay to lie to you?"

"Maybe not okay, but necessary. If I were in your position, and I thought the twins were in danger, I would have done anything to keep them safe. And what my brother did to you…" He shook his head, as if it was almost too painful to say. "It was so wrong, Sierra. He never should have taken the twins from you. He should have owned up to his responsibility."

"But his marriage—"

"To hell with his marriage. He made a mistake and he should have been man enough to admit it. I love my brother, and I appreciate all the sacrifices he made for me, but I just can't excuse the things he did. I'll never believe it was okay. And I will always take care of you and the twins, the way that he should have."

Her heart sank. She didn't want him to see her as some debt he had to repay. That just wasn't good enough for her anymore. "Because you feel guilty," she said.

He cradled her face in his hands. "No, because I *love* you. I asked you to marry me, and you put your faith in me and the first time things got a little hard I bailed. But it isn't going to happen again. I'm dedicated to making this work. I don't have a choice. I need you too much, love you too much to let you go."

"I love you, too," she said.

"And just so you know, I'm calling my lawyer first thing tomorrow and telling him to tear up the prenup."

Not this again. "But, Coop—"

"I don't need it. And I'm going to tell him to get the ball rolling on having your rights as the twins' mother fully restored."

She sucked in a soft breath. The most she had hoped for was to someday be their adoptive mother. She never thought that she would ever be recognized as their biological mother. "Are you sure, Coop?"

He touched her cheek. "They're your daughters. Of course I'm sure. Then after we're married, I'll adopt them. They'll belong to both of us."

It sounded almost too good to be true, and this time she wasn't going to take a second of it for granted. "I'm going to be the perfect wife," she told him. "I'll figure out how to cook a decent meal and learn to clean if that's what it takes."

He shook his head. "Nope."

She blinked. "What do you mean?"

"I don't want the perfect wife."

"You don't?"

He grinned down at her, with that sweet, crooked smile—the one she would get to look at for the rest of her life—and said, "I only want you."

* * * * *

THE NANNY WHO
KISSED HER BOSS

BY
BARBARA McMAHON

Barbara McMahon was born and raised in the south USA, but settled in California after spending a year flying around the world for an international airline. After settling down to raise a family and work for a computer firm, she began writing when her children started school. Now, feeling fortunate in being able to realize a long-held dream of quitting her "day job" and writing full time, she and her husband have moved to the Sierra Nevada mountains of California, where she finds her desire to write is stronger than ever. With the beauty of the mountains visible from her windows, and the pace of life slower than the hectic San Francisco Bay Area where they previously resided, she finds more time than ever to think up stories and characters and share them with others through writing. Barbara loves to hear from readers. You can reach her at PO Box 977, Pioneer, CA 95666-0977, USA. readers can also contact Barbara at her website: www.barbaramcmahon.com.

CHAPTER ONE

SAVANNAH Williams rolled over on her right side and pulled the covers over her head. It was morning, she could tell by the bright sunlight flooding her bedroom. But she was not ready to get up. She'd arrived home late last night after the airplane trip from hell. It had routed her all over the United States and got her to New York long after midnight when she'd been up before dawn on the west coast to make that first flight.

The apartment was quiet. Her sister was on assignment. She relaxed and tried to fall back asleep. Why hadn't she put a blackout shade on the window? She just wanted a few more hours of rest.

The ring of the phone jarred.

"Oh, for heaven's sake!" She threw back the sheet and stalked to the living room where the apartment phone was ringing. She'd turned off her cell, so naturally this phone had to ring.

"It better be good," she snapped into the receiver when she snatched it up.

"Good morning, Savannah. It's Stephanie. Did you have a good trip?" The cheerful voice was not what Savannah wanted to hear this early.

"The cruise was okay except it snowed two days. So much for lying on the deck while the children napped. And the two darling dears of Dr. and Mrs. Lightower were not the angels the parents purported them to be. I was never so thankful to end an assignment. Talk about spoiled brats! The flight home—or should I say the *flights* home—were horrible. I was routed from Alaska to LA to Dallas then Chicago, then I swear I thought I was going to be sent through Atlanta, but fortunately bad weather kept that airport off the schedule, so I got sent to Boston before ending up in New York at two o'clock in the morning!" She was practically yelling the last, but only heard Stephanie's giggles in the background. So much for sympathy.

"I was trying to sleep in," she grumbled.

"Oh, poor you. Go back to sleep in a minute. You have a new assignment and the client actually postponed his trip to make sure it coincided with your availability. This one's right up your alley—one child, a teenager. Parents are divorced, mother has custody. However, the teen is with her father now and will be for the summer apparently. Could be a bonding experience for them, I suppose."

"What could?" Savannah asked. She was growing wider awake the longer Stephanie kept her on the phone. For what? She was off the clock and wanted to catch up on sleep and fun before taking another assignment from Vacation Nannies.

"Backpacking in the High Sierras," Stephanie said.

Savannah stared out the window to the sliver of a view of the Hudson River she and her sister enjoyed from their apartment. Glass and concrete and that tiny sliver compared to endless vistas of mountain ranges? Clear blue sky instead of the heavy layer of smog over New York?

But backpacking?

"How come Stacey gets to lounge around at the beach on the Med and I'm stuck lugging a heavy backpack on a trail where there won't even be hot and cold running water?"

"Luck of the draw. Plus you're our resident expert on troublesome teens."

"Oh, joy, another challenge. When do we meet?" she asked. Rule number one of Vacation Nannies was that both parties had to agree to the assignment. Which usually worked to make sure the match between nanny and children was harmonious, but she had seriously been off with the Lightower children. Who expected them to behave so nicely at the initial meeting and then turn into terrors? Not that she hadn't been able to cope, but the carefree cruise she'd anticipated had not been the case.

"Friday. If everything goes okay, you'll depart next week and be gone three weeks."

"How old's the teen?" Savannah had specialized in adolescent behavior when getting her degree in education. She had a special bond for children who had reached the whacked-out stage of teenagedom, which included recalcitrant and defiant behavior.

"She's fourteen. Lives here in New York."

Savannah could hear papers being turned over, Stephanie was obviously referring to interview notes. She plopped down on the sofa, giving up any thought of going back to sleep until later. "Never mind giving me all the info. I'll be by later to look at the file. Anything else I should know?"

"Do you have hiking boots?"

"Of course, remember my trip to the Adirondacks last fall? It was a glorious week tramping round the forest and enjoying at all the colorful foliage. The pair I got then are well worn in. How cold is it in the High Sierras in June?"

"Check the national weather outlook. I'll confirm you'll be there on Friday at eleven. Oh, and, Savannah…" Stephanie sounded hesitant.

Savannah sat up at her tone.

"What?"

"The dad is Declan Murdock."

Savannah frowned, almost hearing Stephanie holding her breath after delivering that bombshell.

"I'm not going," she said. *Declan Murdock.* It had been seven years since she'd seen him. Seven lonely years of trying to forget the man she'd loved with all the fresh bright hope of first love—and who had dumped her so unceremoniously.

"He asked especially for you."

"That's hard to believe." And was like a knife twisting in her. He'd left her because of Jacey. Now he wanted her to watch her while he was off doing what—oh yeah, backpacking. What had happened to Jacey's mother? They were divorced—again?

"Why backpacking in the mountains? Why isn't he just sticking around New York while he has Jacey? They could see shows, visit museums, go to the shore. Bond in New York."

"I don't inquire as to why our clients do things. Friday morning at his office. I think you know where." Stephanie hung up before Savannah could utter another word.

She slammed down the phone. "For this I had to get up early?"

Declan Murdock. She hadn't seen him in years, hadn't thought about him in—well, at least maybe one year. She wished she could say she'd forgotten him as fast as he'd probably forgotten her. But she'd been incredibly hurt by their parting. She'd been dreaming of a wedding and he'd been lured back to his ex-wife because of a daughter he hadn't known existed.

For the longest time she'd gone over everything, replaying in her mind every word he'd uttered at that final meeting, trying to see where things could have gone differently.

"Water long under the bridge," she muttered, going to get coffee to jump-start her brain. Did Stephanie really think she'd take the job? Be alone with Declan and his daughter for three weeks?

"Why not ask me to plunge a knife into my heart to begin with. It would be just as painful," she mumbled, watching the coffeemaker drizzle the brew into the carafe. Divorced, Stephanie had said. So when had that happened? What about Declan's determination to make a go of his marriage for the sake of a daughter he'd just discovered?

No one would blame her for turning down a request for an assignment from the man who had broken her heart. The man against whom she had judged all other men ever since—and had usually found them lacking.

Maybe she should have asked the Lightowers to extend her services—even the horrible brats looked better than facing Declan again.

Taking her coffee, she went back to the sofa and gazed out the window. She wondered if he'd aged much. She'd learned how successful his sporting goods chain had become. Everything he touched seemed golden.

Divorced. Her curiosity got the better of her. Dare she risk her peace of mind by seeing him again? Any feelings she'd had for him seven years ago had evaporated. She'd become much more wary, much more cynical about men's intentions.

And how could she watch his daughter—the reason he'd left her. She'd been so in love, and she'd thought he had, as well. How could he so easily have tossed that love aside to marry Margo—or rather to remarry her when she'd shown up years after their divorce saying Declan was a father. He'd had the paternity tests done and had then been convinced he needed to marry Jacey's mother again and build a strong family unit.

Forget about the college student who had adored him. Forget about the plans and dreams they'd had. Once he'd uttered the fateful words, Savannah had wished him well and left the coffee shop, tears not falling until she was home.

So what had happened to his precious plans that had brought him full circle back into her life?

Curiosity won. She'd go to the interview. It wouldn't go well, she already knew that. But the reputation of Vacation Nannies was on the line. She didn't want him bad-mouthing the company because of personal feelings. Feelings that should have died seven years ago.

"That *did* die seven years ago!" she repeated aloud. "I'm so over you, Declan Murdock."

Friday, Savannah dressed with care. She was no longer the college student dating an up-and-coming business-man. She went with the most trendy outfit she had, and spiked her short hair the way she liked it. Her outfit was the fourth she'd tried on this morning, wanting to get just the right look of successful businesswoman and capable nanny. The navy slacks, white blouse and sassy scarf de-clared her achievement.

He'd done well, she'd learned a couple of years ago. Well, so had she and her sister. Maybe not on the scale he'd reached, but wildly prosperous. She and Stacey had planned their business long before they were able to start it. The one course she especially wanted to take in her se-nior year in college was Start-ups on a Shoestring—taught by visiting guest lecturer Declan Murdock shortly after he began his sporting goods company. She'd hung on his every word. First for what she could learn about business, then for what she could learn about the man himself. When he'd asked her out, she'd gone. There were rules at the college against faculty dating students but as a guest lecturer, he wasn't really faculty.

Only a few years older than she, he'd captured her imagination and fired her enthusiasm about her business model for Vacation Nannies. Before long the business talk had turned personal and by Christmas that year she'd fallen in love. She remembered their talk about surfing together off the coast of Maine, the fun she'd had slugging a softball out of the park to his wild cheering, the thrill of rollerblading in Central Park together. Visiting museums and art galleries when the weather was bad, lost in a world of two despite the crowded places.

She shook off the memories. She was an accomplished businesswoman in her own right. She would see him, refuse the job and that would be that.

She gave the cabdriver the address. Savannah knew exactly where the company headquarters was for Murdock Sports. She'd met him there many evenings, to give them more time together. She didn't want to remember, but ever since Stephanie's call the memories had flooded in.

At least she had the teensy consolation that she wasn't still some lovestruck idiot pining for a man who'd married a woman he didn't love for the sake of a daughter who had been kept from him the first seven years of her life.

Maybe he'd say or do something so outlandish at the interview she could instantly say no. Highly unlikely, but she lived in hope. Truth was, she could turn down the assignment for no reason at all. She didn't answer to him.

But Vacation Nannies thrived on referrals. He probably moved in such rarified air these days he could give their company a big boost.

Three weeks was a mere twenty-one days. She could do anything for a short time.

The first thing Savannah noticed when she stepped into

the building was the major renovations since she'd last been there. The reception area was larger and very upscale. Most suitable to the image of a very successful company. *Let the public believe you're highly successful, and you'll be highly successful,* had been one of his axioms. So his business instincts had been right on. He was a huge success. Despite her heartbreak, she'd picked up some information over the years from the local business news. If nothing else, she'd learned solid business techniques and how to focus on the main goal from Declan's class.

Add the fact that the address of Vacation Nannies made a major impression on clients, also thanks to Declan. Granted she sometimes thought they paid way too much for the tiny offices they had, but the clientele they drew demanded the very best.

Savannah gave her name to the receptionist and was asked to wait. No hardship since she'd put off the interview entirely if she could. But there was no other nanny as suitable from their company so Stephanie had explained to her when she'd showed up at the office to read the file before the interview. The most important thing was to keep up the reputation of Vacation Nannies.

The concept—provide short-term, temporary nannies to watch children while the family was on vacation—had proven surprisingly popular. Savannah and Stacey had begun the business because of their own desire to travel and see the world. With the little money they had that would be unlikely. So they'd found a way to travel on someone else's dime.

After a degree in education, plus some business courses at NYU, Savannah had been instrumental in getting the business going. Soon there were more requests than she and Stacey could handle, so Stephanie had been hired to handle the scheduling aspect. Other nannies, trained at the prestigious Miss Pritchard's School for Nannies, were carefully vetted and hired. Now they had a dozen others on the payroll, and during the summer months everyone was fully booked.

To ensure the nannies weren't stuck for weeks with horrendous children or parents, the interview aspect went both ways. Either the prospective client could decline after meeting the nanny or the nanny could refuse to take the assignment.

So far there had only been a handful of refusals. She winced, thinking she'd make this another one.

She grew more nervous the longer she waited. What was she doing coming here? She didn't want to spend three weeks with Declan. Or with his daughter.

"Mr. Murdock can see you now," the receptionist said, rising and heading for the hall on the left. Her sleek toned looks gave mute testimony to the healthy lifestyle a sports aficionado could expect—especially if they used Murdock equipment.

Savannah wished she could have checked her makeup and hair one more time. It would never do not to be immaculately turned out and polished-looking. She hoped Declan didn't remember the casual clothes she'd worn in college. Money had always been tight in her family. After the first six months with their new venture, however, that had changed. Now she and her sister enjoyed high-end fashionable clothing, makeup and a professional hair stylist. No more letting her hair grow long like Stacey. Savannah liked it short and spiky. And the kids usually liked it, too. It was easy to care for. And if she were in the sun for long, the blond bleached out to almost white. Which was always a startling contrast to her tanned skin.

The receptionist handed her off to a personal assistant who took her to Declan's office—still located in the back corner of the warehouse-converted-to-offices. But the extremely modern look of chrome, leather and fine woods was a huge step up from when she'd visited before. His business model had obviously propelled his own firm into the stratosphere.

"Savannah," he said when the PA opened the door to usher her in. He stood behind the desk, studying her as she stepped into the office.

Savannah felt a catch in her breath. He looked the same. She'd forgotten how tall he was. While she was only five foot four when she stretched, Declan had to be close to six feet. Muscular and fit, he didn't look a day older than when she'd last seen him. His hair was still dark, not a strand of gray could she find. His eyes were a rich chocolate-brown, focused on her now. She could have stared back forever. For a moment she felt as tongue-tied as that college student who had been so in love. She nodded slightly, clinging to her composure with all she had. Wishing he'd aged, grown a pot belly and lost his hair.

"Hello, Declan." Yippee, her voice hadn't cracked. She hadn't stuttered or slapped his face. She also hadn't expected the jolt of awareness that spiked through her. Taking a slow breath she tried to relax, to treat him like any other prospective client. She wished she could forget the past that seemed to spring to the forefront. Why did long-dormant emotions have to blossom now?

"Connie, coffee for us both." He said to his PA, then looked at Savannah with an eyebrow raised in silent question.

"Thank you, that would be nice." They both had shared a love of strong coffee. Their final meeting had been at a coffee shop. She'd often wondered if he'd done that deliberately to make sure she didn't cause a scene in public.

"Thanks for coming. This is a bit awkward."

"You need a professional nanny for a trip you're taking. That's what our company specializes in. The past is dead, Declan."

He sat after she did and glanced away. Was he remembering their time together, their last meeting? She hoped he found this meeting *extremely* awkward. She would do nothing to ease the situation. After a long moment, she broke the silence.

"Do you still guest-lecture?" she asked.

He shook his head. "No time now. The business grew faster than I expected. The spring class that year was the last one I did. We've expanded to major markets around the country—which is the reason for the trip. I'm exploring the possibility of opening boutique stores in some resorts. So I'm combining business with pleasure. I want to spend a day or two at the San Francisco facility. It's fairly new. Then on to the mountains to test some new equipment. Then to one of the resorts in California that wants to discuss opening a boutique outlet there, offering only the sporting goods suitable for their resort."

She listened, but kept her expression impassive. So he was doing well, good for him. She was here merely to talk about the proposed trip.

He waited a moment and then cleared his throat. Was he as nervous as she felt? She hoped so. And hoped he rued the day he'd dumped her for Margo—daughter or not.

"I hear your company's doing well."

She nodded.

"I don't think I'd have pegged a firm like yours as a contender for growth, which shows how wrong I'd have been. I have friends who had one of your nannies for their trip to South America last year, the Spencers?"

"I think Stacey had that assignment. They visited Machu Picchu," Savannah said.

"Right. They highly recommend the agency to anyone who listens. And as many of us who socialize together have children, we all listened."

Connie brought in a tray with a carafe of coffee, sugar and cream and two mugs.

"Thanks," Declan said. She nodded, smiled at Savannah and left, closing the door behind her.

Once they both had their coffee, Declan leaned back and studied her for a moment. "So tell me how this works."

"Stephanie didn't explain?" Savannah asked. Usually the prospective client got the complete rundown. Fees, limitations, expectations—the works.

"Mainly what I took away from meeting her was we both have to suit each other. I know you'd suit, what do you want to know about Jacey?"

"I need to meet your daughter," Savannah said. He'd been divorced when she'd known him before. Now according to the interview at the office, he was divorced again. What had happened to that second go-round of marriage? Had he ended up dumping Margo as he had her?

"So your office manager said. Jacey will be with me all summer. So if you come by the apartment tomorrow you can meet her. I want to fly to San Francisco on Monday. If you two don't suit, I haven't a clue what I'll do. I heard you specialize in teenagers."

"I do. Is she a problem?"

"I rarely see her. Now I have her for the summer and am not sure what to do with her."

Savannah's attention was caught by his comment. Why didn't he see his daughter? He'd said he wanted to make a good family life with her. What had happened?

"What time?" she asked. Maybe she'd learn a bit more once she met Jacey.

"Say tenish?" His home address was on the questionnaire he'd filled out at the office. She knew the general area—affluent, but not outrageously so. Close to work and other amenities of downtown Manhattan. Was she seriously considering taking the assignment?

She hesitated a moment, still unable to make up her mind. She hadn't expected to be so drawn to him. They'd been lovers, always touching, kissing, delighting in just being with each other. Now it was awkward, as he'd said, to sit opposite him and pretend he was merely a client. To ignore the past, the heartache that threatened again. To refrain from demanding he tell her he'd been wrong to lose the best thing that ever happened to him.

She blinked. She was over this man!

"Tell me about the trip," she said, stalling before making up her mind. One part wanted to learn more about what he was like now. Another wanted to run as fast as she could.

"A couple of days in San Francisco, then we'll head for the Sierra Nevada mountains in California. We'll hike part of the Pacific Crest Trail for a few days to test a new tent and camping gear. Also I want to get Jacey away from New York. Her mother's made other plans this summer and she's sulking about it. The sweet little girl I knew is long gone. Now it's a phone glued to her ear, clothing that's totally inappropriate for her age and makeup that could clog a sewer pipe. All part of growing up, so Margo says, but I don't like it."

Savannah said nothing, but to her Jacey sounded like a normal teenager, maybe carrying things a bit to the extreme, but that was teenagers. And ones with divorced parents often went to the edge for attention, reassurance, love.

"Then we'll spend a few days at a resort in the mountains. It's an exclusive destination resort with hiking trails, some white-water rafting nearby and all the amenities you'd expect to find at a five-star resort." He shrugged. "I think the trip will be good for Jacey."

"Sounds like you would be with her most of the time. Why a nanny?"

"There will be times when I won't be with her. She's too young to leave on her own in San Francisco or the resort. While we're on the trail, it'll be just the three of us."

She slammed the door shut on the image that immediately sprang to mind—starlit nights, quiet conversation, kisses in the dark.

"San Francisco's a favorite city of mine," she murmured. She loved the crisp breeze from the Pacific, the dazzling white buildings against the deep blue sky. The excitement unlike New York's but special in its own way. "Has Jacey been before?"

"No. And I'm not getting an enthusiastic response when I bring it up. I'm hoping she'll come around."

He hesitated a moment, then said slowly, "There's one small thing, though." He narrowed his eyes slightly as he watched her.

Savannah's instincts clamored for caution. Something about his change in tone suggested this could be a deal breaker. Was his daughter more of a problem than a typical teenager?

"I, ah, need you to keep the past in the past. She need not know we once—" He floundered for the word, his expression one of regret.

Savannah stared at him. That was the absolutely last thing she expected. And the last thing she'd ever do—tell anyone how he'd chosen someone else over her.

"I assure you, I keep my private life my own with all my clients. I would never tell your daughter—" Never tell her of her heartbreak. Never tell her how she had so loved her father and been devastated when he'd chosen Jacey and Margo over her.

The feelings of the past threatened to swamp her. She drew a deep breath. Things changed in seven years. She was a bit disconcerted to discover she was still very aware of him as a man. But she had a life she loved, friends and a work ethic she'd spent years developing. And a definite hands-off attitude for any of her employers. She would never risk her heart a second time with a man who threw her love back in her face.

"Say something," he urged softly. "Will you take this job?"

"Why me? Surely there are others in the field you could find to accompany you two." There were other nannies in her own firm who could have gone.

"Stephanie said you had the most experience with teenagers. That you have a way with them. I need someone who will help Jacey. I think she's long overdue for some good moral values and—"

"I still have to meet her before making a decision," Savannah said. Sure, she was good enough to hire to watch his daughter for three weeks, but not good enough to marry and present as a stepmother back in the day?

"Give her a fair shot, Savannah. It wasn't her fault what happened."

She looked up and was met with steady brown eyes. What if she fell for him again?

Never! The trust they'd shared had been shattered. She would not make that mistake a second time.

For three weeks she'd have be around Declan—some of that time 24/7. She'd have to keep all thoughts of the past from mingling with the present. And she'd have to look after his daughter by another woman. She didn't know if she wanted that. It was like lemon juice hitting a cut. Sharp and painful.

Carefully putting down her cup, she prepared to leave. "I have your address from the application. We'll meet at your flat tomorrow at ten." She had to think this through. Maybe talk to Stacey or Stephanie to get an impartial view. Maybe have her head examined that she was even considering it.

"You'd need to understand about Margo, as well."

"What about her?" Savannah didn't want to even think about his wife. Ex-wife.

"We divorced before I started Murdock Sports. She left New York, but when she came back, she had Jacey. I really wanted to do the right thing by my daughter. It was a mistake from the beginning—except for Jacey. She's been the light of my world for years. However, ever since the second divorce, this company's really grown. Margo's been haranguing me for more money. She wants a share. That's the last thing I'll agree to." The hard edge of his tone reminded Savannah that as fascinating as she'd found him, he was still a hard-driven businessman.

"And she's using your daughter as a weapon," Savannah guessed. She'd dealt with other divorced parents in her job. Some could be so thoughtless around their children.

"Exactly. At least I have her for three months this summer. My hope is that we build some kind of relationship like we had a few years ago. That's the reason I wanted to start with a couple of weeks in the wilderness. Cut off from outside influences, just focusing on rebuilding our relationship, maybe she'll realize what's important in life."

There was definitely the chance to build something when it was only Jacey and her father, away from her mother, friends and cell phones.

Declan continued, "She used to love going on hikes,

camping. We did a lot of it when she was younger. I'm hoping that enjoyment will surge forth again. The Sierras are the prettiest mountains in the west, I think. Clean, fresh air, beautiful country, wildlife. Perfection."

If Savannah had a lick of sense, as her grandmother used to say, she'd turn down the job so fast it'd make Declan's head swim. But she liked the outdoors. She liked to hike and camp and see nature's beauty. And she'd never seen the Pacific Crest Trail.

She was intrigued and tempted.

Yet could she set aside her resentment of his daughter? Despite his cutting her out of his life when Margo had returned, he'd helped both her and her sister and the others who now worked for Vacation Nannies by fine-tuning her business plan with her. No one else might think so, but she owed him. She had a dream job, plenty of money for her chosen lifestyle, went on assignments to some of the world's most beautiful and sought-after locations—all because Declan Murdock had taken time to teach a class.

She could handle anything for three weeks. As long as she remembered every day it was only temporary! She would be the most professional nanny in the world. And at the end of three weeks, she'd walk away without a backward look.

CHAPTER TWO

DECLAN stared at the doorway after Savannah left. He was surprised she'd agreed to proceed. He wouldn't have blamed her if she'd refused outright.

Rubbing his hand on the back of his neck, he looked at the stack of reports in front of him. Not that he saw them. Instead, images of Savannah danced in front of his eyes. Her laughter that time they'd taken the paddle boat around the lake at St. Anne's. The way her eyes grew a deeper blue when he kissed her. The evenings they'd made dinner together, stopping between tasks to kiss, touch, promise silently that even more would come later.

The worst mistake of his life had been turning his back on Savannah, thinking he and Margo could make a marriage just for Jacey's sake.

He wasn't sure what he'd expected when he saw Savannah again, but it hadn't been that mature sophisticated businesswoman instead of the fun-loving student on the brink of life.

It looked as if she'd succeeded. He'd learned a lot about her business, but nothing about the woman. What had she been doing these past seven years beyond Vacation Nannies?

Did she have a boyfriend?

The thought twisted his gut.

He had no rights. Any he'd had years ago he'd forfeited when he'd told her goodbye.

"You need to do what you need to do and have no regrets," she'd said at that coffee shop when he'd told her he was breaking it off with her to remarry Margo.

He wished he could have lived with no regrets.

The past was past. Now he needed her in a different way—to help with his daughter.

He remembered Vacation Nannies' office manager telling him the nanny had to approve the children or they would not take the job.

He hoped Jacey would behave. He needed someone to be there for his daughter when he had to work. He'd know by tomorrow shortly after ten.

The next morning Declan was up early and back at work to finish up loose ends before the trip. His housekeeper was with Jacey. She herself would be taking a vacation while he was gone. Had she been a younger woman, he would have prevailed on her to go with them to California. But, in her late fifties, she was not interested in backpacking in the mountains.

His vice president would be in charge of the business for the next few weeks. Declan knew he'd do a good job. It was hard to leave with so many different irons in the fire, but he was determined that while Jacey was with him, he'd do what he could to get his daughter comfortable around him. He wanted his sweet little girl back.

The trip was not all about bonding with Jacey. He was interested in adding an entirely new direction to the company. The fact he was combining business with their time away was prudent. He'd show his daughter some of what he did for a living, thus correlating work with earning money.

Her mother was filling her head with an entitlement attitude that drove him crazy. Nothing in life came free.

Some things came with a steep price. He thought about Savannah and couldn't help but feel a stirring of anticipation. He'd see her soon. He had told Jacey about hiring a nanny and hoped she'd behave.

He'd forgotten over the past seven years how pretty Savannah was. Or had he deliberately suppressed the memory? He'd genuinely tried to make the marriage work. It took two, however, and Margo's agenda had been different from his.

Marrying Margo a second time had been a huge mistake almost from the beginning. Granted, she was stunning. Long dark hair, mysterious eyes, a sly, catlike smile. He'd been captivated the first time around. If she'd told him she was pregnant before they'd divorced, he might have stayed in the marriage. She was high maintenance from the get-go, always wanting to party, to be seen in all the trendy places, to acquire clothes and jewelry and anything else that could be construed as a status symbol. Nothing had changed the second time they married. She'd hired a housekeeper and fobbed Jacey's care off on her.

But she hadn't told him. They'd divorced and he'd met Savannah.

She'd been a small-town girl, new to New York and focused on the business idea she and her sister had of nannies for vacations only. He'd never felt so young and carefree as he had in the months they were together. That time still remained a special memory.

She'd been the first person he'd thought about when he decided to take Jacey backpacking in the wilderness. Savannah was no longer a shy country mouse. From her hair to her attire to her attitude, she was just what he wanted Jacey to be like when she grew up. Trendy without being over the top. Confident, assured, pleasant.

And she probably hated his guts.

He stared at the numbers in the reports he was skimming. None of them made any sense. All he could see was the cool manner in which Savannah had deliberated before giving him an answer. Her final agreement was predicated on her meeting with Jacey going well.

He checked his watch. Time to head for home. What wasn't done wouldn't get done. The world wouldn't end.

Jacey was watching television when he entered his flat a short time later. Mrs. Harris, his housekeeper, was sitting with his daughter, crocheting. Jacey looked up and then deliberately looked back at the television without any greeting.

He had to admit the all-black attire, the dark circles around her eyes and the straight, flat black hair had taken him aback when Margo had brought her by unexpectedly a week ago. Where was the sunny smile Jacey had had when she was younger? The enthusiasm she'd evidenced when she saw him? She used to run to hug him.

"Hi, Jacey," he greeted her, going across the room to give her a kiss on her cheek.

She pulled back and glared at him. "When's the babysitter coming? I called Mom. She'll want to know you plan to pawn me off on some stranger."

"Since your mother didn't consult me at all about this summer, I suspect she'll be happy enough to go along with what I have planned. I thought she was in the Hamptons."

Mrs. Harris, his housekeeper, rose and smiled at her employer. "I'll just finish up in the kitchen," she said and took off without even a glance at Jacey. She did not like confrontations and there'd already been a couple of major storms since the evening Margo had arrived unexpectedly with Jacey, announcing she had plans for the summer and Declan could take a turn with his daughter.

Declan rarely saw Jacey. While he had visitation rights, Margo had demanded full custody. And many of the times he'd planned to see his daughter, Margo had had other plans and couldn't have Jacey spend time with him.

"She has a life, too, you know," Jacey said. "She has a hard time making ends meet. She's going to petition for more child support. And I think you could help out your only child. It's tough living in New York on a small salary."

He looked at her, hearing Margo's voice in his child's words.

"I send more than adequate child support. If she wishes to challenge it in court, maybe we should consider you coming to live with me. That way all her money could go straight to her own needs."

"I don't want to live with you. I'm stuck here this summer when I could be going to the Hamptons with Mom's friends."

He smiled without humor. "Yet your mother brought you here."

Jacey frowned. The fact was she was as angry with her mother as much as with Declan. He was angry with Margo for putting such ideas in his daughter's head. If he could audit his ex-wife's finances, he knew he'd find more of the support money was spent on Margo than on his daughter. He knew how much he sent each month. He doubted Jacey saw much of it, however. Margo had always been high maintenance.

Jacey pouted and looked away, studying the toes of her black shoes. "I wish I was at home."

"What do you normally do at home?" he asked easily.

"Hang out with my friends, for one thing."

"Maybe when we get back from California we can see about having some come over here. Or you can visit."

"It's not like I can walk there."

"I'll provide transportation."

"Whatever."

"Until then you have San Francisco, then backpacking in the High Sierras to look forward to. Remember how we used to go camping?"

"Oh, pul-ease, not camping. I was a kid then. What did I know? When I hear California I think beaches in LA, maybe go to Hollywood, see something worth seeing."

"I understand the views from the Pacific Crest Trail in Yosemite are amazing."

The doorbell sounded. Declan took a breath. Make-or-break time.

Jacey looked at the door but didn't move.

He rose and went to open it. Savannah stood there. Today she wore a light blue silk blouse that made her eyes shimmer. Her slim white pants showed her shapely figure. He wished she'd at least smile at him instead of looking like someone going to a funeral.

Jacey came to Declan's side and looked at Savannah.

"Are you the babysitter?" she asked rudely.

"I'm a certified nanny, but you can call me a babysitter if you think that fits better," Savannah said calmly.

Jacey looked at Savannah and then at her dad. "Did you hire her for me or you?" she asked.

"That's enough," Declan snapped out. "Come in, please, Savannah. As you probably guessed, this is my daughter, Jacey." He turned to Jacey and introduced Savannah.

"If she's going, I'm not. I'm calling Mom." Jacey turned

and went back to the sofa, pulling her cell phone from her pocket. She glowered at both her father and Savannah.

Savannah sighed softly. She really didn't need another assignment that didn't go well. Her last one had been enough to drive a saint crazy. And she wasn't anywhere near being a saint. While her gaze was focused on Jacey, she was very aware of the girl's father standing near enough that she caught a whiff of his aftershave, which spiraled her right back to when she'd been close enough to nuzzle his neck and be flooded with sensations of scent and touch.

Still, having come this far she felt obligated at least to give this interview a fair shake. Trying to ignore Declan, she put herself in Jacey's shoes. She found a bit of empathy. Teen years were hard. Being shunted back and forth between parents was hard. And if Jacey's mother was allowing her to dress like this, she wasn't getting a lot of parental guidance at home.

She sat on one of the chairs, looking at Jacey as the girl stared back at her.

Declan stood nearby. "Does anyone want something to drink?"

"Like what?" Jacey asked.

"Coffee, tea, hot chocolate, a soft drink?"

"I'll have coffee," Savannah said.

"I don't want anything," Jacey growled.

"I'll be right back," Declan said and disappeared into the kitchen area. Suddenly she felt sorry for Declan. He appeared to be trying so hard. Faced with the rebellious teen before her, Savannah knew he'd be in for a bumpy road.

"I don't need a babysitter," Jacey said defiantly.

Savannah took the time to study the girl while she tried to come up with an answer. Jacey could be really pretty if she'd wash her face and wash out whatever dye she'd used on her hair. And put on a colorful shirt. Black leached the color from her skin.

"I'm sure your father knows best," she ended up saying.

"I'm not going."

"Oh? Have the plans changed?"

Jacey frowned. "I don't think my mom's going to let me go to California."

Declan returned, carrying a tray with two mugs of coffee. He glanced between the two and then placed the tray on a table. "You like it black," he said to Savannah, handing her the cup.

Jacey looked at her father with suspicion.

"Jacey says she isn't going on the trip," Savannah said, taking the cup and meeting Jacey's gaze over the rim.

"Well, Jacey's wrong. She's not only going, she's going to have a great time," he said, sitting on another chair facing the sofa.

"When Mom calls back and I tell her what you want to do, she'll come get me."

Savannah watched as she sipped her coffee. Here was a very frustrated, unhappy young person anxious to make things go her way, and they weren't going to. What could she do to distract her? Get her off that line of thinking and on to exploring the possibilities the summer offered?

Jacey faced her father defiantly. "She'll be calling soon."

"Honey, your mother said when she brought you here that she wants you to spend the summer with me. I want you to have a good time. But if you decide to make it painful, so be it. We're still going to California, all three of us."

"Did you tell her we'll be shopping in San Francisco?" Savannah asked. She looked at Jacey. "I've been to the City by the Bay before. It's a fabulous place. They have the crookedest street in the world there. Yummy seafood at the wharf. And the stores are to die for."

"Manhattan has the coolest stores," Jacey said, not at all interested.

"Other places can be cool, too, if you give them a chance," Declan said.

"I hate you!" Jacey jumped up. "Mom said you were always difficult. She was right!"

She ran from the room. A moment later a door slammed.

Savannah looked at Declan. "That went well," she said. "Not. Is she always like that?"

"Before Margo brought her over the other day, I hadn't seen her since April. The hair and makeup is new since then. I think today was a new high in rudeness. Or maybe I mean a new low. With that attitude, we're all going to be miserable."

He looked at her. "You're still going, right? I know you have the right to refuse, but see her for what she could be, not how she's acting today."

Savannah hesitated. She was a professional and knew she was good at her job. But this assignment would be more difficult than any other she'd had. Not only was the child rebellious and going through a definite Goth stage, Savannah was having trouble not focusing on the man sitting across from her.

"I could try it. If nothing else, I'll stick through the San Francisco portion. If it is untenable you'll be on your own for the hiking part. But you'd be with her there and really not need a nanny."

He nodded. "I can handle that. It's not what I want, but if it's the best you'll offer, I'll take it. And hope you change your mind by the time we leave San Francisco."

"We don't always get what we want," Savannah said, rising. "I'll meet you at the airport on Monday. What airline and flight? I imagine the next few days will prove challenging." In more ways than dealing with his daughter.

"I think getting her away from her mother will be the best thing for her. I haven't told her yet there's no cell service in the mountains," Declan said, his expression one of bewilderment and frustration.

"Won't that be fun when she finds out," Savannah said. She studied Declan, seeing his frustration beneath everything. It would prove interesting to see how he handled his daughter.

Savannah hadn't known her own father; he'd died when she was very little. But she'd have loved to have had a father like Declan, good-looking, successful and obviously concerned about his daughter.

Suddenly she hoped the trip would go as planned for his sake.

She walked to the door as he rose and followed her. She could almost feel the vibrations between them. Time and distance—that's what she needed.

He looked at her and caught her gaze, lifting an eyebrow in silent question.

She looked away, too many memories.

"We leave from JFK at ten, arrive in San Francisco shortly after noon." He gave her the airline and said he could have a car pick her up.

"Not necessary, I'll be there."

She reached the door and ventured one more look at him. "Strictly business, right, Declan?"

"Absolutely. Do you want to go over the itinerary before you go?" he asked.

Savannah hesitated again, then shrugged. "I guess." Every instinct clamored for her to leave, but curiosity got the better of her.

"I have brochures and maps on the dining-room table,"

he said. "Jacey, come in here, please. I want to show you something."

Jacey came out of her room by the time Savannah was seated. A couple of maps were spread out on the table, a scattering of brochures nearby. Jacey sat opposite Savannah while Declan took the head seat.

"We'll fly to San Francisco Monday. We're staying right in the heart of the city. I'll take you both with me to check in with the store and get our hiking gear. Want to do anything special after that?" he asked Jacey.

When she merely shrugged, he turned to Savannah.

"There's so much to San Francisco. I think Jacey would enjoy the wharf, especially Pier 39. Then there's the crookedest street in the world, everyone should see that. We can walk down or drive, it's like a corkscrew. Chinatown's fun. And we have to ride the cable cars."

She tried to put as much enthusiasm into the suggestions as she could. She watched Jacey as she spoke, wondering if anything would spark her interest.

"There's also some fabulous shopping around Union Square," she added.

"New York has fabulous shopping," Jacey spoke up.

Savannah nodded. "If you know where to shop."

"You don't like my clothes?" Jacey immediately took up the challenge.

"Not at all," Savannah said.

Declan frowned at her.

"What? I'm supposed to pretend I do when I don't? One thing I insist upon is absolute honesty with children," Savannah said. Time this teen learned not everyone would kowtow to her behavior.

"If you're so honest why not say you're interested in my dad and that's why you're going?"

Savannah burst out laughing. "Oh, no, you have that wrong. I'm the reluctant one on this trip"

Jacey looked at Declan, her expression puzzled. "Why?"

"Various reasons. Anyway, I'll be glad to show you some of the attractions in San Francisco while your father's working. You can pick or I will," Savannah said.

"Whatever," Jacey mumbled, staring at the map.

"So we buy lots of stuff at your San Francisco store," Savannah said, changing the subject and looking at Declan. "I have my own boots. I don't need new ones. But a few new tops and cargo pants wouldn't hurt."

"I don't have anything like that. I don't want to go hiking," Jacey said.

"We'll have a couple of days in San Francisco, and we're ending the trip at a resort in the mountains. You'll need clothes for that, too," Declan said.

Jacey looked bored, her gaze on the map in front of her.

Savannah nodded at the maps. "Show us where we'll be hiking."

Declan rose and leaned over the map of California, showing where San Francisco was and Yosemite National Park. He drew a marker along the Pacific Crest Trail showing where it became the John Muir Trail in Yosemite.

"It's a high elevation," Savannah murmured, following as he pointed it out.

"Some of it's above ten thousand feet. And we'll have higher peaks surrounding us."

"Where are we staying?" Jacey asked, leaning forward to look.

"Camping out on the trail. We'll backpack our stuff—clothes, tent, sleeping bags, food, everything. This is true wilderness. But the resort is here," Declan said, pointing to a spot on the map not too far from Yosemite National Park.

Jacey pulled out her cell phone to check it. "Mom should be calling me," she said.

"Maybe your mother has already started her summer," Declan said.

"What does that mean?" she asked suspiciously.

"She obviously had plans this summer that didn't include you. Why else would you be here for three months?"

"She likes to have me there."

"I know she does. But she's an adult and would like some time to herself," Declan said.

"She can't do much. She has to work all the time. We don't have money for extras," Jacey said.

"I have to work," he said easily.

"Most people on the planet have to work," Savannah added. Wow, Margo had done a number on this child. Money wasn't that important in the greater scheme of things. Family, friends, experiences, all went together to make a rich, fulfilling life. Money helped, but there was more to life than money.

"You're rich, you could do more for us," Jacey said to her father, ignoring Savannah.

"What more do you want, Jacey?" he asked, looking directly at her.

"We're always pinching pennies," she grumbled.

"I send your mother a lot of money each month. It's supposed to all go for you. What're you lacking that my generous child support doesn't provide?" he asked.

"I didn't go skiing with my friends in February. Mom said we didn't have enough money and you wouldn't give her any more."

"You're old enough to understand a few things," Declan said. "First we'll discuss the money I send." He told her how much money he sent each month. Judging from the way Jacey's eyes widened, she'd had no idea. "Granted, some of it goes to supplement the rent and food and basic expenses like that. But if your mother managed the money well, there'd be plenty for extras like a ski trip in February. And, by the way, this is the first time I've heard about that."

"It's expensive to live in New York," Jacey said.

"Your mother's not managing the money I'm sending. Next time something like that comes up, call me directly. I'll consider paying for the trip."

"Mom needs money this summer," she said.

"Now isn't that interesting? I continue to pay the same amount every month, no reduction for the time you stay with me."

Declan glanced at Savannah who was watching the interchange closely. He disliked airing dirty laundry in front of strangers, not that she was a stranger precisely, but he didn't know her now. She'd changed over the years. He hadn't a clue what she was thinking. Probably that all his problems served him right. He'd made a major mistake and could never forget that.

"So we leave in two days," she said, trying to change the subject.

He nodded, suddenly wondering if his idea had been such a good one after all. Jacey was behaving worse than he'd expected. He hoped their time together would prove beneficial.

What really startled him was the anticipation he felt at the thought of spending the next three weeks with Savannah Williams. She'd done nothing even to hint she wanted to resume a friendship, much less anything more. And he couldn't blame her. Looking back, he'd shattered something precious.

No one could go back to the past. Knowing what he now knew, he'd have held on to Savannah for all he was worth.

What would it be like to take this trip with her? What

if they could have taken it alone? Spend days hiking spectacular country and then nights with nothing but the starry sky overhead and endless miles of empty land surrounding them? He knew the reality of their trip would be different, but, for a moment, he almost pretended.

CHAPTER THREE

TIME flew by and before she knew it Savannah was boarding a plane for the flight to San Francisco Monday morning. All weekend she'd dithered, talking things through with Stephanie because she couldn't reach her sister. In the end, she decided to go. It might be a mistake, but she'd made plenty of those in her life. What was one more?

Declan had booked three seats in first class, a luxury she'd grown used to in her line of work. Most of the families who could afford Vacation Nannies had plenty of money and wanted their children to enjoy first-class travel as much as they did—as long as the nanny was there to watch them.

Sitting by the window, Savannah settled in with pleasure. Her lifestyle was so different today from what she'd experienced growing up in that small house on the outskirts of Palmerville, West Virginia.

"Want to sit by the window?" Declan asked Jacey when they boarded the plane.

"Whatever," she said, going in first. Their two seats were together. Savannah's was across the aisle.

Settling in, they watched as the rest of the passengers for the flight boarded. Once they were airborne, Declan got out of his seat and leaned over to talk to Savannah.

"There was a mix-up in the room reservation at the hotel

in San Francisco. We have a suite, but only two bedrooms. Would you find it horrible to share with Jacey? I was confirmed for a larger suite, but found out this morning we got bumped to the smaller one. Some special envoy or something."

She looked into his dark eyes. He looked tired. How stressful was it having his teenage daughter fighting him at every step? Jacey stared out the window, looking mad and unhappy.

"That's what you've hired me for, to be with Jacey. It'll be fine."

"Thanks. If she says anything—I mean, I expect she'll be a bit of a brat."

"Remember you asked for a teen expert. I've handled recalcitrant teenagers before. Relax, Declan. She's being a teenager. They really do better with boundaries and adults running the show. Start as you mean to go on."

He nodded and sat back in his seat.

Savannah smiled at her seat companion and turned to gaze out the window. She had her own problems. Like not getting to sleep last night for thinking about the trip with Declan Murdock. She'd been so in love with him years ago. She thought she'd put all romantic notions behind her when he left. But he was even more interesting now that she'd seen more of the world, spent time among dynamic men who moved in the highest circles. He had a special appeal, and it wasn't all based on the past.

Declan could hire a raft of people to watch his daughter. But he'd chosen her. Not for old times' sake, but because she'd come so highly recommended. And he did need help with his daughter if he so rarely saw her. Savannah was here to do a job, not to dream about her temporary employer.

Savannah brought out a novel she'd picked up in Boston,

not having had a moment to read it after she'd landed in New York—was it only a couple of days earlier? Reading would while away the flight.

As they prepared to land several hours later, Savannah looked over to see Jacey peering out the window as the plane banked over San Francisco. The city gleamed in the sunshine. The buildings of downtown were predominantly white. The water of the San Francisco Bay were deep blue. It was a gorgeous day. Savannah hoped that the teenager would let herself experience some emotion at visiting one of the world's most exciting and beautiful cities.

When they reached the hotel near Union Square, Savannah was pleased with the ease at which Jacey accepted the room assignments. They went into the room they'd share. Two double beds left plenty of room for a dresser and television. The sitting room of the suite also had a large-screen television and two sofas, several easy chairs and a wet bar.

They had a small view of Union Square and when they opened the old-fashioned window, they could hear the famous cable cars clanging as they reached the turntable near Market Street.

Jacey plopped on her bed and leaned back, staring at the ceiling.

"It's only midafternoon. Want to go out?" Savannah asked. The advantage of traveling west was arriving in time to do things.

"Is Dad going?"

"He said he wants to go to the store right away. We could go with him. Or wait until tomorrow to go shopping for our hiking stuff. I know a couple of places where we could find some trendy clothes. Maiden Lane has some fabulous shops."

Jacey sat up. "Whatever."

Savannah resisted rolling her eyes. She wished that word had never been invented. However, she was sure Jacey and teens everywhere would find another equally annoying if that were the case.

Shopping proved more fun than Savannah had expected. In the first shop, Savannah pulled out a lollipop-pink sundress. "My sister's favorite color is pink," Savannah said. "I wouldn't be caught dead in this."

"If you were dead, you wouldn't know what you were wearing," Jacey said.

Savannah laughed. So maybe the kid could be fun to be around. "Good point. What's your favorite color—and don't say black."

"What if that's my favorite color?"

"It's no one's favorite color. Lots of people wear it, but not because it's a favorite color. Purple's my favorite, but I don't wear a lot of it."

"Why not?"

"I don't want to look like a plum?" Savannah suggested.

Jacey actually giggled. "I'd like to see you in purple."

"Okay, find something. I'm not buying, but I'll try it on."

Jacey searched through dresses, finally finding a deep purple one.

"Okay, wait here." Hoping she could trust the teen not to dart away as soon as her back was turned, Savannah went to the changing room. Stepping out a couple of minutes later she was relieved to see Jacey still looking at dresses.

Turning to see Savannah, Jacey began to laugh. "You do look like a tall, thin plum."

"You try it on and see what you look like, Miss Smarty-Pants. You'd look like a plum, too," Savannah retorted, delighted to finally hear a laugh from the girl.

"Purple's not my favorite color."

"What is, then?"

"Blue."

"Powder, navy, aqua?"

"Powder."

Savannah pulled out a light blue dress. "So try it on. Maybe you'll look like a robin's egg."

Jacey rolled her eyes but followed Savannah back to the dressing rooms. While Savannah changed back into the outfit she'd worn on the plane she could hear clothing shuffle in the changing stall next to hers. She was surprised to see how pretty Jacey looked when she stepped out in the blue dress. The makeup was still garish, the hair too dark, but she looked more like a pretty young girl.

"Nice," Savannah said casually. "Want to try on another dress? We don't have to buy anything. It's fun to play dress-up. You should've seen me and my sister when we first moved to New York. We'd spend all Saturday afternoon shopping at high-end stores, just trying on clothes."

They'd done it to find out what looked good and what didn't, making notes on what styles best suited each of them. It made a big difference in the way two country girls were able finally to fit in.

Over the next hour Jacey tried on several different outfits, but she never returned the blue one to the rack.

As it grew closer to the time to meet Declan for dinner, Savannah wondered if she dare buy the blue dress for Jacey.

"Ready to go?" she asked.

"I guess. This has been fun. I think I could be a model."

"Sure, once you learn the tricks of the trade."

"Like?"

"How to walk, pivot, fix your hair and makeup." She was taking a chance very early in their tenuous relationship, but Savannah only had three weeks with Jacey, if that. Anything she could do for Declan would be worth the risk. "Maybe we could get a makeover at one of the department stores on Union Square. I bet their makeup selection is huge."

"Ummm." Jacey didn't exactly jump at the chance, but Savannah was relieved not to have her turn it down completely.

"I like the blue dress," Jacey said casually.

"I do, too. Shall we buy it?" She held her breath.

"Whatever."

Savannah laughed. "Deal."

They reached their hotel room before Declan returned.

"Time for a shower and shampoo before dinner," Savannah said when Jacey dropped the bag from the store on her bed. "Want to go first?"

"I guess. You could use Dad's bathroom since he isn't here," she suggested. "Then I can take as long a shower as I want."

She was once again trying to reach her mother by phone. Savannah didn't know if Margo had ever called her daughter over the weekend. If not, Jacey must be getting annoyed at being ignored.

"Okay, that'll work," she said. Judging how much longer until the dinner time Declan had suggested, she figured she'd have time to be in and out before he returned.

Savannah walked through Declan's bedroom to his bath a few moments later. She kept her gaze averted from the bed, ignoring the few things of his on the dresser. But stepping into the bathroom brought back even more memories. His scent permeated the air. She saw his razor on the bath counter, his aftershave in a bottle beside it. For a moment she was immobile, remembering.

Shaking off the past, she stepped into the shower and soon felt the soothing beat of the hot water. *Focus on your job,* she admonished herself. Jacey had been cordial most of the afternoon—actually, almost friendly toward the end. Trying on clothes was fun no matter what kind of attitude she was trying to maintain.

Still, it felt good to have a few moments to herself. She wondered what Declan had been doing while they shopped. Not that she cared. Maybe she should suggest he take Jacey to dinner and let her stay behind to order room service. It would give the two of them time alone. And she would be spared dining with him again.

Not him precisely. Nothing like before. Despite all the pep talks she'd given herself, it was hard not to feel something around him. An innate curiosity, a feeling of déjà vu, an attraction that sprang forth as strong as ever before. And a memory of his hard words, the end of her love.

After drying off a few moments later, Savannah slipped on one of the thick terry robes the hotel provided. She towel-dried her hair, needing to get the mousse on it. Now it was flat and boring. She didn't know how her sister stood having such long hair. Short hair was so easy to care for. And she liked the sassy look it gave her.

Opening the door she stopped suddenly when she saw Declan lying on the bed. His legs were crossed at the ankles, one arm under his head, as he stared at her coming from his bathroom. Heat flooded, her heart raced. So he'd looked many times before when they'd spent a weekend somewhere. Swallowing hard, she tried to breathe.

"Oh."

"Oh, indeed," he said, rising. He crossed slowly over to her as his gaze traveled down the length of the terry robe. Her heart flipped over, pounded harder than ever.

"Jacey and I wanted showers before dinner. You weren't here. I hope I didn't hold you up," she said. She also hoped he wasn't getting any ideas about her appropriating his bathroom. Obviously she'd misjudged how long he'd be at the store.

He stopped inches away. She wore only the robe, closed with a sash that with one flick of a wrist could be undone. Trying not to think of how little she had on beneath the robe—like, nothing but bare skin—she edged sideways toward the door. He stepped closer and for a split second she thought he was going to reach for her. The surge of longing to feel his arms around her one more time caught her by surprise. Her gaze flicked to his mouth, her own almost tingling in yearning to feel those lips against her again, drawing a response from her that she'd once so freely given.

Then the echo of the words he'd said that had ended everything sounded in her mind.

She was fantasizing about him ripping off the robe and taking her into his arms, kissing her for real, a full-blown lip lock that would blow her mind, when he'd so cavalierly thrown her over for Margo. Now Margo was gone. Did he think he could step back in where they'd left off?

She took another step, watching him warily. What could she say to make sure he knew she was so over him it wasn't funny? That she'd taken this job only for Jacey's sake.

Declan stepped closer. She could feel the warmth from his body. Her eyes locked with his as her imagination ran wild.

"Declan," she started, but that husky voice didn't sound like the crisp professional tone she was striving for. She cleared her throat, took two more steps to the door and opened it.

"How did it go with Jacey today?" he asked.

She turned and looked at him over her shoulder.

"Actually, better than I expected. She actually thawed a bit by the time we reached the second store. I had her trying on any dress she wanted as long as it wasn't black. She even let me buy her a blue one. If she wears it tonight, be complimentary, but don't make a big deal over it."

"Any luck with the makeup?"

"Young girls need to experiment. I'd say you have a typical teen. Once in the wilderness, no makeup for a few days and a compliment or two thrown her way, and I bet she doesn't go back to it. I suggested we could go to one of the major department stores and have a makeover. But her response was tepid at best. Maybe when she gets back to New York you can take her to one of the stores there."

"The resort has a day spa connected. She could go there." He checked his watch. "I have reservations for seven at a place in North Beach."

"I thought maybe you and Jacey should go alone. More time for you to get better acquainted with what she's been up to lately," Savannah said. Even more than before she wanted some distance from Declan. Using his bathroom had been another mistake. She needed to keep tabs and change her behavior or she risked serious heartbreak again.

He stared at her for a long moment, then shook his head. "I need you to buffer."

Savannah shivered and shrugged. "Okay. We'll be ready." Scooting away, she tried to ignore the aching longing that seemed to invade every cell. Why did she have such a hard time remembering he had been the one to end their relationship years ago? How could she let herself be snared by his attractiveness again? Once burned, she needed to guard her defenses.

But for a moment, she could almost feel his mouth on hers.

Jacey was standing in front of the full-length mirror studying herself when Savannah almost burst into their bedroom. She wore a slinky black dress with spaghetti straps and an uneven swirling hemline. Her midnight-black hair hung straight down her back. She had not yet put on the makeup and her sweet face looked pale and drawn against all the black. Savannah couldn't help but wonder why Jacey couldn't see that black was not her color.

She spun around when Savannah entered. "I thought you and my dad would be longer," she said. "I heard him come in a few minutes ago."

"I finished my shower, now it's his turn," Savannah responded, going to the closet to pull out a silvery dress. Black didn't look good with her fair coloring so she rarely wore it. This color was a smoky silvery gray, and looked great with her eyes. To her, the best feature was how well the dress traveled. She glanced at Jacey and considered telling her to put a shirt on, but Jacey wasn't her child and she wasn't going to get into a free-for-all over clothes. If her mother didn't have better taste in clothes for a four-teen-year-old, Savannah hoped her father would.

"I've got to get my hair done," she said, heading for their en suite bath. "You finished in here for a bit?"

"I need to do my makeup, but I can wait until you're done," Jacey called, turning back to the mirror.

Savannah truly hoped the child hated what she saw. Once she had on her macabre makeup, she'd look like the wicked witch from the *Wizard of Oz*.

Savannah had to get her own hair and makeup under control. Shouldn't she get hazardous-duty pay for even contemplating trying to change a teenager? She saw Jacey's clutter on the bathroom counter. The black eyeliner and mascara and the bright rosy blush. Tempting though it was to hide everything, Savannah resisted. She had to get the girl to want to change, not force it on her.

Once dressed, Savannah went into the lounge to give Jacey the bedroom and bath to herself. She walked to the window to enjoy the slight view of Union Square. One of the renowned cable cars was passing. She hoped they got to ride one from one end to another. How could Jacey be blasé about that?

Declan stepped into the lounge. Savannah turned and her eyes widened slightly. He looked amazing. The dark suit contrasted with the snowy shirt and maroon tie. He looked like the very successful businessman he was. His gaze went to her immediately. For a second Savannah could imagine that the two of them were going to dinner and she'd dressed her best to please him.

"You look lovely," he said.

No employer had to say that! "Thank you, I could say the same. Be warned, Morticia will be joining us for dinner."

He grimaced. "Didn't wear the blue dress?"

"Nope."

He ran his hand across the back of his neck. "I don't understand what Margo's thinking, letting her dress that way."

"She thinks she looks sophisticated. Does your ex-wife wear a lot of black?

"I don't know what she does these days. She didn't, back when we were married."

"Well, I think this is a stage," Savannah said.

The bedroom door opened and Jacey walked out. Her eyes were heavily lined in black, her hair had been teased a bit and looked more like a black football helmet than anything else. The high heels she wore made Savannah wonder how she didn't teeter over and fall on her face. She turned back to look at Declan and almost laughed aloud at his dismayed expression.

"So, now we're all ready," she said brightly, hoping to catch his eye.

He looked at her. "Not—"

"—a minute too soon, I know."

Fortunately Declan caught on fast. "Right. Then, if we're all ready, I have reservations at a good restaurant in Little Italy. Everyone likes Italian, right?"

"Sounds wonderful," Savannah said. She glanced at Jacey and felt a moment of sympathy for the girl. Did she even know what she wanted?

Declan bowed to Savannah's hints, but his initial reaction had been to send Jacey back to her room to wash her face. How could Margo let their precious little girl end up like this? The dress was totally inappropriate for someone so young. And a bit over the top for the restaurant they were going to. Some wild night club would be more suitable for the dress—not his daughter.

Savannah looked lovely. Why couldn't Jacey want to look like her?

The cab took them swiftly through the San Francisco traffic and they arrived at the restaurant just before seven. Once seated, Jacey looked around with a frown. Declan watched her. One of the things he and Margo had enjoyed was dining out. Of course, back then, they hadn't had a lot of money. With what he sent each month, she could still enjoy a dinner out from time to time. Did she never take their daughter? Jacey seemed to be bemused by all she saw.

"Do they have pizza?" Jacey asked.

"I'm sure they do," Savannah said. "Did you know the flatbread food we call pizza only had tomato sauce after the Spanish conquistadors brought tomatoes to Europe?"

"What is this? A history lesson?" Jacey asked.

Savannah laughed. "Sorry, my sister and I are always

trying to find out obscure facts to dazzle the other one with. Sometimes that spills over."

"I didn't know it," Declan said. "In fact, I didn't know tomatoes were indigenous to America."

"South America, actually, though the Spaniards spread them all around. Since we've grown up eating tomatoes, I, for one, never questioned where they originated before I went to college." She folded her menu and smiled at him. "But in a fine restaurant like this one, I want more than pizza. I'll have the linguine Alfredo."

"I'm having the veal," he said.

He glanced at Jacey "Pizza's fine if that's what you want."

She closed her menu and looked around. The uncertainty and vulnerable look tugged at his heart.

"Tomorrow we'll go to the store and pick out some clothes for our hike," he said once the order had been taken.

"I still don't see why I have to go," Jacey said. "Why don't you leave me and Savannah here and go on without us? Camping's not fun."

"You used to enjoy camping," he said.

"Well, I enjoyed a lot of different things when I was a kid. I'd like to stay in San Francisco, if we're not going back to New York right away."

"So tell me about camping. Where did you two used to go?" Savannah said.

"The Adirondacks, Poconos, nothing like western mountains. Remember, Jacey, we'd take off after school on Fridays, get a good spot. Then we'd hike, swim if it was warm enough to. Or we'd follow a trail looking for wildlife. Evenings we'd have a campfire and roast marshmallows." Declan spoke about several of their trips.

Savannah watched as the happy memories spilled from him. When she'd glance at Jacey she didn't see fond memories. Why couldn't she unbend long enough to agree with her father about the fun they used to have?

"One more day here in the city and then we leave," Declan said. "I sure am looking forward to the Pacific Crest Trail."

"Me, too." Savannah said. "I brought my hiking boots and some old clothes, but I don't mind buying a few new things. I'd love to see your store here. I've been in the one in Manhattan. Do you have different things for sale in different stores?"

"Depends on where the store is located. For instance, we have more surfboards for sale on the west coast than in our east-coast stores. We can ship in anything from our catalogue, but we don't normally stock surfboards in Manhattan."

Jacey played with her silverware, looking totally bored.

"Remember, Jacey, when you used to come to the store and play with all the balls we had?" Declan said in an effort to include her in the conversation.

She shrugged. Looking at Savannah, she asked, "What do you get out of being a nanny?"

"Actually, quite a lot of enjoyment and a chance to travel. I'm co-owner of the business with my sister, Stacey. We make enough to live the lifestyle we like, and we don't need to depend on anyone else."

"Unlike your mother," Declan murmured.

Jacey turned and glared at him. "She works. They don't pay well in New York."

"I make a comfortable living, Savannah makes a comfortable living. Your mother could if she wanted," Declan said.

"She has an image to uphold. That doesn't come cheap," Jacey defended.

"An image?" Savannah asked. Was this a clue to getting closer to Jacey?

"She works in a very exclusive boutique and has to look the part. Even with ten percent off the clothes she buys, they're incredibly expensive." Jacey looked at her father. "You can't say our apartment's glamorous. It's barely in an acceptable area."

"I'm not discussing your mother's life with you. If you have a problem with her, you talk to her."

"I don't have a problem with her—it's you. You have millions. You could be a little more generous to your only daughter!" Jacey almost shouted the last.

Heads turned, eyes searched for the source, then were averted when Declan glared around the restaurant.

Savannah almost reached out and touched the back of the fist he had clenched on the table. He took a breath and looked at her. He was furious.

Savannah wanted to help. She turned to Jacey.

"So your mother's a buyer in an exclusive boutique dress shop?"

"She's a sales clerk. But if they'd give her the chance, she'd be a buyer. Until then she has to sell clothes to rich people like she'd be if Dad would send more money. He's loaded."

Savannah nodded. She could hear the echo of Declan's ex-wife in those words.

Just then Jacey's phone rang. She snatched it out of her purse, checked the number calling, then opened it eagerly. "Mom, where have you been? I've been calling and calling."

"Jacey, not at the table," Declan said.

She glared at him. "Hold on, Dad doesn't want me talking to you."

"That's not what I said," he said with restraint. "Take it in the lobby so you aren't disturbing the other customers."

"Like I care about them," she mumbled as she rose and quickly headed for the lobby.

"So her mother doesn't call as often as Jacey wants?" Savannah asked as the teen quickly walked away from their table.

"Margo hasn't talked to Jacey since she dropped her at the apartment. And since your interview, Jacey's called her a dozen times with no response until now. Despite what Jacey says, Margo wanted this summer for her own ends."

"If she works at a high-end shop, shouldn't she know better how to dress her daughter?"

"I'm sure she does, but it's easier to let Jacey do her own thing. Margo wasn't much on discipline when we lived together. I expect nothing's changed. I wish she'd stop filling Jacey's head with the idea I owe them more money. I send child support, I'm not planning to support Margo in the lifestyle she'd like."

Savannah nodded. She did not want to get involved in the family dynamics. She wondered how things would have gone if he hadn't tried a second marriage with Margo. Would they have found an easier way to relate, or would Jacey still be going through this stage? This trip was not going to be as easy as Declan thought.

The waiter had begun to serve their plates when Jacey came back.

"Mom was at the Hamptons this weekend. She left her phone at home," she said, slipping into her chair. She looked at Savannah. "She said she didn't know about you."

"Why would she? We live different lives," Declan said easily.

Savannah was glad to see he'd regained his composure.

He'd been angry with his daughter but had let it go. She suspected there would be a lot of that in the days to come.

"I think you and Mom should get back together," she said, challenging her father with her look.

Savannah glanced at Declan.

"It's never going to happen, Jace. Your mother and I tried that when she came back to New York with you. You know that. Eat up. I'll satisfy your clothing requirements at the store tomorrow. You can buy anything you want."

Savannah wondered how much black hiking gear would be found.

"I still don't want to go. Don't I count for anything?" she said sulkily.

"You count for a lot. But the plans are made. I hope you'll remember how much you liked camping when you were little. We'd see deer and beavers and other wildlife."

She shrugged. "Big whoop. I can see animals in the zoo."

"I hope we see them. I can go to the zoo, too, but would love to see some in the wild," Savannah said. "What's your favorite animal?"

The rest of the meal passed pleasantly with Savannah doing her best to draw Jacey out, and Declan paying close attention to all Jacey said. Gradually the conversation grew broader. He told her about his favorite tourist attraction in San Francisco, what he hoped to see while hiking. And how she and Savannah could help evaluate the products he was testing.

"I want the tent to be easy enough for novice hikers as well as suitable for seasoned backpackers," he said.

Jacey listened but didn't say anything. Savannah thought she saw a spark of interest when Declan talked about evaluations, but she wasn't sure. *Something* had to interest this child.

When they were finished, Declan called a cab to return to the hotel. As the three of them rode silently up in the elevator, Savannah wondered if she was helping in any way. The two didn't seem a bit closer than they had been when she'd first met Jacey. And the tension in the elevator car was thick enough to cut with a knife. She still had another day or two to decide whether to stay the course or to return to New York when they headed for the hiking trail. If she had to decide right now, Savannah would opt for home.

CHAPTER FOUR

THE next morning Savannah woke early. Jacey was still sleeping, so she kept as quiet as possible while she dressed. It was awful to feel this way, but she didn't want to confront the teen any earlier than she had to. This was not going to be the dream assignment she always hoped for.

Slipping into the lounge once dressed, she was surprised to find Declan fully dressed, an empty plate beside him, sipping coffee as he studied his laptop. For a moment she wanted to turn and slide back into the bedroom.

He looked up before she could do so. "Good morning. Sleep well?"

"Yes. I'm still on New York time I guess."

"Me, too. I've already eaten. Call room service and order breakfast. I'm catching up on some work. Tomorrow we head for the mountains and I'll be out of touch for a while." He studied her for a moment, then looked back at the computer.

"Actually, I thought I'd take a quick walk around Union Square before the day fully starts. By the time I get back, Jacey might be up and we can eat together." She headed for the door, anxious to escape.

"Sure." He leaned back in the chair and looked at her. "Sorry she was such a brat last night."

Savannah shrugged. "I've handled worse. Teen years are hard."

"Yet that's your age specialty, so I was told."

"It is. They are hard sometimes, but other times, I see amazing transformations and that makes it all worthwhile. Plus I remember being a teenager and all the angst that goes with it. Especially if one is out of step with others in her peer group. I took several courses on adolescent behavior. Wow, that was an eye-opener. I could have applied what I learned to my own life. So I figure I'm a good advocate for them."

"As I remember, you came from a small town in West Virginia."

She nodded, remembering all the things they'd shared. "Palmerville. How did you remember that?"

He looked at her directly. "I never forgot one thing about you, Savannah. I remember your goal was to make enough money to live well. It looks as if you succeeded at that."

She nodded. "We've done what we set out to do. My sister and I have all we wanted. Our company's growing, both in reputation and in the number of nannies who now work for us. The apartment we have isn't in the best of neighborhoods, but since we're rarely home more than a couple of days at a time, it suits us."

"Do you really travel that much?"

"Spring, summer and holidays, yes, I'm gone most of the time. But I love it. I've been on every continent except Antarctica. I've been to carnival in Rio, seen the Pope's blessing in Rome, visited Uluru in Australia. What's not to like?"

He nodded. "Margo should try something like that. It might assuage her desire for expensive life experiences."

She didn't want to discuss his wife. Or even to remember he'd chosen Margo over her when she'd been so very much in love with him. And had thought for a few glorious months that he'd loved her.

"I need to go," she said, opening the door.

"The store opens at ten. I have nothing planned before then, so I'll be here when Jacey wakes," he said.

Out into the hall, she felt as if she'd already gone for a run. Being around Declan was not getting easier, she thought, gulping air. *He remembered everything about me.*

Truth to tell, she remembered every minute they'd spent together. The walks around Central Park, watching skaters at Rockefeller Center at Christmas, even helping out when he had that bad case of strep throat. Tears filled her eyes and angrily she dashed them away. Tough times, but gone. Head held high, she walked to the elevator.

Savannah loved San Francisco. She'd visited each September for the past three years with the Thompson family and their children, Sean and Irene. The children loved riding on the cable cars, exploring Fisherman's Wharf and the Exploratorium. They were still at a fun age. This year they'd be ten and eleven. Approaching the dreaded teen years, but still young enough not to have attitudes that sometimes drove her crazy.

She stepped out of the hotel and headed for Union Square. There was a crispness in the air due to the marine fog. San Francisco wasn't exactly a hot spot in summer as the marine fog kept the temperatures cooler than New York. But it felt good today. The park was tiny compared to Central Park, but it offered a spot of green surrounded by high-rises. The breeze was cool. Setting off briskly, Savannah almost did a quick dance step. It was a beautiful day and she was in her favorite city.

When she returned to their suite thirty minutes later, Jacey was sitting on a chair, one leg slung over the arm, reading a book. Declan was still at his computer. The teen looked up when Savannah entered.

"I'm starved. Dad said I had to wait for you to eat."

"I'm sorry. I should have told you I have my cell. You could have called to let me know you were up. Maybe tomorrow if you're still sleeping I'll wake you up. You could have come with me, it's gorgeous out."

"Dad says we'll walk to the store from here. I'm hungry."

"Be good exercise and preparation for the trail," Declan said with a smile for his daughter.

"I still don't want to go," Jacey said.

Savannah didn't feel she was any closer to getting to know Jacey than when they'd started. The hours were ticking down to decision time. Did she plan to extend her stay, or leave to return home when Declan and his daughter left for the backpacking trek?

When they entered the Murdock Sports store shortly after ten, Savannah compared it to the one she'd visited in Manhattan. This one was larger. The staff was young and friendly. Each sales clerk she saw looked as if he or she had just come in from running or biking or surfing. A healthy glow and trim body epitomized each one.

Declan introduced Jacey and Savannah to the manager, who in turn called one of her most knowledgeable staff members to assist. When Declan went back to the office with the manager, Savannah and Jacey went with their guide to search for their supplies and clothes.

As Savannah had suspected, there was very little in black.

Savannah quickly picked out several shirts and cargo pants to try on. She waited as Jacey listlessly pushed the hangers along or looked through the shirts folded on shelves.

"Don't see anything you like?" she asked after a few minutes.

"I don't know why I have to do this. I'd rather be in New York with Mom."

"What would you be doing there?" Savannah asked. "I thought your mother worked."

"She does. I'd watch TV until she gets home."

"And then?"

She shrugged. "Hang out, I guess."

"Instead, now you have the opportunity to see an amazing national park, with views I hear are spectacular. A entire week to be out in the fresh air and sunshine and do something rather than sit around."

Jacey looked at her, eyes narrowed. "Are you a PE teacher?"

Savannah laughed. "Hardly. But you're young. Don't you like to keep your body moving? I'm excited about the trip—to see the scenery I've only heard about."

Jacey looked at her a moment, then looked back at the shirts. She picked up a navy one, the closest thing to black on the shelf. "I guess I'll take this one."

"We're not going to be able to wash clothes where we're going so if they get sweaty or dirty, you don't want to wear one more than a day. You need a week's worth," Savannah said.

Grumbling, Jacey picked out another couple of colors and bought two shirts in each color. The sales clerk would earn her salary for today, Savannah thought, as she almost pushed Jacey into getting all the clothes she needed. A hint of enthusiasm or gratitude wouldn't go amiss.

Declan joined them when almost everything had been tried on and decided upon. He went to Jacey and rested his arm across her shoulders. She seemed surprised by the gesture but didn't shake him off.

"How are you doing?"

"I picked out what I want. Savannah said there won't be any washing machines, so I got enough for every day."

She held out the stack of shirts in her hands in navy, pink, yellow and minty green. Savannah didn't say a word, but the look she shared with Declan behind Jacey's back signaled progress with colors.

When they went to the register, Savannah took her clothes to a different clerk from the one Declan stopped at.

"I'll buy those," he called over.

"I'll buy my own clothes, thank you," she said, pulling out her credit card. This was strictly business and she wasn't going to confuse the issue no matter what Declan thought. Even back when they'd been a couple she had paid her way many times. She never wanted to be totally dependent on anyone.

In the cab back to the hotel, Jacey asked Savannah why she hadn't let her dad buy her clothes.

"First, it's inappropriate. Second, I told you, I'm capable of supporting myself, I don't need anyone else helping me."

"He's paying you to babysit me, why not let him pay for the clothes you need for that job?"

Savannah wanted to ask if her mother took stuff, but that would be too personal. "He's paying me to do my job," she said. "I pay my own way when it comes to everything else."

"So you're really not looking for my dad to be your meal ticket," Jacey asked, confused.

Savannah laughed. If she only knew. "Nope."

Obviously the idea was new to Declan's daughter.

Savannah wondered what life lessons she was learning

from her mother. Maybe Declan should explore obtaining custody of her during her impressionable teen years.

When they'd sent their new clothes into the hotel laundry, with a guarantee they'd be ready the next morning, Declan asked Jacey what she wanted to do for the rest of the day.

"Whatever."

"So maybe we could look at the maps again to see where we're going, talk about the trek?" he suggested.

"Boring," Jacey said. "Can we go ride the cable cars?"

"I thought you didn't want to go sightseeing?" Declan said.

"Better than staying here and looking at maps," she said.

"How about you?" he asked Savannah.

"I've a few things to do. You two don't need me for that. Go, have fun."

He raised an eyebrow in surprise. What could she have to do? Not go with him, that was obvious. He wondered what it would be like if she weren't here almost under duress. If she still enjoyed time spent with him.

Of course, any fantasies he entertained surrounding Savannah would not include a fourteen-year-old daughter tagging along.

Not that he needed to be having any fantasies right now. He was here for Jacey. He still couldn't believe Savannah had gone along with his job offer. Sometimes—like once or twice a minute—he wished he could turn back the clock. Make a different choice seven years ago.

"Then let's go ride a San Francisco landmark," he said. With enough distractions, he could forget about his growing awareness of his daughter's nanny.

"Why do I have to go if the babysitter doesn't?" Jacey asked.

"Savannah is entitled to some time off. It'll just be you and me."

The rest of the day proved to be the most fun Declan had had with his daughter in a long time. By the time their cable car reached Fisherman's Wharf, Jacey had seemed to forget her surly teenage persona and thrown herself into the ride. The wind blew from the Bay as they walked to Pier 39 and all the shops and restaurants there. For a few moments, he caught a glimpse of his little girl. She laughed once at two little girls holding on to their carousel horses and waving at their parents from the carousel.

They stepped into the chocolate store and browsed the endless array of chocolates. A short time later, strolling along eating delicious chocolate truffles, Declan almost recaptured those first years with the child he hadn't known about. She'd been adorable at seven when they'd first met. And even until last year, he'd thought they had a special bond.

Jacey was especially enthralled with the sea lions that had appropriated several docks. When hoarse barking drew them along the pier, she laughed aloud at the fat animals. Declan thought he could have stayed there forever, watching his daughter make faces at the sea creatures, hearing her laugh, enjoying the perfect weather.

They ate fish and chips for an early dinner, strolled back along the wharf, watching those who were flying kites in the brisk afternoon breeze. The elaborate structures swerved, dipped and soared on the constant sea breeze.

Riding the cable car back to downtown, Jacey stood on the running board, holding on to one of the poles. She'd lean back and let the wind blow through her hair and Declan feared she'd fall off. But her enjoyment kept his mouth shut with cautions.

Still, he was glad when they reached their hotel suite safe and sound.

"I'm going to call Mom," Jacey said heading to the bedroom.

Declan went to sit on the sofa, leaning aback against the cushions. Savannah wasn't here. What had she to do in San Francisco? Did she have friends here? A special someone?

He frowned, not liking that thought. Since Margo, he'd been very wary of getting involved with anyone. Business gave him plenty to do and, until the past few months, he had tried to see Jacey as much as possible.

Still, being around Savannah, seeing her reserve after remembering the carefree, loving woman he'd known before, hurt. He knew he was the reason for that wariness and he hated himself for causing such a change.

And for thinking he was doing right at the time to try to make a family for his daughter. The two years he and Margo had been together that time had probably been almost worse for Jacey than if he'd been a weekend dad. He hated that, and in the end that was what he'd ended up being.

It was growing dark when Savannah let herself into the suite. Jacey was watching television and Declan was again at the computer. He looked up, relieved to see her. He hadn't been worried, precisely. But had wondered all evening where she was.

"Have a nice time?" he asked.

Jacey looked at her.

"Where did you go?"

He wanted to hug her for asking the question that was at the forefront of his mind.

"Sightseeing. Then I had dinner at a fabulous Chinese restaurant. Did you enjoy the cable-car ride?"

Jacey nodded. "I got to stand on the platform. It was cool."

Declan wanted to know where Savannah had been. Had she been with someone she knew, or had she gone sightseeing alone? He looked back at his computer. He regretted no longer having the right to ask.

"The laundry sent back our clothes," Jacey said. "Dad showed me how to pack the backpack. Want me to help you?"

Savannah hid her surprise and nodded. "Sure."

The two of them headed for the room they shared. Declan watched as his daughter displayed more energy than she had the entire time she'd been staying with him. He hoped she'd continue going back to being the lively, happy child he so longed for.

But it was his awareness of Savannah that had him staring at the open doorway for so long. It had started in New York and wouldn't let go.

He wished she'd gone with them today. She would have made the excursion even more fun and given him time with her—precious minutes that he'd never expected to have.

"So riding the cable cars was fun," Savannah said as she folded her shirts and then rolled them to stuff in the backpack.

"I had a good time," Jacey said, sitting yoga-fashion on her bed watching. "Did you ride them?"

"I did."

"Maybe the trip won't be so bad," Jacey said thoughtfully.

"Your dad just wants to make you happy," Savannah said. If only Jacey knew how much the man had tried to make her happy would her attitude soften a little?

"I guess. Did your dad want to make you happy?"

"He died before I could remember him."

"Oh." The teenager was silent for a moment. "That must have been tough."

"Both my parents died before I was four. My sister and I went to stay with our grandmother."

"What was that like?"

"We didn't have much. Grams was old when Stacey and I went to live with her. She had arthritis pretty bad, too. But she did her best for us. And I had my sister. While we lacked material things, we never lacked love. Grams died shortly after I left for college. Stacey and I often think she held on until we were out of the nest."

"Oh."

"Cherish your parents, Jacey. You don't know how long you'll have them," Savannah said lightly. She didn't want to scare the child, but maybe she needed a nudge to begin to appreciate what she did have.

"Dad said we'll get the rest of the supplies and pick up the car in the morning. We'll leave around nine. It'll take several hours to get to the trailhead where we're leaving the car," Jacey said. "I called Mom again, but she didn't answer."

"What were her plans for the summer?" Savannah asked.

"Spend it with friends," Jacey mumbled, pulling out her phone and looking at it.

"Nice for her to have a break, don't you think?"

"From me?" Jacey looked up sharply at that.

"From watching out for you, making sure you're safe, growing, learning. Being a parent isn't an easy job. Working as a nanny, I know exactly what parents have to do to raise children. Everyone needs a carefree break now and then."

"Normally she doesn't," Jacey said slowly. "I wanted

her and my dad to get married again. I don't think Dad will. They fought a lot before they got divorced."

Savannah had seen this hope with other children she'd watched who were living with one or the other divorced parent. "I understand. Truly I do. However, did you ever have any indication your dad wanted to marry your mother again?"

Jacey shook her head. "But Mom says she never should have divorced him. They struggled all the time and then when she was gone, he became a millionaire. She wants to get married again."

"Money's not the best reason to marry someone," Savannah said, hoping she could say the right words. "Love, respect, enjoying being with the other person, those count more. Not everyone's a millionaire. If people only married millionaires, there wouldn't be many people left on the earth."

"I think he loves her," Jacey said. "She told me he doesn't date much. Doesn't that sound like he wishes he was with her?"

"No. You'll only keep yourself unhappy if you think like that. What they had sounds like it was over a long time ago."

"I wish we were back in New York," the girl said, but less vehemently than before.

"We will be soon enough. There, I've squeezed everything in, including my mousse." Savannah lifted the backpack and was surprised at the weight.

Jacey giggled. "They're heavy, aren't they? I don't know how I'm going to manage and I'm used to heavy schoolbooks."

"We'll get used to it, I'm sure." Savannah shrugged into her backpack, fastened the strap in front and walked around a little. "Not too bad."

She took it off and looked at Jacey. "Dibs on the first use of the bathroom."

Jacey nodded and leaned back on her pillows.

It was a long time before Savannah fell asleep. She had only hours left to decide to stay or go. So far she'd not rocked the boat by even mentioning she was still considering letting the two of them go on their trek together. If Declan really wanted to bond with his daughter, it would easier if it were the two of them.

Yet she could already see the change in Jacey. Maybe his plan was working. And if she could help, she wanted to. When she'd first left Declan's office after that initial interview, she'd expected to resent Jacey. She was the reason Declan had broken off their relationship. At first she didn't warm to the child, but the past day or two had shown her how delightful the girl could be.

Or was it that she was still aware of Declan and didn't know how she would keep from falling in love with him again if they stuck close? He hadn't changed that much. Yet she refused to let herself be caught up in some silly daydreams. He'd proven once that she took second place to his daughter. If she let herself go for even a second, she would likely bring only more heartache on herself.

Being around him was like slow torture. She remembered ever touch, caress, special look. Savannah hoped she wouldn't fool herself into thinking he'd changed. That he'd ever put anyone ahead of Jacey.

She was never going to get to sleep thinking about him. She threw on her robe and went to the lounge.

They were leaving their city clothes in the car when they parked at the trailhead. If she went with them, it would be jeans and T-shirts and sleeping in sleeping bags. No amenities, no comforts. Just roughing it on the trail, man against nature.

"Like the pioneers," she said softly as she switched on a lamp and lifted the phone receiver to call room service for some warm milk. She'd do okay. She'd been raised without much comfort or modern conveniences. They'd made do. She could do it again if needed.

She stood at the window overlooking the city while she waited for the milk to be delivered. The lights sparkled. Tendrils of fog drifted by, hiding then revealing the buildings in front of her. Few cars traveled the street. She saw no pedestrians. Glancing at the clock on the shelf she saw it was almost three o'clock. No wonder it looked almost deserted outside. Everyone was asleep. Was she the only person awake at this hour?

When the discreet knock came at the door, she answered it, signing the chit and taking the tray with a solitary glass of warmed milk. Taking off the cover they'd placed on it, she saw it had a sprinkling of cinnamon.

Declan's door opened and he stepped into the lounge as she was taking her first sip.

"I thought I heard something," he said. He wore only pajama bottoms, no top. And Savannah let her gaze feast on his strong solid chest, the glass poised halfway to her mouth. He looked amazing. She remembered running her hands all over that chest, feeling the warmth of his skin, the strength of his muscles. Being held against him as they danced. Crushed against him in passion. Snuggling against him as they watched favorite television shows.

Dragging her gaze away was an effort she almost couldn't handle.

"I, um, couldn't sleep, so I thought warm milk might help," she said, moving back toward the window.

"Is Jacey giving you trouble?" he asked, standing by

the open door to his bedroom. When Savannah glanced over at him, she could see the rumpled bed behind him. She quickly looked back out the window. It was safer than letting her mind go down memory lane.

"No. In fact, I'm a bit surprised at how cordial she was when I got in this evening."

"I haven't said anything, nor have you. Will you be continuing on the trip?"

Decision time. She hesitated a moment, trying to find some reason to leave, wanting just a little more time with him before saying goodbye.

"I guess I'll go," she said, taking another sip of milk.

"Good."

She didn't hear anything and thought maybe he'd returned to his room. She turned and almost spilled the milk. He was only inches away, his dark eyes gazing down at her.

"Remember when—"

"No, don't. The past is past. Let's not drag it up," she said quickly. If he only knew. Since seeing him last week she'd done nothing but drag up the past. "If I go, same rules apply. No talking about the past."

"Will you ever forgive me?" he asked slowly, reaching out to feather his fingertips over her short hair. After her shower, she had not moussed it.

"It doesn't matter if I do or don't," she said, gripping her glass so tightly she was afraid it might break.

"I was wrong, you know. It didn't work. I should have made other arrangements. Margo and I married too young and it didn't work then. I don't know why I thought it would a second time around," he said, his eyes beseeching.

She stepped back before she could drop the glass and throw herself into his arms, begging him to kiss her the way he used to.

"I understand why you went back to her. But you had to have known before you told me…you had been seeing her, right?"

He nodded. "But only with Jacey. She seemed to dote on our daughter. And she seemed older and wiser. It wasn't until after we remarried that she showed more of her true colors. I wanted to believe her so she and I could provide a good home life for Jacey. Only Margo's agenda wasn't the same as mine."

"Some things are only discovered when proven." She turned and walked back to her bedroom. "I'm sorry things didn't work out for you the way you wanted," she said softly, and closed the door. Leaning against it she let her eyes adjust to the lack of light. Once the ambient light from the street filtered through the drapes, she made her way to her bed. Sitting on the side, she sipped the milk, wishing with all her heart that things had been different. As her grandmother had often said, if wishes were horses, beggars would ride. Wishing never changed a thing.

Life moved on. She was sadder than that happy young college girl, but wiser and more prudent. Declan Murdock was nothing but heartache, and she had learned to avoid that state.

The drive from San Francisco to where they'd leave the car at Yosemite National Park took several hours. Declan had Jacey sit in the front to navigate. For several hours Savannah watched as they talked. Gradually she was seeing the Jacey Declan wanted back. It had not been a vain dream to make a family with his daughter. With another mother, they might have succeeded. But then, if Margo had been a different woman, he might not have divorced the first time and he never would have found Savannah.

She'd never had a long-term boy friend after Declan.

First she was focused on her studies in school, and she nursed her heartache. Once Vacation Nannies took off, she was gone more than she was home. Which definitely didn't help in the relationship department.

So to be cherished as Declan had once seemed to cherish her was a pipe dream. It had been fun to be part of a couple. They'd planned activities together, spent their free time doing things both enjoyed, and, she'd thought, built a stronger relationship for the future.

All the more devastating when he'd told her goodbye.

She refused to look too far into the future. She enjoyed her life. She loved children and appreciated the opportunity to explore the world. She'd seen some places others only dream about. There were still a myriad of other exotic vacation spots she'd like to visit.

Was it odd she'd never thought about getting married and having a family? Had Declan derailed that dream? Or was it just natural hesitancy because of her parents? She knew her parents hadn't planned to die so young. Life was uncertain. If something happened to her today, at least there'd be no one whose life she'd alter. Stacey would grieve but move on. She'd not leave some child or children behind bewildered by the change in the family, raised in an environment totally different from their early years.

Savannah realized they'd been traveling in silence for a while when Jacey said,

"I'm bored." As if it were the worst of fates.

"So listen to your radio," her father suggested.

"There's no reception here. No phone reception either or I could call Mom."

Declan glanced at Savannah in the rearview mirror. He had not told Jacey yet that there would be no phone service where they were going. Savannah shrugged. Time would let the teen know. No point in saying anything. She'd support his decision. For the next couple of weeks she was his employee. And she believed in absolute loyalty.

"Want to play a game?" Savannah asked. As a seasoned nanny, she knew kids of all ages got bored on long car trips. She had several car games in her tote.

"Like what?"

"There are tons of games for car play. We can play car bingo—I have some cards with things like signs or state license plates and the first one to get all in a row wins. Or we can spot license plates and the first one to read all fifty wins."

"Like all cars from all fifty states are going to be around here," Jacey said.

"You never know. California is a very popular state. I have some Mad-Lib cards. Or how about Truth or Dare?"

"What's that?"

"Whoever goes first asks the next person a question. That person then has to say truth or dare. If truth, he or she has to answer whatever question you ask. If they say dare, you have to dare them to do something."

"Like what?"

"Like crow like a rooster."

Jacey giggled and turned to look at her. Savannah smiled back. "Want to try?"

"Okay, if I get to go first."

"Go for it."

"Dad, truth or dare?"

"Truth."

"Why did we come on this dumb trip?"

"Truth—I wanted to reconnect with my little girl."

"Oh, brother," Jacey said.

"Okay, my turn," Declan said. "Savannah, truth or dare?"

She looked at him consideringly. "Okay, truth."

"What's your favorite memory?"

"Easy, lying on the bank of the river near home watching the stars at night with my sister and Grams. She knew all the constellations and told us God knows the name of every star. I couldn't fully understand at the time, but I remember I thought that was awesome."

"Okay, your turn," Declan said.

"Jacey, truth or dare."

"Truth."

"What's your favorite memory?" Savannah asked.

There was silence for a moment.

Declan glanced at his daughter. She stared out the window.

"My daddy tucking me into bed," she said in a low voice, looking away.

He felt the clutch of emotion grab hold and threaten to strangle him.

"Dad, what's yours?"

"Like Savannah said, easy. The day you and I went to the zoo for the first time. Actually I have a bunch of favorite memories all centering around you but that's my very favorite. I had a daughter I'd just found out about. Nothing is more special than that."

"This is a mushy game," Jacey said. "Can we play bingo?"

Savannah pulled out the cards and soon she and Jacey were deep into trying to outdo the other. Declan had to drive, so he was excused from the game. When Jacey gave a shout of triumph, he smiled. She was as excited as if she'd won something big.

The games were a hit and Jacey didn't complain about being bored the rest of the trip.

It was midafternoon when they reached the ranger station where they'd get their permit and leave their car. From now on, it was backpacking the High Sierras.

When they were loaded up and ready to go, Jacey complained her backpack was heavy.

"Each of us brings our own stuff. In addition, I'm carrying the tent and the cookstove, so I have the heavier load," Declan said, anxious to get started. He hoped to reach one of the recommended camping sites before it got too dark to set up.

"I bet Savannah's is lighter."

"I'll switch," Savannah said, taking hers off and holding it out to Jacey. The teen studied the backpack for a moment, then took hers off and handed it to Savannah. She almost dropped Savannah's and her eyes widened. "Wait, this is much heavier than mine. You're shorter than me, how can you carry all that?"

"It's my stuff, I've told you before, I'm responsible for me."

Jacey took her own pack back and put it on. "Ready," she said to her father. She opened her cell. "No bars. How am I going to charge it during the trip?"

"No electricity until we get back," her father said.

"And no bars," Savannah said.

Jacey looked up, horrified. "How can I call my mom? What about my friends?"

"We're going into the wilderness like people have done for years. You can live without your phone for a week or two," her dad said, starting off.

Savannah followed, keeping an ear out to make sure Jacey followed. They had gone several yards before the teen scrambled behind them to catch up.

"That's so unfair. I have a life, you know."

"This is life. Seeing the beauty of nature, learning how we can be one with it. Living off the grid," her father said.

"Oh, brother," Jacey said.

* * *

They reached the site Declan wanted before full dusk. Quickly he directed each of them in setting up the camp. When he unloaded the tent, Jacey complained how small it was.

"It's just to keep the dew off us and provide some shelter from the cold. It's not the Hilton," he said. "But I want to see how easy it is to set up. I know the basics, so you two follow the directions and see if you can do it. That's part of the trip, to try out this new gear."

Savannah looked at Jacey. "Now we know the real reason we're here, to wait on your father."

Jacey giggled. "Only if we can figure out how to set up the tent."

Savannah walked over and leaned closer. "Maybe we can figure out how to have part of it collapse on him tonight."

Jacey giggled again.

Declan smiled, turning away so she wouldn't see. Trust Savannah to know how to get the girl in a better frame of mind. He knew now what the Spencers had been talking about. Vacation Nannies did have top-notch nannies. He felt proud of her success. And of knowing he'd been in on the early planning stage.

Amidst much arguing and constantly checking the directions, Savannah and Jacey had the tent erected in less than thirty minutes.

"Ta da," Jacey said when it was up.

"Great job, only the manufacturer thought it should go up in ten," Declan said.

"We'll be faster tomorrow," Savannah promised.

"Now what, oh slave driver?" Jacey asked, sitting on the ground and looking up at her father.

Declan directed the rest of the camp setup. Each followed his directions. Soon Savannah had some water boiling on the fire. The freshwater creek was cold and beautiful. Due to parasites in the water, however, it had to be boiled to be potable. Once the water was deemed safe, she put in the dried ingredients to make a savory stew.

Jacey said little once she finished laying out all the sleeping bags and throwing a rope over a limb of a tree for hoisting their provisions later to keep them safe from bears.

When she finished, she sat on the ground near the fire staring at the flames.

Savannah would give a lot to know what was going through the child's mind. Despite the fun they'd had setting up the tent, she wasn't sure Jacey had decided to enjoy herself. Working, activity, that was no threat. But introspection wasn't her thing and the silence seemed to bother her.

By the time dinner was finished, it was full dark. They washed the plates, banked the fire and prepared for bed.

Once ready for bed, the three of them sat on the ground cloth next to the small fire. It was peaceful. The night sky was full of sparkling stars. The moon was low on the horizon. The setting was silent except for the low murmur of the nearby stream.

"So can you tell us constellations or have you forgotten them?" Declan asked Savannah.

"Oh, we never forget things our Grams taught us. She'd make us learn it." She pointed out the Big and Little Dippers, and several other constellations.

"They're just stars that don't look like anything," Jacey said.

"I have a hard time envisioning the figures they are supposed to represent. Except for Leo and Orion," Savannah said. "They're so clear up here, however. In New York, there's too much ambient light to see any but the brightest stars. There's the Milky Way."

Savannah indicated several other constellations, then stopped. "You'll never remember them all," she said.

"No, but it's fun to have them pointed out," Declan said.

"There's nothing else to do up here. I can't get cell service, don't have a flush toilet or anything," Jacey said. "What's that one over there?"

The flickering fire was small, giving little warmth. Savannah shivered. It had grown colder ever since the sun had set.

"I'm getting cold," she said. "I think I'm going to get into my sleeping bag."

Grateful Declan had known what to get for the trip, Savannah got into her down sleeping bag a few moments later. In only seconds she grew warmer. Snuggling down, she let herself relax. Let father and daughter have time alone. She was tired and glad to get to bed early and be alone for a little while even if she could hear every sound within fifty feet.

Her solitude didn't last. In less than five minutes Jacey followed her into the tent and scrambled into her sleeping bag, turning her back on Savannah. A moment later Declan banked the fire and joined them.

Once in their respective sleeping bags, the tent zipped closed, Declan questioned the wisdom of his sleeping arrangement. Why had he thought it a good idea to be in a confined space with Savannah? He could smell her scent, the sweet floral fragrance that seemed so much a part of her.

She'd made it perfectly clear last night she was not interested in him. The job was solely for Jacey. Still, he wished she'd stayed up and Jacey had gone to bed early. He'd welcome some calm adult conversation. And even some insights from a professional on how to continue to get better acquainted with his daughter.

She'd given him such a sweet smile during the hike that had encouraged him, made him glad he was doing this when Jacey had him doubting every move. She was happy in the trek, that was all. He wished it had held special meaning.

Yet his goal remained steadfast. He wanted his daughter back. Surely the child of younger years was there, waiting to come out again to be the joy of his life.

Declan turned and looked at Savannah. There was little light in the tent. The fire had been banked. The only illumination came from the moon, climbing in the sky. The back of her head was toward him. Her hair was still spiky. He looked forward to the morning to see how she fared. Had she been teasing about always carrying her mousse? Or did she really fix her hair every day?

He liked it that way, it was sassy, just like he remembered her.

He'd liked it longer, too. When he could run his fingers through the softness, let the strands drift through. The sweet smell had permeated every bit of her—including her silky hair.

He'd missed her.

The next morning—more complaints. Jacey didn't have a mirror to use for her makeup. She didn't have a place to take a shower. She was cold and wanted to go home. Had she known there would be no cell service she never would have come.

"After breakfast, we'll heat some water to wash in. You don't need makeup here, there's no one around to see you. And we'll go home when our trip is finished. Time enough then to call or text your friends," he said, barely holding on to his temper. One step forward, two back. Or at least it seemed like it.

"Where are we going?" Jacey asked.

"Up the trail. We're not on a schedule. We'll stop when we want, push forward when we want. There're several overnight stopping areas along the route we're taking today, we can choose wherever we want to stop."

She grumbled again. Savannah listened with some amusement as Declan tried to reason with his daughter.

He found he was best to change his focus to Savannah. He engaged her in conversation and she didn't like it. She was trying to keep a distance, but she sensed the genuine interest he had and that made it easier to tell him—them—more about the operations of Vacation Nannies.

She remembered their long talks into the night when he'd shared his business knowledge with her. She'd taken all the suggestions and applied them to their start-up company. When they paid off, she had so many times wished she could have shared that with him. Here was the perfect opportunity for payback.

"So then we tried the office in a prestigious location. And business doubled almost overnight."

He nodded, his eyes holding hers. The silent "Well done" warmed her heart.

Breaking eye contact she looked at her plate of reconstituted scrambled eggs. She was grateful, but the gratitude was mixed with sadness.

Once they'd cleaned up, Declan had Savannah and Jacey break down the tent, as further testing. He took notes on the things they complained about to see if he could find a way around difficulties in the instructions. Or where they weren't clear.

They started out on the trail. Tall evergreen trees

flanked both sides. The air was cooler than yesterday, perfect for hiking. The sun shone in a cloudless sky and once or twice she heard the screech of an eagle. Looking up, she saw a magnificent bird floating on thermals, wings widespread.

Despite the awkwardness of dealing with Declan, Savannah was glad she'd accepted this job. The scenery was spectacular, the air so clean and fragrant with pine and cedar. She glanced at Declan once or twice. He seemed in his element here. His hiking clothes were worn in spots, like a well-loved pair of cargo pants that had seen many hikes. How did he stand being cooped up inside during the year when he could be here, exploring one of the scenic wonders of the world?

That was another aspect of her job she liked. So often families had some kind of back-to-nature adventure for vacation—whether at the beach, hiking or at a destination resort that catered with water, sun and fun. She would not like to be an office worker.

As the morning progressed, Savannah tried remembering all she could about her adolescent psychology classes. She wished she could find the key to getting Jacey to drop the act and be herself. She suspected from some of the comments the girl made from time to time that she had a great sense of humor and could even be nice. But only if she'd lose the chip on her shoulder. Normally Savannah could relate with teens quickly. Was this more difficult because of the divorce, or because of her feelings for Jacey's father?

The day grew warmer as they hiked along the narrow trail. The higher they climbed, the cooler the air was. Pockets of snow still dotted the landscape in shady sections. Wildflowers pushed up through the damp soil, yellow, blue and red. In the distance snowcapped peaks rose.

Declan had started their trek with a fast pace, but soon slowed to accommodate Savannah and his daughter. As they climbed, Jacey lagged behind, dragging her feet and scowling as she looked only at the ground immediately in front of her toes.

When Declan and Savannah stopped, Jacey almost ran into Savannah.

She looked up. Declan pointed to his left. Silently she turned to see a small herd of deer grazing in a meadow about fifty yards away. The three of them watched in silence for long moments; the deer didn't seem to notice they were sharing the area with them. Two small fawns jumped around, then went to stand near two does.

"They're adorable," Savannah said softly, the delight showing on her face. This alone made the assignment worthwhile. She was enchanted.

Declan glanced beyond her to Jacey. She seemed equally enthralled. Miracle of miracles, there was a smile on her face.

Another group of hikers could be heard coming up behind them. They were laughing and talking. The deer lifted their heads, then in the blink of an eye bounded into the grove of trees beyond and vanished.

"Oh," Jacey said, turning to look behind her with a scowl.

Three couples came into view. They seemed completely oblivious to the scenery surrounding them, too intent on their conversations.

"Hi," they said as they drew closer, glancing around. "Is there something to see from here?"

"Just taking a breather," Declan said easily. "Great day, isn't it?"

"Sure is. Enjoy." They passed and continued with their talk and laughter.

"They're going to miss a lot being so noisy," Jacey said. "I wish they hadn't scared the deer."

"We'll see more—if we let them get far enough ahead of us," Declan said.

"Until then, we can spot wildflowers," Savannah said. "I brought a chart of Sierra wildflowers. It's rolled up in my backpack, can you get it, Jacey?"

"Geez, are you sure you aren't a teacher?" Jacey grumbled, but she reached into Savannah's backpack as instructed.

"I'm sure. I think it's fun to learn new things. I've never been here before, and who knows if I'll ever come back. I want to enjoy everything today I can."

Jacey blew out a breath as she pulled out the laminated chart. The three of them looked at it when Savannah unrolled it, then looked at some of the flowers growing in the meadow.

"Okay. The flowers are sort of pretty," Jacey said.

Declan had to hand it to Savannah, she was making headway. He was grateful for that.

The rest of the day was actually enjoyable. Jacey and Savannah began a contest to see who could spot a new flower. They checked each one that could compare with the chart Savannah had. Stepping off the trail at one point, Jacey's foot got covered with water and mud. The snow melt made everything soggy. But instead of complaining, she just shook off the water and stepped back on the trail.

Savannah had Declan sharing the wildflower descriptions and tried to spot them, as well. But he spent more time watching Savannah and her genuine delight in recognizing flowers from the chart she had. She found life exciting. He wanted that for his daughter. And himself.

They passed another group of hikers going the opposite

direction and had another couple pass them in midafternoon, going at a strong, fast pace.

"Now, *they're* in shape," Savannah murmured as they nodded and passed in seconds.

"But they're going too fast to see the flowers," Jacey said. "Or any deer. I wish we'd see another bunch."

"Look there," Declan said, pointing skyward. Another eagle soared above them

"Wow, is that an eagle?" Jacey asked.

Jacey stepped closer and Declan threw his arm around her shoulders, leaning down so his face was close to hers as they watched the bird.

Savannah watched the father and daughter. They looked right together. With no makeup on, Jacey looked like the young teenager she was. Her hair was still that awful flat black, but at least for a few days, she'd have a healthier look without the makeup. She hoped this would work for Declan's sake. He was trying so hard.

They picnicked with trail mix and bottled water in the shade of a huge cedar. The ground was damp, so they used a ground cloth to sit on.

"This is nice," Savannah said. "It's hard to believe people back home are hurrying to work, hurrying home from work, doing errands and all the while I'm lounging in beautiful country, enjoying myself."

"Guilt-free," Declan said.

She looked at him. "What does that mean?"

"You can't do anything here, so all the ought-to-dos are gone. You can enjoy doing nothing guilt-free."

Jacey laughed.

Savannah turned to look at her. "What are you ignoring guilt-free?" she asked, delighted to see the girl's spontaneous laughter.

"Chores around the apartment. And no homework."

"You wouldn't have homework anyway over summer."

"Yeah, but it's hard sometimes to make the switch. I find I still feel like I should be doing something about studying even after school gets out."

"Then I'll see what more I can do to help," Savannah teased.

"Hey, flowers are enough for today. At least I don't have to take a test."

Savannah pretended to be in deep thought. "Maybe I can have a geology lesson. Talk about the mountains here."

"I'd rather learn map-reading. Dad's map is topographical, how do you know how to read that?"

Declan reached for the map in an outside pocket of his backpack. "I can show you," he said flipping it open. "It's easy once you get used to it. It shows the terrain so we know if we'll be going uphill, finding a valley or a wide meadow."

"Too bad it doesn't show where there'll be more deer," Jacey said, looking over at the map.

"We're about here," Declan said, pointing. "And we'll follow the trail here. See where it opens up for a while? That'll be a meadow."

The two studied the map for a few minutes. Then Declan suggested they move on to reach the meadow as a stopping place for the night. "There's no water there, so if we don't find a snowbank, we'll have to use what we're carrying," he said as they donned their backpacks.

"And if we find a snowbank, remember the first rule of winter—don't eat yellow snow," Jacey said.

Declan laughed. "You remembered."

"Always, how many times did you tell me that when we went to the snow in Vermont that Christmas? And you always laughed. It's not that funny."

"Maybe not, but at the time it was," Declan said a look of amusement still on his face.

Savannah looked away. It hurt to be excluded from special moments in his life. She had thought they would share them. And look where they were today.

The hike that afternoon after their lunch stop was delightful. Jacey began to talk without the attitude. Mostly with Declan, but now and then she'd say something to Savannah. By the time they stopped for dinner, Savannah was beginning to think Declan's idea was working exactly as he wanted. By the end of the hike, his sweet child would be back, and she hoped the surly teenager was gone for good.

Thinking about the end of summer reminded her she might not ever know the outcome. She was hired to be with Jacey only for this trip; the assignment ended when they returned to New York. She kept up with some families, but others were a one-time holiday, never to be heard from again.

The agency sent cards at Christmas, and she sometimes wrote a personal note to the families she'd really liked. Sometimes they asked for her again. But there were children growing up now she'd enjoyed watching a few years ago, about whom she knew nothing more. Ships passing in the night, never to see each other again.

As it would be with Declan and Jacey.

Whether discussing his business, his family or remembering happy memories, she couldn't help seeing them all through the eyes of might-have-been.

Still, she thought as she gazed around her, while her sister had an assignment on the beach in Spain, Savannah wouldn't trade this hike for anything. Painful memories and all.

CHAPTER FIVE

ON THE fourth day, Declan woke early. The trek was going better than he'd expected. Which was fortunate. If he'd been continually subjected to Jacey's attitude as she'd so charmingly displayed it when she'd been left with him, he didn't know if he could have coped. He ran a multimillion-dollar company, but his daughter baffled him at every turn.

As did Savannah. It was easy to understand why she kept her distance from him. He deserved it for the way he'd treated her. He couldn't help but wonder if she'd hold that decision against his daughter. But she showed no evidence of it at all. Granted she treated him like a stranger—kept him at arm's length, but with Jacey, she was friendly and was gradually working with his daughter to build her confidence, tease her out of sulks, and show that she could have a good time despite her initial reluctance.

Today was the turning point. They'd be heading back to the car and then on their way to the resort in Taylor. Much as he was enjoying the time with his daughter, he was also anticipating discussions with the resort. Murdock Sports already had several major stores across the country. This would be a different kind of outlet—high-end clothes and gear—specialty shopping tailored for that particular resort.

He'd debated taking Jacey along when he saw how she looked these days. But since they'd arrived in California the outrageous aspect of her attire had softened. He hoped, with Savannah's help, she'd not be a detriment at the resort. If it didn't work out, he'd have them driven back to San Francisco. He thought they'd enjoy the resort and give him space to deal with the opportunity to expand.

After breakfast they packed up. Their backpacks were lighter now as the food was being consumed. No more complaints from Jacey first thing each morning. And Savannah had never given a single complaint. She still moussed her hair every day. Fascinated, he loved to watch, hoping she didn't notice.

In fact, he loved watching her do anything. From working with Jacey to setting up the tent, which they could do in under seven minutes now, to her enchantment with the wildlife they'd seen, to her sparring gently with his daughter. She had a great sense of humor and was able to draw the same from Jacey.

"Today we head back down the trail," he said, pulling on his load. "By the time we reach the car in a few days, it'll be time to move on to the resort."

"If it has a hot shower, I'm all for it," Jacey said.

"I wouldn't mind one myself," Savannah added. "I guess I thought we'd be hiking a bit longer."

"It'll take us three days to return. Then you'll get to rest."

"But you'll be working," Jacey said.

"Not all the time."

"What'll we do there?" she asked.

"There are tennis courts and swimming pools, hiking trails. And a day spa—maybe you and Savannah would like that."

"No maybe about it, that's right up my alley," Savannah said.

"What's a day spa?" Jacey asked.

"You'll love it. You get to be pampered all day—massages, manicures and pedicures, hair styled—though I like mine the way it is," Savannah said.

Declan looked at her. "I do, too."

She looked at him in astonishment.

Jacey looked at her. "Would I have to get my hair styled?"

"You don't have to do anything. It's usually buffet style—you pick and choose the aspects you want. They do makeovers which are really fun. I'm sold."

Instead of the scowl Declan expected, Jacey looked thoughtful.

They retraced their steps, seeing the scenery a second time from the opposite direction. Once they saw a mother bear and a cub at a distance. Declan had them go quietly so the bears wouldn't notice three hikers. But Jacey and Savannah insisted they stop for a moment to watch the cub's antics. When Jacey laughed aloud, he hurried them along.

He had enjoyed the trek more than expected. Even with Savannah. He wished he could turn the clock back.

It seemed to Savannah as if the next days passed in double time. They were familiar with the terrain and better suited to walking long stretches than they had been when they started. They saw more wildlife on their way and passed more hikers as the weather was warming and people were taking advantage of the open trail.

Declan gradually shifted his own focus from testing the new hiking gear to the business opportunity ahead. He spent less time in conversation. Twice she saw him lost in thought when his daughter asked a question. She'd call his name loudly before he'd react.

The day before they were to reach the car it rained.

A sudden storm came upon them before they knew it. Declan quickly erected the tent and the three of them and their backpacks huddled together inside as the rain poured down.

"This'll melt the snow," he said. The temperature had dropped; the dampness in the air made it seem even colder.

"We weren't walking in the snow," Savannah reminded him. She lay down on the ground cloth, using her backpack as a pillow. "I guess we were lucky we didn't have rain before."

"The forecast didn't call for it when we left San Francisco," Declan said. "But maybe it's just a local storm. Quickly started, quickly over."

"Or maybe it'll rain until tomorrow and we can't even cook dinner," Jacey said, gloomily.

"We have trail mix."

"For dinner?" The horror in her voice had Savannah smiling again.

"Think of this as an adventure. Won't it be fun to tell your friends when you get back?"

"None of them will care a bit about my summer vacation. They're doing cool stuff like exploring New York or going to Coney Island or the Hamptons."

"Ummm," Savannah said, looking at Declan. In such close quarters it was hard not to. So maybe neither of the others would suspect she looked at him when she could, when he was not watching her. It make her heart race and gave her squishy feelings inside. Determined to ignore the sensations, she listened to the rain and wondered if she could get Jacey to have a makeover. And new hairstyle.

Their last night camping, and they were stuck in the tent. When Declan excused himself to "use the facilities," as he said, Jacey looked at Savannah. "I wish we weren't going to this resort after all," she said softly.

"Because?"

"Dad's not the same. When we were hiking today he didn't see the deer until I pointed them out and I had to call him twice."

"I'm sure he's thinking about business."

"What about me?"

"What about you? He hasn't forgotten you. He's taking you on this great trip. And I expect you'll love the resort."

"But he won't be with us, I bet. He'll be all business. Like he is at home."

"It takes a lot to run a successful company like your dad's," Savannah said. She'd seen the change in Declan as well and hoped once he was at the resort he'd remember to spend time with Jacey. "Try getting him to talk about it. After all, you have a good shot at being the president of that company someday."

Jacey looked at her in surprise. "Me?" she squeaked.

"You're his only heir. Who else is he leaving everything to?"

The teenager was silent for a moment. Then she shrugged. "He could get married again and have more kids."

"Still, he adores you. Even if he has other children in the future, you'll always be his first-born precious child. And if he has a boy, what's to say the boy would want to work in sporting goods? He might want to be a soldier or a banker or artist."

"I don't know if I want to work in sporting goods," Jacey said thoughtfully.

"So find out about the business, see if it's something you'd be interested in. Get him talking—he'll love that you're interested, even if in the future you decide to do something else," Savannah said.

Declan came back shaking the rain off himself as much

as he could before sitting down and looking at the two of them sitting so close. "What's up?"

"The moon," Jacey said, then laughed.

"The stars," Savannah said and smiled at Jacey.

"The rain clouds." The teenager laughed again. "So, Dad, tell me about the boutique at the resort."

If Declan was surprised at the question coming out of the blue he didn't show it. He relayed a brief version of what he planned to propose and what he was looking to find out on their visit. Savannah was pleased at some of the questions Jacey asked. They showed genuine interest—perhaps for the first time. When they turned in that night, Savannah also knew much more than she had before. Quietly, in the dark, with only the gentle sound of the rain for background, Jacey asked more questions.

Savannah liked listening to Declan talk. His thoughtful approach to the opportunity reminded her of his warnings and guidance when she was in class. Not for Declan the exciting pie-in-the-sky outlook. He was a firm business-man wanting to make sure his business ran efficiently and profitably. She remembered the discussions they'd had in the class she'd attended. Some of his ideas flew in the face of long-established traditional business models. Yet he was now living proof his ideas worked.

As they had worked with Vacation Nannies.

Savannah listened to Jacey and her father talk and felt a twinge of envy. She didn't remember her parents. Grams was the only family she'd known except for her sister. How often had she longed as a child to have the normal family unit of parents and kids? Too numerous to count. She wished Jacey would appreciate what she had. Even with her parents divorced, she still had the love from both, and she could spend time with them.

"It's getting late. I'm going to sleep," Savannah said.

They had unpacked in the limited space and spread their sleeping bags.

"Dad and I'll stay up. We're talking," Jacey said proudly.

Savanna hid a smile. Gone, for now, was the attitude. There was hope for the teen.

"We'll be quiet soon," Declan said.

"I'm so tired, I won't even notice," she said. Savannah fell asleep listening to the murmur of Declan's voice, a smile on her face and an ache in her heart.

The next morning they awoke to a cloudless day. Everything dripped from the rain, but the tent had kept them dry. After a hasty breakfast, they were on their way. They'd reach the car by midday, drive to the resort and be there in time for dinner. During the walk, Declan fell into step with Savannah.

"What caused Jacey's interest last night?" he asked.

"Shouldn't your daughter be interested in what you do?" she asked, glancing over her shoulder to glimpse Jacey studying the trees they were walking through.

"Never happened before," he said.

"Just be glad she's interested."

"I am, just wondering what brought about the change. Are you glad to be going to the resort?"

"In some ways, of course, but I think this hiking idea was good. Look how much she's changed in such a short time. A few more days and she might even want to change her hair back."

He laughed softly. "Wish that was so." He smiled at her. "I appreciate your hanging in there. She's still snippy but definitely improving."

Jacey caught up with them. "I hope we see some more deer before we reach the car," she said, from her dad's left. Savannah was on his right but dropped behind them as they walked.

"Me, too. But we always have the memory of that first day," Declan said.

"We should have brought a camera. I could take pictures to send Mom," Jacey said, head up, looking around.

Declan nodded. "We can get a disposable one at the resort and take some picture there."

"But we missed those deer," she said.

"We'll take others. That image you'll have in your head anytime you want to think about it," he said. Declan was pleased with the change in Jacey in just a few short days. Granted she still lapsed into sulky behavior. She hadn't exactly warmed up to Savannah, but they interacted in a way that was good for his daughter. With the heavy makeup gone she looked much more like the sweet little girl he remembered.

He glanced at Savannah. Opportunity lost. He wished the two of them had been on the trek alone. Spending nights together in the tent. Seeing the splendor of the mountains, the soaring eagles together. Sharing.

Even with the distance she kept, he wished they had a few more days in the wilderness. He knew once they reached the resort his free time would be limited.

Savannah looked up at the sky and smiled. He felt it like a fist to the chest. He wanted one of those smiles directed toward him.

He scanned the trail ahead. How soon would they reach the car? The sooner they were at the resort, the sooner he could get to work and avoid so much time with her.

He had dated occasionally over the years since he and Margo had split the second time. Not often, and not for long. More time was devoted to building the firm. Now he could coast a little—but that didn't mean he wanted to get entangled with some woman. None had compared with Savannah in making him feel like the most important man in the world.

Frowning, he focused on the immediate future, getting to the resort, checking in with the New York office, starting the ball rolling with the potential negotiations. He needed to let go of all thoughts of Savannah. He hoped he could.

They arrived at the resort around four o'clock. Once again they had a suite, but this one had three bedrooms. Declan showered, shaved and dressed in casual clothes, pulled out the laptop and called his second in command. It was evening in New York, but Nick had been expecting his call and was still at the office.

Leaving the lounge area available for Jacey and Savannah, he settled down to business in his room, forgetting all else but the business model Nick had been working on since Declan had called from San Francisco.

Savannah didn't know the plans for dinner, so after she showered she dressed in one of her new casual hiking outfits and regular cross trainers, prepared to wander around the place and get her bearings. She'd barely noticed the amenities of the resort when they arrived, Declan had been in too much of a hurry to contact his New York office.

She wandered into the common room of the suite, wanting to explore the resort but not leaving Jacey behind. She knocked on her door. In seconds the teenager opened it. Her hair was still damp, hanging straight down her back. No makeup so far. But the black was back. Black T-shirt, black jeans, black shoes.

"Want to explore the resort?" Savannah asked.

"Where's Dad?"

"I think still in his room talking with New York, that's

what he said he'd be doing. We can walk around, check out stuff and be back in time for dinner."

"I guess."

They retraced their steps to the large lobby then took one of the halls branching off that held the allure of shops. A gift shop, a clothing store, a jewelry store and a small office area opened along the hall.

"Why would someone want to buy jewelry when on vacation?" Savannah mused as she gazed into the window display with large rings, bib necklaces and assorted tennis bracelets.

"Maybe someone gets engaged here and the guy wants to buy something for her," Jacey said, also looking at the sparkly items.

"Which do you like best?" Savannah asked.

"That blue one, on the right there," Jacey responded promptly, pointing to the sapphire ring.

"That's pretty, I like that necklace," Savannah said, pointing to a simple diamond pendant hung from a long platinum necklace.

"It's sort of plain," Jacey said.

"So's your ring."

"But chunky rings would be hard to wear and not hit against things. I'd think you'd like that necklace," Jacey pointed to an elaborate diamond and ruby bib necklace that had to be worth a fortune. "It's the one my mom would want," she finished.

"Ummm, different tastes. Come on, let's check out the clothes. I bet this is as upscale as your mom's place of work."

"Yeah, I've only been there once. She said it's not for kids."

They looked at the clothes; Savannah was slightly startled at the high prices. Fortunately, she wasn't planning to buy anything, just look. But when Jacey seemed drawn to another light blue dress, Savannah made a mental note to see if Declan would get it for her.

"Paging Savannah Williams, Savannah Williams." A uniformed hotel employee was walking down the main hall.

Savannah looked at Jacey and hurried from the shop. "I'm Savannah Williams," she called to the man.

"A message for you." He handed her a white slip of paper with a note on it from Declan.

Where are you two? Let's get ready for dinner.

"Shopping postponed," she said with a grin to Jacey. "Your dad's hungry. We need to get ready for dinner."

Jacey walked beside her back to the elevators, eyeing the other guests as they walked along. There were families, singles, young couples and retirees—a wide assortment of ages and interests. But it seemed to Savannah that Jacey paid the most attention to the other teenagers. None of whom were dressed in black.

From a couple of sidelong glances and giggles that followed, Savannah suspected the teenagers were having a great time. She glanced at Jacey who looked at them with longing. Could she find a way to have Jacey hook up with other teens at the resort? Maybe there were special activities for that age group.

Savannah wore the same dress and sandals she'd worn in San Francisco. She'd planned more for hiking the High Sierras than dining at a fancy resort. Not that she didn't have other appropriate dresses, but only two more. This remained her favorite.

When she stepped into the lounge shortly before seven, Declan was already waiting. He wore his suit and white shirt. She saw the gleam of appreciation in his eyes and was glad she'd worn the dress again. Not that it meant anything. But every woman likes to be appreciated when she takes the time to dress up.

"Jacey and I were in one of the dress shops when you paged. I think she saw another dress she liked that wasn't black. Maybe she'll try it on tomorrow," she murmured, wishing she could just stop and stare at the gorgeous man in front of her.

"Have her charge it to the room," he said casually. "Where is she?"

"Coming. Where are we eating?"

"The Montgomerys have asked us to join them in the Mariposa Room. I said we'd be there at seven."

"Oh, I shouldn't go then."

"Why not?"

"If it's business, I have no need to be there."

"It's not business, it's dinner. Jacey and you are included."

Savannah still wasn't sure she should attend. This assignment was as unlike any other as she'd ever had. First, she'd never been so aware of a child's father as she was of Declan. No matter how often she told herself she couldn't allow herself to trust him, it didn't stop the awareness that grew daily.

Awareness exacerbated by the memories of his touch, his kisses, his very presence in her past. Funny how she hadn't thought about him in years and suddenly it was as if they'd parted only yesterday. Every memory she had popped to the forefront of her mind and she was hard-pressed to ignore the longing that grew.

A yearning for what could never be.

"Did you get all your work done?" she asked for distraction.

"Enough. It's late back in New York and so I sent them home. We'll get going again in the morning."

Jacey opened her door and both Savannah and Declan turned toward the door. She stepped out, looking warily at both of them, defensively, as if in challenge.

She wore the blue dress bought in San Francisco. No makeup and her dark hair was pulled back from her face and tied at her neck with a white ribbon.

"Don't you look nice. Ready to go? We'll be eating with Harry and Ada Montgomery. They own the resort, though their children run it now," Declan said.

"I'm ready. What'll we talk about?" she asked, looking back and forth between Savannah and her father.

"Business, mostly, I expect. You okay with that?" Declan asked.

"I guess." She darted another questioning look at Savannah.

"You look very nice," Savannah said with a smile.

"Thanks," she mumbled and went to the door.

"Actually, you look beautiful," Declan said as he held the door for them to pass through.

Jacey ducked her head, but Savannah saw the happy smile.

Dinner went better than Savannah had expected. Ada Montgomery was a delightful older woman who was immediately taken with Jacey. Declan had been right, Jacey had a delightful personality when she wasn't convinced she needed to make a statement designed to drive her father up the wall.

Ada was originally from New York City and spoke of the fun she'd had growing up there. Soon she and Jacey were comparing notes. Savannah was pleased that the woman drew out the teen, but was shocked when Jacey said, "I need to get my hair fixed. Does the spa here do things like that?"

"Of course, dear, we have some of the best people on the west coast. How about you and me, and Savannah, of course, do a full day tomorrow at the spa. It'd be my pleasure to treat you both. And you'll love all the pampering."

Jacey glanced at Savannah. "She said spas were wonderful."

"Ah, a wise young woman."

Jacey seemed unconvinced. "She's my nanny. Not that I need one, but Dad's old-fashioned that way."

"Ah, a properly chaperoned young lady. Nicely done by your father," Ada said wisely.

Jacey stared at her in surprise, then her expression grew thoughtful. "Yeah, I guess she is more like a chaperone. Not that I need one of those either. She's almost like an older friend."

Savannah couldn't believe her ears.

"Friends are important to have. And I also have friends of varying ages. Makes life so much more enjoyable," Ada said with a friendly smile at Savannah.

Jacey stared at her. "Really?"

"Friends are those you can confide in, too. I've been my husband's confidante for forty years. He talks with his men friends, but I know what's really important to him. We're best friends."

"You're his wife, that's your job."

"Oh, no. Many husbands and wives are not best friends," Ada said.

Jacey looked at her dad. "My mom and dad aren't friends."

"Were they once?" Ada asked.

"I don't know. I only see them arguing."

"Not best friends, then. What does your mother do?" the older woman asked, changing the topic smoothly.

The talk centered on Margo for a while. Savannah listened, picking up on some of Jacey's comments. She wondered if she should share with Declan. Jacey wasn't telling her, she was telling Ada. So no confidentiality involved. He should know what she was going through. Savannah had an idea he hadn't a clue.

After dinner they thanked the Montgomerys and returned to the suite.

"She's nice," Jacey said in the elevator. "And she's going to treat us to the spa tomorrow."

"Sounds like fun," Declan said.

When they reached the suite, Jacey went straight to her room, but Savannah stared at Declan hoping he'd pick up on not retiring immediately. He did.

Once the door closed behind his daughter, he turned to Savannah. "Want a brandy or something before we go to bed?"

"A small one. I wanted to talk to you about Jacey."

"I figured as much." He poured the brandy and brought it to one of the sofas, gesturing for Savannah to sit. He sat beside her, handed her a glass then touched his lightly to hers.

"Thanks for all you're doing," he said.

"That's why you hired me. I think you should know some of how Jacey spends her life with her mother. Alone many evenings, no one to attend school activities and a series of men in and out of their lives who may or may not be her future stepfather."

She relayed what she'd learned that evening. Declan grew more frustrated the more she revealed.

"I thought she'd be better off with her mother," he said finally, standing and pacing to the window. It was black out except for the lights on the grounds. He turned. "I've thought over the past couple of years I should ask her to live with me. Or at least spend more time with me. I want her to grow up with my values and ideals. Not only her mother's."

"Are you going to devote any more time to her than Margo does? Your business seems all-consuming," Savannah asked. "Or are you planning to have Mrs. Harris fill in full-time?"

He studied her for a moment, lost in thought.

"Balance, remember?" she said. "That was one of the tenets you pounded into our heads in the class. Don't let the business become all-consuming. At the end of the day, leave it behind, refresh and hit it hard the next day."

"I hate it when people quote things I said back to me," he grumbled.

She laughed, setting her glass on the coffee table. "Touché. Pay attention, Professor, the words hold true. More so when children are in the equation. They grow so fast. I bet it seems like yesterday she was that little seven-year-old you had just met."

He nodded, studying the last of the brandy in his glass. Tossing it back, he put the empty glass on the windowsill.

"I don't want her to exchange one neglectful family situation for another," he said. "I'll have to think about it and feel Jacey out about it, as well. There'd still be the problem of her coming home from school while I was working. Mrs. Harris would be there, but not to entertain her."

"She could entertain herself. Or, you could find her a spot at the company where she could do her homework, then ride home with you. Encourage her interest in the business. She might surprise you," Savannah suggested, sipping her brandy.

"You mean she might have a genuine interest, not just one forced on her because she was bored on the hike?"

"Exactly." Savannah rose and joined him by the window. "Don't neglect her while you work. We know you need time, but the expectation when we left New York was devoting exclusive time to recapturing the fun you had camping and hiking when she was younger. You need to make sure she knows she still has your full attention when she needs it."

He reached for her hand, lifted it to his lips and kissed it. "You're amazingly astute about children. You've changed over the years."

Savannah stared at her hand in his, feeling the tingling down to her toes. She refused to meet his eyes, afraid of her own weakness. She wanted to draw him closer, kiss him, hold him. To forget for a little while that they were no longer strangers.

"Not necessarily. These are my suggestions, who knows what's going to work with her?"

Her focus wouldn't move from Declan, on the hand that held hers, on the warmth on the back of her hand that had been kissed. Chancing it, she looked up. His eyes gazed into hers.

"Want to take a walk?" he asked slowly.

"Where?"

"Outside. I miss the night sky, the freedom we had on the trail."

"It'll be cold out."

"Get a jacket."

"Oh, won't that look nice with this dress."

"I'll give you ten minutes to change."

Savannah hesitated. She was being foolish. A prudent woman would bid him good-night and go to bed. Temptation proved too strong. She knew their time together was fleeting. Throwing caution to the wind, she decided to give in to desire for tonight.

"Deal." She whirled and hurried to her room.

Stepping outside from the lobby a few minutes later, Savannah felt as giddy as a schoolgirl with her latest crush. This was probably a stupid move, but she pushed her doubts away. She'd told Jacey they were going out for some fresh air. The teen was listening to music and didn't care.

The sweatshirt and long pants felt good in the cool mountain air. The lights around the resort blotted some of the stars, but many could still be seen overhead. They took a path away from the buildings and soon were surrounded by tall pines and firs, blocking the resort light while permitting only limited light from the stars.

"If we get lost, it's on you," she said taking a deep breath of the crisp air.

He reached for her hand. "As long as we stay on this trail and then turn around, how can we get lost? Remember when we went for a stroll at that place in the Adirondacks? There'd been no moon that night."

"But we had flashlights. I remember Stacey and I used to sneak out of Grams' house some nights to go on fishing trips with some of the kids from school. We thought at the time no one knew, but now I suspect every detail was known, but deemed safe enough. Palmerville, West Virginia, isn't exactly a hotbed of crime. Or anything else for that matter. It was always a little spooky in the dark. I was younger then, of course."

"So you'd go to the local fishing hole. Ever catch anything?"

"No. Who catches fish at night? And if we had, how would we explain that to our parents or Grams?"

"I'm sure you would have come up with something."

"Ever go night fishing?"

"No. Our greatest activity was playing softball then baseball by the time I got into high school. I hated to go home from the park as I remember. Those were great days."

"Are your parents still doing well?" Savannah had never met them. But Declan had spoken about them from time to time.

"My dad is. He lives in Albany. Married again about three years after my mom died. They're happy."

"I'm sorry. I didn't know she'd died. I bet your dad's proud of you."

"I hope so. And if so, it's more because I'm a good man than for all the money I've made. He was disappointed my marriage didn't take. I don't think he cared that much for Margo, but he adores Jacey."

"Jacey needs as much family as she can get. To gain different perspectives. Her mother sounds like a self-centered, money-hungry woman."

"Makes you wonder, doesn't it? I'd think you'd have more reasons to crave money, coming from a poor background. Margo never had it as bad as you. Yet you have balance and she doesn't."

"I have much more than I ever had before, and actually more than we anticipated when we started Vacation Nannies. I'm living just the way I want. I have savings in the bank. What more could I want?"

"Millions?"

"Why? It'd just swell my bank account. Money for money's sake doesn't do much for me. But having enough to live like I want to does."

"You wouldn't have to work if you had millions," he suggested.

"I love my work. I adore children, and I really like visiting exotic locations."

"You could travel if you had millions."

"Like you do?" she asked, teasing. It was easier walking in the dark to forget the past and future, to live in the moment. She was enjoying herself.

"Hey, I'm here aren't I? This is a vacation."

"Yes, selling more product to another client. Making even more money."

"You make money when you go to exotic locales," he countered.

"True, but I'm also enjoying myself. And someone else is paying for my trip, so why should I quit work to pay for my own trips?"

"You have fun with every assignment, don't you?" he asked.

"Pretty much, why would I do it if I didn't? Don't you like what you do?" she asked.

"Yes, but for the challenge, for the testing of my business acumen, not for fun."

"So, different strokes and all that. The end result is the same. We're happy."

He stopped and turned to face her. "Are you, Savannah? Really happy? I didn't mess up your life? I didn't ruin everything, did I?"

The serious question caught her by surprise. She considered it for a moment. "No one else has the ability to mess up my life. Only me. I like where I am now." She hoped that would suffice. She didn't want to tell him how much he'd hurt her. And in the end, she did like where she was in life.

He was silent a moment, then said, "You're making a difference in my life and my daughter's and for that I thank you, Savannah. I hope by the end of the vacation she'll be happy. And maybe you'll find it in you to forgive me."

He leaned over and kissed her.

When the first instant of surprise had vanished, Savannah sank into the kiss. For a few moments she was transported to the happiest time of her life. The sensations that raced through her heated her blood and made her wish for things that could never be.

She pushed even closer, wrapping her arms around him and kissed him back. Endless moments passed. Or did time stand still?

Floating, feeling, fantasizing. Forever felt just a heartbeat away.

Then slowly, he pulled back, trying to see her in the darkness.

Her breath came fast and hard. Reality returned. She let her arms fall and stepped back.

"Do you want me to apologize?"

"Not at all." She tried to keep her voice level, free of the swirling emotions that threatened to swamp her. What was she doing? He was off-limits.

"I never forgot you," he said softly. His voice was low, caressing her. She wanted to close her eyes and savor every second of the past five minutes.

"Ready to return? Did you see there's a hot tub by the pool? It's open until midnight. Want to test it out?"

Another temptation. She almost asked if he would kiss her again. If he said yes, would she go or flee to her room wherein lay safety?

"That sounds exotic, it's cool enough we'd enjoy the heated water. But we'll probably freeze when we leave it." She decided she could be the sophisticated woman she'd become. A kiss was merely a kiss.

"We're hardy people, we can do it," he said.

She laughed, trying to enjoying his playful mood. Aware that every second drew her closer to danger. The danger of losing her heart again to this man. Every aspect of Declan Murdock appealed to her.

"I'd love to, however, since our plans were to hike the high country, I didn't bring a bathing suit."

"The hotel shops are open, I bet. Let's check at least."

His hand held hers as they hurried back. She couldn't help thinking about the kiss he'd just given. It had hit her with more emotion that she expected.

I will not fall in love with Declan Murdock, she repeated all the way back to the hotel. She only hoped she could keep to her vow. She knew she was tempting fate to continue to spend time with him alone. But for one night she could indulge. Their time together was fleeting. She yearned for some closure. Until then, she wanted to explore what being with Declan now would be like.

Savannah found a swimsuit at the gift shop. She also purchased a cover-up and put her clothes in the bag.

They entered the pool area a few minutes later. One man swam in the pool, two couples sat in chairs near the edge talking. No one was in the hot tub.

"Is the resort not full?" Savannah asked as she shed her cover-up and walked to the bubbling hot tub, feeling slightly self-conscious in the suit. It had been the only one in her size in the boutique and she'd been grateful to have something. Normally she didn't even think about her employers when she took children swimming. Tonight, however, as she turned, she caught Declan's decidedly masculine appraisal. Those flutter-feelings started again. She stepped into the hot tub and sat down, the water coming to her chin. It was getting harder and harder to remember what was in the past and what was in the present.

"Mmm, this feels heavenly in the cool night air," she said.

He joined her a moment later and the water rose another

notch. He rested his arms along the edge, tipped back his head and stared at the sky. "I might have to get one of these."

"And put it where?"

"Do you think the building manager would let me put it on the roof?"

"As long as it didn't crash into the apartment below, he might."

"Naw, too many other tenants would then want to use it. I like it like this—just us."

Her heart skipped a beat. She liked it with just the two of them, as well. She always had.

"Tell me more about your grandmother," he said. "And about growing up in Palmerville."

"Not a lot to tell." She thought a moment and then began to talk about her early feelings when her parents had died so unexpectedly and she and her sister had arrived at their grandmother's.

Time seemed to fly by. When the attendant came to close the pool area, Savannah was surprised it was so late. They'd discussed their respective childhoods and first impressions of New York when they'd moved there.

To her disappointment, there were no more kisses, or any hint of a move on his part while in the hot tub. Was he having regrets?

They dried off as best they could with the pool-side towels. Covering up, they returned to the suite. Would he kiss her again? she wondered.

"Good night, Declan," she said, ready to retreat to her room.

"Thanks for spending the evening with me, Savannah." He brushed his lips lightly against hers.

She went to her bedroom and closed the door quietly. Her heart raced. The kiss had her silently chanting the mantra to keep her heart whole, but the emotions that swirled through her had her dreaming things that would never be.

She was years older than that naive coed and wiser. She refused to fall again for the man. She'd met dozens of dynamic captains of industry, gone to events with high-level politicians, businessmen, even with some European aristocracy. Why did this one man flood her with awareness and attraction and sensual feelings that wouldn't go away?

Declan stood in the lounge for a long moment after Savannah left. He felt he was balanced on a high wire, one misstep and he'd crash below. He'd wanted his funny, sweet Jacey back. Now he wanted Savannah—in a totally different way. She was beautiful, sexy. Did she have any idea how that spiky blond hair had him yearning to touch it, feel the softness beneath the mousse, run his fingers through it to see what happened?

Did she have any idea how much he longed for the trust and love she'd once so freely given? Had he made any progress tonight? Her kiss would likely keep him up tonight, remembering the feel of her body against his, her mouth moving against his, sending his desire off the scale.

Was there any probability of them becoming a couple again?

He turned and headed to his room. At least he knew where he stood with business. With women—it was an entirely different matter. Yet, even as he thought about his parting remarks so long ago, he wondered if he could change her mind. There wasn't another woman in the world like Savannah. Too bad he'd learned that too late.

CHAPTER SIX

SAVANNAH woke early the next morning. After dressing, she went to take a quick walk, expecting Jacey to sleep in as late as she could. Teenagers loved to sleep to noon. To her surprise, Declan was standing by the window in the lounge looking out.

"Good morning," she said.

He turned and she caught her breath. He looked so amazing. Her heart picked up speed. She felt suddenly tongue-tied.

"Did you sleep well?" he asked.

"I did, you?"

"Short but good. I waited for you to have breakfast. I thought we could have it together."

Savannah considered the invitation. She wanted to spend more time with him. Not to rekindle anything, but because she could.

"Okay, sounds good."

"I'll leave a note for Jacey and we can go downstairs. Too cool to sit out on the terrace, I think, but we ought to be able to get a window table."

When they entered the dining room, they were quickly shown a table by the window. The breakfast was buffet style and once they filled their plates they sat down. Coffee appeared and Savannah took a sip as she looked at Declan over the rim of the cup.

"Anything special you wanted to talk about?" she asked.

"No. You enjoying the trip?"

"Very much. And I believe Jacey is, as well. She especially is looking forward to the spa day with Ada."

"Women love to be pampered," he murmured with a smile.

"Right on that. She's in for a treat. Apparently your ex-wife doesn't indulge as much as you think. Jacey didn't even know what a spa was."

"I don't know what Margo does now. Do you have any hints on keeping Jacey happy for the rest of the trip? I'd hoped we'd build a closeness like that we had when she was younger. But it's not moving as fast as I wanted."

"I think you need to give her time. It's only been a couple of weeks. She's with her mother all the time, and it sounds as if Margo gives her a slanted view of things."

Declan took a moment to eat some of his omelet and gaze out the window, then moved his gaze to Savannah.

"I'm giving serious thought to asking Jacey to come live with me for the next few years. She's not going to be living at home for much longer. I've toyed with the idea for a while. Seeing her as she is now, I think it'd be for the better. Her mother's had her for her entire life, sharing her reluctantly lately. Once she graduates from high school, she'll be off to college and then on to life. If I ever want a chance to really get to know her, I need more time with her now."

"She's very protective of her mother. And I think she has a very biased outlook on the situation—Margo's position all the way."

"My fault. I should have made more of an effort while we were married. And then even more these past couple of years. I've enjoyed talking with her this trip, learning her take on things. I might have been able to head off some of the ideas Margo implanted. I should have insisted on every weekend I was scheduled."

"It's not too late. When you have free time in the next few days, spend it with her. She needs to know you care. I mean she needs to *really* know it, by your asking her opinion on things, getting her ideas. And one other bit of advice, don't come across as defensive. She'll be quoting her mother and you'll hear Margo in the words or tone. Don't react."

"You think I wouldn't come across cool and collected?"

She grinned and shook her head. "I think your first impulse would be to defend the situation and present your side as the only one."

"Isn't it?" he teased.

"Only in your mind," Savannah retorted.

"Ah, so I should do what? Turn my feelings and opinions aside?"

She shrugged. "I don't know, maybe role-play or something."

"You sound like a shrink. I hate role-playing."

"When did you ever go to a shrink?"

"Never, but I watch TV."

"Ah, but when you set the rules, you get to be the hero. Anyway, it'll help her to get inside your head, and if she reacts differently from how you'd do it, you can correct her and teach her at the same time."

He nodded thoughtfully.

Savannah wasn't convinced he'd try it, but at least he hadn't laughed outright. She admitted she had difficulty seeing him in role-playing. But she recognized his sincere desire to reconnect with Jacey. And she wanted to help.

"Tell me your favorite vacation spot," he said, changing the subject.

"They're actually work places for me, vacations for my clients. I think my favorite was the cruise in Alaska. Not the children I watched, but the spectacular scenery I saw."

"The children were brats?"

Savannah laughed and then regaled him with an exaggerated story of some of the trials and adventures she'd had over the years with unruly kids or difficult parents. She kept the information vague enough that he'd never know of whom she spoke. But in retrospect some of her experiences *were* funny.

They sipped their coffee companionably when they'd finished eating.

"Has Vacation Nannies fulfilled all the expectations you had in class?" he asked.

"More, even," she said with enthusiasm. Savannah began telling him how they began each stage of development, watching to see if he was growing bored. He seemed as interested as if it were his own company. He had questions, made complimentary comments from time to time. She basked in his approval, still grateful for the information he'd so freely shared with the students in his class. She felt she and her sister had benefited tremendously because of it.

"Yours is the only company I know of that has succeeded so well. Makes me feel the time I spent was worthwhile," he said slowly.

"You never know when the others will venture forth and take the chance. In our case, we had nothing to lose because we started with nothing. Most of the students in that class were either focused on an MBA, which lends itself more to bigger corporations, or they already had jobs.

It's hard to walk away from a steady paycheck to try something never done before," she said.

"Maybe."

Jacey pulled out a chair at their table and plopped down. She eyed the empty coffee cups. "If you'd finished, why didn't you come back to the room?" she asked.

"Good morning to you, too, sunshine," Declan said.

"Good morning," she mumbled, throwing a quick glance at Savannah. "Ada called and said we should meet her at ten at the spa. I didn't know when you were coming back to the room."

"I'm glad you joined us," Declan said. "Go pick out your food and come back."

"We'll sit with you while you eat," Savannah suggested.

"I'll get my plate." Jacey served herself and ate quietly while Declan and Savannah discussed some of the locales she'd worked in.

"How did you like celebrating the new year in London?" he asked.

Jacey looked up at Savannah. "You were in London at New Year's?"

Savannah nodded. "We had the best visit. We saw lots of the sights there and took day trips on the train to Salisbury and Bath. I'd love to have taken a car trip, but I didn't want to chance driving, and my employers were happy staying in London. I don't drive much in Manhattan, I sure didn't want to try the English roads."

"Did you spend Christmas there, too?" Jacey asked.

"Nope, I was in Paris for Christmas. Ooo la la!" Savannah grinned at her, noticing Declan's attention from the corner of her eye.

Declan watched his daughter's eyes light up.

"So you travel a lot?" Jacey asked.

"Wherever my clients are going. This was my first visit to Yosemite, however," Savannah said.

Jacey looked at her dad. "I like that we came here," she said, almost shyly.

Savannah felt a thrill of delight when Declan smiled broadly at his daughter. Maybe his plan would work better than he thought.

Savannah and Jacey met Ada at the spa promptly at ten. They were given a brief brochure describing the different stations offered, from massage to hairstyling, manicures, facials, makeovers and full-body wraps. There was even a gym where they could use any of the exercise machines. They selected similar treatments, from the facials and makeovers to the manicures. Those could be done at the same time so they could visit as they were pampered. The massages were individual and they chose those first, planning to meet for their manicures, break for lunch and then have the facials and makeovers.

Savannah enjoyed spa services whenever she could. She loved the boneless way she felt during and after a massage. She took a warm soak in the hot tub after the massage thinking of her evening with Declan. In fact, her thoughts centered more and more on Declan. She enjoyed their time together, talking, learning more about each other and where they were now. It seemed as if they'd come to an unspoken truce and she liked that. Breakfast had been almost as enjoyable as his kiss last night.

Uh-oh, she'd best not dwell on that. It only caused more craving, more yearning for what would never be.

A short time later, she dressed in the robe the hotel furnished and went to have her manicure. Ada was there, Jacey not yet.

"This is a wonderful treat for Jacey," Savannah told the older woman. "It's wonderful for me, too. Thank you!"

"My pleasure. I think it's so delightful. I admit I indulge myself a couple of times a month."

"If I worked here, I'd probably do it once a week," Savannah said. She was shown to an elevated chair with a foot rest and swing table. Ada sat next to her just as Jacey bounded in.

"Did you like it?" Savannah asked with a smile. The girl's energy was amazing.

"Wow, it's totally awesome! I never knew." She hopped up on the chair next to Ada. "I'm having a blast. Thanks, Ada. Wait until I tell my mom. I don't think she's ever been to a spa. She'd love it."

"You must invite her here," Ada said.

"I can't, we live in New York. But I bet there're spas there."

"Of course. Maybe the two of you could have a day together like this," Ada suggested.

"Awesome!"

They chatted while they were having their toenails and fingernails buffed, shaped and polished. When Jacey learned small designs could be painted on her fingernails she insisted on daisies.

"What a great idea," Ada said. "How about we all have one finger with a daisy to commemorate our day together?"

"Yes," Jacey said. "Sounds fun. Wait until my dad sees."

Huge step, Savannah thought.

"Did you go to a spa in London?" Jacey asked.

"No time," Savannah said.

"When were you in London?" Ada asked.

"New Year's," Jacey answered before Savannah could say a word. "She travels a lot."

"Sounds like such an exciting job. Getting to see the world."

"I specialized in adolescent behavior and education. But I can watch any age group. It was my way to earn a living and get to see the world."

"My, how interesting. How did you come to do that?" Ada asked.

"My sister and I don't come from a very wealthy background, so we tried to figure out what we could do to earn enough to live on and still see the world. Our service is unique and highly sought after, I'm proud to say. My sister and I own the agency and have a dozen other nannies working for us."

"I love seeing women own their own business," Ada said. "Of course, in my generation it wasn't as common, but now I believe woman can do almost anything they wish with a little imagination, hard work and commitment."

"Me, too," Savannah said.

"Don't you get attached to the kids and miss them when you get home?" Jacey asked.

"Most of the time. But I try to remember I'm part of their vacation experience, so I want them to have the best time and go home with happy memories. And for some families, I'm requested each year for vacation so I get to see the kids again as they're growing up."

"Have you been doing this long?"

"Almost seven years now. My sister and I have been all over. She's in Spain right now."

"So you'll be gone all summer?" Jacey asked.

Savannah smiled and nodded.

They ate a lovely lunch beside the pool. The day was warm and sunny though there were few swimming. They still had time after eating before returning to the spa. A group of teens were sitting at one table, laughing and talking. Jacey glanced over once or twice. Ada noticed. "Want an introduction?" she asked.

Jacey shook her head quickly. "No, we're only here a couple of days."

"There's a film showing tonight. You could go to that. Let me introduce Melissa to you. I know her parents well."

Savannah watched as Ada took Jacey over to the group and made introductions. The teens quickly moved to include her in their group, and before long Jacey was sitting with them and Ada returned.

"I hope that's all right. Did you want her to stay with us?" she asked as she sat down.

"I'm happy as long as she is. In fact, it might be a good thing for her to be around normal teens. I don't know if you noticed, but black is her favorite color at the moment, and she's far too young to pull it off."

"I know, but it's a stage. I'm sure you are aware of that," Ada said.

The afternoon passed swiftly with more luxury treatment. When they met at the entrance at the end of their session, Savannah smiled broadly when she saw Jacey. Her hair had been treated and looked normal, soft and pretty, with highlights and a glossy sheen. It was shades lighter, almost brown with a hint of copper.

The light makeup was suitable to her age and enhanced her eyes.

"Wow, you look terrific. Wait until your dad sees you," Savannah said with enthusiasm.

"Oh, we have to buy at least one new outfit to go with our new looks," Ada said. "You do look lovely, Jacey. Come on, let's visit the boutique near the lobby. I have just the outfit for you in mind."

Some time later Savannah and Jacey entered the suite.

Jacey looked disappointed when she didn't see her father waiting. "Oh, I thought he'd be here."

"He's meeting with the resort managers. He'll be along for dinner."

Jacey licked her lips and looked at herself in one of the large mirrors on the wall. "It's kind of hard to believe this is really me."

"Why? You're pretty. Now, with the extra added enhancement from the spa, your true beauty shows."

Jacey stared at the mirror. "I am sort of pretty, aren't I?"

Savannah came to stand beside her, studying her reflection. "Jacey, girl, you are *very* pretty, not sort of. And I bet you'll have those teenage boys tonight shoving each other to sit by you."

Jacey giggled. She looked at Savannah. "I guess you and Dad'll have the evening to yourselves."

"I guess we will," Savannah said neutrally, while her heart rate kicked up a notch. Would Declan want to spend the evening with her?

"Don't do anything I wouldn't," Jacey said audaciously.

Savannah laughed and turned away, already thinking about what she'd like to do with Declan—if this had been a true romantic relationship. If it had been seven years ago and he hadn't left her.

Declan finished the negotiations and rose to shake hands all around. The final touches would be handled by the attorneys, but it looked as if the deal had been hammered out to the satisfaction of both parties. If this worked, he'd look into offering boutique shops in other resorts. An entirely new facet to Murdock Sports, Inc.

He walked into the suite a short time later and stopped when he saw his daughter.

"Hi, Daddy," Jacey said, jumping up from the sofa where she'd been sitting with Savannah.

"Jacey?" he asked, taking in her glossy brown hair, the pretty girl he remembered from before. The sherbet-pink dress was perfect for a young teenager. What miracle had happened? Where was the sullen girl dressed in black with the look of a zombie?

She giggled and nodded. "Didn't you recognize me?"

"I almost didn't. You look fantastic."

Jacey exchanged a smile with Savannah, who winked.

Declan walked over and then walked around his daughter, noting that the hair color was almost her natural shade. The makeup was so subtle she had that freshly scrubbed girl-next-door look. And the dress—he thought it perfect on his daughter.

"Ada thought this was a perfect dress for me and I didn't want to hurt her feelings."

"It is perfect. You are now grounded to your room until you are twenty-five," Declan said, teasing.

For a second Jacey didn't get it, then she giggled again.

"That'll have to wait," Savannah said. "Jacey's been invited to join some other young people tonight for dinner and the movie the resort is showing."

"Do I know them?"

"No, but Ada does and she vouches for them," Jacey said. "I can go, can't I?"

Declan gave Savannah a questioning look.

"I see no reason why not," Savannah said. "If Ada Montgomery knows them and vouches for them, how could there be a problem?"

"Okay, then."

"Thanks, Daddy." Jacey hugged him and then did a little dance. "I'm to meet them in just a few minutes. I didn't think you'd get back in time."

"Then Savannah could have given permission," he said. He looked again at Savannah. She was wearing a dress he hadn't seen before. The mint-green dress fitted her perfectly, displaying her feminine figure to advantage. He studied her for a minute. "So this means you and I have dinner alone."

She nodded, her expression a bit wary.

The spark that arced between them had Declan wishing for more than dinner. Not that anything like that would happen while his daughter was around. But they wouldn't always be here in California. Once they returned to New York, Declan had plans to get in touch with Savannah— and not with business in mind. There were many years to catch up on, and a woman's mind to change. If he could.

He'd had a lot of time to think last night, since sleep had proved impossible. He'd made a mistake. A monumental one, granted. But if she was the woman he knew her to be, he hoped he could talk her into forgiveness, into forgetting. Into seeing what they could build together.

Jacey left in high spirits, and shortly thereafter Declan and Savannah went to one of the dining rooms that also had dancing. They were early. Service was prompt. In no time they had a window seat that gave way to the expanse of forest and distant mountains. It was growing dark and before the meal ended, they'd only have the lighting on the grounds to illuminate the view.

"It's so beautiful here," Savannah said. "I love the feeling of open space, of seeing land where no one has ever walked."

"You think no one has walked the land? We saw a lot of people on the trail. And even more here," Declan said. "What about the early explorers or before them the indigenous people?"

She waved her hand. "There's so much. Sure some of

it has been crossed, but I bet there are miles and miles of untouched land, seen only from a distance."

"Do you want to be the first?"

She laughed and shook her head. "No thanks. I like looking at it, walking the trail like we did, but I don't need to be on that pristine land. It's just amazing to think about it, that's all. You have to admit there is not a square inch in Manhattan that hasn't been touched."

"True." She was a romantic. He remembered that from before.

"There's dancing later. I thought we could stay and enjoy that," Declan said as they waited for their meal. A lot would depend on her answer.

She hesitated a moment and then nodded. "Sounds like fun," she said, but her eyes didn't meet his.

He looked at her and caught one hand, his thumb rubbing softly over the back.

She looked at him then.

"I want you to enjoy the evening," he said slowly.

She nodded. "Thank you for asking. I love to dance. And I don't often get a chance, unless it's dancing around the nursery with a little kid in my arms."

Declan felt the attraction grow stronger. He had not expected this when he hired her.

"Tell me about Jacey's amazing transformation. I had hoped by summer's end, maybe, but she looks like her old self. How did you do it?" he asked.

"I wish I could claim credit, but it's all Ada. Jacey really admires the woman and hung on her every word today. Compliments made her happy, and they make her see herself in a different light."

"I don't want her to change back into the sullen teenager who showed up for the summer," he said.

"She's smart, Declan. I think it was a stage and now if

things go well, she'll be happy with herself and not want to make such a shocking declaration. Especially if she gets involved in the activities the resort has for teenagers."

"I hope so."

"So how are the negotiations going?" she asked.

"Finished most of the details today. It looks good. I'll try it for a few months and if it continues to look profitable, I will think about a new branch to the company."

Savannah nodded, pleased for him, but not so happy to hear the negotiations were finalized. There really would be no reason for her to remain. He could spend time with his daughter. After almost not taking the assignment, now she didn't want to cut it short.

Looking down at her plate, she hoped the sudden realization didn't show. She couldn't help remembering how once she'd foolishly thought they might get married, have a family.

She wanted children. She wanted to tell them the old family stories her grandmother had told her. She wanted to see how their eyes would light up when they learned new things. Seeing the world through the eyes of a child was always so special. She wanted her own children to be enchanted with everything the world had to offer. And she wanted to be there to see it.

A little boy with Declan's eyes or unruly hair. Another girl to give him fits when she started dating.

"You've gone very quiet," he said.

She looked up and smiled, hoping he couldn't read anything into her expression. "Just trying to remember if I've ever had the rainbow trout before. It's quite delicious."

He accepted her explanation easily and the conversation veered into food they enjoyed. Many dishes she remembered from before. Now it seemed he'd also developed a taste for sushi.

When the small band stepped into place, Declan and Savannah had long since finished their meal and moved to the bar where they had after-dinner brandy and coffee. The music was familiar and both seemed glad to take to the dance floor for the first song. From faster songs to slower ones, Declan insisted they dance the night away. Savannah had a grand time. She truly loved to move her body in rhythm with the music. And an attentive dance partner made it all the more enticing.

Her favorites, however, were the slow songs when Declan drew her into his embrace and moved with the music. She encircled his neck with her arms, pressing against him, delighting in the feel of his strong muscles against her. She could spend every night like this. Knowing the trip would wind down soon, however, she savored the moments.

She wished she could spend every night with Declan.

They stayed until after midnight then walked to the suite hand in hand.

"I enjoyed the evening," Declan said as he opened their door.

"Me, too," she said.

"Do you think Jacey's back?" he asked.

"I'll check." Back to the job. Savannah crossed the living room and peeked into Jacey's room. The teenager was sound asleep in her bed, her clothes pooled on the floor. Typical teenager, Savannah thought with amusement as she closed the door.

"In bed and asleep," she reported. "Which is where I'm heading—bed and sleep. Thanks for a wonderful evening," she said, moving to her door. She was in her room in no time. So no awkward will-he-kiss-me-good-night-or-not moment to deal with. No giving herself away by throwing herself into his arms and clinging like a vine.

She regretted the move as soon as the door closed behind her. Taking a breath, she opened it to say she would rejoin him if he wanted, but he was already moving to his room. She closed the door quietly and leaned against it. She was so dumb sometimes.

Or wise. It depended upon how she looked at things.

Over the next two days, Declan, Savannah and Jacey were treated as special guests at the resort. They followed one of the trails for a day of hiking. They enjoyed the pools, especially the one overlooking the valley, with the waterfall they could swim beneath. Nights Jacey spent with the other teenagers and Savannah and Declan spent as if they were a courting couple—dancing, spending time together walking around the grounds to enjoy the evening coolness. They shared time in the hot tub with another couple.

Thursday dawned overcast with the threat of rain. Declan spent most of the morning on the phone with his office. Jacey was going on a trail ride, if the rain held off. The resort had arranged it for the teenagers who were interested.

"You could go to the day-care center and watch the little kids," Jacey said to Savannah as she prepared to leave.

"Do I look like I need something to do?" Savannah asked, amused Jacey would volunteer her.

"What will you do if I'm gone all day?"

"I might have another day at the spa," Savannah said. It wasn't often she got the luxury. She'd pay for it herself, of course, but it might be fun. She wasn't needed to watch Jacey—between her daytime activities with other teens and her evenings spent telling her father all she'd done, Savannah felt superfluous.

Every night Jacey had other plans leaving Savannah and Declan together. She knew she was falling again for

Declan in a big way. And that would give her nothing but heartache. She wished she'd stop trying to guess the future. He was attentive. But he had been before. Could she ever stop making comparisons?

Savannah was lying on the massage table almost asleep when a woman from the spa knocked on the door.

"Sorry to interrupt," she said, sticking her head in when she opened it. "There's an emergency and Mr. Murdock has asked to have Miss Williams return to their suite as soon as she can."

"What's happened?" Savannah asked, sitting up and wrapping the sheet around her. "What emergency?"

"I'm not sure, but he wants you to hurry."

In less than five minutes Savannah entered the suite in a rush. No one was there. She went to his room, it was empty. Checking hers and Jacey's, which were also empty, she turned and headed downstairs. Reaching the front desk, she told the woman she'd been asked to return to the suite but no one was there.

"They're in the infirmary." She beckoned over one of the bell men. "Show Miss Williams to the infirmary, please."

What had happened? Savannah hurried after the man, glad he walked quickly, as if knowing it was urgent.

When she entered the area, she immediately heard Declan. Following the sound of his voice, she peeped around a cubicle curtain and saw Jacey crying, her dad leaning over her, hugging her and rocking her gently.

"What happened?" She rushed to the side of the high bed.

"I fell and broke my ankle," Jacey wailed, crying.

"Honey, don't cry so, it'll be all right," Declan said, hugging her again.

"It hurts," she complained.

"They'll have you fixed up in no time."

"But I won't be able to ride the horses anymore."

"Did you fall from the horse?" Savannah asked, standing by the opposite side of the bed from Declan, brushing back the hair from Jacey's forehead.

"No. We got off at a look-out point. We were playing around and then I slipped on some rocks and fell a little way, but my foot landed wrong. Stupid old bones. It wasn't that big a fall."

"Sometimes just the oddest angle will be enough," Savannah said. She looked at Declan. He looked totally distraught.

"She'll be okay," she said softly, reaching over to touch him, to offer what support and comfort she could.

"That doesn't make it any easier to deal with," he said. "This changes everything. As soon as her ankle's set, I'm making arrangements to return home."

CHAPTER SEVEN

Less than twenty-four hours later they arrived at Declan's apartment. Jacey was exhausted and unhappy. She'd wanted to stay and spend more time with the new friends she'd made at the resort. Declan, however, had finished his business and saw no reason to remain at the resort when it would be easier to care for her at home.

"Want to go lie down?" he asked his daughter when they reached their flat.

"I guess. I'm so tired." Jacey had been grumpy on the flight, unable to become totally comfortable even in the spacious first-class seats. She had not mastered the crutches yet and was clumsy and awkward. Stubborn to the end, however, she managed to go down the hall to her room.

"I'll settle her," Savannah said, following.

A few minutes later she returned to the living room. "She'll be asleep in no time," she murmured. "If you don't need me anymore, I'll head out."

He turned and looked at her.

"Technically, I guess you could say the job's ended. But if you'd stay a few more days of the assignment, it'll help with the transition. The doctor said she could be switched to a walking cast in another week or two. Until then, she's going to need extra help. The venue's changed, but not the timing. Stay, please. Finish the week at least."

"I can't stay beyond that. I have another assignment starting soon."

"Until then."

"You have a housekeeper and are only a few minutes away when you're at work. She's fourteen, she doesn't need a babysitter at home."

He rubbed the back of his neck and shook his head. "We can't just end this like that."

For a moment Savannah felt a spark of hope. Could she finish the assignment here in Manhattan? Spend a few more days—and evenings?—with Declan? The trip was over, but it didn't have to mean *they* were.

"I could come during the day. I do have to check my schedule. When my next assignment comes up, I need to take it," she said, already deciding to extend her interaction with Declan as long as she could.

He nodded. "I appreciate your help now."

The way his dark eyes looked into hers, Savannah couldn't help hoping. Was it her own imagination, her own yearning? Or was there something more?

She was far too interested and attracted to the man for her own good. And she feared spending more time in his own home would only strengthen that attraction until she'd be in for another huge heartbreak when she left.

A few kisses, quiet times together, dancing the night away—these did not add up to a confession of undying love.

Still, there was nothing to be done about it now. She'd guard her heart and do the best she could.

"Actually, there won't be a housekeeper for a few days. I gave Mrs. Harris the same time off as I was planning to take. I thought we'd be gone. I can have food brought in. You won't have to cook or anything."

"Oh, I don't mind. I enjoy cooking and rarely get to since I travel so much. When I'm home, I do all the cooking. Stacey doesn't like it that much so the kitchen is my domain." She was already thinking of some of his favorite meals, the ones they'd made together and shared before.

"I'd love some home cooking. But don't feel obligated. You were hired for a different role."

It came down to that. She'd been hired to spend time with his daughter. Any romantic overtones were only in her imagination. Turning away, she tried to catch her breath against the pain that hit her sharply. Was that his way of saying don't get involved? Don't read more into anything?

"Maybe Jacey likes to cook, too. Once she's on her feet again, maybe she'd want to help."

His expression sobered. "I don't even know that about my own daughter. How could a father not know that?"

"Probably because you never gave her a chance. With her mother cooking at home and Mrs. Harris here, it'd be surprising if she did cook."

"Something more to learn. My hope is now that she changed back to the girl I know, she doesn't revert to the Goth creation because we're home."

"It might help if she had friends over."

"Unless they dress all in black."

He walked over to her and placed his hands on her shoulders. Savannah raised her gaze to his, longing for him to pull her close and kiss her.

"I appreciate your help. I'm still technically on vacation, so I won't go into the office for a couple of days. Between the two of us, maybe we can keep the change going."

She felt butterflies in her stomach. His eyes looked into hers and she felt as if she were beginning to float away.

Involuntarily her gaze dropped to his mouth. His lips had kissed her, drawn a response from her that had her feeling giddy. Was she the only one to feel it? Once before she'd been in love with Declan Murdock. She felt the same way again.

He squeezed her shoulder and removed his hands, turning to go into the kitchen. "We can check the supplies and see what we need to get to eat for the next few days," he said.

She took a breath, trying to get her racing heart under control. She couldn't have been so foolish as to fall for him again. Had she learned nothing from the past?

But a voice seemed to whisper—again? Had she ever fallen out of love with him? She'd been hurt, incredibly hurt. Yet she had understood his actions after years of questioning things. He'd tried to do the honorable thing for his daughter, for the mother of his child.

Truth be told, had he known the extent of her love? They'd said it a few times, but only in passion. She'd never told him how she counted the moments until she saw him again. That a part of her felt missing when he was gone. Of the dreams she'd had of the two of them together against the world.

In the end, it hadn't mattered. She doubted if he would have made a different decision.

Savannah stood rooted to the spot. He still hadn't a clue how deeply she felt about him. She should be grateful, but a small part of her wished he felt the same pull of attraction. Wished that he found it hard to act casually and not give in to desire that rose every time they came near each other.

Playing house. That's what it felt like. Declan leaned against the counter in the kitchen and watched as Savannah and Jacey prepared dinner. They were having hamburgers and salad, but the elaborate concoction they were making was fancier than any hamburger he'd ever eaten. He enjoyed watching them. Quite a change from the beginning of the trip two weeks ago. Gone was the sullen girl determined to stay with her mother.

It was like a family ought to be, he thought. Working together, enjoying each other's company. It didn't take money or exotic locales to make him happy. This is what he'd wanted for Jacey all along, once he'd learned of her existence.

The sad part was that this was all make-believe. His second go-round with Margo had ended in shambles despite all the effort he'd made. He wanted the best for his daughter. His ex-wife wanted the best for herself.

What would life have been like if he'd stayed with Savannah, married her and made a home for Jacey with Savannah? That choice had only briefly been entertained seven years ago. She'd still been in college. He couldn't saddle her with a seven-year-old daughter, limit her own activities and future to take on his daughter.

He hadn't wanted Jacey shuttled back and forth between two homes. Yet that's how it ended up.

Some said love conquered all. Love lasted forever.

He didn't think he'd ever loved Margo. Not the way he should have. Never the way he'd felt about Savannah. But he'd tried to do what he thought was right. He wanted to have a family, do things the way his parents had done. Margo had not changed. It appeared she never would.

"Declan, is one enough?" Savannah asked. The way both of them were looking at him, he suspected it wasn't the first time she'd asked.

"Yes. You're making them huge."

"They'll shrink up a bit when cooking," she said, shaping a patty.

Jacey looked at him. "These'll be the best burgers you ever ate."

"Think so?"

"Definitely." She shaped another patty and soon the burgers were broiling in his oven. Savannah instructed Jacey on the next stage. The teen followed instructions perfectly and beamed with the praise Savannah gave when the task was finished.

Once again Declan wondered what things would have been like if he'd made a different choice. He looked at Savannah and felt the desire rise as it did every time he looked at her. She was beautiful, inside and out. She gave more than she took. She was settled and content with her life.

Which was both good and bad. Settled meant she didn't want to change.

He pushed away from the counter. "I'll be back in a minute," he said, leaving the kitchen. He'd made his choice seven years ago. It hadn't worked out at all like he'd hoped. Now, he was stuck with the fallout of that decision.

It didn't matter that some nights he was so lonely he walked outside just to escape the thoughts that crowded his head. That he felt awkward at his own company's picnics in the summer, odd man out because he didn't have his family with him.

He went to the window and stared out across Central Park. It was a windy day, he could see the trees limbs moving. If Jacey were more mobile, they could go to the park. Or someplace. Staying at home, playing house, seeing how well Savannah fitted into his life brought too many conflicting emotions to the forefront.

The phone rang and he picked it up, hoping it might be work with an emergency needing his attention.

It was Margo.

"I got a text from Jacey that she broke her ankle. Now you're home. How is she?"

"Healing. She'll get a walking cast in another couple of weeks. Until then she's on crutches."

"How did that happen? Were you too busy with work to pay attention to your own daughter?"

"She was well looked after. She was horseback-riding with friends. They stopped and got to playing around. She slipped on some rocks," he answered patiently, ignoring the other part of her comment.

"She should come back home."

"She is home, with me. For the summer. I thought you wanted it that way."

"I did, things changed. You'll be away at work more than you'll be home," Margo said.

"You work, how is that different?" Declan asked.

The silence lasted only a moment, then she said, "I could take a leave if you'd make up the difference in pay. Then I'd be home with her all summer."

"Not going to happen. She's mine for the summer."

"I'm coming to see her," Margo said.,

"Not today. Come tomorrow if you like. We'll be here."

Hanging up, Declan wished he could keep the woman as far away from Jacey as possible. Maybe he should consider asking his daughter now if she'd like to live with him for the next few years. All too soon she'd be off to college and her own future. If she was to be his only child, he should spend more time with her. He'd hoped waiting until later in the summer would give her a sense of how they would live, which would help her make up her mind. Maybe waiting would be a mistake.

"Dad, dinner's ready," Jacey called.

Back to playing house. Savannah would be gone soon and life would return to normal.

The next morning Savannah headed for Declan's early. She planned to make omelets for breakfast and had picked up some cinnamon buns for an extra treat. Normally she didn't like sweets with breakfast, but she had a soft spot for cinnamon buns. She hoped Declan and Jacey did, too.

Riding the elevator, she tried to quell her anticipation of seeing Declan again. Last night had been low-key, and when she'd left for home Jacey had even asked if she'd be back. When she'd heard Savannah would bring breakfast, she'd seemed delighted. "You can teach me how to make omelets. I've always wanted to know."

Declan's daughter was turning out to be a lot of fun. He was right in insisting she stay with him, the change in such a short time was amazing. Savannah even hoped Jacey liked her, as well.

Knocking on the door, she was impatient for it to open. When Jacey opened it, she smiled.

"Good morning."

"Did you bring the eggs?"

Savannah held up one bag.

"Something smells good," Jacey said, looking at the other one.

"Cinnamon rolls."

Savannah held the bag out of reach and headed for the kitchen, telling Jacey what she'd brought.

"I want one," the teen said, following on her crutches.

"After the omelet. You'll love my omelets, they are light and full of goodies."

"Like what?" Jacey lumbered along on her crutches.

Savannah smiled at Declan when she entered the

kitchen. He was standing by the coffeemaker, waiting for the pot to fill. "Good morning to you." Seeing him had her catching her breath again. He looked so inviting. If Jacey weren't around, would he have kissed her? His gaze flicked to her mouth and she felt it almost like a caress.

If Jacey wasn't around, however, there'd be no need for Savannah to be there.

"I heard about the food. Maybe we should eat the buns while you're cooking the omelets," he suggested, eyeing the white paper bag.

"Nice try. I want you both to appreciate my cooking expertise."

Jacey stood by the door. "I'm making a notebook for cooking. I'll be right back. Don't start without me."

She turned and thumped down the hall toward her bedroom.

Declan grinned and stepped forward, sweeping Savannah into his arms, bending her back theatrically and giving her a big kiss. She clung—to avoid falling she assured herself. But for an instant, all thought fled and only the feelings his kiss engendered roiled through her. All too soon he brought her back upright and released her.

"Wow," Savannah said, staring at him in surprise.

"I didn't get a good-night kiss last night," he said, turning and taking cups from the cupboard.

Jacey could be heard returning.

Savannah turned and began blindly searching for a bowl, her mind roiling. The kiss had been over too soon. Her heart pounded. She desperately hoped he couldn't tell. It was one thing to play along, something else again to hide her true feelings.

Breakfast was accompanied by laughter and jokes and plans for the rest of the summer. Savannah listened and joined in where she thought appropriate. She felt a hint of

sadness that she wouldn't be participating in all the activities Declan planned, like trips to the beach when the
ankle was healed, a weekend in the Adirondacks. She remembered one weekend they'd spent there. Would she ever
remember the past without the weight of the end of their
relationship?

While she was washing the dishes, Declan and Jacey
still sat at the table, Jacey looked over at her. "Do you know
where you'll be next?"

"I'm leaving next week for a cruise of the Norwegian
fjords," she said. She'd checked in with Stephanie at the
office and been given her next assignment. The days were
counting down.

"For how long?" Declan asked.

"Two weeks."

"You'll be gone for two weeks?" Jacey repeated. "I
thought you'd be around and go with us to the movies or
a play or something."

"Your father hired me for the trip to California, not the
entire summer. This is my busiest time."

Savannah felt oddly bereft thinking of leaving at the end
of the week and not seeing Declan or Jacey again. But that
was the way Vacation Nannies worked. She had a new assignment and would have another after that.

Jacey looked perplexed. She looked at her dad. "Can't
you hire her for the rest of the summer?"

He drew his coffee closer and looked at his daughter.
"Savannah has a job to do. You and I don't need her. We'll
manage fine on our own. Establish routines that suit us."

"But you could pay her to stay with me," Jacey said.

"I could. But she has other obligations. She's already
agreed to go with the other family to Norway. She can't
go back on her word."

Jacey studied her father for a moment. Declan nodded

slowly, hoping Jacey would understand. He was having a hard time himself, but dared not show it.

Jacey was quiet for a long moment, then said, "Like Mom does?"

He didn't know how to answer that. The truth was hard to take. "It's different with your mother. She and I had a relationship. We were married. But we changed. The marriage didn't last. I'm sorry that it didn't. It wasn't your fault."

"It was Mom's fault," Jacey said slowly. "I think she just wants your money."

"I'm not obligated to support her once the legal tie was severed," Declan said slowly.

"That doesn't mean your dad doesn't want to help you," Savannah said when Jacey looked as if she were contemplating what Declan had said. "He sends money for you. If you lived with him instead of your mother, he'd still spend money on you. You're his daughter—he'll support you until you're grown."

"And then I have to stand on my own two feet?" Jacey asked, looking at Savannah and then her father.

He nodded. "For the most part."

"Even though you have oodles of money?"

"It's your dad who has oodles of money, not you," Savannah said softly.

"That's not fair," Jacey said.

"How is it not fair? If you earned a lot of money, wouldn't you want the right to choose how you spent it? Would you want to feel obligated to give it to someone else—even a close family member?" Savannah asked.

The teen considered the situation for a few moments, then reluctantly shrugged. "I guess I'd want to have the final say in how my money was spent. But I'd want my family to be happy, too."

"Money doesn't buy happiness," Declan said, with a look at Savannah.

"It buys a lot of stuff," Jacey retorted.

"More to clean, store, worry about breaking or being taken," Savannah suggested, wiping the last of the counter and rinsing the cloth.

"I like a lot of things," Jacey said.

"All the more reason to do well in school, go to college and get a good-paying job," Declan said.

Jacey rolled her eyes and shook her head. "You're always saying that."

Declan laughed. "Is it sinking in?"

Jacey wrinkled her nose and shrugged. "I guess."

There was a knock on the door.

"Who even knows we're home?" he asked, rising.

Jacey watched him walk to the door. "My mom knows," she said slowly as her father left the kitchen.

Savannah heard the voices and suspected Jacey was right, Margo had arrived.

Jacey got up and clumped to the living room. Savannah followed.

Margo Murdock was tall and thin with brown hair and a frown on her face. She had been talking with Declan, but now looked at her daughter, who was struggling to get to her mother on her crutches.

"Oh, my poor baby. Look at you. Does it hurt?" She walked swiftly across the room and gave Jacey a hug, almost knocking her over as one of the crutches was dislodged.

"Let her get to the sofa first, Margo," Declan said, moving to intercept.

"I'm going to be okay, Mom. My ankle throbs a little, but it's not too bad." She lumbered to the sofa and then sank down, placing the crutches on the floor.

Margo followed and sat beside her. She brushed back her daughter's hair. "I see you've changed your hair again."

"Yeah. I went to a spa and a complete makeover was included. It was really cool. They had massages, and did my toenails." Jacey wiggled her toes and looked hopefully at her mother, but Margo turned away and glared at Declan.

"She needs to come home. You need to provide a nurse so she'll be taken care of."

"Mom, I'm okay."

"I thought you wanted her to spend the summer with me. What happened to your plans that made it impossible for Jacey to stay home with you?" Declan asked.

Savannah stood by the table, watching the scenario unfold. She'd have been a lot more frustrated than Declan appeared to be. From all Jacey had said since she'd met her, Savannah felt Margo would propose anything if she thought she'd get more money.

How had Declan fallen for her? Granted she was a beautiful woman, but some of that was due to cosmetics and clothes. Too bad her personality didn't match.

Meow, she thought. For a moment she considered leaving. But something kept her in place. Jacey was scowling. Margo looked peeved and Declan had lost that easygoing air and now looked decidedly angry.

"Coffee anyone? I can make some," she said, to break the tension.

"I'll take a cup," Declan said.

"I'd like a cup, as well. You remember how I like it, Declan," Margo said, still sitting beside her daughter.

"Black?" he asked.

She pouted for a second and shook her head. "Cream and just a small teaspoon of sugar."

Declan reached Savannah and put his arm across her shoulders, urging her into the kitchen. "The more I'm around that woman, the more I want to pull my hair out. She drives me up the wall," he said, dropping his arm when they were out of view.

Savannah pulled down three mugs and put them on the counter, then waited for the coffee to drip into the pot.

"You hide that so well," she murmured.

He gave a short laugh. "I made a mistake even talking to her last night. I wish she hadn't come today. I can't believe her nerve, wanting me to pay her to watch our daughter if she took a leave of absence from work. She just wants a summer off."

Savannah didn't know how to respond. She was totally unimpressed with Margo Murdock. How had Declan ever thought the two of them were suited?

Declan leaned against the counter, watching Savannah prepare the coffee mugs. "Actually I think Jacey *wants* to stay here this summer."

"Good for her. I think the two of you have recaptured some of the relationship you had before," Savannah said, taking the full pot and pouring coffee into three mugs.

He reached over and cupped Savannah's chin, turning her face toward him. "I have you to thank for the change."

The touch of his fingers tingled through her as she watched him. His frustration rolled off him. Then he seemed to really see her and his touch softened. His thumb caressed her jaw gently.

"I know it's above and beyond what you usually get when hired. But I needed your help."

"I owe you for all the information you so freely shared in class. Vacation Nannies wouldn't be the success we are if you hadn't."

For a second Savannah thought she glimpsed disappointment.

He dropped his hand and nodded. "Gratitude? Was

that—never mind. Not that I need it. I was paid for my lectures."

She picked up his cup and the one prepared for Margo and handed them both to him.

"Ready for round two?"

She nodded. "Wait a minute."

Both his hands were full, but she didn't pick up her own cup. Instead, she reached up to cradle his face in her palms and pulled his head down to kiss him on the mouth. She could feel his startled surprise. A moment later she pulled back, studying him for a moment.

"For luck," she said.

"Next time give a bit of warning. I almost dropped the cups."

If there ever will be a next time, she thought sadly.

Margo looked suspiciously at them both when they returned. Taking her cup, she glared at Savannah.

"This is a family matter," she said.

"Savannah stays," Declan said.

Margo changed her gaze. "Honestly, Declan," she said, ignoring Savannah, "how could you put Jacey at risk like that? She could have been more seriously injured."

"Chill, Mom, it was my own fault. And it wasn't as if I fell off the horse. I was already on the ground, scrambling around some rocks."

Margo glanced at her daughter then back at Declan. "She needs someone with her."

He shrugged. "I'll take more time off. Mrs. Harris will be back next week. Jacey will get a walking cast soon and be good to go—right, sweetheart?"

"Yep," Jacey said, grinning at her father.

Margo fumed.

Jacey looked at her. "Maybe Mom could see me on a weekend," she suggested.

"I don't think that's a good idea," Declan said.

"I don't see why you two can't get married again and we'd all live together!"

Savannah saw the work of the past two weeks unraveling with the presence of Jacey's mother. She looked at Declan and her heart went out to him. He'd tried too hard to let this happen now. Desperate for something that would help, she racked her brains. Then an idea hit.

"I know someone who lives in the Hamptons," she said. Looking directly at Margo, she continued, "How about if I ask if you can use their guest cottage for a week or two this summer? You'd have to work around any guests they've already invited, but I bet there would be a couple of weeks still available. Free, of course."

Margo narrowed her eyes. "Why would you do such a thing?"

"To get you to leave," she said frankly.

Declan swung his gaze to Savannah in astonishment. Jacey looked at her mother and back at Savannah.

"I can get two weeks off in August," Margo said slowly. "That would give me time to get some new clothes, too."

"Mom, what about me?" Jacey asked.

"Honey, you're going to be incapacitated for weeks with that cast, most of your summer actually. You don't want to get a tan line from midcalf up. We'll talk on the phone. It's obvious your father doesn't want me around."

Jacey frowned. "But I do."

"Honey, this is your time with your father. Once fall gets here, we'll be like we were."

Jacey didn't looked convinced.

Declan wanted to hug Savannah right then and there. Was this going to work? Would Margo just up and leave now that she had something she wanted? And how did Savannah know anyone in the Hamptons? He wouldn't have thought Vacation Nannies moved in those circles. Unless—it had to be a former client. Someone she'd worked for before. Did she have such a good relationship that they'd do her such a huge favor? He felt a ping of jealousy. He wished he knew more about her life, more about her friends.

Margo glanced at her watch. "Oh, dear, I need to get going. I'm only going in a bit late, not taking the day off." When she rose, she looked at Savannah. "Jacey has my phone number. Call and let me know so I can get the time off."

Savannah nodded.

Once Declan shut the door behind Margo he turned back to the room. "A stroke of genius," he said. "Do you really have friends there who might let her use their guest cottage for two weeks?"

She nodded. "The Hendersons. I'll call this morning."

"Are they old?" Jacey asked.

Savannah looked at her in surprise. "What does that matter?"

"'Cause I think Mom only wants to go there so she can meet a rich husband. She's said so the last two times she's gone. But those have only been weekend parties and no available men were there."

"The Hendersons are probably a few years older than your mother. I watched their kids a couple of times. Your mother would not be part of their social network, just have use of the cottage. But she could go into town, find friends there."

Declan couldn't believe Margo would be so forthright with their daughter about her desire to marry money. He didn't want to marry again without love and the happy union his parents had had. He didn't want Jacey to think of marriage as a way to get money or an extravagant life-style.

He looked at Savannah, calmly sitting sipping her cof-fee. He wished he could emulate her serenity. Seeing Margo always hit a hot button. It reminded him of his loss seven years ago. Of a foolish decision that had never gone the way he'd hoped, but that had ended the best thing in his life.

"I'm going to my room," Jacey said, struggling to get off the sofa.

When she'd left, he turned to Savannah. "Now what?"

"Up to you."

"I want to spend time with her. I'll have to go into work from time to time, a couple of days a week, but this is my summer to get to know my daughter in all her facets."

"Jacey's lucky to have you for a dad," she said.

"Not so lucky in her mother," he replied.

Savannah shrugged. "Margo has different values. She wants to get ahead, like everyone else."

"She wants to get ahead the easy way, the best way for Margo. I want my daughter to be caring and content, not constantly unhappy because of the way her life is going."

"So tell her. Spend time sharing your values and expec-tations. Let her know what you want for her life, and then support her the best you can."

"How did you get so smart about teenagers?"

She laughed. "Not so smart, just some common sense. I was a teenager once."

"And not too long ago."

"Long enough to look back and see things a bit more objectively. Anyway, if you don't need me any longer, I'll take off."

"I do need you. Stay. Don't let me face Jacey alone yet."

"You're joking, right?"

"Maybe a little. But things do go more smoothly when you're around."

It was on the tip of Savannah's tongue to say things could go more smoothly always if he'd keep her around. She'd stay, she'd make memories, and when she left she wouldn't look back.

CHAPTER EIGHT

SAVANNAH called the office to check in and to get the phone number for the Hendersons. She then called them and chatted for a few moments before asking her favor. They discussed the situation for a little while, Savannah implying Margo was a friend, though she knew the two of them never would be. Still, for the sake of getting her away from Declan and Jacey for the summer, she'd say almost anything.

"Great, thanks a bunch. I appreciate this more than you'll know," she said when they'd agreed to two weeks in August. "May I talk to Patty now?" The little girl was a special favorite of hers. She'd watched her several times in the past three years and was scheduled again at Thanksgiving when the entire family was flying to Hawaii.

She spoke with Patty for almost ten minutes, then said goodbye.

"You really like her, don't you?' Declan asked. He'd been lounging on the sofa during her call, watching Savannah's animation as she talked to both the parents and the child, amazed she would do such a favor for his ex-wife.

"Patty is a little doll. She had the sweetest disposition I've ever come across. I keep in touch with some of my kids."

"Come sit by me and tell me more," he said.

She rose and sat beside him on the sofa. He was glad she hadn't argued.

But as he took her hand and laced their fingers, resting them on his thigh, he remembered back to when they'd sit after dinner and talk. As she talked about some of her kids he remembered how much he'd liked listening to her. She was entertaining, yet her own values shone through. She was the kind of person he wanted his daughter to grow up to be. Caring, kind, taking delight in mundane things, yet charting her future with goals and working to achieve everything on her terms.

He watched her as smiles lit her face. She genuinely liked the children she watched. And obviously she loved the travel. It tugged at his heart. He'd missed her over the years. Was there any chance—

Jacey came out of her room a short time later, while both of them were laughing at a story Savannah had told.

His daughter sat on a chair and looked at them, noting the held hands. Her eyes widened and Declan quickly released Savannah's hand.

"What's funny?" she asked.

"Savannah has a way of telling a story that has me laughing," Declan said. "Tell her about Maisie May."

Savannah smiled. "You want to hear it again?"

"Why not? I bet it's just as funny the second time."

So Savannah related the experience she'd had with a Cajun woman who was sure she could cast a spell to find her a husband. She embellished it a bit more this time around and before long Jacey was laughing.

"How did you meet her?" she asked at the end of the story.

Savannah explained how she'd had a few days extra in New Orleans and had gone exploring. That led to more questions from Jacey about her job.

After she finished there was a moment of quiet. Jacey looked at her dad again.

"You're never going to marry Mom again, are you?"

He shook his head.

"Are you and Savannah going to get married?"

Declan went on alert, his gaze seeking Savannah's.

"No," Savannah said, rising.

"But if Dad asked you, why wouldn't you say yes, then if you two got married, I could live here, couldn't I?"

Declan felt his heart catch. "You could live here with me whether or not I ever marry again," he said, trying not to give away how much it meant to him.

"I think I'm in Mom's way," she said slowly.

"Oh, honey, I'm sure that's not true. I'd love for you to come live with me if you want to. You already have your room, know the neighborhood. It'd mean changing schools, but you could handle that easily enough."

Jacey smiled. "Well, I'll think about it."

"You do that, honey. I'd love to have you spend your high school years here. Before you know it, you'll be grown and out the door and on your own," Declan said.

Jacey looked thoughtful as she nodded again. "I'll think about it. I don't have to decide now, do I?"

"No, we have all summer to decide. But we do need to let your mom know when you're ready," Declan said.

Savannah wondered how Margo would take the news. Maybe Jacey was cramping her style, but she also was the reason Margo got a generous child support check each month. How would she feel about that vanishing?

"So, what shall we do today?" Jacey asked. "How about a movie? That way I can sit most of the time."

They agreed on a movie and once lunch was over, they headed out to the nearest theater. It wasn't crowded, even though school was out. Sitting near the center, Declan sat between the two of them, and once the theater went dark, he reached for Savannah's hand.

She looked at him but only saw him studying the screen as the previews played.

She would be hard-pressed to concentrate on the movie when her entire focus was on the sensations cascading through her at his touch. She sat in the dark, eyes on the big screen, her thoughts tumbled and confused. The more she was around him, the more she wanted to be with him. Yet he never spoke of the past or the future.

When the lights came on at the end, she blinked and pulled her hand away. Following Jacey and Declan out of the row, she made up her mind to go home now, not to spend another minute with the man. She had to gain some distance and perspective. The only change she'd seen this summer was that her love had been brought to the forefront. It had been hidden and now she had to face it again.

Letting Jacey get ahead of them a little bit as they exited the theater, she said softly, "I'm going home. If you need me tomorrow I'll come over. But I think the two of you get along better than ever now. You don't need me any longer." It was hard to say the words.

"Stay for dinner."

"No. You need time alone with Jacey and I need some time alone myself."

His eyes looked into hers. "Why?"

"Why what?" She felt her senses scatter.

"Why do you need time alone?"

"I just do." She looked away, seeing Jacey near the doors to the outside, watching them.

"We're limited in what we can do while she's in that cast. Another summer we could go to the beach, do some museums, other things, but not right now. You have ideas on how to entertain children. I need you. You said until the end of the week. Come on with us, Savannah."

I need you. How she wished it was for more than entertaining his daughter.

"Okay, I'll come back for a little while. We could play board games. Do you have any?"

"No."

"Then we need to swing by a toy store on the way back to your place."

Jacey balked initially at the suggestion of playing games, declaring it was too childish. But once they were back at Declan's apartment, she grew more enthusiastic. And once she beat her father at Yahtzee, she wanted to play even more.

Declan called for dinner from a nearby Chinese restaurant. Once dinner was finished, he said he'd take Savannah home.

"I can grab a cab," she said, putting away the games.

"I'll take you. You'll be okay here for a short while, right?" he asked his daughter.

"Sure. I'll watch television until you get back. Then I want a rematch on checkers." That had been the game Declan beat her on every time.

"Better study up on strategy, then," he teased.

She laughed. Coming over to Savannah, she balanced on her crutches and gave her a hug. "Thanks for today, it was fun."

"I had fun, too." Savannah was touched at the teen's show of affection. What a difference in such a short time.

Declan flagged down a cab and they settled in the back seat.

"I can't believe she might want to come live with me," he said as the cab pulled out into traffic.

"I think it's great. You'll be a better influence on her than her mother," Savannah said.

"There might be a problem getting Margo to agree to changing the custody agreement."

"Probably not as much as you think. You should ask your attorney," Savannah said.

"I will. Thanks for today. It's the most fun I've had in ages. And all because of you."

"Now you have some ideas of how to entertain her until she's more mobile. I hope you both have the best of summers."

"That sounds like goodbye."

"It is. Declan, you hired me for the trip to California. That's been cut short. The longer we play at this, the harder it's going to be at the end."

He was silent for a moment, staring out the side window. Then he turned and looked at her. "What if we don't stop seeing each other?"

"What do you mean?" For a moment, hope blossomed. Then her spirits fell. "I'm booked most of the summer. I won't be around."

"Can't someone else take your assignments? I can pay for the entire summer."

Pay for her time? She was hoping for a renewed relationship and he was talking about hiring her to spend time with his daughter.

She shook her head. "Some of these families are repeat clients and asked especially for me. I'm not going to send someone else in my place."

They arrived at her apartment building.

"Wait, please," Declan told the cabdriver. "I'm just escorting her to her apartment." He slipped the man a twenty-dollar bill and opened the car door.

The ride in the elevator was silent. Savannah wished

things could end differently, but she didn't see how anything had changed.

Declan walked beside her to her door, trying to find a compelling reason she should stay.

"How about dinner tomorrow night, just you and me?" he said as she took her keys from her purse.

She looked at him. "Dinner?"

"That's right, the evening meal. Dress up, we'll go some place nice."

He could tell she didn't think it was a good idea. "Consider it a bonus for the excellent job you did for me." *And give me the opportunity to change your mind about leaving,* he added silently.

"Okay then. Will Jacey be all right?"

"I'll make sure. Maybe she could invite a friend over to keep her company. I'll pick you up at seven."

Savannah hesitated, then nodded. "Okay. Good night."

She had the door open. But he wasn't going to let her go so easily. He pulled her gently into his arms and kissed her, letting her know the only way he knew how that she was someone special. He didn't understand why he was so anxious to stay involved, but he wasn't letting her go so soon. He wanted more time with Savannah.

When she responded, he deepened the kiss. Her sweet curves met his harder muscles in all the right places. He could have held her all night. Memories crowded, the present vanished and it was as if he was reluctantly parting from her for the night seven years ago. She had a class early in the morning or he had a new product to consider. They'd meet again tomorrow night.

For a moment he forgot what had happened. Reality crashed down when she pushed him slightly. He let her go, staring down into her big blue eyes. He saw the hurt, the uncertainty and the distrust. All the emotions he'd caused.

He wanted to rail at fate for the way things had ended. The way he'd thought to make things right. How could doing wrong to this lovely woman ever have seemed right?

"Good night, Declan."

He stood in front of her closed door for another minute. She'd entered her apartment too quickly. And for a moment, he'd felt her farewell was final. At least he had tomorrow evening to get her to change her mind. Slowly he returned to the cab.

"Take a longer route home, I have some thinking to do," he instructed the cabby.

"You got it, mister. That's a first, asking for a longer way," the man replied, shaking his head in amazement.

When Declan returned home, Jacey was snuggled down on the sofa, a light afghan over her. The show on the TV was a comedy. She looked up when he came in. "I've been thinking," she said, sitting up and switching off the TV with the remote. "I would like to come here to live."

"I'd do almost anything to have you live with me a few years. You're sure?"

"Yes. I think Mom'll like being on her own. She complains sometimes that I take a lot of work. It won't be too much work for you, will it?"

"Never." He felt love sweep through him for this sweet child of his.

"What are you going to do when I'm gone off to college? You'll be all alone."

Did every woman no matter what the age think being alone was worse than being in a marriage just for the sake of companionship?

"I'll manage. I've been alone these past few years."

"But I used to come to visit on weekends and the summer."

"You won't drop in from time to time once you're off to college?" he asked.

"Sure, sometimes. But I'll be busy at school and with friends. Dad, you should think about marrying Savannah. She's nice."

He sat up and looked at her seriously. "Let's discuss your moving here—what ramifications we can expect and when to tell your mother." He didn't even want to think about marrying Savannah. If he'd only done so when he'd had the chance. How different would all their lives be now?

When Declan picked up Savannah at seven the next evening he had a good game strategy in mind. Jacey was going to live with him. He was very appreciative of that. Next week he'd return to the office and work a minimum schedule, making up any lost time when at home in the evenings. The rest of the day he and Jacey could spend together.

Knocking on the door, he thought he should have asked Savannah out before, after he'd divorced Margo. He hadn't because he'd thought she'd moved on. He hadn't been able to bear the thought of finding a new man in her life.

Savannah opened the door looking as lovely as he'd ever seen her. The blue dress she wore reflected her own eyes. Her smile rocked him to his toes. He'd missed her over the years.

"You're on time and I'm ready. Just let me get my purse." She picked up a small clutch and put her keys inside.

He stepped in, crowding her a bit and leaned for a quick brush of his lips against hers. She reminded him of happiness, love, family and youth.

She looked up in surprise.

He had kept the cab waiting and soon they were off to the Bradbury, one of the latest trendy restaurants. Situated on the top of one of the high-rise hotels on Broadway, it was a short cab ride. They rode an outside glass elevator which gave them a beautiful view of Times Square and surrounding buildings. Soon they reached the top floor and stepped right into the restaurant.

Savannah had heard about this place, but had never eaten here before. She was surprised to see that beyond the bar there was a dance floor. The seating for the restaurant was to their right. Declan had obviously made reservations. After escorting them to one of the tables beside the floor-to-ceiling windows, the maître d' pulled out a chair for Savannah.

"Wow, good thing I'm not afraid of heights," she said a moment later when Declan sat opposite her. "This view is amazing. And I feel like I'm a bird perched somewhere, able to see for miles."

"Glad you like it. I've only been once before. The food's good, too."

Declan waited until they'd ordered then told her about his day with his daughter.

Savannah listened and smiled a time or two. He couldn't help feel that the day would have been even more special had she been with them.

Then he told her of their discussion on Jacey's moving in. "I want expectations to be clear on both ends. And to make sure she's really going through with it. I'm worried about Margo's reaction. She's not going to be happy and I don't want her pressuring Jacey."

"Jacey will have to be very sure of her decision to stand up to her mother. But I think it'll be the best thing for both of them in the long run," Savannah said.

Savannah looked out the window. He followed her gaze and studied the view for a few minutes. It was spectacular. The sky would turn red with the sunset soon and once darkness fell the lights of the city would glimmer like stars.

"I have news," Savannah said. "My sister's engaged! To the man who hired her to watch his children on the trip to Spain. She got the assignment because she speaks the language. Now she'll spend some of her time there and some here in New York."

"What's she going to do about Vacation Nannies?" Declan asked.

"We haven't discussed that in depth yet. She's asked Stephanie to stop booking her until she gets back and we discuss things. I see big changes ahead. I hope we can get another Spanish-speaking nanny, we have a call for one several times a year."

"You don't speak it?" he asked.

"No, English only. I think we should have planned for something like this, but both of us were so full of starting our business and getting ahead, we never planned for one of us bailing out."

"Is that how it feels, as though she's bailing out?"

Savannah tilted her head in thought. Declan loved that look.

"Not really. She'll still be involved. Mostly I'm happy for her. She sounded so happy on the phone. And I spoke with her fiancé and the two boys. They arrived in New York, and then two weeks later turned around and flew back to Spain to celebrate with his family."

"Do you think she'll keep working?"

"Not if traveling is needed. I think she plans to stay home with Luis's boys—at least initially."

"Does that happen often—a nanny leaves for marriage?"

"Usually that's the only way our nannies leave. We have a great business and properly trained nannies love the idea of all the travel."

Declan changed the subject of conversation to veer away from marriages. If things had gone differently seven years ago, he and Savannah might have married. Had children by now.

The thought hit him in the gut. He could have had a home full of children by now. Funny he had no doubt that he and Savannah would have made their marriage work. Would she ever consider marrying him after all that had happened?

When they finished eating, he suggested they stay longer and enjoy the music and dancing. He felt a wave of satisfaction when she agreed. He couldn't wait to hold her in his arms while they danced.

The rest of the evening went perfectly. They danced, enjoyed a nightcap, danced again. When it was finally late enough that he knew they had to leave he requested one more dance.

"I've enjoyed the evening," he said softly. His chin rested against her forehead. He could breathe in her sweet light scent. He'd forever associate it with Savannah and dancing the night away.

"I have, too."

"Come by the house tomorrow. We'll play games, plan the trip to the beach."

"You and Jacey need to do that without me," she said.

"Come anyway," he urged.

She was silent for so long he thought she'd refuse. Finally, she said, "Okay, but for the last time. I'm leaving for two weeks soon and have chores to do around the apartment."

For a moment he wanted to argue. But there was no denying that next week Savannah would be off to another assignment. Off to another country and another family. He didn't like the thought.

The drive back to the apartment took only moments. He felt as if he'd left his best friend behind. Tomorrow he'd ask her out again. Spend as much time as he could with her before she took off on the next assignment. He didn't examine closely why or consider what he'd do if she said no.

CHAPTER NINE

SAVANNAH took the subway to Declan's neighborhood the next morning and walked the rest of the way. It was one of those perfect New York days. The sky was clear, a light breeze blew. The temperature hadn't risen to an uncomfortable level. She loved New York on days like this. If Jacey hadn't had her broken ankle, they could have walked to the river and enjoyed watching the boats. Or was that too childish for a teenager? She almost laughed aloud. She bet the thought of other teens around would have Jacey jumping at the chance.

She greeted the doorman and was escorted right to the elevator. Rising swiftly to Declan's floor, her anticipation rose as she walked down the hall to his flat.

Knocking on the door, she smiled. She couldn't wait to see him.

Declan opened the door a moment later, a frown on his face. "We have a problem," he said, opening the door wider and motioning her in.

Jacey sat on the sofa, crying, her crutches leaning against the arm.

"What happened?" Savannah asked, glancing between Jacey and Declan.

"Margo was in a hit-and-run accident last night. She was in a crosswalk and someone knocked her several feet.

She's in a coma at the hospital. We were waiting until you got here to go."

"She could be dying," Jacey said, rubbing her face with a soggy handkerchief. "We had to wait until you got here because you didn't answer your phone."

Savannah frowned, remembering she'd left it in the charger when she headed for the bakery this morning. "I'm sorry. You should have gone. You could have left a note."

"I said that to Dad, but he insisted we wait for you."

"They aren't going to let us in to see her anyway, Jacey," Declan said gently. He looked at Savannah. "She's hurt pretty badly. I still need to find out how much."

"What if she dies?" Jacey asked, scared.

"I'm hoping she won't die," he said. "Don't think the worst until we know more facts."

"What can I do?" Savannah asked.

He hesitated a moment, then said, "Can you come with us? I know you probably don't want to, but I could use the support."

Savannah nodded. "I brought cinnamon rolls again. Have you two eaten?"

"I don't want to eat. I want to see Mom," Jacey said, struggling to her feet. "Dad, you said we could leave as soon as Savannah got here."

"I did and we can. Bring the rolls, we'll eat them on the way."

"I'm not hungry," Jacey said. "I hope Mom's going to be okay. You'll help, right, Dad?"

"As much as I can," Declan said.

For a moment Savannah was taken back seven years. This reminded her of what had happened then. Margo needed Declan; he left Savannah to go to her.

Granted, this was a bit different. Margo needed both

Declan and Jacey. But was this a pattern that would always be repeated? Declan going to Margo?

"Here," Savannah thrust the white bag into Declan's hands. "I can't go after all. Sorry." She had decided two days ago to make the break. This was the perfect chance. All her insecurities and uncertainties rose.

Nothing had changed, much as she had wished for it. Seven years ago Margo had arrived back in New York with a child Declan had not known they had. She'd beckoned and he'd gone to her. Now she was injured and needed help. He was going again.

It didn't matter to her that anyone would go to help someone with a tie to the past as Margo had to Declan. It mattered only that Declan was going.

She was not going to be left behind this time.

If she really had a spot in Declan's life, she'd jump in to help as much as she could. But despite a few kisses, nothing had changed. He had never given a hint he wanted anything beyond her services as nanny to his daughter. Her assignment had really finished when they returned to New York. She should have stood firm at leaving then. She might have wondered, but nothing like this would have happened.

"Where are you going?" Declan asked. "I need you."

Savannah shook her head. "You have your family. It's not mine." Foolishly she'd let her love blossom, but she'd known all along heartbreak would follow.

He reached out and took her shoulders gently, turning her so she faced him.

"There's something between us, you know it, I know it."

She gazed into his dear dark eyes. She hoped she never forgot this moment. She could almost imagine he was asking her to stay forever, to make a life with him. To help with Jacey and moving on and getting married and having children.

The reality, however was that he wanted her help with Margo. He'd left her once before for the woman—the woman and child. They were still in the picture.

Could a person feel her heart break? Surely it was just fantasy, yet the pain gripping her chest belied that. She thought it at least cracked.

She wanted to tell him she loved him, see if he'd be willing to open his mind to the possibility of a future together. But nothing he'd said or done gave her hope, it was her own dreamy fantasy.

"I have to go," she said, her voice cracking a bit. Blinking back tears, she reached up to kiss him. He pulled her into his arms, holding her tightly against him, pouring out the attraction and desire that had shimmered between them into that kiss.

Both were breathing hard when Savannah pushed herself free. She tried a smile, but tears welled. Turning swiftly, she went to the door.

"Wait, Savannah," he called.

She shook her head and let herself out of the apartment. Not wanting to wait for the elevator, she slipped out into the stairs, the door closing as she heard him call again. Was he coming after her? Wanting to change the parameters of their agreement? Wanting to say he loved her?

Walking swiftly down the stairs, she listened for any sounds from above. All was silent.

It took her several minutes to go down all the floors. When she pushed open the outside door into the sunshine, she stopped a moment to draw a breath.

The day was still beautiful. The sun shone. The light

breeze kept the temperatures moderate. How could the world look so bright and happy when her life had become dark and dismal?

CHAPTER TEN

DECLAN stood in the doorway staring down the empty hall. She had gone. Slowly he closed the door. Why had the accident happened? Was fate constantly going to intervene just when he thought he was getting his life the way he wanted it?

Instead of a day together, a day in which he might suggest future outings, he had a heartsick, scared teenager and an empty spot where Savannah had been moments before.

He rubbed his face with his hands. Maybe she'd come back when she'd had a chance to consider.

Consider what? For a long moment he stared at the hall. Something about this reminded him of his leaving last time.

Margo. Was he to have her in his life forever?

"Dad, can we go?" Jacey came over to him, her worried expression touching his heart. Her mother had been injured. Right now he needed to take care of his daughter. He'd go after Savannah later.

Their original assignment was over. She'd delivered all he'd expected and more. He had nothing more to hold her with. She would be leaving next week on another assignment. For a bright businessman who had built a major company, he had acted like a dumb kid in this.

"Yes, Jacey, we'll go now."

"Why did Savannah kiss you?"

He shrugged. He wasn't going to try to explain why. He could still see the tears in her eyes. "For comfort, I expect."

Savannah went back the her apartment. She was totally unhappy. After a day of feeling sorry for herself, however, the next morning she decided she wasn't giving in to it.

She called her sister. She wanted to hear Stacey's voice and to listen to her happiness with her plans. She exclaimed at all the right places, wishing she had something equally exciting to tell her.

She didn't say a word about her personal situation. If she'd begun, she didn't think she could stop. Her sister would either tell her she was crazy or offer some insight that would help her deal with the situation. But it would dim some of Stacey's happiness and Savannah wouldn't have that for anything.

Once they finished talking, Savannah couldn't sit still. She had a new job in a couple of days. If nothing else, she'd go shopping. She longed for the hustle and bustle of stores, of being anonymous in a crowd. Of something to take her mind off Declan.

She found two outfits that would be suitable for the cruise of the fjords of Norway. She also saw a pretty sundress that would look good on Jacey. Holding it up, she studied it for a moment. On impulse, she added it to the clothes she'd already chosen. A new outfit never failed to raise a woman's spirits—so she suspected that applied to teenagers, as well. She hoped the teen's mother would be okay. Despite resenting Margo and the impact she'd had on her life, Savannah wouldn't wish her harm.

She indulged herself with a large sundae for lunch, then took her purchases home. She'd arranged for the store to deliver Jacey's dress.

The afternoon stretched out. She thought about Declan. She did laundry. And remembered dancing at the resort in California. Painted her nails and thought about his desire to do the best he could for his daughter. She vacuumed the apartment, even though she and Stacey splurged and had a weekly housekeeper. It helped when they were both gone for up to several weeks at a time. However the mindless activity didn't do anything but offer more opportunities to think about Declan—his dark hair, his eyes gazing into hers, the feel of his mouth on hers.

Calculating the time difference she decided she'd talk to her sister just before bedtime in Spain. She was leaving in another day for Norway; it would be a while before she could talk to Stacey again.

She dialed and waited impatiently for Stacey to answer.

"Hi," she said when she heard her sister's voice. And promptly burst into tears.

"Savannah? What happened? What's wrong?" Stacey's concern came across the line clearly.

"I'm such an idiot."

"As in?"

She heard the concern in her sister's voice.

"My last assignment was with Declan Murdock."

The silence on the line told her how shocked Stacey was.

"Couldn't you have refused?"

"I considered it," Savannah said.

"But?"

"But I went anyway. I still love him."

Stacey's voice was warm with love. "Oh honey, I always wondered. You never found another guy you felt was special. I hoped you'd gotten over him."

"Me, too. Actually, I thought I had. Until I spent the past three weeks with him."

"I take it you aren't seeing him anymore?"

"No. And it's almost the same reason. His wife was injured and he rushed to her side."

"Shall I fly home?" Stacey asked.

Savannah wiped her eyes with the back of her hands. "No. I'm leaving for Norway and would be gone by the time you got here. I just wanted to talk a little."

"I have the rest of the night," Stacey said softly.

Savannah leaned back on the sofa, closed her eyes and told her sister about Declan and Jacey and the time in California. Especially about when she'd realized she loved Declan and how she'd tried to put some distance between them, while spending as much time as she could with him—just for a few memories to cling to down through the years.

As she wound down, she ended with, "He's no more interested in me this time than last time. Why can't I find some darling man who is single, unattached, no baggage and who would love me to distraction?"

"The heart loves whom it loves," Stacey said. "Sometimes the person loves back, sometimes not. Your love is still there, not diminished by his not returning it. I'm so sorry it's bringing you pain instead of happiness. I can relate. I didn't know Luis loved me until he finally proposed. I thought I was going to end up at home nursing a broken heart, so I feel for you, sis."

"At least I only have the next couple of days to get through and then my next assignment takes me to Norway. I'm counting on the country to be as pretty as Alaska."

They spent a few minutes talking about the coming weeks and tentative plans Stacey and Luis had made.

Savannah hung up feeling marginally better. Her sister had the dilemma of having to fulfill contracts when all she wanted was to stay with Luis. Savannah looked forward to her busy schedule to keep her from dwelling on Declan.

Sunday night her cell rang. Jacey. Savannah almost answered, but decided she didn't need another confrontation the night before she left. She let it go to voice mail—if the girl would even leave a message. She could listen to it when she felt not so fragile.

Finished with her packing, she went to the kitchen to pull out the small container of chocolate-chocolate-chip ice cream. It was her favorite comfort food. The small container was still too much for one person, but she made serious headway through it. Putting the remainder back, she took a shower and went to bed early.

To lie awake for endless hours as she had the past three nights, thinking about Declan, the kisses they'd shared, the discussions they'd had. Trying to remember that the whole adventure had been just an assignment, not the prelude to a long life together.

Savannah met up with the family she'd accompany the next morning at JFK airport, just before boarding the plane to Oslo. Too busy now to think about might-have-beens, she greeted the three children and once on board had them occupied with coloring books and handheld games. For the next two weeks she'd enjoy Norway, make sure her charges were happy and that the parents had a carefree vacation. She did her job well.

And her plan worked—except at night. No matter how tired she was, it was hard to fall asleep. And once asleep, more than once she dreamed of Declan. Some dreams were sweet—he laughed and held her hand. Others had them plunging off cliffs on a mountain trail. She never dreamed about Jacey. But every once in a while when she had a free few minutes, she wondered how Declan was faring with his daughter. Had her mother recovered? Was she still planning to live with him for the next few years? She hoped so. He deserved to be happy. Just because she wasn't the one to make him happy, she still wished him well.

Her heart ached for him. He'd been so happy to see the change in his daughter, so delighted when she'd said she wanted to live with him for the next few years. Savannah hoped that hadn't changed—for both their sakes.

The two weeks ended on a happy note and Savannah gave her charges a hug when they parted at JFK upon their return to the U.S. She'd miss those kids. They had been so enchanted with Norway. She laughed, remembering some of their attempts to speak Norwegian—her own included. Fortunately, all those on whom they'd tried out the language had been friendly and helpful.

She got her luggage, hailed a cab and settled back, glad to be home if only for a couple of days.

She had her cell phone with her, but had stupidly left the charger at the apartment. Not that she could have used it in Norway, it was strictly a U.S. phone, but she'd be able to check in with Stephanie now. Was Stacey home or had she thrown caution to the wind and canceled her assignments to spend more time with Luis and his boys? She didn't think her sister would have backed out of an assignment without someone to take over despite being a woman in love.

She sighed and watched as the familiar scenery sped by. She didn't think she would have forsaken Vacation Nannies instantly if Declan had been more interested in her. But she would have been tempted not to spend a day apart from him. Now they'd spend a lifetime apart.

She didn't know what had happened to him in the past

two weeks. She remembered the weeks and months after he'd left before. She didn't want a repeat this time.

When she reached her apartment, she kicked off her shoes and dragged her suitcase into the bedroom. She'd unpack later. Right now she wanted to open windows and air the place out. Being shut up for a couple of weeks in summer made it more than stuffy.

After a slight breeze began to permeate the apartment, she fished out her phone and plugged in the charger. She went to see if there was anything edible in the kitchen or if she needed to do some quick shopping. She wrinkled her nose at the stale bread and over two-week-old eggs. Dumping both, she went to shower and change. Shopping next and then she'd call Stephanie. Saturdays the office manager worked until noon, as some people found it more convenient to come in for interviews on the weekend.

Once showered and dressed, Savannah went to the phone and called the office.

She got an answering machine. Stephanie was probably busy with a client. Grabbing her purse, she headed out. She knew her next assignment wouldn't start before Monday, so had time to herself for at least a day and a half. Which meant—a lunch at her favorite deli and then grocery shopping. Better on a full stomach anyway, she rationalized. She loved Sol's. It was the best deli in the area and always packed. Today was no exception. It was good to be home, and back in her routine.

Slipping the key into her lock a couple of hours later, Savannah was feeling good. She was full, had two bags of fresh fruit and salad fixings, and a new carton of chocolate-chocolate-chip ice cream. Could life get much better?

Just as she finished putting everything away, the phone rang.

"Home safe and sound?" Stephanie said when she answered.

"I am and will have my report on the family in by Monday. I can mail it if I'm leaving right away." They kept records of the childrens' likes and dislikes, favorite toys or games, and other facts that would help the next time around. And so often that made the second or subsequent assignments that much easier on all. "Are you still at the office?"

"No, I'm home, just calling to see that you made it back. I left the Pendergasts' folder on my desk if you go in before Monday. You don't have to meet up with them until four. It's a late flight to Maine. Also, I never got a report on Murdock," Stephanie murmured.

Savannah looked at the ceiling. She didn't want to write Declan up as a client. She felt a pang of longing to see him again. See how he was doing. Find out what had happened between him and his daughter and his ex-wife. Did Jacey get her walking cast?

"I'll include that one, as well," she said as the silence ticked on. She didn't want Stephanie questioning her closely on that assignment.

"Did you have fun in Norway?"

"It was amazing." Savannah told her about the beautiful scenery she'd enjoyed. She had had a good time, despite thinking of Declan all the time.

"Want to have dinner tomorrow night?" Stephanie asked.

"Sure, we can catch up even more. How about Antoine's on Fourth?" Savannah suggested.

"Meet you at seven."

That gave Savannah more than a day to decide what she'd say about Declan and the assignment to California.

And to hope she could pass it off as a regular assignment enough to pass Stephanie's alert.

She went to check on her phone. It was fully charged—and there were forty-seven missed calls.

As she thumbed through them, she saw they were all from one phone—Declan's. Her heart jumped. The first bunch were the second day she was gone. Then several each day since then. The last one had been two hours ago.

Why was he calling her?

Almost afraid to find out, she debated returning the calls. Maybe later. She put the phone down and went to unpack. She had enough to do to keep her busy. She didn't need to respond to calls from a one-time client.

But as the afternoon went on she couldn't help obsessing about his calls. What did he want? Was everything okay? How was Jacey doing? Tempting as it was to call him, she resisted. Almost as if testing her resolve.

Savannah was curled up on the sofa watching reruns that evening and eating her favorite ice cream when her phone rang. Hesitating only a moment, she rose and went to answer, already knowing who was on the other end of the line.

"Savannah?" It was Declan.

"Hi."

"You're home now?"

"Yes, I arrived home today." She wished her heart didn't race just hearing his voice. She closed her eyes to better picture him.

"I've been trying for weeks to reach you."

"I only have U.S. service and have been in Europe. I didn't hear any messages."

"No, I, uh, didn't want to leave messages. Are you free?"

"For what?"

"I'd like to see you."

"Why?"

"Because I've missed you?" he said tentatively.

She sure had missed him, but she thought they might put different emphasis on their version of missed.

"It's too late for dinner, I'm sure you've eaten," he said.

She looked at the clock, it was after eight. "I did, and right now I'm enjoying dessert."

"Want to go out for a drink or coffee or something?"

"No, thank you. It's really late in Europe and I'm still on that time zone. I'm going to bed soon."

"Tomorrow for breakfast then?"

Her heart raced. He wanted to see her. She had a million reasons why she should refuse. But—she wanted to see him again.

"I'll pick you up at seven," he said when she didn't respond.

"So no sleeping in for me tomorrow," she murmured, trying to come up with a reason why she should refuse. A reason that wouldn't tell him how foolish she'd been to fall in love with him again.

"Too early?"

"No." She wished she felt up to seeing him tonight. But she was tired and she wanted all her senses fully alert when meeting Declan again.

"See you then."

"Right." She ended the call, wondering what he had meant by *missing* her.

She should have asked about Jacey. Maybe the teen would be at breakfast in the morning.

Finishing what she wanted of the ice cream, she put it away and went to bed. She was tired, but even so, as on every other night for the past two weeks, she didn't fall asleep right away. Her thoughts dwelt on Declan. She would see him in a few short hours. To what end? Nothing had changed.

Not that she cared. At least she'd see him for a little while.

She wore a pretty lavender sundress the next morning and white sandals. Her hair was done to her satisfaction. Her eyes sparkled as she stared at herself in the mirror and counted the minutes until he'd arrive. She hoped—well, she wasn't going to set herself up for disappointment. She'd see what he had to say.

When the knock came at the door, Savannah was ready. She threw it open and stared a moment, surprised by her delight at seeing him. He looked wonderful in a dark shirt, dark slacks and wind-blown hair.

"Ah, ready, I see. You were always prompt."

"I learned that from my business teacher," she said, picking up a small purse and pulling the door closed. He didn't move and for a moment she wondered—then he leaned over to kiss her. His lips were warm and firm and so exciting she almost dropped her purse. Her knees grew wobbly as he kissed her and kissed her. Finally he stood tall and looked into her eyes, his own questioning. "I've been wanting to do that for two weeks."

What could she say? This meeting ranked right up there with the top ten stupid things she'd ever done. They had no future together. She knew that. She'd wanted so much more than a kiss, but couldn't reveal that. Yet she couldn't deny she'd been a willing and active partner in the kisses. Floundering around for something to say, she grasped on Jacey.

"How's Jacey doing?"

"Getting around like a pro on her walking cast. She doesn't seem at all hampered by it, though she says her ankle itches all the time and she's careful not to get any tan until it comes off."

"Ah, following her mother's advice. And how is Margo?" Not that she really wanted to know. Better to keep reminding herself about the other woman. She was never going away.

"Doing better than the doctors originally expected. She's in a convalescent hospital in Queens."

"Doing all right without your help?" she couldn't resist asking.

"Yes, well, that's another situation. Best saved for later. I thought we could walk to Marney's on the Battery. It's still cool enough to enjoy eating outside. And I hope everyone else in the city wanted to sleep in so we won't have to wait for a table."

They walked the few blocks to Battery Park and followed a pathway to the small café that had a view of the harbor. Declan had his wish, as well—there were several vacant tables. Taking the one with the best view, they soon ordered and settled back, sipping hot coffee. The day would grow hot soon, but right now the temperature was ideal.

"So update me about Jacey," she said.

"She had a hard few days while Margo was still in a coma. Once she woke, she's improved daily. Jacey visits her almost every day. She's still set on moving in with me, however, which was in doubt for a few days. Her mother's dead set against it, so there's a lot of tension there."

"It's the money, isn't it?" she said.

He nodded.

"Putting Jacey right in the middle of it all."

"I know. I don't like it, but she is taking a more pragmatic view of her mother these days. She told me when Margo starts complaining about money, she changes the subject."

"Is Margo any good at what she does—selling high-end fashion?" Savannah asked after a moment. "Surely that should bring in enough money for her."

He shrugged. "To hear her tell it, one day she's leading sales person, the next she's so poor she needs more child support. It's hard to know what's what with her. But she's had the job for several years, so I expect she's doing something right."

Breakfast arrived and the conversation turned away from the Murdock family.

"Tell me about your trip," he invited.

Glad for the safe topic, Savannah told him about the cruise, the gorgeous scenery and the fun she and the children had had. He asked questions which showed his interest. He watched her as she talked, his eyes delving deep into hers. A couple of times Savannah felt flustered by so much attention.

He looked around when she finished.

"It's pretty here, too," he said.

"Of course. New York is home. But I'm glad I got to see the fjords. Reminded me of part of Alaska on my other cruise."

He studied her for a moment. "You love the travel part, don't you?"

"I do. And I'll forever be grateful for learning enough from your course to make Vacation Nannies a success."

He nodded, his face losing expression.

"What?" she asked.

"Nothing." He took a sip of coffee. "Oh, I almost forgot. Jacey told me to be sure and give you this." He fished an envelope out of his pocket and handed it to her. It was yellow and small. She lifted the flap and drew out a thank-you card. Smiling, she opened it and read, "Savannah, thank you for the dress. It's very pretty and I will love wearing it once I can walk again. It's okay if you and my dad see each other. I wish he'd marry someone who would make him happy. If it can't be my mom, I want it to be you."

It was signed with X's and O's and a big *Jacey*.

"A thank you for her dress," she murmured, replacing it in the envelope and tucking it into her purse.

"That was nice of you. She really likes it. Hasn't worn it yet, though."

"She says she will when she can walk again."

"Or when we go someplace where she'd need a dress. We haven't done all that much while she's been hampered by the cast."

His phone rang and he glanced at who was calling, then with a quick, "Excuse me," he answered. "Hi, Jacey, what's up?"

Savannah watched his expression change as his daughter spoke to him. She could tell he was getting angry again, or at least extremely frustrated.

"Tell your mother—never mind, I'll call her myself. Don't worry about it. She and I will discuss the situation."

He hung up and glared at Savannah for a moment, not seeing her. Margo made him so angry he wanted to throw something.

"That was good," she said.

"What?"

"That you are not putting Jacey in the middle of you and Margo. At first I thought you were going to give her a message to relay."

"That would be too easy. I need to get it through her head that Jacey is old enough to decide and she's decided to live with me."

He looked over the river, still seething with Margo's attempted manipulation of their daughter.

"May I make a suggestion?" Savannah said hesitantly.

He wondered what she had to offer in this mess. For a second he hoped she'd offer to watch Jacey until she was better—or for the entire summer.

"If a manager hasn't been hired yet, put her in charge of that little boutique sports store you're putting in the resort in California."

"Have you lost your mind?" he asked. "Why in the world would I have anything more to do with Margo than I need to? I certainly—" He stopped talking and looked at her. She looked as pretty as he remembered. She'd been the smartest, quickest student in the class he'd taught. But how could she think he'd want to work with Margo?

"You're an astute businessman—listen for a minute. You said she's good at selling, or could be. That new shop will be in a high-end resort with tons of luxury items and amenities. Rich people come to stay. She might meet her rich husband there. The pay will probably be excellent. You could arrange for her to live at the resort. And she'd be three thousand miles away from your daughter when you and Jacey need time to get your own family traditions and routines started."

For a moment all he could do was rail against the idea of doing anything to help the woman who had caused such havoc in his life. But slowly his temper cooled and he began to see the merit in what Savannah suggested. He'd have to play around with the idea for a little while, assess the pros and cons, but the more he thought about it, the more he liked the idea. He could have Margo train in the San Francisco office. She'd love that city. Then she could settle in at the resort before the cold weather hit, so she'd see it in the best season.

"She couldn't report directly to me," he murmured.

Savannah smiled slowly. He caught his breath, wanting to reach across the table and kiss her.

"Something to think about," she said.

"It has some merit," he said cautiously.

"I think Jacey will be fine with the idea, knowing her mother's being taken care of. Some of her hesitation in moving in with you was concern for her mother. She's seen the resort, seen San Francisco, so she can picture where her mother's living. Jacey would love visiting her at the resort maybe for the full summer next year."

"Giving me the summer free," he said pensively.

"Did you want that?"

"Maybe, in the future," he said. He looked at her plate. She was finished. He was finished. Summoning the waiter for the bill, he paid then looked at Savannah. "Want to walk along the water for a while?"

"Sure. I have no plans until tonight."

"What's tonight?" he asked as they rose and wound their way through the other tables. Every one was occupied now.

"I'm meeting a friend for dinner," she said.

Declan felt the words like a blow. He didn't want her seeing anyone else. They'd spent almost three weeks together and she had not mentioned a special man in her life. Yet he'd done nothing to make sure that never happened. Had he left it too late?

He turned toward the right and they walked along the wide asphalt pathway.

"Now or never," he murmured, glancing around. Except for the couple on the rollerblades moving away from them, they were alone on the path.

"Now or never for what?" she asked.

He turned, picking up her hand in his. Hands linked, he looked at her.

Took a breath.

"Savannah Williams, will you marry me?"

She stared at him dumbfounded.

"The thought of you going out with someone else is driving me nuts. I was going to wait for the perfect setting. See you a few more times. Take you for dinner, dancing. Have you see I'm not the man I was seven years ago? I want you to trust me. I want you to want me as much as I want you. I let you down, I know I did, and you suffered the most for my stupid decision seven years ago. I thought I was doing the right thing. It turned out to be a disaster. For all of us, but most of all for you."

She nodded slowly. He couldn't read her expression.

"Say something."

"I'm thinking," she replied.

Declan frowned. "About?"

"There's so much to consider. Jacey, Margo. I want—well I wanted this seven years ago. Instead you walked away without a backward look. You'll never know how much that hurt."

The pain in her eyes told him. "It wasn't without a backward look, or regrets. I hardly had the marriage vows out of my mouth before I knew it was a mistake. I tried—I really tried, for both Jacey's sake and yours."

"Mine?" Savannah said in surprise.

"I knew I had hurt you badly. It couldn't have been in vain. I had to make a go of the marriage or I would have to face the fact I threw away the best thing I'd ever had for nothing. And that was too hard to accept."

"We're not the same people," she said slowly, her eyes seeking his, searching for…what?

"No. I hope I'm a better man. You are still the bright young woman who gave me such joy. If you can find it in you to forgive me, I will spend the rest of my life making up for that hurt."

"What if you change your mind again?" she asked tentatively.

He felt her words like a slap. Yet how could he blame her?

"I won't. I didn't even years ago—I just pushed you away to do my duty. I found it wasn't enough. I didn't seek you out when the divorce was final. I didn't try to regain our trust or love then. But I thought about you every day. Much as I hated the way Jacey was behaving, I saw it as a way to have you back in my life. To see how you were, if there was anything there for you and me."

"It was a ploy?" she asked.

"No. A gift. I looked at it as a miracle—your taking the assignment. The more I was around you the more my love strengthened. I've loved you for eight years. With you or without you, I'll always love you, Savannah. I just hope it'll be with you."

"Why? Why are you asking me and why now?"

"Why? Because we're meant to be together. I knew that seven years ago. I hurt you. I'm so sorry. I didn't feel good myself or about myself when I left the café that night. But I was focused on the daughter I'd never known I had."

Savannah watched his eyes carefully

"I honestly thought I was doing the best thing for her. It wasn't until a few days later I realized how much doing that would end up costing me. Margo is nothing like you. I loved you. I should have married you on the spot and dealt with Jacey in another fashion."

Savannah tilted her head slightly. "As in?"

"Gotten custody, introduced her to you. She was adorable at seven. You two would have hit it off."

"Yet when Margo was hurt you rushed to her side," Savannah said slowly. Her heart beat so fast she could hardly think.

"I rushed her daughter to her side—there's a difference. I don't blame you for not trusting me. I don't know how to build trust back except to ask you to give me a chance. I swear you'll never regret it."

Savannah pulled her hand from his and turned slightly. "I have to think about this," she said.

"Look at the weeks we spent together. Everything meshed. You enjoyed the hiking as I did. Never complained. At the resort you introduced Jacey to all those amenities as if you were born to them. You talk as well with businessmen as their wives. You don't mind getting dirty. And you clean up really good." He wasn't going to talk about their kisses, the touches that drove him crazy, the yearning and desire and everything else that he felt around her.

She shook her head. "Those are not reasons to get married."

Declan felt a wave of panic. He'd asked her and she was going to say no. He'd apologized for his thoughtless rejection years ago. He'd promised to do better. He thought they'd rediscovered each other in California. He would have asked her the day she came for the interview when he realized his feelings were as strong as ever. But he needed some hint from her that she returned his feelings. Only Margo's accident and Savannah's next assignment had delayed the proposal.

Now he couldn't imagine going through the years ahead alone. Savannah had shown him what a real family could be like. And he wanted it—with her.

He floundered around for something else to offer. "Jacey would love to have you for a stepmother."

"I wouldn't be marrying Jacey," she said.

"You're not making this easy," he said with a frown.

She looked back at him, her expression impossible to read.

"I love you, Savannah. I have for years. Even when I

was exchanging vows with Margo, determined to make that second marriage work for Jacey's sake, I almost stopped, knowing it wasn't her I loved but you. I can't imagine my life without you. It would be dead and empty. It's already been dead and empty for seven years. Please, join your life with mine and let me cherish and love you the rest of our lives."

She laughed and flung herself against him, hugging him tightly. "You love me? You've always loved me?" she asked, then kissed him as if there was no tomorrow.

He didn't question her reaction, just kissed her with all the years of pent-up love. If they lived to be a hundred, it would never be enough time to make up to her for the lost years.

People walked by, he didn't care. He'd kiss her until dark if she'd let him.

She pushed back a fraction and opened her blue eyes, gazing up into his. "My answer is yes, in case you were still wondering."

"I had hoped that with the kiss. But for a few moments, I wasn't sure." His heart raced with her response. "How soon before we can get married?"

"Months yet. I have assignments to fulfill. My sister to marry off. And a future to plan. Plus you'll need that time to cement the bond with Jacey so she doesn't feel threatened when we get married."

"I love you. I don't know if I can wait months. We have lost time to make up."

"Yes, you can wait. Did I mention I love you, too? Declan, I have since before you left me that night in that café. I've never been back. I tried so hard to get over you. And I even convinced myself I had when you interviewed me. But that was so bogus. I first fell in love with you at your class, and I never did get over it."

He hugged her tightly. "I am so sorry we wasted the years."

"You did what you thought best. Even though I hated it, I understood it. I'm sorry for your sake it didn't work."

"I never loved Margo, not then, certainly not now. Everything I did was for Jacey. And rushing to the hospital was the right thing to do for my daughter."

"It felt like the past all over again. Margo before me."

"I'd figured that out by the time we left the hospital," he said, brushing his lips against hers again. "I should have gone after you right then. But Jacey needed me. The thing is, Savannah, she might need me a lot in the next few years."

"I've never resented Jacey. It was only Margo."

"You never had competition there."

"It didn't seem like it when you married her!" she said.

He grimaced. "I will never marry again unless it's you and only you. I plan for it to be forever. My dad and mom were happy up to the day she died. That's what I want for us. And for Jacey when she gets married. Let's show her how a great marriage works."

"I'd love to be part of that project," Savannah said, reaching up to kiss him again. "I love you, Declan. I always have, and I believe I always will."

"I'm counting on it," he said, kissing her again. The future was theirs. He didn't know why he got her forgiveness, only that Savannah was the most loving person he knew. And she loved him. Together they'd forge a loving and happy partnership that would last a lifetime.

* * * * *

MILLS & BOON®

Why shop at millsandboon.co.uk?

Each year, thousands of romance readers find their perfect read at millsandboon.co.uk. That's because we're passionate about bringing you the very best romantic fiction. Here are some of the advantages of shopping at www.millsandboon.co.uk:

* **Get new books first**—you'll be able to buy your favourite books one month before they hit the shops

* **Get exclusive discounts**—you'll also be able to buy our specially created monthly collections, with up to 50% off the RRP

* **Find your favourite authors**—latest news, interviews and new releases for all your favourite authors and series on our website, plus ideas for what to try next

* **Join in**—once you've bought your favourite books, don't forget to register with us to rate, review and join in the discussions

Visit **www.millsandboon.co.uk**
for all this and more today!

MILLS_WEB

MILLS & BOON®

Why not subscribe?

Never miss a title and save money too!

Here's what's available to you if you join the exclusive **Mills & Boon® Book Club** today:

✦ *Titles up to a month ahead of the shops*
✦ *Amazing discounts*
✦ *Free P&P*
✦ *Earn Bonus Book points that can be redeemed against other titles and gifts*
✦ *Choose from monthly or pre-paid plans*

Still want more?

Well, if you join today, we'll even give you
50% OFF your first parcel!

So visit **www.millsandboon.co.uk/subs**
to be a part of this exclusive Book Club!

MILLS & BOON®
By Request

RELIVE THE ROMANCE WITH THE BEST OF THE BEST

A sneak peek at next month's titles...

In stores from 7th April 2016:

- **His Most Exquisite Conquest** – Elizabeth Power, Cathy Williams & Robyn Donald

- **Stop The Wedding!** – Lori Wilde

In stores from 21st April 2016:

- **Bedded by the Boss** – Jennifer Lewis, Yvonne Lindsay & Joan Hohl

- **Love Story Next Door!** – Rebecca Winters, Barbara Wallace & Soraya Lane